The Cromptons

Mary Jane Holmes

The Cromptons

BY

MARY J. HOLMES

G. W. DILLINGHAM COMPANY

PUBLISHERS   NEW YORK

" Here by this grave I promise all you ask."—Page 39.

CONTENTS

PART I

PART II

THE CROMPTONS

PART I

CHAPTER I

THE STRANGER AT THE BROCK HOUSE

The steamer " Hatty " which plied between Jacksonville and Enterprise was late, and the people who had come down from the Brock House to the landing had waited half an hour before a puff of smoke in the distance told that she was coming. There had been many conjectures as to the cause of the delay, for she was usually on time, and those who had friends on the boat were growing nervous, fearing an accident, and all were getting tired, when she appeared in the distance, the puffs of smoke increasing in volume as she drew nearer, and the sound of her whistle echoing across the water, which at Enterprise spreads out into a lake. She had not met with an accident, but had been detained at Palatka waiting for a passenger of whom the captain had been apprised.

" He may be a trifle late, but if he is, wait. He must take your boat," Tom Hardy had said to the captain when engaging passage for his friend, and Tom Hardy was not one whose wishes were often disregarded. "Them Hardys does more business with me in one year than ten other families and I can't go agin Tom, and if he says wait for his friend, why, there's nothing to do but wait," the captain said, as he walked up and down in front of his boat, growing more and more impatient, until at last as he was beginning to swear he'd wait no longer for all the Hardys in Christendom, two men came slowly towards the landing, talking earnestly and not seeming to be in the least hurry, although the "Hatty" began to scream herself hoarse as if frantic to be gone.

"How d'ye, Cap," Tom said, in his easy, off-hand way. "Hope we haven't kept you long. This is my friend I told you about. I suppose his berth is ready?"

He did not tell the name of his friend, who, as if loath to cross the plank, held back for a few more words. Tom gave him a little push at last, and said, "Good-bye, you really must go. Success to you, but don't for a moment think of carrying out that quixotic plan you first mentioned. Better jump into the river. Good-bye!"

The plank was crossed and pulled in, and a mulatto boy came forward to take the stranger's bag and pilot him to his stateroom, which opened from what was called the ladies' parlor. Coiled up in a corner on the deck was a bundle of something which stirred as they came near to it, and began to turn over, making the stranger start with a slight exclamation.

"Doan you be skeert, sar," the boy said, "dat's nottin' but Mandy Ann, an onery nigger what b'longs to ole Miss Harris in de clarin' up ter Ent'prise. She's been hired out a spell in Jacksonville,—nuss to a little gal, and now she's gwine home. Miss Dory done sent for her, 'case Jake is gone and ole Miss is wus,—never was very peart," and turning to the girl the boy Ted continued: " You Mandy Ann, doan you know more manners not to skeer a gemman, rollin' round like a punkin? Get back wid yer."

He spurned the bundle with his foot, while the stranger stopped suddenly, as if a blow had been struck him.

"Who did you say she was? To whom does she belong, I mean?" he asked, and the boy replied, " Mandy Ann, a no count nigger, b'longs to Miss Harris. Poor white trash! Crackers! Dis your stateroom, sar. Kin I do somethin' for you?"

The boy's head was held high, indicative of his opinion of poor white trash and Crackers in general, and Mandy Ann in particular.

"No, thanks," the stranger said, taking his bag and shutting himself into his stuffy little stateroom.

" 'Specs he's from de Norf; looks like it, an' dey allus askin' who we 'longs to. In course we 'longs to somebody. We has ter," Ted thought, as he made his way back to Mandy Ann, who was wide-awake and ready for any war of words which might come up between herself and Ted, " who felt mighty smart 'case he was cabin boy on de ' Hatty.' "

As Ted suspected, the stranger was of Northern birth, which showed itself in his accent and cold, proud bearing. He might have been thirty, and he might have been more. His face did not show his age. His features were regular, and his complexion pale as a woman's. His eyes were a cross between blue and gray, with a look in them which made you feel that they were reading your inmost secrets, and you involuntarily turned away when they were fixed upon you. On this occasion he seemed colder and prouder than usual, as he seated himself upon the stool in his stateroom and looked about him,—not at any thing that was there, for he did not see it, or think how small and uncomfortable his quarters were, although recommended as one of the staterooms *de luxe* on the boat. His thoughts were outside, first on Mandy Ann,—not because of anything about her personally. He had seen nothing except a woolly head, a dark blue dress, and two black, bare feet and ankles, but because she was Mandy Ann, bound slave of " ole Miss Harris, who lived in de clarin'," and for that reason she connected him with something from which he shrank with an indescribable loathing. At last he concluded to try the narrow berth, but finding it too hard and too short went out upon the rear deck, and taking a chair where he would be most out of the way and screened from observation, he sat until the moon went down behind a clump of palms, and the stars paled in the light of the sun which shone down upon the beautiful river and the tangled mass of shrubbery and undergrowth on either side of it.

At last the passengers began to appear one by one, with their cheery how dye's and good mornings, and curious glances at this stranger in their midst, who, although with them, did not seem to be one of them. They were all Southerners and inclined to be friendly, but nothing in the stranger's attitude invited sociability. He was looking off upon the water in the direction from which they had come, and never turned his head in response to the loud shouts, when an alligator was seen lying upon the shore, or a big turtle was sunning itself on a log. He was a Northerner, they knew from his general make-up, and a friend of

Tom Hardy, the captain said, when questioned with regard to him. This last was sufficient to atone for any proclivities he might have antagonistic to the South. Tom Hardy, although living in Georgia, was well known in Florida. To be his friend was to be somebody; and two or three attempts at conversation were made in the course of the morning. One man, bolder than the rest, told him it was a fine day and a fine trip, but that the "Hatty" was getting a little too *passée* for real comfort. At the word *passée* the stranger looked up with something like interest, and admitted that the boat was *passée*, and the day fine, and the trip, too. A cigar was next offered, but politely declined, and then the attempt at an acquaintance ceased on the part of the first to make it. Later on an old Georgian planter, garrulous and good-humored, swore he'd find out what stuff the Yankee was made of, and why he was down there where few of his kind ever came. His first move was the offer of tobacco, with the words: "How d'ye, sir? Have a chew?"

The stranger's head went up a little higher than its wont, and the proud look on the pale face deepened as he declined the tobacco civilly, as he had the cigar.

"Wall, now, don't chew tobacky? You lose a good deal. I couldn't live without it. Sorter soothin', an' keeps my jaws goin', and when I'm so full of vim,—mad, you know,—that I'm fit to bust, why, I spit and spit,—backy juice in course,—till I spit it all out," the Georgian said, taking an immense chew, and sitting down by the stranger, who gave no sign that he knew of his proximity, but still kept his eyes on the river as if absorbed in the scenery.

The Georgian was not to be easily rebuffed. Crossing his legs and planting his big hat on his knees, he went on:

"You are from the North, I calculate?"

"Yes."

"I thought so. We can mostly tell 'em. From Boston, I reckon?"

"No."

"New York, mabby? No? Chicago? No? Wall, where in—" the Georgian stopped, checked by a look in the bluish-gray eyes which seldom failed in its effect.

Evidently the stranger didn't choose to tell where he lived, but the Georgian, though somewhat subdued, was not wholly silenced, and he continued: "Ever in Florida before?"

"No."

"Wall, I s'pose you're takin' a little pleasure trip like the rest of us?"

To this there was no response, the stranger thinking with bitterness that his trip was anything but one of pleasure. There was still one chord left to pull and that was Tom Hardy, who in a way was voucher for this interloper, and the Georgian's next question was: "Do you know Tom well?"

"Do you mean, Mr. Hardy?" the stranger asked, and the Georgian replied. "In course, but I allus calls him Tom. Have known him since he wore gowns. My plantation jines old man Hardy's."

There was no doubt, now, that the stranger was interested, and had his companion been a close observer he would have seen the kindling light in his eyes, and the spots of red beginning to show on his face. Whether to talk or not was a question in his mind. Cowardice prompted him to remain silent, and something which defied silence prompted him at last to talk.

"I was with Mr. Thomas Hardy in college," he said, "and I have visited him in his home. He is my best friend."

"To-be-sure!" the Georgian said, hitching nearer to the stranger, as if there was a bond of relationship between them.

The man had given no inkling of the date of his visit, and as it was some years since Tom was graduated the Georgian did not dream of associating the visit with a few weeks before, when he had heard that a high buck was at old man Hardy's and with Tom was painting the neighborhood red and scandalizing some of the more sober citizens with his excesses. This quiet stranger with the proud face and hard eyes never helped paint anything. It was somebody else, whose name 'he had forgotten, but of whom he went on to speak in not very complimentary terms.

"A high buck, I never happened to see squar in the face," he said. "Had glimpses of him in the distance ridin' ole man Hardy's sorrel, like he was crazy, and oncet reelin' in the saddle. Yes, sar, *reelin'*, as if he'd took too much. I b'lieve in a drink when you are dry, but Lord land, whar's the sense of *reelin'?* I don't see it, do you?"

The stranger said he didn't and the Georgian went on, now in a lower, confidential voice.

"I actually hearn that this chap,—what the deuce was his name? Have you an idee? He was from the North?"

If the stranger had an *idee* he didn't give it, and the Georgian continued: "These two young chaps—

Tom ain't right young though, same age as you, I
reckon—called on some Cracker girls back in the
woods and the Northern feller staid thar two or three
days. Think of it—Cracker girls! Now, if 'ted been
niggers, instead of Crackers!"

"Ugh!" the stranger exclaimed, wakened into
something like life. "Don't talk any more about that
man! He must have been a sneak and villain and a
low-lived dog, and if there is any meaner name you
can give him, do so. It will fit him well, and please
me."

"Call him a Cracker, but a Florida one. Georgy
is mostly better—not up to so much snuff, you know,"
the Georgian suggested, while the Northerner drew a
quick breath and thought of Mandy Ann, and wondered where she was and if he should see her again.

He felt as if there was not a dry thread in one of his
garments when his companion left him, and returning
to his friends reported that he hadn't made much out
of the chap. He wasn't from New York, nor Boston,
nor Chicago, and "I don't know where in thunder
he is from, nor his name nuther. I forgot to ask it,
he was so stiff and offish. He was in college with
Tom Hardy and visited him years ago; that's all I
know," the planter said, and after that the stranger
was left mostly to himself, while the passengers busied
themselves with gossip, and the scenery, and trying to
keep cool.

The day was hot and grew hotter as the sun rose
higher in the heavens, and the stranger felt very uncomfortable, but it was not the heat which affected
him as much as the terrible network of circumstances
which he had woven for himself. It was the harvest
he was reaping as the result of one false step, when

his brain was blurred and he was somebody besides
the elegant gentleman whom people felt it an honor
to know. He was himself now, crushed inwardly, but
carrying himself just as proudly as if no mental fire
were consuming him, making him think seriously
more than once of jumping into the river and ending
it all. He was very luxurious and fastidious in his
tastes, and would have nothing unseemly in his home
at the North, where he had only to say to his servants
come and they came, and where, if he died on his
rosewood bedstead with silken hangings, they would
make him a grand funeral—smother him with flowers, and perhaps photograph him as he lay in state.
Here, if he ended his life, in the river, with alligators
and turtles, he would be fished up a sorry spectacle,
and laid upon the deck with weeds and ferns clinging
to him, and no one knowing who he was till they sent
for Tom Hardy at that moment hurrying back to his
home in Georgia, from which he had come at the
earnest request of his friend. He did not like the
looks of himself bedraggled and wet, and dead, on the
deck of the " Hatty," with that curious crowd looking at him, Mandy Ann with the rest. Strange that
thoughts of Mandy Ann should flit through his mind
as he decided against the cold bath in the St. John's
and *to face* it, whatever it was. Occasionally some
one spoke to him, and he always answered politely,
and once offered his chair to a lady who seemed to be
looking for one. But she declined it, and he was
again left alone. Once he went to the other end of
the boat for a little exercise and change, he said to
himself, but really for a chance of seeing Mandy Ann,
who of all the passengers interested him the most.
But Mandy Ann was not in sight, nor did he see her

2

again till the boat was moving slowly up to the wharf at Enterprise, and with her braided tags of hair standing up like little horns, and her worldly goods tied up in a cotton handkerchief, she stood respectfully behind the waiting crowd, each eager to be the first to land.

The Brock House was full—" not so much as a cot or a shelf for one more," the clerk said to the stranger, who was last at the desk. He had lingered behind the others to watch Mandy Ann, with a half-formed resolution to ask her to direct him to " ole Miss Harrises" if, as Ted had said, she was going there. Mandy Ann did not seem to be in any hurry and sauntered leisurely up the lane a little beyond the Brock House, where she sat down and stretching out her bare feet began to suck an orange Ted had given her at parting, telling her that though she was " an onery nigger who belonged to a Cracker, she had rather far eyes and a mouth that couldn't be beat for sass, adding that he reckoned that thar tall man who didn't speak to nobody might be wantin' to buy her, as he had done ast him oncet how far it was to the clarin', an' he couldn't want nobody thar but her." Mandy Ann had taken the orange, but had spurned what Ted had said of the tall man's intentions. She had been told too many times, during her brief stay in Jacksonville as a nurse girl, that she was of no manner of account to believe any one wished to buy her, and she paid no attention to the tall man, except to see that he was the last to enter the hotel, where he was told there was no room for him.

" But I must have a place to sleep," he said. " It is only for the night. I return on the ' Hatty.' "

"Why not stay on her then? Some do who only come up for the trip," was the clerk's reply.

This was not a bad idea, although the stranger shuddered as he thought of his ill-smelling stateroom and short berth. Still it was better than camping out doors, or—the clearing—where he might be accommodated. He shuddered again when he thought of that possibility—thanked the clerk for his suggestion—and declined the book which had been pushed towards him for his name. No use to register if he was not to be a guest; no use to tell his name anyway, if he could avoid it, as he had successfully on the boat, and with a polite good-evening he stepped outside just as Mandy Ann, having finished her orange, peel and all, gathered herself up with a view to starting for home.

CHAPTER II

THE PALMETTO CLEARING

The stranger had asked Ted on the boat, when he came with some lemonade he had ordered, how far it was from the Brock House to the palmetto clearing, and if there was any conveyance to take him there. Ted had stared at him with wonder—first, as to what such as he could want at the clearing, and second, if he was crazy enough to think there was a conveyance. From being a petted cabin boy, Ted had grown to be something of a spoiled one, and was what the passengers thought rather too "peart" in his ways, while some of the crew insisted that he needed " takin' down a button hole lower," whatever that might mean.

" Bless yer soul, Mas'r," he said, in reply to the question. " Thar ain't no conveyance to the clarin'. It's off in de woods a piece, right smart. You sticks to de road a spell, till you comes to a grave—what used to be—but it's done sunk in now till nuffin's thar but de stun an' some blackb'ry bushes clamberin' over it. Then you turns inter de wust piece of road in Floridy, and turns agin whar some yaller jasmine is growin', an fore long you're dar."

The direction was not very lucid, and the stranger thought of asking the clerk for something more minute, but the surprise in Ted's eyes when he in-

quired the way to the clearing had put him on his
guard against a greater surprise in the clerk. He
would find his way somehow, and he went out into the
yard and looked in the direction of the sandy road
which led into the woods and which Mandy Ann was
taking, presumably on her way home. A second time
the thought came to him that she might direct him,
and he started rather rapidly after her, calling as he
went: " I say girl, I want you. Do you hear?"

Mandy Ann heard, gave one glance over her
shoulder, saw who was following her, and began at
once to run, her bare feet and ankles throwing up the
sand, and her sunbonnet falling from her head down
her back, where it flapped from side to side as she
ran. She remembered what Ted had said of the
stranger, who might be thinking of buying her; this
was possible after all, as he had said he wanted her,
and though her home in the clearing was not one of
luxury, it was one of ease and indolence, and she had
no desire for a new one—certainly not with this man
whose face did not attract her. Just why she ran,
she did not know. It was of no use to appeal to *ole
missus,* who would not know whether she belonged
to her or some one else. Miss Dory was her only
hope. With promises of future good behavior and
abstinence from pilfering and lying, and badness generally, she might enlist her sympathy and protection
till Jake came home, when all would be right. So she
sped on like a deer, glancing back occasionally to see
the stranger following her with rapid strides which,
however, did not avail to overtake her. The afternoon was very warm—the road sandy and uneven—
and he soon gave up the chase, wondering why the
girl ran so fast, as if afraid of him. The last sight he

had of her was of her woolly head, turning off from the
road to the right, where it disappeared behind some
thick undergrowth. Ted had said, "Turn at the
grave," and he walked on till he reached the spot,
and stood by the low railing enclosing a sunken
grave, whether of man or woman he could not tell,
the lettering on the discolored stone was so obscure.
Studying it very carefully, he thought he made out
" Mrs." before the moss-blurred name.

" A woman," he said, with a feeling how terrible it
must be to be buried and left alone in that dreary,
sandy waste, with no human habitation nearer than
the Brock House, and no sound of life passing by,
except from the same place, unless—and he started,
as he noticed for the first time what Ted had said was
the worst road in Florida, and what was scarcely
more than a footpath leading off to the right, and to
the clearing, of course—and he must follow it past
tangled weeds and shrubs, and briers, and dwarf palmettoes, stumps of which impeded his progress.

Mandy Ann had entirely disappeared, but here and
there in the sand he saw her footprints, the toes
spread wide apart, and knew he was right. Suddenly
there came a diversion, and he leaned against a tree
and breathed hard and fast, as one does when a shock
comes unexpectedly. His ear had caught the sound
of voices at no great distance from him. A negro's
voice—Mandy Ann's, he was sure—eager, excited,
and pleading; and another, soft and low, and reassuring, but wringing the sweat from him in great drops,
and making his heart beat rapidly. He knew who
was with Mandy Ann, and that she, too, was hurrying on to the clearing, still in the distance. Had there
been any doubt of her identity, it would have been

swept away when, through an opening in the trees, he caught sight of a slender girlish figure, clad in the homely garments of what Ted called poor white trash, and of which he had some knowledge. There was, however, a certain grace in the movements of the girl which moved him a little, for he was not blind to any point of beauty in a woman, and the beauty of this girl, hurrying on so fast, had been his ruin, as he in one sense had been hers.

" Eudora !" he said, with a groan, and with a half resolve to turn back rather than go on.

Tom Hardy in their talk while the boat waited for them at Palatka, had told him what *not* to do, and he was there to follow Tom's advice—though, to do him justice, there was a thought in his heart that possibly he might do what he knew he ought to do, in spite of Tom.

"I'll wait and see, and if—" he said at last, as he began to pick his way over the palmetto stumps and ridges of sand till he came upon the clearing.

It was an open space of two or three acres, cleared from tanglewood and dwarf palmettoes. In the centre was a log-house, larger and more pretentious than many log-houses which he had seen in the South. A Marshal Niel had climbed up one corner to the roof, and twined itself around the chimney, giving a rather picturesque effect to the house, and reminding the stranger of some of the cabins he had seen in Ireland, with ivy growing over them. There was an attempt at a flower garden where many roses were blooming. Some one was fond of flowers, and the thought gave the stranger a grain of comfort, for a love of flowers was associated in his mind with an innate refinement in the lover, and there was for a moment a tinge of brightness in the darkness settling upon his future. Around the house there was no sign of life or stir, except a brood of well-grown chickens, which, with their mother, were huddled on the door step, evidently contemplating an entrance into the house, the door of which was open, as were the shutters to the windows, which were minus glass, as was the fashion of many old Florida houses in the days before the Civil War. With a shoo to the chickens, which sent some into the house and others flying into the yard, the stranger stepped to the door and knocked, once very gently, then more decidedly—then, as there came no response, he ventured in, and driving out the chickens, one of which had mounted upon a table and was pecking at a few crumbs of bread left there, he sat down and looked about him. In the loft which could hardly be dignified with the name chamber, he heard a low murmur of voices, and the sound of footsteps moving rapidly, as if some one were in a hurry. The room in which he sat was evidently living and dining-room both, and was destitute of everything which he deemed necessary to comfort. He had been in a Cracker's house before, and it seemed to him now that his heart turned over when he recalled his visits there, and his utter disregard of his surroundings.

"I was a fool, and blind, then; but I can see now," he said to himself, as he looked around at the marks of poverty, or shiftlessness, or both, and contrasted them with his home in the North.

The floor was bare, with the exception of a mat laid before the door leading into another and larger room, before one of the windows of which a white curtain was gently blowing in the wind. A rough, uncovered table pushed against the wall, three or four chairs, and a haircloth settee completed the furniture, with the exception of a low rocking-chair, in which sat huddled and wrapped in a shawl a little old woman whose yellow, wrinkled face told of the snuff habit, and bore a strong resemblance to a mummy, except that the woman wore a cap with a fluted frill, and moved her head up and down like Christmas toys of old men and women. She was evidently asleep, as she gave no sign of consciousness that any one was there.

"Old Miss," the stranger said, and his breath again came gaspingly, and Tom Hardy's advice looked more and more reasonable, while he cursed himself for the fool he had been, and would have given all he was worth, and even half his life, to be rid of this thing weighing him down like a nightmare from which he could not awaken.

He was roused at last by the sound of bare feet on the stairs in a corner of the room. Some one was coming, and in a moment Mandy Ann stood before him, her eyes shining, and her teeth showing white against the ebony of her skin. In her rush through the woods Mandy Ann had come upon her young mistress looking for the few berries which grew upon the tangled bushes.

"Miss Dory, Miss Dory!" she exclaimed, clutching the girl's arm with such force that the pail fell to the ground and the berries were spilled, "you ain't gwine for ter sell me to nobody? Say you ain't, an' fo' de Lawd I'll never touch nothin', nor lie, nor sass ole Miss, nor make faces and mumble like she does. I'll be a fust cut nigger, an' say my prars ebery night. I'se done got a new one down ter Jacksonville. Say you ain't."

In her surprise Miss Dory did not at first speak; then, shaking Mandy Ann's hand from her arm and pushing back her sunbonnet she said: "What do you mean, and where did you come from? The 'Hatty,' I s'pose, but she must be late. I'd given you up. Who's gwine ter buy yer?"

"Ted done tole me mabby de man on de boat from de Norf, what got on ter Palatka, an' done as't the way hyar, might be after me—an'—— "

She got no further, for her own arm was now clutched as her mistress's had been, while Miss Dory asked, "What man? How did he look? Whar is he?" and her eyes, shining with expectancy, looked eagerly around.

Very rapidly Mandy Ann told all she knew of the stranger, while the girl's face grew radiant as she listened. "An' he done holler and say how he want me an' follered me, an' when I turn off at the grave he was still follerin' me. He's comin' hyar. You won't sell me, shoo'," Mandy Ann said, and her mistress replied, "Sell you? No. It was one of Ted's lies. He is my friend. He's comin' to see me. Hurry!"

Eudora was racing now through the briers, and weeds, and palmetto stumps, and dragging Mandy Ann with her.

"Never mind granny," she said, when they reached the house and Mandy stopped to say how d'ye to the old woman in the chair. "Come upstairs with me and help me change my gown."

"Faw de Lawd's sake, is he yer beau?" Mandy Ann asked, as she saw the excitement of her mistress, who was tearing around the room, now laughing, now dashing the tears away and giving the most contradicting orders as to what she was to wear and Mandy Ann was to get for her.

They heard the two knocks and knew that some one had entered the house, but Mandy Ann was too busy blacking a pair of boots to go at once, as she had her hands to wash, and yet, although it seemed to him an age, it was scarcely two minutes before she came down the stairs, nimble as a cat, and bobbed before him with a courtesy nearly to the floor. Her mistress had said to her. " Mind your manners. You say you have learned a heap in Jacksonville."

" To be shoo'. I've seen de quality thar in Miss Perkins's house," Mandy Ann replied, and hence the courtesy she thought rather fetching, although she shook a little as she confronted the stranger, whose features never relaxed in the least, and who did not answer her. " How d'ye, Mas'r" which she felt it incumbent to say, as there was no one else to receive him.

Mandy Ann was very bright, and as she knew no restraint in her Florida home, when alone with her old Miss and young Miss, she was apt to be rather familiar for a negro slave, and a little inclined to humor. She knew whom the gentleman had come to see, but when he said. " Is your mistress at home? " she turned at once to the piece of parchment in the rocking-chair and replied. " To be shoo. Dar she is in de char over dar. Dat's ole Miss Lucy."

Going up to the chair, she screamed in the woman's ear, " Wake up, Miss Lucy. I'se done comed home an' thar's a gemman to see you? Wake up! "

She shook the bundle of shawls vigorously, until the old lady was thoroughly roused and glared at her with her dark, beady eyes, while she mumbled, " You hyar, shakin' me so, you limb. You, Mandy Ann! Whar did you come from?"

"Jacksonville, in course. Whar'd you think? An' hyar's a gemman come to see you, I tell you. Wake up an' say how d'ye."

"Whar is he?" the old woman asked, beginning to show some interest, while the stranger arose and coming forward said, "Excuse me, madam. It is the young lady I wish to see—your daughter."

"She hain't her mother. She's her granny," Mandy Ann chimed in with a good deal of contempt in her voice, as she nodded to the figure in the chair, who, with some semblance of what she once was, put out a skinny hand and said, "I'm very pleased to see you. Call Dory. She'll know what to do."

This last to Mandy Ann, who flirted away from her and said to the stranger, "She hain't no sense mostly—some days more, some days littler, an' to-day she's littler. You wants to see Miss Dory? She's upstars changin' her gown, 'case she knows you're hyar. I done tole her, an' her face lit right up like de sun shinin' in de mawnin'. Will you gim me your caird?"

This was Mandy Ann's master-stroke at good manners. She had seen such things at "Miss Perkins's" in Jacksonville, and had once or twice taken a card on a silver tray to that lady, and why not bring the fashion to her own home, if it were only a log-cabin, and she a bare-foot, bare-legged waitress, instead of Mrs. Perkins's maid Rachel, smart in slippers and cap, and white apron. For a moment the stranger's face relaxed into a broad smile at the ludicrousness of the situation. Mandy Ann, who was quick of comprehension, understood the smile and hastened to explain.

"I done larn't a heap of things at Miss Perkins's, which we can't do hyar, 'case of ole Miss bein' so quar. Miss Dory'd like 'em right well."

"Certainly," the stranger said, beginning to have a good deal of respect for the poor slave girl trying to keep up the dignity of her family.

Taking a card from his case he handed it to Mandy Ann, who looked at it carefully as if reading the name, although she held it wrong side up. There was no silver tray to take it on—there was no tray at all—but there was a china plate kept as an ornament on a shelf, and on this Mandy Ann placed the card, and then darted up the stairs, finding her mistress nearly dressed, and waiting for her.

"Oh, his card? He gave it to you?" Eudora said, flushing with pleasure that he had paid her this compliment, and pressing her lips to the name when Mandy Ann did not see her.

"In course he done gin it to me. Dat's de way wid de quality both Souf and Norf. We livin' hyar in de clarin' doan know noffin'," Mandy Ann replied.

On the strength of her three months sojourn with Mrs. Perkins, who was undeniably quality, she felt herself capable of teaching many things to her young mistress, who had seldom repressed her, and who now made no answer except to ask, "How do I look?"

She had hesitated a moment as to the dress she would wear in place of the one discarded. She had very few to select from, and finally took down a white gown sacred to her, because of the one occasion on which she had worn it. It was a coarse muslin, but made rather prettily with satin bows on the sleeves,

and shoulders, and neck. Several times, since she had
hung it on a peg under a sheet to keep it from getting
soiled, she had looked at it and stroked it, wondering
if she would ever wear it again. Now she took it
down and smoothed the bows of ribbon, and brushed
a speck from the skirt, while there came to her eyes
a rush of glad tears as she put it on, with a thought
that he would like her in it, and then tried to see its
effect in the little eight by twelve cracked glass upon
the wall. All she could see was her head and shoulders, and so she asked the opinion of Mandy Ann,
who answered quickly, " You done look beautiful—
some like de young ladies in Jacksonville, and some
like you was gwine to be married."

" Perhaps I am," Eudora replied, with a joyous
ring in her voice. " Would you like to have me get
married? "

Mandy Ann hesitated a moment and then said,
" I'se promised never to tole you no mo' lies, so dis
is de truffe, ef I was to drap dead. I'd like you to
marry some de gemmans in Jacksonville, or some
dem who comes to de Brock House, but not him
downstars ! "

" Why not? " Eudora asked, and there was a little
sharpness in her voice.

" 'Case," Mandy Ann began, " you as't me, an' fo'
de Lawd I mus' tell de truffe. He's very tall an' gran',
an' w'ars fine close, an' han's is white as a cotton
bat, but his eyes doan set right in his head. They
look hard, an' not a bit smilin', an' he looks proud as
ef he thought we was dirt, an' dem white han's—I
do' know, but pears like they'd squeeze body an' soul
till you done cry wid pain. Doan you go for to marry
him, Miss Dory, will you? "

At first Mandy Ann had opened and shut her black fingers, as she showed how the stranger's white hands would squeeze one's body and soul; then they closed round her mistress's arm as she said, "Doan you marry him, Miss Dory, will you?"

"No," Eudora answered, "don't be a silly, but go down and bring me a rose, if you can find one two-thirds open. I wore one with this dress before and he liked it, and as't me to give it to him. Mebby he will now," she thought, while waiting for Mandy Ann, who soon came back with a beautiful rose hidden under her apron.

"Strues I'm bawn, I b'lieve he's done gone to sleep like ole Miss—he's settin' thar so still," she said.

But he was far from being asleep. He had gone over again and again with everything within his range of vision, from the old woman nodding in her chair, to the bucket of water standing outside the door, with a gourd swimming on the top, and he was wondering at the delay, and feeling more and more that he should take Tom Hardy's advice, when he heard steps on the stairs, which he knew were not Mandy Ann's, and he rose to meet Eudora.

CHAPTER III

She was a short, slender little girl, not more than
sixteen or seventeen, with a sweet face and soft brown
eyes which drooped as she came forward, and then
looked at him shyly through a mist of tears which she
bravely kept back.

" How d'ye. I'm so glad to see you," she said,
looking up at him with quivering lips which were so
unquestionably asking for a kiss that he gave it, while
her face beamed with delight at the caress, and she
did not mind how cold, and stiff, and reserved he grew
the next moment.

He did not like her " How d'ye," although he knew
how common a salutation it was at the South. It
savored of Mandy Ann, and her accent was like
Mandy Ann's, and her white dress instead of pleasing
him filled him with disgust for himself, as he remembered when he first saw it and thought it fine. She
had worn a rose then, and he had asked her for it,
and put it in his pocket, like an insane idiot, Tom
had said. She wore a rose now, but he didn't ask her
for it, and he dropped her hand almost as soon as
he took it, and called himself a brute when he saw
the color come and go in her face, and how she
trembled as she sat beside him. He knew she was
pretty, and graceful, and modest, and that she loved

him as no other woman ever would, but she was un-
trained, and uneducated, and unused to the world—his
world, which would scan her with cold, wondering
eyes. He couldn't do it, and he wouldn't—certainly,
not yet. He would wait and see what came of his
plan which he must unfold, and tell her why he had
come. But not there where the old woman might
hear and understand, and where he felt sure Mandy
Ann was listening. She had stolen down the stairs
and gone ostensibly to meet a woman whom Eudora
called Sonsie, and who, she said, came every day to do
the work now Jake was away.

"Who is Jake?" the man asked, and Eudora replied, "The negro who has taken care of us since I
can remember. He is free, but does for us, and is in
Richmond now, valleying for a gentleman who pays
him big wage, and he spends it all for us."

The stranger flushed at her words indicative of her
station, and then suggested that they go outside
where they could be sure of being alone, as he had
much to say to her.

"Perhaps you will walk part way with me on my
return to the 'Hatty,'" he said, glancing at his watch
and feeling surprised to find how late it was.

Instantly Eudora, who had seemed so listless, woke
up with all the hospitality of her Southern nature
roused to action. "Surely you'll have supper with
me," she said. "Sonsie is here to get it and will have
it directly."

There was no good reason for refusing, although
he revolted against taking supper in that humble
cabin, with possibly that old woman at the table; but
he swallowed his pride and, signifying his assent, went
outside, where they came upon Mandy Ann in a

3

crouching attitude under the open casement. She was listening, of course, but sprang to her feet as the two appeared, and said in response to her mistress's "What are you doing here?" "Nothin', Miss Dory, fo' de Lawd, nothing, but huntin' on de groun' for somethin' what done drap out de windy upstars."

The stranger knew she was lying, and Eudora knew it, but said nothing except to bid the girl get up and assist Sonsie with the supper. Mandy Ann had once said of her mistress to Jake, "She hain't no sperrit to spar," and Jake had replied, "Lucky for you, Mandy Ann, that she hain't no sperrit, for ef she had she'd of done pulled every har out of your head afore now."

Mandy Ann knew that neither her hair, nor any part of her person, was in danger from her young mistress, and after a few more scratches in the dirt after an imaginary lost article, she arose and joined Sonsie, to whom Eudora gave a few instructions, and then with her guest walked across the clearing to a bench which Jake had made for her, and which was partially sheltered by a tall palm. Here they sat down while he unfolded his plan, plainly and concisely, and leaving no chance for opposition, had the crushed, quivering creature at his side felt inclined to make it. As Mandy Ann had said she hadn't much spirit, and what little she had was slain as she listened, while her face grew white as her dress, and her hands were linked together on her lap. The sun had just gone down, and the full moon was rising and throwing its light upon the clearing and the girl, whose face and attitude touched her companion, cold and hard as he was, but he must carry his point.

"You see it is for the best and you promise; you

will remember," he said, taking one of her hands and wondering to find it so cold.

"Yes, oh, yes," she replied, every word a gasp. "I thought—I hoped—you had done come to take,—or to stay—not here, but somewhar—but I see you can't. You know best. I ain't fittin' to go yet, but I'll try, and I promise all you ask; but don't let it be long. The days are so lonesome since I come home, and things seem different since I knew you; but I promise, and will remember and do my best."

Half his burden rolled away. He could be very kind now, for he knew he could trust her to the death, and putting his arm around her, he drew her close to him and said, " You are a good girl, Eudora. I shall not forget it; but why do you tremble so? Are you cold?"

" Yes—no," she answered, nestling so close to him that the rose in her dress was loosened and fell to the ground.

He picked it up, but did not put it in his pocket as a keepsake. He gave it back to her, and she fastened it again to her dress, saying, " I do' know why I shake, only it seems 's if somethin' had died that I hoped for. But it is all right, becase you care for me. You love me."

She lifted up her face on which the moonlight fell, making a picture the man never forgot to the last day of his life. He did not tell her he loved her, he could not; but for answer he stooped and kissed her, and she—poor, simple girl—was satisfied.

" If I could tell Jake, it would be some comfort," she said at last, timidly, and her companion answered quickly. " Tell Jake! Never! You must not be too familiar with your servants."

"Jake is more than a servant. He is everything to me," the girl answered, with rising spirit. " He would die for me, and if anything happened to me and you did not come, I think he would kill you."

There was something of Southern fire in her eyes as she said this, which made the stranger laugh as he replied, " Nothing will happen, and I'm not afraid of Jake."

In his heart he was glad the negro was not there, for something warned him that in the poor black man he might find a formidable obstacle to his plan. Meanwhile in the house Mandy Ann had been busy with the supper-table. They ought to have a good deal of light, she thought, remembering the lamps at Mrs. Perkins's, and as there were only two candle-sticks in the house her fertile brain had contrived two more from some large round potatoes, cutting a flat piece from one end, making a hole in the centre to hold the candle, and wrapping some white paper around the standard. She had taken great pains with the table, trying to imitate Mrs. Perkins's, and the imitation was rather satisfactory to herself. The best cloth had been brought out, and though it was yellow with disuse it showed what it had been. A few roses in a pitcher were in the centre of the table, and ranged around them were the four candles, spluttering and running down as tallow candles are apt to do. The dishes troubled her, they were so thick and nicked in so many places, that it was difficult to find one which was whole. The stranger had the china plate, which had done duty as a tray for his card, and he had the only plated fork in the house: a Christmas gift from Jake to the ole Miss, who scarcely appreciated it, but insisted that it be wrapped in several folds of tissue paper and kept in her bureau drawer. Mandy Ann did not ask if she could have it. She took it and rubbed it with soft sand to remove some discolorations and laid it, with a horn-handled knife, by the china plate.

" Ef we only had napkins," she said, while Sonsie, who had lived all her life near the clearing, and knew nothing of the fashions of the world, asked what napkins were. With a toss of her head indicative of her superior knowledge, Mandy Ann replied, " You'd know if you'd lived wid de quality in Jacksonville. Miss Perkins's allus had 'em. Dey's squar little towels what you holds in yer lap to wipe yer fingers on when you've done eatin'. Dat's what they is, an' de gemman or to hev one."

" Can't he wipe his hands on de table cloth, for oncet?" Sonsie asked, with a sudden inspiration which was received with great scorn by Mandy Ann, to whom there had also come an inspiration on which she at once acted.

In one of ole Miss's bureau drawers was a large plain linen handkerchief which was never used. ·It would serve the purpose nicely, and Mandy Ann brought it out, holding it behind her lest it should be seen by the old lady, who sometimes saw more than Mandy Ann cared to have her see. It was rather yellow like the table cloth, and the creases where it was folded were a little dark, but Mandy Ann turned it, and refolded and pressed it, and laid it on the china plate, while Sonsie looked on and admired. Everything was in readiness, and Mandy Ann called across the clearing. " Hallo, Miss Dory. Supper's done served."

She had caught on to a good many things at Miss

Perkins's, and " served " was one of them. " I don't
s'pose Miss Dory will understan'," she thought, " but
he will, and see dat dis nigger know sumptin'."

It was a novel situation in which the stranger found
himself, seated at that table with Eudora presiding
and Mandy Ann waiting upon them, her tray a
dinner-plate which she flourished rather conspicuously.   He was quick to observe and nothing escaped
him, from the improvised candlesticks to the napkin
by his china plate.   He knew it was a handkerchief,
and smiled inwardly as he wondered what Tom
Hardy would say if he could see him now.   The old
lady was not at the table.   Mandy Ann had managed
that and attended to her in her chair, but as if eating
brightened her faculties, she began to look about
her and talk, and ask why she couldn't sit at her own
table.

" 'Case thar's a gemman hyar an' you draps yer
vittles so," Mandy Ann said in a whisper, with her
lips close to the old woman's ear.

" Gentleman? Who's he? Whar's he from? " the
old woman asked—forgetting that she had spoken to
him.

" I told you oncet he's Miss Dory's frien' an' from
de Norf.   Do be quiet," Mandy Ann blew into the
deaf ears.

" From the Nawth.   I don't like the Nawth, 'case
I—" the old lady began, but Mandy Ann choked her
with a muffin, and she did not finish her sentence and
tell why she disliked the North.

Eudora's face was scarlet, but she did not interfere.
Her grandmother was in better hands than hers, and
more forceful.

" Granny is queer sometimes," she said by way of

apology, while her guest bowed in token that he understood, and the meal proceeded in quiet with one exception. Granny was choked with eating too fast, and Mandy Ann struck her on her back and shook her up, and dropped her dinner-plate and broke it in her excitement.

"For de Lawd's sake, 'tan't no use," she said, gathering up the pieces and taking them to the kitchen, where Sonsie laughed till the tears ran at Mandy Ann's attempt " to be gran'," and its result.

Meanwhile the stranger ate Sonsie's corn cakes and muffins, and said they were good, and drank muddy coffee, sweetened with brown sugar out of a big thick cup, and thought of his dainty service at home, and glanced at the girl opposite him with a great pity, which, however, did not move him one whit from his purpose. He had told her his plan and she had accepted it, and he told it again when, after supper, she walked with him through the clearing and the woods to the main road which led to the river. He did the talking, while she answered yes or no, with a sound of tears in her voice. When they reached the highway they stopped by the sunken grave, and leaning against the fence which inclosed it, Eudora removed her sunbonnet, letting the moon shine upon her face, as it had done when she sat in the clearing. It was very white but there were no tears now in her eyes. She was forcing them back and she tried to smile as she said, "You are very kind, and I think I understand what you want, and here by this grave I promise all you ask, and will do my best—my very best."

Her lips began to quiver and her voice to break, for the visit from which she had expected so much had proved a blank, and her high hopes were dead as the woman by whose grave she stood. She had folded her hands one over the other upon the top rail of the fence, and her companion looked at them and thought how small they were and shapely, too, although brown with the work she had to do when Jake and Mandy Ann were both gone and Sonsie came only at meal times. He was not a brute. He was simply a proud, cold, selfish man, whose will had seldom been crossed, and who found himself in a tight place from which he could not wholly extricate himself. He was sorry for Eudora, for he guessed how desolate she would be when he was gone, and there was nothing left but that home in the clearing, with old granny and Mandy Ann. He had not seen Jake, of whom Eudora now spoke, saying, " Our house never seemed so poor to me till I seen you in it. It will be better when Jake comes, for he is to fix it up —he knows how."

It was the only excuse she had made, and she did it falteringly, while her companion's heart rose up in his throat and made him very uncomfortable, as he thought of Jake and Mandy Ann caring for this girl, while his income was larger than he could spend. It had not occurred to him to offer her money till that moment, and he did not know now that she would take it. Turning his back to her as if looking at something across the road, he counted a roll of bills, and turning back took one of the little brown hands resting on the rail in his and pressed the roll into it. Just for an instant the slim fingers held fast to his hand—then, as she felt the bills and saw what they were, she drew back and dropped them upon the sand.

" I can't; no, I can't," she said, when he urged

them upon her, telling her it was his right to give and hers to take.

As usual his will prevailed, and when at last he said good-by and walked rapidly towards the river, while she went slowly through the woods and across the clearing to the log-house, where Mandy Ann was having a frightful time getting ole Miss to bed, she had in her possession more money than Jake would earn in months.

" I would send it all back," she thought, " if we didn't need it badly, and he said it was right for me to take it, but some of it *must* go. I'll send it just before the ' Hatty ' sails."

There was no one to send but Mandy Ann, who, after many misgivings on the part of her mistress, was entrusted with a part of the money, with injunctions neither to look at nor lose it, but to hold it tight in her hand until she gave it to the gentleman. Eudora had thought of writing a note, but the effort was too great. Mandy Ann could say all she wanted to have said, and in due time the negress started for the boat, nothing loth to visit it again and bandy words with Ted. The " Hatty " was blowing off steam preparatory to starting, when a pair of bare legs and feet were seen racing down the lane to the landing, and Mandy Ann, waving her hand, was calling out, " Hol' on dar, you cap'n. I'se sometin' berry 'portant for de gemman. Hol' on, I say," and she dashed across the plank, nearly knocking Ted down in her headlong haste. " Whar is 'ee? " she gasped, and continued, " Leg-go, I tell ye. Le' me be," as Ted seized her arm, asking what she wanted, and if she was going back to Jacksonville.

" No; leg-go, I tell you. I wants the man from de

Norf, what comed to see Miss Dory. I've sometin'
for him very partic'lar."

She found him in his seat at the rear of the boat,
where he had sat on his way up, and had again appro-
priated to himself, with no one protesting or noticing
him beyond a civil bow. They called him Boston,
knowing no other name, and wondered why he had
visited the Harrises as they knew he had. Ted, who
was allowed nearly as much freedom of speech on the
boat as Mandy Ann had at the clearing, had aired
his opinion that the gentleman wanted to buy Mandy
Ann, but this idea was scouted. Boston was not one
to buy negroes. Probably he was some kin to old
Granny Harris, who had distant connections in the
North, some one suggested. This seemed reasonable, and the people settled upon it, and gave him a
wide berth as one who wished to be let alone. When
Mandy Ann rushed in and made her way to him
curiosity was again roused, but no one was near
enough to hear her as she put into his hands a paper,
saying breathlessly, " Miss Dory done send some of
it back with thanks, 'case she can't keep it all, and she
wants to know how d'ye, an' I mus' hurry, or dey
carries me off."

The stranger took the paper, opened it, and
glanced at the bills; then at the girl who stood as if
she expected something. Taking a dollar from his
pocket he gave it to her saying, " Take this and be a
good girl to your young mistress, and now go."

Mandy Ann did not move, but stood with her lips
twitching and her eyes filling with tears. No one had
ever given her a dollar before, and her better nature
cried out against what she had done.

" Fo' de Lawd, I can't help 'fessin," she said,

thrusting her hand into her bosom and bringing out a crumpled bill which she gave to the gentleman, who saw that it was a ten and looked at her sternly as she went on: " I done promised Miss Dory I'never tache a thing, if she wouldn't sell me to you, but dar was sich a pile, an' I wanted some beads, an' a red han'-kercher, an' a ring, an' I done took one. I don'no how much, 'case I can't read, an' dat's why I was late an' had to run so fass. You're good, you is, an' I muss 'fess—may de Lawd forgive me."

At this point Ted, who had been on some of the large boats between Jacksonville and Charleston, and had heard the cry warning the passengers to leave, screamed close to her. " All asho', dat's gwine asho'!" and seizing her arm he led her to the plank and pushed her on to it, but not until she had shaken her bill in his face and said, " Licke-e-dar, a dollar! All mine—he done gin it to me, an' I'se gwine to buy a gown, an' a han'kercher, an' some shoes, an' some candy, an' some—" the rest of her intended purchases were cut short by a jerk of the plank, which sent her sprawling on her hands and knees, with a jeer from Ted sounding in her ears. The " Hatty " was off, and with a feeling of relief the stranger kept his seat on the rear deck, or staid in his stateroom until Palatka was reached, where he went on shore, lifting his hat politely to the passengers, shaking hands with the captain, and giving a quarter to Ted, who nearly stood on his head for joy, and could scarcely wait for the next trip to Enterprise, where he would find Mandy Ann and tell her of his good fortune, doubling or trebling the amount as he might feel inclined at the time.

CHAPTER IV

HOPING AND WAITING

The curiosity concerning the stranger at Enterprise had nearly died out when it was roused again to fever heat by the arrival at the clearing of a little girl, whom the young mother baptized with bitter tears, but refused to talk of the father except to say, " It was all right and people would know it was when he came, as he was sure to do."

He didn't come, and the girl's face grew sadder and whiter, and her eyes had in them always an expectant, wistful look, as if waiting for some one or something, which would lift from her the dark cloud under which she was laboring. Jake, who had returned from Richmond, suffered nearly as much as she did. His pride in his family—such as the family was—was great, and his affection for his young mistress unbounded.

" Only tell me whar he is an' I'll done fetch him, or kill him," he said, when in an agony of tears she laid her baby in his lap and said, " Another for you to care for till he comes, as I know he will."

Eudora had said to the stranger that Jake would kill him if anything happened to her, but now at the mention of killing him she shuddered and replied, " No, Jake, not that. You'll know sometime. I can't explain. I done promised more than once. The last

time was by that grave yonder, when he was sayin'
good-by. It was same as an oath. I was to go to
school and learn to be a lady, but baby has come, and
I can't go now. It will make some differ with him
perhaps, an' he'll come for baby's sake. You b'lieve
me, Jake?"

"Yes, honey—same as ef 'twas de Lawd himself
talkin' to me, an' I'll take keer of de little one till he
comes, an' if I sees somebody winkin' or hunchin'
de shoulder, I'll—I'll——"

Jake clenched his fist to show what he would do,
and hugging the baby to him, continued, "Dis my
'ittle chile till its fader comes; doan' you worry. I'se
strong an' kin work, an' Mandy Ann's done got to
stir de stumps more'n she has."

He cast a threatening look at Mandy Ann, who had
at first been appalled at the advent of the baby, and
for a while kept aloof even from Ted, when the
"Hatty" was in. Then she rallied and, like Jake, was
ready to do battle with any one who hunched their
shoulders at Miss Dory. She had two good square
fights with Ted on the subject, and two or three more
with some of her own class near the clearing, and as
she came off victor each time it was thought wise not
to provoke her, except as Ted from the safety of the
"Hatty's" deck sometimes called to her, when he
saw her on the shore with the baby in her arms and
asked how little Boston was getting along. Mandy
Ann felt that she could kill him, and every one else
who spoke slightingly of her charge. She had told
Jake over and over again all she could remember of
the stranger's visit, and more than she could remember when she saw how eager he was for every detail.
She told him of the card taken to her mistress on a

china plate, of the table with its four candles, and ol(
Miss's handkerchief for a napkin, and of her waiting
just as she had seen it done at Miss Perkins's.

"The gemman was gran' an' tall, an' mighty fine
spoken, like all dem quality from de Norf," she said,
although in fact he was the first person she had ever
seen from the North; but that made no difference with
Mandy Ann. "He was a gemman—he had given her
a dollar, and he was shoo to come back."

This she said many times to her young mistress,
keeping her spirits up, helping her to hope against
hope, while the seasons came and went, and letters
were sometimes received or sent, first to Tom Hardy
and forwarded by him either to the North or to Eudora. There was no lack of money, but this was not
what the young girl wanted. Mandy Ann had said she
had not much *sperrit,* and she certainly had not enough
to claim her rights, but clung to a morbid fancy of
what was her duty, bearing up bravely for a long
time, trying to learn, trying to read the books recommended to her in her Northern letters, and sent for by
Jake to Palatka, trying to understand what she read,
and, most pitiful of all, trying to be a lady, fashioned
after her own ideas, and those of Jake and Mandy
Ann. Jake told her what he had seen the quality do
in Richmond, while Mandy Ann boasted her superior
knowledge, because of her three months with Miss
Perkins's in Jacksonville, and rehearsed many times
the way she had seen young ladies "come into de
house, shake han's an' say how d'ye, an' hole' thar
kyard cases so" (illustrating with a bit of block),
"an' thar parasols so" (taking up granny's cane),
"an' set on the aidge of thar char straight up, an'
Miss Perkins bowin' an' smilin' an' sayin' how glad

she was to see 'em, an' den when dey's gone sayin'
sometimes, 'I wonder what sent 'em hyar to-day,
when it's so powerful hot, an' I wants to take my
sester '—dat's her nap, you know, after dinner, what
plenty ladies take—an' den you mus' sometimes speak
sharp like to Jake an' to me, an' not be so soff spoken,
as if we wasn't yer niggers, 'case we are, or I is, an'
does a heap o' badness; an' you orto pull my har f'or
it."

Confused and bewildered Eudora listened, first to
Jake and then to Mandy Ann, but as she had no card
case, no parasol, and no ladies called upon her, she
could only try to remember the proper thing to do
when the time came, if it ever did. But she lost heart
at last. She was deserted. There was no need for
her to try to be a lady. Her life was slipping away,
but for baby there was hope, and many times in her
chamber loft, when Mandy Ann thought she was taking her *sester*, and so far imitating "de quality," she
was praying that when she was dead, as she felt she
soon would be, her little child might be recognized
and taken where she rightfully belonged.

And so the years went on till more than three were
gone since the stranger came on the " Hatty," and
one morning when she lay again at the wharf, and
Mandy Ann came down for something ordered from
Palatka, her eyes were swollen with crying, and when
Ted began his chaff she answered, " Doan't, Teddy,
doan't. I can't fought you now, nor sass you back,
'case Miss Dory is dead, an' Jake's done gone for de
minister."

CHAPTER V

That day was one of the hottest of the season, and the sun was beating down upon the piazza of the Brock House where the Rev. Charles Mason sat fanning himself with a huge palm leaf, and trying to put together in his mind some points for the sermon he was to preach the next Sunday in the parlor of the hotel to the few guests who came there occasionally during the summer. But it was of no use. With the thermometer at ninety degrees in the shade, and not a breath of air moving, except that made by his fan, points did not come readily, and all he could think of was Dives' thirsting for a drop of water from the finger of Lazarus to cool his parched tongue. " If it was hotter there than it is here I am sorry for him," he thought, wiping his wet face and looking off across the broad lake in the direction of Sanford, from which a rowboat was coming very rapidly, the oarsman bending to his work with a will, which soon brought him to the landing place, near the hotel. Securing his boat, he came up the walk and approaching Mr. Mason accosted him with, " How d'ye, Mas'r 'Mason. I knows you by sight, and I'se right glad to find you hyar. You see, I'se that tuckered out I'm fit to drap."

The perspiration was standing in great drops on his face as he sank panting upon a step of the piazza.

" 'Scuse me," he said, " but 'pears like I can't stan' another minit, what with bein' up all night with Miss Dory, an' gwine 'crost the lake twiste for nothin', 'case I didn't find him."

By this time Mr. Mason had recognized the negro as one he had seen occasionally around the hotel selling vegetables and eggs, and who he had heard the people say was worth his weight in gold.

" How d'ye, Jake," he said, pleasantly. " I didn't know you at first. Why have you been across the lake twice this morning? "

Jake's face clouded as he drew his big black hand across his eyes.

" Miss Dory done died at sun up," he replied. " You know Miss Dory, in course."

Mr. Mason was obliged to confess his ignorance with regard to Miss Dory, and asked who she was.

Jake looked disgusted. Not to know Miss Dory was something inexcusable.

" Why, she's Miss Dory," he said, " an' ole Miss is her granny. We live up in the palmetto clearing, back in de woods, an' I take keer of 'em."

" You mean you belong to Miss Dora's grandmother? " Mr. Mason asked, while Jake looked more disgusted than ever.

Not to know Miss Dory was bad enough, but not to know who he was was much worse.

" Lor' bless your soul, Mas'r Mason, I don't belong to nobody but myself. I'se done bawn free, I was. But father belonged to ole Miss Lucy, an' when my mother died she took keer of me, an' I've lived with her ever sense, all but two or three times I hired out

4

to some swells in Virginny, whar I seen high life. They's mighty kine to me, dem folks was, an' let me learn to read an' write, an' do some figgerin'. I'se most as good a scholar as Miss Dory, an' I tole her some de big words, an' what the quality in Virginny does, when she was tryin' so hard to learn to be a lady. She's dead now, the lam', an' my cuss be on him as killed her."

"Killed! Didn't she die a natural death?" Mr. Mason asked.

"No, sar. She jest pined an' pined for him, an' got de shakes bad, an' died this mornin'," Jake replied, "an' ole Miss done gone clar out of her head. She never was over-bright, an' 'pears like she don't know nothin' now. 'I leave it to you to do,' she said, an I'm doin' on't the best I kin. I seen her laid out decent in her best gownd—that's Miss Dory—an' sent to Palatka for a coffin—a good one, too—an' have been across the lake for Elder Covil to 'tend the burial, 'case she done said, ' Send for him; he knows.' But he ain't thar, an' I'se come for you. It'll be day after to-morrer at one o'clock."

Mr. Mason felt the water rolling down his back in streams as he thought of a hot drive through the Florida sand and woods, but he could not say no, Jake's honest face was so anxious and pleading.

"Yes, I'll come, but how?" he asked.

"Oh, I'll be hyar wid de mule an' de shay. Noon, sharp," Jake replied. "Thankee, Mas'r Mason, thankee. We couldn't bury Miss Dory without a word of pra'r. I kin say de Lawd's, but I want somethin' about de resurrection an' de life what I hearn in Virginny. An' now I mus' go 'long home. Ole Miss'll be wantin' me an' de chile."

"What child?" Mr. Mason asked, in some surprise.

Jake's face was a study as he hesitated a minute, winking to keep his tears back before he said, "Sartin', thar's a chile. Why shouldn't thar be, but fo' God it's all right. Miss Dory said so, an' Elder Covil knows, only he's done gone Norf or somewhar. It's all right, an' you'll know 'tis the minit you see Miss Dory's face—innocent as a baby's. Good day to you."

He doffed his hat with a kind of grace one would hardly have expected, and walked rapidly away, leaving the Rev. Mr. Mason to think over what he had heard, and wonder that he didn't ask the name of the family he was to visit. "Miss Dory, ole Miss, and Jake," were all he had to guide him, but the last name was sufficient.

"Oh, yes," the landlord said, when questioned. "It's old Mrs. Harris and her grand-daughter out in the palmetto clearing; they're Crackers. The old woman is half demented, the whole family was queer, and the girl the queerest of all—won't talk and keeps her mouth shut as to her marriage, if there was one."

"Who was the man?" Mr. Mason asked, and the landlord replied, "Some Northern cuss she met in Georgia where she was staying a spell with her kin. A high blood, they say. Attracted by her pretty face, I suppose, and then got tired of her, or was too proud to own up. I wasn't landlord then, but I've heard about it. I think he was here once three or four years ago. He came on the 'Hatty' and staid on her— the house was so full. Didn't register, nor anything— nor tell his name to a livin' soul. One or two ast him square, I b'lieve, but he either pretended not to hear 'em, or got out of it somehow. Acted prouder than Lucifer. Walked along the shore and in the woods,

and went to the clearin'—some said to buy that limb
of a Mandy Ann, but more to see Miss Dory. All
the time he was on the boat he was so stiff and
starched that nobody wanted to tackle him, and that
girl—I mean Miss Dóry—has kept a close mouth
about him, and when her baby was born, and some of
the old cats talked she only said, ' It is all right, I'm
a good girl,' and I b'lieve she was. But that Northern
cuss needs killin'. He sends her money, they say,
through some friend in Palatka, who keeps his mouth
shut tight, but neither she nor Jake will use a cent of
it. They are savin' it to educate the little girl and
make a lady of her, if nobody claims her. A lady out
of a Cracker! I'd laugh! That Jake is a dandy. He's
free, but has stuck to the Harrises because his father
belonged to old Mrs. Harris. He is smarter than
chain lightnin', if he is a nigger, and knows more than
a dozen of some white men. He drives a white mule,
and has managed to put a top of sail cloth on an old
ramshackle buggy, which he calls a ' shay.' You'll
go to the funeral in style."

Mr. Mason made no reply. He was thinking of
Dory, and beginning to feel a good deal of interest
in her and her story, and anxious to see her, even if
she were dead. At precisely twelve o'clock on the
day appointed for the funeral Jake drove his white
mule and shay to the door of the Brock House. He
had on his Sunday clothes, and around his tall hat was
a band of black alpaca, the nearest approach to
mourning he could get, for crape was out of the question. If possible, it was hotter than on the previous
day, and the sail cloth top was not much protection
from the sun as they drove along the sandy road,

over bogs and stumps, palmetto roots and low
bridges, and across brooks nearly dried up by the
heat. The way seemed interminable to Mr. Mason,
for the mule was not very swift-footed, and Jake was
too fond of him to touch him with a whip. A pull at
the lines, which were bits of rope, and a " Go 'long
dar, you lazy ole t'ing, 'fore I takes the hide off'n
you " was the most he did to urge the animal forward, and Mr. Mason was beginning to think he
might get on faster by walking, when a turn in the
road brought the clearing in view.

It had improved some since we first saw it, and was
under what the natives called right smart cultivation
for such a place. Jake had worked early and late to
make it attractive for his young mistress. He had
given the log-house a coat of whitewash, and planted
more climbing roses than had been there when the
man from the North visited it. A rude fence of
twisted poles had been built around it, and standing
before this fence were three or four ox-carts and a
democrat wagon with two mules attached to it. The
people who had come in these vehicles were waiting
expectantly for Jake and the minister, and the moment they appeared in sight the white portion hurried
into the house and seated themselves—some in the few
chairs the room contained, some on the table, and
some on the long bench Jake had improvised with a
board and two boxes, and which threatened every
moment to topple over. There were a number of old
women with sunbonnets on their heads—two or
three higher-toned ones with straw bonnets—a few
younger ones with hats, while the men and boys were
all in their shirt sleeves. Some of them had come

miles that hot day to pay their last respects to Miss
Dory, who, in the room adjoining where they sat, lay
in her coffin, clad, as Jake had said, in her best gown,
the white one she had worn with so much pride the
day the stranger came. She had never worn it since,
but had said to Mandy Ann a few days before she
died, " I should like to be buried in it, if you can
smarten it up." And Mandy Ann who understood,
had done her best at smartening, and when Sonsie
and others said it was " yaller as saffern, an' not fittin'
for a buryin'," she had washed and ironed it, roughly,
it is true, but it was white and clean, and Sonsie was
satisfied. Mandy Ann had tried to freshen the satin
bows, but gave it up, and put in their place bunches
of wild flowers she had gathered herself. With a part
of the dollar given her by " the man from the Norf,"
she had commissioned Ted to buy her a ring in Jacksonville. It had proved too small for any finger, except her little one, and she had seldom worn it. Now,
as she dressed her mistress for the last time an idea
came to her; she was a well-grown girl of sixteen,
and understood many things better than when she
was younger. Going to Jake, she said, " Ain't thar
somethin' 'bout a ring in that pra'r book you got in
Richmon' an' reads on Sundays? "

" Yes, in de weddin' service," Jake replied, and
Mandy continued: " Doan' it show dey's married for
shoo'! "

" For shoo? Yes. I wish Miss Dory had one,"
Jake answered.

Mandy Ann nodded. She had learned what she
wanted to know, and going to the little paper box
where she kept her ring she took it up, looked at it
lovingly, and tried it on. She had paid fifty cents

for it, and Ted had told her the real price was a dollar, but he had got it for less, because the jeweler was selling out. It tarnished rather easily, but she could rub it up. It was her only ornament, and she prized it as much as some ladies prize their diamonds, but she loved her young mistress more than she loved the ring, and her mistress, though dead, should have it. It needed polishing, and she rubbed it until it looked nearly as well as when Ted brought it to her from Jacksonville.

"I wish to de Lawd I knew ef dar was any partic'lar finger," she thought, as she stood by the coffin looking at the calm face of her mistress.

By good luck she selected the right finger, on which the ring slipped easily, then folding the hands one over the other, and putting in them some flowers, which, while they did not hide the ring, covered it partially, so that only a very close observer would be apt to think it was not real, she said, " If you wasn't married with a ring you shall be buried with one, an' it looks right nice on you, it do, an' I hope ole granny Thomas'll be hyar an' see it wid her snaky eyes speerin' 'round. Axed me oncet who I s'posed de baby's fader was, an' I tole her de gemman from de Norf, in course, an' den made up de lie an' tole her dey had a weddin' on de sly in Georgy—kinder runaway, an' his kin was mad an' kep' him to home 'cept oncet when he comed hyar to see her, an' I 'clar for't I doan think she b'lieve a word 'cept that he was hyar. Everybody knowd that. I reckon she will gin in when she see de ring."

Pleased with what she had done, Mandy Ann left the room just as the first instalment of people arrived, and with them old granny Thomas. In the little

community of Crackers scattered through the neighborhood there were two factions, the larger believing
in Eudora, and the smaller not willing to commit
themselves until their leader Mrs. Thomas had done
so. On the strength of living in a frame house, own-
ing two or three negroes and a democrat wagon, she
was a power among them. What she thought some
of those less favored than herself thought. When she
" gave in " they would, and not before. Up to the
present time there had been no signs of " giving in "
on the part of the lady, whose shoulders still hunched
and whose head shook when Eudora was mentioned.
She should go to the funeral, in course, she said. She
owed it to ole Miss Harris, and she really had a good
deal of respect for the nigger Jake. So she came in
her democrat wagon and straw bonnet, and because
she was Mrs. Thomas, walked uninvited into the room
where the coffin stood, and looked at Eudora.

" I'd forgot she was so purty. It's a good while
sense I seen her," she thought, a feeling of pity rising
in her heart for the young girl whose face had never
looked fairer than it did now with the seal of death
upon it. " And s'true's I live she's got a ring on her
weddin' finger! Why didn't she never war it afore an'
let it be known? " she said to herself, stooping down
to inspect the ring, which to her dim old eyes seemed
like the real coin. " She wouldn't *lie* in her coffin,
an' I b'lieve she was good after all, an' I've been too
hard on her," she continued, waddling to a seat outside, and communicating her change of sentiment to
the woman next to her, who told it to the next, until
it was pretty generally known that " ole Miss Thomas
had *gin in*, 'case Miss Dory had on her weddin' ring."

Nearly every one else present had " gin in " long

before, and now that Mrs. Thomas had declared he
self, the few doubtful ones followed her lead, an
there were only kind, pitying words said of poc
Dory, as they waited for the minister to come, an
the services to begin.

CHAPTER VI

THE SERVICES

The blacks were outside the house, and the whites inside, when Jake drove his shay to the door, and the Rev. Mr. Mason alighted, wiping the sweat from his face and looking around with a good deal of curiosity. A mulatto boy came forward to take charge of the mule, and Jake ushered the minister into the room where the coffin stood, and where were the four men he had asked to be bearers.

"I s'pose I'd or'ter of had six," he said in a whisper; "but she's so light, four can tote her easy, an' they's all very 'spectable. No low-downs. I means everything shall be fust-class."

Wrapped in shawls, with her head nodding up and down, old Mrs. Harris sat, more deaf and more like a dried mummy than she had been on the occasion of the stranger's visit. Jake had bought her an ear trumpet, but she seldom used it, unless compelled by Mandy Ann, who now sat near her with the little girl who, at sight of Jake, started to meet him. But, Mandy Ann held her back and whispered, "Can't you done 'have yerself at yer mammy's funeral an' we the only mourners?"

The child only understood that she was to keep quiet, and sat down in her little chair, while Jake motioned to Mr. Mason that he was to see Miss Dory.

During her illness her hair had fallen out so fast that it had been cut off, and now lay in soft rings around her forehead, giving her more the look of a child than of a girl of twenty, as the plate on her coffin indicated. " Eudora, aged twenty," was all there was on it, and glancing at it Mr. Mason wondered there was no other name. Jake saw the look and whispered. " I wan't gwine to lie an' put on ' Eudora Harris,' for she ain't Eudora Harris, an' I didn't know t'other name for shoo. Ain't she lovely ! "

" She is, indeed," Mr. Mason said, feeling the moisture in his eyes, as he looked at the young, innocent face on which there was no trace of guilt.

He was sure of that without Jake's repeated assertion, " Fo' God, it's all right, for she tole me so. Mostly, she'd say nothin'. She'd promised she wouldn't, but jess fo' she died she said agen to me, ' I tole him I'd keep dark till he come for me, but it's all right. Send for Elder Covil 'crost the river. He knows.' I've tole you this afore, I reckon, but my mind is so full I git rattled."

By this time the bent figure sitting in the rocking-chair, near the coffin began to show signs of life and whimper a little.

" 'Scuse me," Jake said, pulling a shawl more squarely around her shoulders and straightening her up. " Mas'r Mason, this is ole Miss Lucy. Miss Lucy, this is Mas'r Mason, come to 'tend Miss Dory's funeral. Peart up a little, can't you, and speak to him."

There didn't seem to be much " peart up " in the woman, who began at once to cry. Instantly Mandy Ann started up and wiped her face, and settled her cap, and taking the trumpet screamed into it that she was to behave herself and speak to the gemman.

" Dory's dead," she moaned, and subsided into her shawl and cap, with a faint kind of cry.

" Dory's dead," was repeated, in a voice very different from that of the old woman—a child's clear, sweet voice—and turning, Mr. Mason saw a little dark-haired, dark-eyed girl standing by Mandy Ann.

Mr. Mason was fond of children, and stooping down he kissed the child, who drew back and hid behind Jake.

" Me 'fraid," she said, covering her face with her hands, and looking with her bright eyes through her fingers at the stranger.

Something in her eyes attracted and fascinated, and at the same time troubled Mr. Mason, he scarcely knew why. The old grandmother was certainly demented. The landlord had said Eudora and the whole family were queer. Was the child going to be queer, too, and did she show it in her eyes? They were very large and beautiful, and the long, curling lashes, when she closed them, fell on her cheeks like those of her dead mother, whom she resembled. She seemed out of place in her surroundings, but he could not talk to her then. The people in the next room were beginning to get restless, and to talk in low tones of their crops and the weather, and the big alligator caught near the hotel. It was time to begin, and taking the little girl in his arms, Jake motioned to Mr. Mason. In the door between the two rooms was a stand covered with a clean white towel. On it was a Bible, a hymn-book, a cup of water, and two or three flowers in another cup. Mr. Mason did not need the Bible. Jake had asked for the Resurrection and the Life, and he had brought his prayer-book, and began the beautiful burial service of the Church, to which the people listened attentively for a while; then they began to get tired, and by the time the long reading was through there were unmistakable signs of discontent among them. They had expected something more than reading a chapter. They wanted remarks, with laudations of the deceased. Miss Dory was worthy of them, and because there were none they fancied the minister did not believe it was all right with her, and they resented it. Even old Miss Thomas had " gin in," and thar was the weddin' ring, an' no sermon,—no remarks, and they didn't like it. Another grievance was that no hymn was given out, and there was the hymn-book at hand. They had at least expected " Hark from the tombs," if nothing else, but there was nothing. Singing constituted a large part of their religious worship, and they did not mean to have Miss Dory buried without this attention.

As Mr. Mason finished the services and sat down, he was startled with an outburst of " Shall we meet beyond the river." Everybody joined in the song, negroes and all, their rich, full voices dominating the others, and making Mr. Mason thrill in every nerve as the quaint music filled the house, and went echoing out upon the summer air. When the " Beautiful River " was finished some one outside the door took up the refrain:

" Oh, that will be joyful, joyful, joyful;
  Oh, that will be joyful,
When we meet to part no more."

This appealed to the blacks, who entered into the singing heart and soul, some of the older ones keeping time with a swinging motion of their bodies, and one old lady in her enthusiasm bringing down her fist upon the doorstep, on which she was sitting, and shouting in a way which warned Jake of danger. He knew the signs, and putting down the little girl, who had fallen asleep in his lap, he went to the old negress, who was beginning to get under full headway, and holding her uplifted arm, said to her:

" Hush, Aunt Judy, hush; this ain't no place to have the pow'. This ain't a pra'r meetin'; tis a 'Piscopal funeral, this is, such as they have in Virginny."

What Judy might have said is uncertain, for there came a diversion in the scene. The child had followed Jake to the door, where she stood wide-eyed and attentive, and when the last words of the hymn ended, she sang in a clear, shrill voice, " Be joyful when we meet to part no more." Her voice was singularly sweet and full, and Mr. Mason said to himself, " She'll be a singer some day, if she is not crazy first." Nothing now could keep old Judy from one more burst, and her " Yes, thank de Lawd, we'll meet to part no mo'," rang out like a clarion, and the religious services were over.

There still remained what was the most interesting part to the audience—taking leave of the corpse—and for a few minutes the sobs, and cries, and ejaculations were bewildering to Mr. Mason, who had never had an experience of this kind. Jake quieted the tumult as soon as possible, reminding the people again that this was a first-class 'Piscopal funeral, such as the quality had in Virginny. The old grandmother was led to the coffin by Mandy Ann, who shook her up and told her to look at Miss Dory, but not cry much, if she could help it. She didn't cry at all, but nearly every one did in the adjoining room, where they said to each other, " Ole Miss is takin' leave and don't sense it an atom." The little girl was held up by Jake, who made her kiss her mother.

" Mamma's s'eep," the child said, as she kissed the pale lips which would never smile on her again.

There was a fresh outburst of sobs and tears from the spectators, and then the coffin was closed, and the procession took its way across the hot sands to the little enclosure in the clearing, where other members of the Harris family were buried. Remembering the impatience of the people in the house, Mr. Mason wished to shorten the service at the grave, but Jake said: " No. We'll have the whole figger for Miss Dory." Mr. Mason went the whole figure with uncovered head under the broiling sun, and when he was through he felt as if his brains were baked. The Crackers did not seem to mind the heat at all. They were accustomed to it, and after their return from the grave, stayed round until the white mule and sail-topped shay were brought up for Mr. Mason's return to the hotel.

As Jake was very busy, a young negro boy was sent in his place. Naturally loquacious, he kept up a constant stream of talk, but as he stammered frightfully the most Mr. Mason could understand was that Miss Dory was a dandy, ole Miss 'onery, whatever that might mean, and Jake a big head, who thought he knew everything because he was free and could read.

The next day was Sunday, and Mr. Mason took for the subject of his remarks in the parlor of the hotel the story of Lazarus and Dives, and every time he

spoke of Dives receiving his good·things in life, he
thought of the man whom the landlord had designated a " Northern cuss "; and every time he spoke
of Lazarus, he thought of poor little Dory and that
humble grave in the sands of the palmetto clearing.

It was covered before night with young dwarf
palmettoes, which Mandy Ann laid upon it with a
thought that they would keep her young mistress
cool. All through the day she had restrained her feelings, because Jake told her that was the way to do.

" Seems ef I should bust," she said to herself more
than once, and when at last the day was over, and
both ole Miss and the little girl were asleep, she stole
out to the newly made grave, and lying down upon it
among the palmettoes she cried bitterly, " Oh, Miss
Dory, Miss Dory, kin you har me? It's Mandy Ann,
an' I'm so sorry you're dead, an' sorry I was so bad
sometimes. I have tried to be better lately, sense I
got growed. Now, hain't I, an' I hain't tole many
lies, nor tached a thing sense I took that bill from
him. *Cuss* him, wherever he is! Cuss him to-night,
ef he's alive; an' ef his bed is soff' as wool, doan let
him sleep for thinkin' of Miss Dory. Doan let him
ever know peace of min' till he owns the 'ittle girl;
though, dear Lawd, what should we do without her—
me an' Jake? "

Mandy Ann was on her knees now, with her hands
uplifted, as she prayed for *cusses* on the man who had
wrought such harm to her mistress. When the prayer
was finished she fell on her face again and sobbed,
" Miss Dory, Miss Dory, I must go in now an' see to
'ittle chile, but I hates to leave you hyar alone in de
san'. Does you know you's got on my ring? I gin
it to you, an' ole granny Thomas ' gin in ' when she

seed it, an' said you mus' be good. I'se mighty glad I gin it to you. 'Twas all I had to give, an' it will tell 'em whar you've gone that you was good."

There was a dampness in the air that night, and Mandy Ann felt it as she rose from the grave, and brushed bits of palmetto from her dress and hair. But she did not mind it, and as she walked to the house she felt greatly comforted with the thought that she had *cussed* him, and that Miss Dory was wearing her ring as a sign that she was good, and that " ole granny Thomas had gin in."

5

CHAPTER VII,

COL. CROMPTON

He was young to be a colonel, but the title was merely nominal and complimentary, and not given for any service to his country. When only twenty-one he had joined a company of militia—young bloods like himself—who drilled for exercise and pleasure rather than from any idea that they would ever be called into service. He was at first captain, then he rose to the rank of colonel, and when the company disbanded he kept the title, and was rather proud of it, as he was of everything pertaining to himself and the Cromptons generally. It was an old English family, tracing its ancestry back to the days of William the Conqueror, and boasting of two or three titles and a coat-of-arms. The American branch was not very prolific, and so far as he knew, the Colonel was the only remaining Crompton of that line in this country, except the son of a half-brother. This brother, who was now dead, had married against his father's wishes, and been cut off from the Crompton property, which, at the old man's death, all came to the Colonel. It was a fine estate, with a very grand house for the New England town by the sea in which it was situated. It was built by the elder Crompton, who was born in England, and had carried out his foreign ideas of architecture, and with its turrets and square towers it bore some resemblance to the handsome places he had seen at home. It was of stone, and stood upon a rise of ground, commanding a view of the sea two miles away, and the pretty village on the shore with a background of wooded hills stretching to the west. It was full of pictures and bric-a-brac, and statuary from all parts of the world, for the Colonel's father had travelled extensively, and brought home souvenirs from every country visited. Florida had furnished her quota, and stuffed parokeets and red birds, and a huge alligator skin adorned the walls of the wide hall, together with antlers and pieces of old armor, and other curios. A small fortune was yearly expended upon the grounds which were very large, and people wondered that the Colonel lavished so much upon what he seemed to care so little for, except to see that it was in perfect order, without a dried leaf, or twig, or weed to mar its beauty.

It had not always been thus with him. When he first came into possession of the place he was just through college, and had seemed very proud and fond of his fine estate, and had extended his hospitality freely to his acquaintances, keeping them, however, at a certain distance, for the Crompton pride was always in the ascendant, and he tolerated no familiarities, except such as he chose to allow. This genial social life lasted a few years, and then there came a change, following a part of a winter spent in South Carolina and Georgia with his intimate friend and college chum, Tom Hardy. Communication between the North and South was not as frequent and direct then as it is now, and but little was known of his doings. At first he wrote occasionally to Peter, his head servant, to whom he entrusted the care of the house; then his letters ceased and nothing was heard from him until suddenly, without warning, he came home, looking much older than when he went away, and with a look upon his face which did not leave it as the days went on.

" 'Spect he had a high old time with that Tom Hardy, and is all tuckered out," Peter said, while the Colonel, thinking he must give some reason for his changed demeanor, said he had malaria, taken in some Southern swamp.

If there was any disease for which Peter had a special aversion it was malaria, which he fancied he knew how to treat, having had it once himself. Quinine, cholagogue, and whiskey were prescribed in large quantities, and Peter wondered why they failed to cure. He did not suspect that the quinine went into the fire, and the cholagogue down the drain-pipe from the washstand. The Colonel's malaria was not the kind to be cured by drugs, and there came a day when, after the receipt of a letter from Tom Hardy, he collapsed entirely, and Peter found him shivering in his room, his teeth chattering, and his fingers purple with cold.

"You have got it bad this time," Peter said, suggesting the doctor, and more quinine and cholagogue, and a dose of Warburg's Tincture.

The Colonel declined them all. What he needed was another blanket, and to be let alone. Peter brought the blanket and left him alone, while he faced this new trouble which bore no resemblance to malaria. He was just beginning to be more hopeful of the future, and had his plans all laid, and knew what he should do and say, and now this new complication had arisen and brushed his scheme aside. He had sown the wind and was reaping a cyclone, and he swore to himself, and hardened his heart against the innocent cause of his trouble, and thought once of suicide as he had on the St. John's the year before. He spent money, just the same, upon his handsome grounds; but it was only for the pride he had in keeping them up, and not for any pleasure he had in them. He never picked a flower, or sat on any of the seats under the trees, and, unless the day was very hot, was seldom seen upon his broad piazza, where every day Peter spread rugs and placed chairs because his master liked to see them there, if they were not used. His library was his favorite place, where he sat for hours reading, smoking, and thinking, no one knew of what, or tried to know, for he was not a man to be easily approached, or questioned as to his business. If he had malaria it clung to him year after year, while he grew more reserved and silent, and saw less and less of the people. Proud as Lucifer they called him, and yet, because he was a Crompton, and because of the money he gave so freely when it was asked for, he was not unpopular; and when the town began to grow in importance on account of its fine beach and safe bathing, and a movement was made to change its name from Troutburg to something less plebeian, Crompton was suggested, and met with general approval. No one was better pleased with the arrangement than the Colonel himself, although he did not smile when the news was brought to him. He seldom smiled at anything, but there was a kindling light in his eyes, and his voice shook a little as he thanked the committee who waited upon him. To be known as " Col. Crompton of Crompton " was exceedingly gratifying to his vanity, and seemed in a way to lift the malarious cloud from him for a time at least.

It was more than three years since Tom Hardy's letter had thrown him into a chill, and everything as yet was quiet. Nothing had come from the South derogatory to him, and he had almost made himself believe that this state of things might go on for years, perhaps forever, though that was scarcely possible. At all events he'd wait till the storm burst, and then meet it somehow. He was a Crompton and had faith in himself, and the faith was increased by the compliment paid by his townspeople; and as he was not one to receive a favor without returning it, he conceived the idea of giving an immense lawn-party, to which nearly everybody should be invited. He had shut himself up too much, he thought—he must mingle more with the people, and build around himself a wall so strong that nothing in the future could quite break it down.

Peter and the rest of his servants were consulted and entered heartily into his plan. Cards of invitation were issued bearing the Crompton monogram, and a notice inserted in the daily paper to the effect that any who failed to receive a card were to know it was a mistake, and come just the same. There was a great deal of excitement among the people, for it had been a long time since any hospitality had been extended to them, and they were eager to go, knowing that something fine was to be expected, as the Colonel never did anything by halves. The day of the lawn-party was perfect—neither too hot nor too cold—and the sun which shone upon that humble funeral in the palmetto clearing shone upon a very different scene in the

Crompton grounds, where the people began to assemble as early as one o'clock. The grass on the lawn was like velvet, without a stick or stone to be seen, for two gardeners had been at work upon it since sunrise, cutting and raking, and sprinkling, until it was as fresh as after a soft summer shower. The late roses and white lilies were in full bloom, the latter filling the air with a sweet odor and making a lovely background. There were tables and chairs under the maples and elms, and rugs and pieces of carpet wherever there was a suspicion of dampness in the ground. There was a brass band in one part of the grounds, and a string band in another, where the young people danced under the trees. Refreshments were served at five o'clock, and the festivities were kept up till the sun went down, and half the children were sick from overeating—the mothers were tired, and some of the men a little shaky in their legs, and thick in their speech, from a too frequent acquaintance with the claret punch which stood here and there in great bowls, free as water, and more popular. The crowning event of the day came when the hundreds of lanterns were lighted on the piazzas and in the trees, and every window in the house blazed with candles placed in so close proximity to each other, that objects could be plainly seen at some distance.

The Colonel was going to make a speech, and he came out upon an upper balcony, where the light from ten tall lamps fell full upon him, bringing out every feature of his face distinctly. He was rather pale and haggard, but the people were accustomed to that, and charged it to the malaria. He was very distinguished looking, they thought, as they stood waiting for him to commence his speech. All the afternoon he had been the most courteous of hosts—a little too patronizing, perhaps, for that was his way, but very polite, with a pleasant word for every one. He knew he was making an impression, and felt proud in a way as Crompton of Crompton, when he stepped out upon the balcony and saw the eager, upturned faces, and heard the shout which greeted him. And still there was with him a feeling of unrest—a presentiment that on his horizon, seemingly so bright, a dark cloud was lowering, which might at any moment burst upon the head he held so high. He was always dreading it, but for the last few days the feeling had been stronger until now it was like a nightmare, and his knees shook as he bowed to the people confronting him and filling the air with cheers.

No contrast could have been greater than that between the scene on which he looked down—the park, the flowers, the fountains, and the people—and the palmetto clearing in far away Florida. He did not know of the funeral and the group assembled around the log-cabin. But he knew of the clearing. He had been there, and always felt his blood tingle when he thought of it, and it was the picture of it which had haunted him all day, and which came and stood beside him, shutting out everything else, as he began to thank the people for the honor conferred upon him by calling the town by his name.

He didn't deserve it, he said. He didn't deserve anything from anybody.

"Yes, you do," went up from a hundred throats, for under the influence of the good cheer and the attention paid them the man was for the time being a hero.

"No, I don't," he continued. " I am a morally

weak man—weaker than water where my pride is concerned—and if you knew me as I know myself you would say I was more deserving of tar and feathers than the honor you have conferred upon me."

This was not at all what he intended to say, but the words seemed forced from him by that picture of the palmetto clearing standing so close to him. His audience did not know what he meant. So far as they knew he had been perfectly upright, with no fault but his pride and coldness by which he came rightfully as a Crompton. He must have visited the punch bowls too often, they thought, and didn't know what he was talking about. After a pause, during which he was trying to thrust aside the clearing, and the log-house, and the old woman in her chair, and Mandy Ann, and to pull himself together, he went on to say:

" You have been for a long time discussing the site of a new school-house, in place of the old one which stands so near the marshes, that it is a wonder your children have not all died with fever and ague. Some of you want it on the hill—some under the hill—some in one place, and some in another. Nobody wants it near his own premises. A school-house with a lot of howling children is not a desirable neighbor to most people. For my part I don't object to it. I like children."

Here he stopped suddenly as the image of a child he had never seen came before him and choked his utterance, while the people looked at each other, and wondered how long he had been so fond of children. It was generally conceded that he did not care for them—disliked them in fact—and he had never been known to notice one in any way. Surely he had been too near the claret bowls. He detected the thought of those nearest to him, and continued:

"I am not one to show all I feel. It is not my nature. I am interested in children, and as proof of it I will tell you my plan. There are two acres of land on the south side of the park. I fenced it off for an artificial pond, but gave it up. There is a spring of good water there, with plenty of shade trees for the children to play under. I will give this land for the new school-house."

Here he was obliged to stop, the cheers were so deafening. When they subsided he went on rapidly:

"I will build the house, too. Such an one as will not shame District No. 5 in Crompton. It shall be a model house, well lighted and ventilated, with broad, comfortable seats, especially for the little ones, whose feet shall touch the floor. It shall be commenced at once, and finished before the winter term."

He bowed and sat down, white and perspiring at every pore, and hardly knowing to what he had committed himself. The cheers were now a roar which went echoing out into the night, and were heard nearly as far as the village on the beach, the people wondering more and more at his generosity, and sudden interest in their little ones. And no one wondered more than himself. He did not care a picayune for children, nor whether their feet touched the floor or not, and he had not intended pledging himself to build the house when he began. But as he talked, the palmetto clearing stared him in the face, shutting out everything from his vision, except a long seat directly in front of him, on which several little girls whose feet could not touch the ground were fast asleep, their heads falling over upon each other, and the last one resting upon the arm of the settee. It was a pretty picture, and stirred in him feelings he had never experienced before. He would do something for the children, expiatory, he said to himself, as he sat down, thinking he ought to be the proudest and happiest of men to have the town called for him, and to stand so high in the esteem of his fellow citizens. What would they say if they knew what he did, and how cowardly he was because of his pride. Sometime they must know. It could not be otherwise, but he would put off the evil day as long as he could, and when, at last, his guests began to leave, and he went down to bid them good-night, his head was high with that air of patronage and superiority natural to him, and which the people tolerated because he was Col. Crompton.

That night he had a chill—the result of so much excitement to which he was not accustomed, he said to Peter, who brought him a hot-water bag and an extra blanket, and would like to have suggested his favorite remedies, quinine and cholagogue, but experience had taught him wisdom, and putting down the hot-water bag and blanket, he left the room with a casual remark about the fine day, and how well everything had passed off, " only a few men a little boozy," he said, " and three or four children with bruised heads caused by a fall from a swing."

The lawn-party had been a great success, and the Colonel knew he ought to be the happiest man in town, whereas he was the most miserable. He could not hear Mandy Ann's curses as she knelt on her mistress's grave, nor see her dusky arms swaying in the darkness to emphasize her maledictions. He didn't know there was a grave, but something weighed him down with unspeakable remorse. Every incident of his first visit South came back to him with startling vividness, making him wonder why God had allowed him to do what he had done. Then he remembered his trip on the " Hatty," when he kept himself aloof from everybody, with a morbid fear lest he should see some one who knew him, or had heard of him, or would meet him again. He remembered the loghouse and his supper, when Mandy Ann served from a dinner-plate, and his napkin was a pocket handkerchief. He remembered the mumbling old woman in her chair; but most of all he remembered the girl who sat opposite him. Her face was always with him, and it came before him now, just as it was in the moonlight, when she said: " You can trust me. I will do the best I can."

She had stood with her hands upon the fence and he saw them as they looked then, and holding up his own he said, " They were little brown hands, but they should have been white like mine. Poor Dory! "

There was a throb of pity in his heart as his remorse increased, and the hot night seemed to quiver with the echo of Mandy Ann's " cuss him, cuss him wherever he may be, and if his bed is soff as wool doan' let him sleep a wink." His bed was soft as wool, but it had no attraction for him, and he sat with his hot-water bag and blanket until his chill passed, and was succeeded by a heat which made him put blanket and bag aside, and open both the windows of his room. The late moon had risen and was flooding the grounds with its light, bringing out distinctly the objects nearest to him. Some tables and chairs were left standing, a few lanterns were hanging in the trees, and in front of him was the long bench on which the little girls had been sleeping, with their feet from the ground, when he made his speech. The sight of this brought to his mind the day three years before when, just as his plans were perfected, there had come a letter which made him stagger as from a heavy blow, while all around him was chaos, dark and impenetrable. In most men the letter would have awakened a feeling of tenderness, but he was not like most men. He was utterly selfish, and prouder than any Crompton in the long line of that proud race, and, instead of tenderness or pity, he felt an intense anger against the fate which had thus dealt with him when he was trying to do right.

What to do next was the question, which Tom Hardy, as cold and unfeeling as himself, answered for him.

"You are in an awful mess," he wrote, "and the only course I see is to keep them supplied with money, and let things run until they come to a focus, as I suppose they must, though they may not. Florida is a long ways from Massachusetts. Few Northerners ever go to Enterprise, and if they do they may not hear of the clearing and its inmates. The girl is not over-bright. I beg your pardon, but she isn't, and will be apt to be quiet when she makes up her mind that she is deserted. The only one you have to fear is that nigger, Jake; but I reckon we can manage him; so cheer up and never make such an infernal fool of yourself again."

Something in this letter had grated on the Colonel's feelings—the reference to the girl, perhaps—but he had decided to follow Tom's advice, and let things run until they came to a focus. They had run pretty smoothly for three years, and only a few letters, forwarded by his friend who now lived in Palatka, and kept a kind of oversight of the clearing, came to trouble him. These he always burned, but he could not forget, and the past was always with him, not exactly as it was on the night after his lawn-party, when it seemed to him that all the powers of the bottomless pit had united against him, and if ever a man expiated his wrong-doing in remorse and mental pain he was doing it. The laudations of the crowd which had cheered him so lustily were of no account, nor the honor conferred by giving the town his name. Nothing helped him as he stood with the sweat rolling down his face, and looked out upon his handsome grounds, which he did not see because of the palmetto clearing, and the little child, and the young mother on whose grave the moon was shining. Mandy Ann's curse was surely taking effect, for no sleep came to him that night, and the next day found him worn and pale, and when Peter, sure of a malarious attack worse than usual, ventured to offer his cholagogue and quinine, he was sworn at, and told to take himself off with his infernal drugs.

"I am tired with yesterday's mob. I shall be better when I am rested, and get the taste out of my mouth of Tom, Dick, and Harry tramping over the premises," he thought.

This was not very complimentary to the Tom's, and Dick's, and Harry's who had tramped through his grounds, but they did not know his thoughts, and were full of the lawn-party, and the new school-house, the work on which was commenced early in August, when a large number of men appeared, and were superintended and urged on by the Colonel himself.

He did not work, but he was there every day, is orders and making suggestions, and in this way aging to dissipate in part the cloud always ha over him, and which before long was to assu form which he could not escape.

CHAPTER VIII

THE CHILD OF THE CLEARING

The school-house was finished, and was a model of comfort and convenience. It was well lighted and ventilated, and every child of whatever age could touch its feet to the floor. If it were in any sense expiatory, it had proven a success, for the palmetto clearing did not haunt the Colonel as it had done on the day of the lawn-party. It was a long time since he had heard from there, and he was beginning to wonder if anything had happened, when Peter brought him an odd-looking letter, directed wrong side up, written with a pencil, and having about it a faint perfume of very bad tobacco. It was addressed to " Mr. Kurnal Krompton, Troutberg, Mass." The writer evidently did not know of the recent change of name, and the letter had been long on the way, but had reached its destination at last, and was soiled and worn, and very second-class in its appearance, Peter decided, as he took it from the office and studied it carefully. No such missive had, to his knowledge, ever before found its way into the aristocratic precincts of Crompton Place. If it had he had not seen it, and he wondered who could have sent this one. He found his master taking his breakfast, and, holding the letter between his thumb and fingers, as if there were contamination in its touch, he handed it to him.

"Fairly turned speckled when he looked at it," Peter thought, as he left the room. "Wish I had seen where it was mailed."

An hour later, Jane, the housemaid, came to him and said, "The Colonel wants you."

Peter found him in his bedroom, packing a satchel with a shaking hand and a face more speckled than it had been when he read the letter.

"Peter," he said, "fold up these shirts for me, and put in some collars and socks. I am going on a little trip, and may be gone two weeks, maybe more. Hold your tongue."

When he wished Peter to be particularly reticent, he told him to hold his tongue. Peter understood, and held it, and finished packing the satchel, ordered the carriage for the eleven o'clock train, and saw his master off, without knowing where he was going, except that his ticket was for New York.

"That smelly letter has something to do with it, of course," he said. "I wish I knew where it was from."

He was arranging the papers on the library table, when he stopped suddenly with an exclamation of surprise, for there, under his hand, lay the smelly letter, which the Colonel had forgotten to put away.

"Phew! I thought I got a whiff of something bad," he said, and read again the superscription, with a growing contempt for the writer. "Nobody will know if I read it, and I shall hold my tongue, as usual," he thought, his curiosity at last overcoming his sense of honor.

6

Opening the envelope, he took out the piece of foolscap, on which was neither date nor name of place.

"Kurnal Krompton," it began. "Yer fren' in Palatky done gone to Europe. He tole me yer name 'fore he went, an' so I rite meself to tell you Miss Dory's ded, an' ole Miss, too. She done dide a week ago, an' Miss Dory las' July. What shal I do wid de chile? I shood of rit when Miss Dory dide, but Mandy Ann an' me—you 'members Mandy Ann— sed how you'd be comin' to fotch her rite away, an' we cuddent bar to part wid her whilst ole Miss lived. But now she's done ded de chile doan or'to be brung up wid Crackers an' niggers, an' den dar's de place belonged to ole Miss, an' dar's Mandy Ann. She doan' or'ter be sole to nobody. I'd buy her an' set her free ef I had de money, but I hain't. She's a rale purty chile—de little girl. You mite buy Mandy Ann an' take her for lil chile's nuss. Jake Harris."

"Jerusalem!" Peter exclaimed. "Here's a go. Who is Miss Dory? Some trollop, of course—and she is dead, and old Miss, too. Who is old Miss? and who is Mandy Ann the Colonel is to buy? I'd laugh, rank Abolitionist as he is! And what will he do with a child? Crackers and niggers? What is a Cracker?"

Peter had no opinion on that head. He knew what a nigger was, and at once detected another odor besides bad tobacco, and opened the window to air the room. Then he began to study the postmark to see where the letter came from. It was not very clear, and it took him some time to make out "Palatka, Fla." The latter baffled him, it was so illegible, but he was sure of "Palatka," and wondered where it was. Hunting up an atlas, he went patiently through

State after State, till he found Palatka, on the St. John's River, Florida.

"Florida! That's where he's gone. There are niggers enough there, but who the Crackers are is beyond me," Peter said. "I believe I'll copy this letter."

He did copy it, and then waited for developments.

Meanwhile the Colonel was hurrying South as fast as steam could take him. Arrived in New York, he found himself in time to take a boat bound for Savannah, and shutting himself up in his stateroom sat down to analyze his feelings, and solve the problem which had for so long been confronting him. A part of it was solved for him. Eudora was dead; but there was the child. Something must be done with her, and Jake's words kept repeating themselves in his mind:

"She doan or'ter be brung up wid Crackers an' niggers."

"No, she don't or'ter," the Colonel thought, involuntarily adopting Jake's dialect; but what to do with her was the question.

If Tom Hardy had been home he would have consulted him, but Tom was away, and he must face the difficulty alone, knowing perfectly well what his duty was, and finally making up his mind to do it. If he chose to adopt a child it was no one's business. As a Crompton he was above caring for gossip or public opinion. To be sure the child would be a nuisance, and a constant reminder of what he would like to forget; but it was right, and he owed it to the mother to care for her little girl. He began to think a good deal of himself for this kind of reasoning, and by the time he reached Jacksonville he had made up his mind that he was a pretty nice man after all, and felt happier than he had in years. Death had closed one page of his life, and the distance between Florida and Massachusetts would close the other, and he was much like himself when he at last stepped on board the " Hatty," and started up the river.

There was room for him at the Brock House this time, and he registered his name. " Col. James Crompton, Crompton, Mass.," and said he had come to look after a family in the palmetto clearing, Harris was the name, and through a friend he was interested in them. The landlord was not the same who had been there on the occasion of the Colonel's first visit, but he knew something about the clearing, and volunteered whatever information he had concerning the family, speaking of the recent death of the demented old woman, and of the little child left to the care of two negroes, and saying, he hoped the gentleman had come to take it to its friends, if it had any.

The Colonel bowed and said that was his business, and early the next morning started on foot along the road he had trodden twice before, and which brought Eudora before him so vividly that it seemed as if she were walking at his side, and once, as some animal ran through the bushes near the grave at the turn of the road, he started at the sound as if it had been the rustle of Eudora's white dress as he heard it that day. He was beginning to get nervous, and by the time the clearing was reached he was as cold as he had been at home, when Peter brought him the hot-water bag and blanket. He noticed the improvements which had been made in the place since he was there last, and knew it was Jake's handiwork. He had never seen the man, and shrank a little from meeting him, knowing how infinitely superior to himself in a

moral way the poor African was. He remembered
Mandy Ann perfectly, and recognized her as she came
to the door, shading her eyes with her hand to look
at him; then she disappeared suddenly, and Jake, who
was at the rear of the house, fixing a barrel to catch
rain-water, was clutched by the arm, and nearly
thrown backwards, as the girl exclaimed: " For the
Lawd's sake, Jake, it's comin'—it's comin'—it's hyar!"

" What's comin'? The las' day, that you look so
skeered?" Jake said, while Mandy Ann continued:
" De man from de Norf, Cunnel Crompton, you call
him—done come for lill chile!"

She put her apron over her face and began to cry,
while Jake wiped his hands, and hurrying round the
house, met the Colonel just as he reached the door.
There was not the least servility in Jake's manner,
although it was respectful, as he said, " How d'ye,
Mas'r Crompton. I'm shoo it's you, an' I'se right
glad to see you, though I 'spects you done come for
the lill chile, an' I feel fit to bust when I think of
partin' wid her. Walk in, walk in; take a cheer, an'
I'll sen' Mandy Ann for de lill chile. She's in de
play-house I made her, jess dis side de graves, whar
she sits an' plays. Thar's a tree thar an' she calls it
de shady."

" Thanks!" the Colonel said, taking a chair, while
Jake went for Mandy Ann, and found her struggling
with the child, not far from the door.

The *chile* had seen the stranger as soon as Mandy
Ann; and as visitors were rare at the cabin, and she
was fond of society, she left her sand pies, and her
slice of bread and molasses, and started for the house,
meeting Mandy Ann, who seized her, saying, " Come
an' have on a clean frock and be *wassed*. Your face

is all sticky, an' han's, too—an' de gemman from de
Norf, de Cunnel, is hyar."

As it happened, the *chile* didn't approve of changing her dress and having her face washed. She was
in a hurry to see the gentleman, and she pulled back,
and fought, and called Mandy Ann an " ole nigger,"
and told her to " leg-go," and finally wrenched herself free, and ran like a little spider to the house, and
into the room where the Colonel was sitting. Starting to his feet he stood looking down at the mite
staring at him with her great dark eyes, in which was
a look which had puzzled the Rev. Mr. Mason when
he saw her at her mother's funeral. She was a very
pretty child, with a round, chubby face just now
smeared with molasses, as were her fat little hands,
while her dress, open at the back, showed signs of the
sand and water with which it had come in contact.
And she stood, holding the Colonel with her eyes,
until he began to feel cold again, and to think of his
hot-water bag. He did not care for children, and this
one——

" Heavens ! " he thought to himself. " Can I do it?
Yes, I must ! "

Then, putting out his hand, he said, " Little girl,
will you shake hands with me."

Nothing abashed she was going forward, when
Mandy Ann rushed in and pulled her back, exclaiming: " Oh, sar, not wid dem han's; dey mus' be
wassed."

" You ole Mandy Ann nigger, you lemme be. I
won't be wassed," was the sharp reply, and the dark
eyes flashed with a fire which made the Colonel think
of himself when roused, and he began to feel a good
deal of respect for the spoiled tyrant.

" Little girl," he said, very gently, but firmly, " Go with Mandy and be washed, and then come and see—" he came very near saying " see what I have brought you," without at all knowing why it should have come into his mind.

It had never occurred to him to bring her anything, but he wished now that he had, and began to wonder what he had that would please a child. He was fond of jewelry, and wore on his watch-chain several ornaments, and among them a very small, delicately carved book in ivory. He could detach it easily, and he began to do so, while the child eyed him curiously. She had seen very few gentlemen, and this one attracted her, he was so tall and imposing; and when he said again, " Go and be washed," she obeyed him, and the Colonel was a second time alone, for Jake was making his ablutions, and changing his working clothes for his best, in which he looked very respectable, when he at last rejoined his guest, and began at once in a trembling voice to speak of the business which had brought the Colonel there.

CHAPTER IX

THE COLONEL AND JAKE

" I 'lowed you had the best right to her because 'twas you that sent the money," he said.

The Colonel neither assented nor dissented, and Jake went on: " Thar is nobody else. Miss Dory never tole nothin'; she was silent as de grave about—him—de fader of de lill chile, I mean. ' It's all right,' she'd say. ' I tole him I wouldn't tell till he came—an' I won't—but, it's all right. Elder Covil knows—send for him.' That's just afore she died."

" And did you send for him ? " the Colonel asked with some alarm, and Jake replied: " I went for him an' he wasn't thar—had moved off—an' another gemman, the Rev. Mr. Charles Mason, what I foun' at the hotel, 'tended de buryin' with his pra'r book, 'case I wanted somethin' 'bout de Resurrection an' de Life. 'Twas as fust class a funeral as we could have out hyer. She wore her white gown—the one Mandy Ann says she wore when you war hyer. You 'members it ? "

The Colonel nodded, and Jake, thinking he could do nothing better than repeat all the particulars, went on: " She had a nice coffin from Palatka, an' Mandy Ann done fixed her rale nice, wid flowers in her han's, an' on her bosom, an', does you 'member givin' Mandy Ann a dollar when you's here afore ? "

Again the Colonel nodded and Jake went on: " Well, she done bought a ring wid some of it—not rale gold, you know, but looked most like it—an' what do you think Mandy Ann did, as the last thing she could do for Miss Dory? "

Jake was growing excited, and the Colonel nervous, as the negro continued: " It was too small for her, to be shue, but she thought a sight on't, but more of Miss Dory's good name."

There was a great ridge in the Colonel's forehead, between his eyes, as he repeated, " Her good name? "

" Yes, sar," Jake answered. " What could you 'spec when dar's a lill chile, and no fader for shoo, as anybody knows, but me an' Mandy Ann, an' Mas'r Hardy. Naterally they'd talk. But I 'shured 'em 'twas all right, an' knocked down one or two Crackers what grinned when I tole 'em, an' Mandy Ann did a power of fitin'. She's great at it—jess like a cat, an' we got 'em pretty much all under, except a few ole women, who never quite gin in till de last. Ole granny Thomas was de worst, an' de rest follered her; but she gin in when she seen de ring Mandy Ann slipped on Miss Dory's weddin' finger, an' dar wasn't a s'picion on de lam' as she lay in her coffin."

The Colonel's lips moved spasmodically, while Jake continued: " Thar was a right smart of 'em hyar, an' the minister read from de pra'r book jest as I seen 'em in Virginny 'mongst de quality, an' when de blacks set up a singin' so loud that ole Aunt Judy nighly had de pow'—dat's a kind of fit, you know, when dey gits to feelin' like kingdom come—I stopped her. I was boun' to have de funeral fust class. When ole Miss died, I let 'em have dar way, an' ole Aunt Judy had de pow' till her missus, who was hyar, shook her out on't.

That was ole Miss Thomas, who stood out agin Miss Dóry till she seen de ring. She says to me, says she, ' Does you know whar de chile's fader is? ' an' says I, ' S'posin' I do? ' ' Then sen' for him,' says she. ' Tain't fittin' de chile to stay on hyar.' ' I'm gwine to sen',' says I, an' I did, an' you've done come. Is you gwine to take her? ' "

Jake's broad chest heaved as he asked this question, to which the Colonel replied, " That is what I came for."

Jake had assumed that he was the child's father, and he did not contradict him, but said, " You call her the child. Has she no name? "

" Yes, Dory; dat's what her mother called her, but to me dar's only one Dory, an' she's dead, an' 'twas handy to say de *lill chile* or *honey*. Is you gwine to take her right away? "

" Yes, when the ' Hatty ' goes back," the Colonel replied, with a feeling of pity for the negro, whose face was quivering, and whose voice shook as he said, " It's best, I s'pose, but 'twill be mighty lonesome hyar, with the chile gone from de ' shady ' whar she plays, an' from de cradle whar I rocks her, an' from dese arms what totes her many a time, when she goes through de clarin' in de woods. You wouldn't be wantin' me an Mandy Ann to go wid you? De chile is wonderfully 'tached to us, an' has some spells only we can manage."

The Colonel shook his head. Jake and Mandy Ann knew too much for him to take them North. The child would soon forget its surroundings. People would stop wondering after a while, and the past would be bridged over, as far as was possible. On the whole the future looked brighter than it had done for years, and on this account the Colonel could afford to be very suave and gentle with this poor negro.

"No, Jake," he said, very kindly. "You would not be happy at the North, it is so different from the South. I cannot take you, nor Mandy Ann, but I shall reward you for all you have done for the child, and for her mother."

The last words came slowly, and there was a kind of tremor in the Colonel's voice.

"I 'specs you are right," Jake said meekly; "but it'll be mighty hard, an' what's gwine to become of Mandy Ann? Who does she 'long to, now Miss Dory an' ole Miss is both dead? I 'longs to myself, but what of Mandy Ann?"

Here was a problem the Colonel had not thought of. But his mind worked rapidly and clearly, and he soon reached a decision, but before he could speak of it the child appeared. It had taken a long time to wash and dress her, for the little hands were grimy, and the face very sticky, and a good deal of scrubbing had been necessary, with a good deal of squabbling, too—and the Colonel had heard some of the altercations—the child's voice the louder, as she protested against the soap and water used so freely. Jake had closed one of the doors to shut out the noise, saying as he did so, " She's got a heap of sperrit, but not from de Harrises, dey hadn't an atom."

It did not puzzle the Colonel at all to know where the *sperrit* came from, and he did not like the child the less because of it. She was in the room now, scrubbed till her face shone, and her hair, which was curly, lay in rings upon her forehead. Mandy Ann had put on her best frock, a white one, stiff with starch, and standing out like a small balloon. The

Colonel liked her better in the limp, soiled gown, as
he had seen her first, but she was clean, and she came
to him and put up her hand as Mandy Ann had told
her to do. It was a little soft, fat, baby hand, such as
the Colonel had never touched in his life, and he took
it and held it a moment, while the old malarious feeling crept over him, and he could have sworn that the
thermometer, which, when he left the " Hatty " had
stood at seventy-five, had fallen to forty degrees. As
a quietus during the washing, Mandy Ann had suggested that " mabby de gemman done brung somethin'," and remembering this the little girl at once
asked, " Has you done brung me sumptin'?   Mandy
Ann tole me so."

The Colonel's thermometer dropped lower still at
the speech, so decidedly African, and his pride rose up
in rebellion, and his heart sank, as in fancy he heard
this dialect in his Northern home.   But he must bear
it, and when, as he did not at once respond to her
question, she said, " Has you done brung me sumptin'? " he was glad he had removed the little ivory
book from his watch-chain.   It was something, and
he gave it to her, saying, " This is for you—a little
book.   Do you know what a book is? "

She was examining the ornament on the back of
which was carved a miniature bar of music, with three
or four notes.   The child had seen written music in
a hymn-book, which belonged to her mother, and
from which she had often pretended to sing, when
she played at a *funeral*, or prayer meeting, as she
sometimes did under the *shady*.   Jake had not
spoken of this habit to the Colonel.   He was waiting
to take him to the graves, and the play-house near
them, and he was watching the child as she examined

the carving. Lifting up her bright eyes to the Colonel, she said, " Moosich—me sing," and a burst of childish song rang through the room—part of a negro melody, and " Me wants to be an angel " alternating in a kind of melody, to which the Colonel listened in wonder.

" Me done sing dood," she said, and her eyes shone and flashed, and her bosom rose and fell, as if she were standing before an audience, sure of success and applause.

Jake did clap his hands when she finished, and said to the Colonel, " She done goes on dat way very often. She's wonderful wid her voice an' eyes. 'Specs she'll make a singer. She's a little quar—dem Harrises——"

Here he stopped suddenly, and asked, " Is you cole? " as he saw the Colonel shiver. He knew the Harrises were *quar*, and this dark-haired, dark-eyed child singing in a shrill, high-pitched, but very sweet voice, seemed to him uncanny, and he shrank from her as she said, " Me sing some mo'."

Jake now interfered, saying, " No, honey; we're gwine to yer mother's grave."

" Me go, too," the child answered, slipping her hand into the Colonel's and leading the way to a little enclosure where the Harrises were buried.

The Colonel felt *quar* with that hand holding his so tight, and the child hippy-ty-hopping by his side over the boards Jake had put down for a walk to the graveyard.

" Dis mine. Me play here," the child said, more intent upon her play-house than upon her mother's grave.

The play-house was a simple affair, which Jake

had constructed. There were two pieces of board for a floor, and a small bench for a table, on which were bits of broken cups and saucers, the slice of bread and molasses the child had left when she went to see the stranger, a rag doll, fashioned from a cob, with a cloth head stuffed with bran, and a book, soiled and worn as from frequent usage. The child made the Colonel look at the doll which she called Judy, "after ole mammy Judy, who came nigh havin' de pow' at de funeral, an' who done made it for her," Jake explained. The book—a child's reader—was next taken up, the little girl saying, "Mamma's book—me read," and opening it she made a pretense of reading something which sounded like "Now I lay me." The Colonel, who had freed his hand from the fingers which had held it so fast, looked inquiringly at Jake, who said, "Miss Dory's book; she done read it a sight, 'case 'twas easier readin' dan dem books from Palatka; an' she could larn somethin' from it, but de long words floored her an' me, too, who tried to help her."

For a moment the Colonel seemed agitated, and taking the book from the child he said, "Can I have it?"

"No, sar!" Jake answered emphatically. "I wouldn't part wid it for de world. It's a part of Miss Dory, an' she tried so hard to read good an' be a lady. Mandy Ann lived a spell wid de quality, an' got some o' dar ways, an' I got some in Virginny, an' we tole 'em to her, an' she done tried till towards de las' she gin it up. ' 'Taint no use,' she said to me. 'I'm 'scouraged. I can never be a lady. Ef he comes after I'm dead, tell him I tried an' couldn't.' She meant the chile's fader, her husband. Ain't you her husband?"

It was a direct question, and Jake's honest eyes were looking steadily at the Colonel, whose lips were white, and opened and shut two or three times before he answered, " I am nobody's husband, and never shall be. I knew your young mistress, and was interested in her, and shall care for the child. Don't ask me any more questions."

Up to this moment Jake had felt quite softened towards the man he had once thought to kill. But now he wanted to knock him down, but restrained himself with a great effort, and answered, " I axes yer pardon, but I'se allus thought so—an'—an'—I thinks so still."

To this there was no reply, and Jake, who had sent home his shaft, which he knew was making the proud man quiver, spoke next of a monument for Miss Dory, and asked where he'd better get it.

" Where you think best," the Colonel answered. " Only get a good one, and send the bill to me."

" Yes, sar; thank'ee, Mas'r," Jake said, beginning to feel somewhat less like knocking the Colonel down. " What shall I put on it?" he asked, and the Colonel replied, " What was on her coffin?"

" Jess ' Eudora, aged twenty.' I didn' know no odder name—las' name, I mean. I was shue 'twan't Harris."

" Put the same on the monument," the Colonel said; " and, Jake, keep the grave up. She was a good girl."

" Fo' de Lawd, I knows dat, an' I thank'ee, Mas'r, for sayin' dem words by de grave whar mabby she done har 'em; thank'ee."

The tears were in Jake's eyes, as he grasped the Colonel's hand and looked into the face which had relaxed from its sternness, and was quivering in every muscle. The proud man was moved, and felt that if he were alone he would have knelt in the hot sand by Eudora's grave, and asked pardon for the wrong he had done her. But Jake was there, and the child looking on with wide-open eyes, and though she did not understand what was said she knew that Jake was crying, and charged it to the stranger—"the bad man, to make Shaky cry—I hates 'oo," she said, beginning to strike at him.

"Hush! honey, hush!" Jake said, while the Colonel began to feel the need of several hot-water bags as he went back to the house where Mandy Ann, remembering the hospitable ways at Miss Perkins's when people called, had set out for him the best the house afforded, including the china plate he remembered so well.

He felt that to eat would choke him, but forced himself to take a sip of coffee and a bit of corn bread. The little girl had remained behind in her play-house, and he was glad of that. She was a restraint upon him. He wanted to talk business, and he did not know how much she would understand. When her great bright eyes were on him he felt nervous as if she were reading his thoughts, and was more himself with her away. He must talk about her and her going with him on the "Hatty," and Jake listened with a swelling heart, and Mandy Ann with her apron over her head to hide her tears. They knew it must be, and tried to suppress their feelings.

"It's like takin' my life," Jake said, "but it's for de best. Miss Dory would say so, but, Mas'r Crompton, you'll fotch her back sometime to de ole place. You'll tell her of her mudder, an' me, an' Mandy Ann. You won't let her done forget."

Nothing could be further from the Colonel's intentions than to let the child come back, and everything he could do to make her forget was to be done, but he could not say so to Jake, and with some evasive answer he hurried on to business, and spoke of the house and clearing, which now by right of inheritance belonged to the child. As he assumed her guardianship he should also assume an oversight of her property, and it was his wish that Jake should stay on the place, receiving a certain sum yearly for his services, and having all he could make besides. For anything of his own which he had spent on the clearing he was to be repaid, and all the money Eudora had put by was to be his. Jake felt like a millionaire, and expressed his thanks with choking sobs. Then, glancing at Mandy Ann, he asked as he had asked before, " An' what 'bout Mandy Ann? I 'longs to myself, but who's she 'long to, now ole Miss an' young Miss is dead? "

" Yes, who's nigger be I? Whar am I gwine? " Mandy Ann cried, jerking her apron from her head.

" In the natural sequence of things you belong to the little girl," the Colonel replied, adding, " I might buy you——"

But he got no further. All of Mandy Ann's animosity, when Ted suggested that the man from the North had come to buy her, and she had begged her mistress to save her from such a fate, had returned, and she exclaimed vehemently, " Fo' de Lawd, not dat ar. Lemme stay hyar. You 'members Ted, de colored boy on de ' Hatty.' We's kep' company,

7

off an' on, a year, sometimes quarrelin', and den makin' up. I can't leave Ted."

Her soul was in her eyes, as she begged for herself and Ted, and the Colonel hastened to say, " You did not let me finish. I couldn't buy you, if I would, and if I did I'd set you free. I will see that this is done some time."

" Bress you, Mas'r, for dat ar," Mandy Ann began, but the Colonel stopped her by saying, " You are young to be keeping company."

" I'se 'most as ole as Miss Dory when lill chile was born," was the reply, which silenced the Colonel with regard to her age.

He had quite a liking for Mandy Ann, and meant to do all he could for her and Jake, and after some further conversation it was arranged that she should stay with the latter, the Colonel promising to see that her wages were paid, and saying that she could keep the money for herself. He was certainly acting generously towards the two blacks, who would have been happy but for the parting with the child, which weighed so heavily upon them. There was not much time left, for the " Hatty " sailed early the next morning, and the Colonel must be on board that night.

Great as was their grief it was nothing compared to the antagonism of the child, when she heard she was to go with the Colonel, and leave Jake and Mandy Ann behind. She would *not* go, she said, and fought like a little tiger when that evening the Colonel came for her, and Mandy Ann tried to dress her for the journey. Under the table, and lounge, and chairs she crawled in her efforts to hide, and finally springing into Jake's lap begged him to keep her, promising to be good and never call him nor Mandy Ann niggers again, and nearly breaking Jake's heart with her tears and pretty coaxings. At last worn out with excitement, and feeling that the battle was against her, she sobbed, " Go wid me, Shaky, if I goes."

" I 'spects I'll hev to go part way—say to Savannah—ef you gets her off quiet. Thar's that in her will make her jump inter de river ef we pushes her too far," Jake said, and the Colonel, who was sweating like rain, and did not care for a scene on the " Hatty," finally consented for Jake to accompany them to Savannah, trusting Providence for what might follow.

Thus quieted the child made no resistance when Mandy Ann changed her soiled white dress for one more suitable for the trip, and then began to pack her few belongings. Here the Colonel stopped her. He did not know much about children's clothes, but he felt intuitively that nothing of the child's present wardrobe would ever be worn at Crompton Place. He did not say this in so many words, but Mandy Ann understood him and asked, " Ain't she to carry nothin'? "

" Nothing but what is necessary on the road," the Colonel replied, and an old satchel was filled with a night-dress, a clean apron, a pair of stockings, and Mandy Ann's tears, which fell like rain as she performed her last office for the little girl, who, now that Jaky was going, began to look forward to the trip with childish delight.

Judy was wrapped carefully in paper and put into the satchel, and then she was ready. Mandy Ann went with her to the boat, where, as it was late, scarcely any one was visible except Ted, to whom Mandy Ann intrusted her charge, bidding him 'muse her when he could, and whispering to him the good luck which had come to her and Jake through the Colonel's generosity. Then with a terrible wrench in her heart, she took the child in her arms and said, " Doan' you forget me, honey, an' some time you'll be comin' agen. Oh, I can't bar it ! " and with a wail which was scarcely like a human cry she dropped the child, and hurrying from the boat ran swiftly up the lane, and was soon out of sight. There were two or three bursts of tears for Mandy Ann, but for the most part the little girl was quiet until Savannah was reached, and she heard Jake was to leave her. Then she showed of what she was capable, and the Colonel looked on aghast, wondering what he should do when Jake was gone. She had played on the way with Judy, whose appearance had provoked a smile from some of the passengers, making the Colonel wonder if there were not something more reputable in looks than Judy, with her features of ink and the sewed-up gash in the side of her neck from which a little bran was still oozing. He didn't know much about dolls, but was sure there must be some in Savannah, and he went on a tour of inspection, and found a gold ring with a small stone in it for Mandy Ann in place of the one buried with poor Dory. This he would give to Jake to take home to the negro girl, he thought, and then continued his search for dolls, finding one which could stand up, and sit down, and was gorgeous in a satin dress, with earrings in its ears. This was more in keeping with his ideas, and he took it to the hotel, hoping he had seen the last of Judy, who, he suggested, should be thrown away. He didn't know children. The little girl was delighted with her new doll, which she handled gingerly, as if afraid to touch it, and which she called Mandy Ann. But she clung to Judy just the same, quite to the disgust of the Colonel.

Poor Jake grew thin during the few days they spent in Savannah, and he knew he was nearing the end.

"I must buy her somfin'," he thought, and one morning when he was walking with her past a dry goods store he saw in the window a little scarlet merino cloak, lined with white satin, and looking so pretty that he stopped to look at it, while the little girl jumped up and down, exclaiming, "Oh, the buffitel cloak. Me wants it, Shaky; me wants it."

Going into the store Jake inquired the price, which was so large that his heart sank. It would take nearly all the money he had with him to buy it, but reflecting that the Colonel was paying his bills, and that on his return home he could eat two meals a day, and light ones at that, until he had saved the required sum, he bought the cloak; and, when the final parting came, wrapped it round the little girl, and carrying her to the steamer put her down, and left hurriedly, while she rolled on the floor screaming for Shaky, and bumping her head against a settee. As the boat moved off, Jake stood on the wharf watching it for a long distance, with a feeling that all the brightness of his life had vanished with the little girl, whom the harassed and half-crazed Colonel would have given much to have left with him had it been practicable.

CHAPTER X

EUDORA

The Colonel had been gone nearly three weeks and no one knew where he was, or thought it strange that they didn't. It was his habit to go suddenly and return just as suddenly. Peter had his opinion, and felt curious to know if the Colonel would bring back Jake and Mandy Ann besides the child, and had many a hearty laugh by himself as he imagined the consternation of the household when this menagerie was turned in upon them. Naturally his master would let him know when to expect him, he thought, and was greatly surprised one morning when a station hack drove into the yard, and the Colonel entered the house looking years older than when he went away.

With him was a little girl, three years old or more, clinging to his hand as if in fear. Her garments were all coarse and old-fashioned, except the scarlet merino cloak. The hood was drawn over her head, and from it there looked out a pair of eyes, which, had Peter ever heard of the word, he would have said were uncanny, they were so large, and bright, and moved so rapidly from one object to another. She dropped the hood from her head, and began tugging at the ribbons of her cloak, while her lip quivered as if she were about to cry. It came at last, not like anything Peter had ever heard, and was more like a howl than a cry, for " Shaky; me wants Shaky."

It was loud, and shrill, and penetrated to all parts of the house, bringing Sally, the cook, Jane, the chambermaid, and Sam, the coachman, all into the hall, where they stood appalled at what they saw.

" Shaky, Shaky," the child wailed on, frightened by the strange faces around her, and as he did not come she threw herself upon the floor, and began to bump her head up and down, her last resort when her paroxysms were at their height.

The Colonel had borne a good deal since leaving Savannah, and had more than once been tempted to turn back and either bring Shaky, or leave the child with him. She had cried for him till she was purple in the face, and the stewardess had struck her on her back to make her catch her breath, and then taken her in her arms, and tried to comfort her. Perhaps it was owing to her color that the child took to her so readily that the Colonel said to her, " Keep her quiet, if you can, and I do not care what I pay you."

After that the little girl staid mostly with the stewardess, and was comparatively happy. Judy was a great comfort to her, and she kept it hugged to her bosom through the day, and slept with it at night, and when she reached the Crompton House it was in the inside pocket of her cloak. Becoming detached from the pocket as she rolled on the floor it fell at Peter's feet, making him start, it was so unlike anything he had seen in years.

" Great guns! " he exclaimed, spurning it with his foot, and sending it near the child, who snatched it up with a cry of " Judy, Judy, my Judy."

" Who is she, and where did she come from? " the

cook asked, while Jane tried to soothe the excited child.

"Her name is Eudora Harris," the Colonel said. "Her father is a sneaking scoundrel; her mother was a good woman, and my friend. She is dead, and there is no one to care for her child but myself. I have brought her home to bring up as my own. Jaky is the colored man who took care of her with Mandy Ann, a colored girl. She will·cry for her by and by."

As if to prove his words true the child set up a howl for Mandy Ann; "me wants Mandy Ann," while the Colonel continued, "She is to be treated in all respects as a daughter of the house. Get her some decent clothes at once, you women who understand such things. Don't mind expense. Give her a pretty room, and I think you'd better hunt up some young person to look after her. Until the girl comes Jane must sleep in the room with her, and don't bother me unless it is necessary; I feel quite used up, and as if I had been through a thrashing-machine. I am not used to children, and this one is—well, to say the least, very extraordinary."

This was a good deal for the Colonel to say at one time to his servants, who listened in wonder, none of them knowing anything except Peter, who kept his knowledge to himself. And this was all the explanation the Colonel gave, either to his servants, or to the people outside who knew better than to question him, and who never mentioned the child in his presence. Gossip, however, was rife in the neighborhood, and many were the surmises as to the parentage of the little girl who for a time turned the Crompton House upside down, and made it a kind of bedlam when her fits were on, and she was rolling on the floor, and bumping her head, with cries for Shaky and Mandy Ann. She was homesick, and cared nothing for the beautiful things they brought her. Against the pretty dresses she fought at first, and then submitted to them, but kept her old one in a corner of her room, and Susie, the girl hired to attend her, sometimes found her there asleep with her head upon it, and Judy held closely in her arms. They bought her a doll-house which was fitted up with everything calculated to please a child, but after inspecting it a while she turned from it with a cry for her " shady " under the palm tree in the clearing. The doll, Mandy Ann, which the Colonel had bought in Savannah, never took the place of Judy, who was her favorite, together with the scarlet cloak, which she would seldom let out of her sight. During the day she kept it round her, saying, " Me's cold," and at night she had it near her bed where she could see it the first thing in the morning.

The Colonel knew the town was full of speculation and surmises, but he did not care. Surmises which went wide of the mark were better than the real truth would have been, and that he could not tell. He had left a large part of his past in Florida, and trusted it would not follow him. He could not leave the little girl, and he meant to do his duty by her, outwardly at least. He had no love for her, and could not manufacture one. He would rather she had never been born; but inasmuch as she was born, and was very much alive, she must be cared for.

There was a private baptism in his library one Sunday afternoon, and she was christened Amy Eudora. Amy was for his mother; Eudora for no one knew whom, except Peter, who thought of the smelly letter, and knew that Eudora was for the young mother, dead somewhere in Florida. But he held his tongue, and tried to make up to the little girl her loss of Shaky, for whom she cried for days. Then, as she grew accustomed to her surroundings, she became contented, and her merry chatter filled the house from morning till night. Every one was devoted to her, except the Colonel. He was kind, but never encouraged her advances; never kissed her, never took her in his lap, or allowed her in his library. She called him father, and he answered to the name, while she was Eudora Harris to others. He tried at first to call her Amy, but she stoutly resisted.

" Me's Dory. Shaky and Mandy Ann calls me Dory," she would say, with a stamp of her foot, refusing to answer to any name but Dory, which came at last to be Dora as she grew older.

She learned to read in the new school-house by the south gate of the park, and when she heard that the Colonel built it, she called it hers, and queened it over her companions with an imperiousness worthy of the Colonel himself. When questioned of her old home her answers were vague. There was a river somewhere, and her mother was sick, and she reckoned she had no father but Shaky.

As she grew older, she became very reticent of her past, and, if she remembered it at all, she held her tongue, like Peter. Once, when she was more than usually aggressive, claiming not only the school-house but everything in and around it, she was told by the children that she lived with niggers till she came to Crompton Place, and they guessed her mother was one, and nobody knew anything about her anyway. There was a fierce fight in which Dora came off victorious, with a scratch or two on her face and a torn dress. That afternoon the Colonel was confronted by what seemed a little maniac, demanding to know if her mother was black, and if she had lived only with negroes until she came to Crompton.

" No, to both questions, and never let me hear another word on the subject as long as you live," was the Colonel's answer, given with a sternness before which the girl always quailed.

She was afraid of the Colonel, and kept aloof from him as much as possible, rarely seeing him except at meal times, and then saying very little to him and never dreaming how closely he watched her, attributing every pecularity, and she had many, to the Harris taint, of which he had a mortal terror. But however much or little there might have been of the Harris blood in her, the few who knew her found her charming, as she grew from childhood into a beautiful girl of eighteen, apparently forgetful of everything pertaining to her Florida home. The doll-house, with all the expensive toys bought for her, had been banished to a room in the attic, and with them finally went Judy and Mandy Ann. The red cloak she seemed to prize more than all her possessions. It was more in keeping with her surroundings than Judy, and she often wrapped it around her as she sat upon the piazza when the day was cool, and sometimes wore it on her shoulders to breakfast in the morning. Once she asked the Colonel where it came from, and he answered " Savannah," and went on reading his paper with a scowl on his forehead which warned her she was on dangerous ground. He was not fond of questions, and she did not often trouble him with them, but lived her silent life, increasing in beauty with every year, and guarded so closely from contact with the outer world that she scarcely had an intimate acquaintance.

It was not the Colonel's wish that she should have any. Indeed, he hardly knew what he did want. He was aristocratic, and exclusive, and wished to make her so, and keep her from contact with the common herd, as he secretly designated the people around him. He knew she was beautiful, with an imperiousness of manner she took from him, and a sweet yielding graciousness she took from her mother. Sometimes a smile, or turn of her head, or kindling in her eyes, would bring the dead woman so vividly to his mind that he would rise suddenly and leave the room, as if a ghost were haunting him. On these occasions he was sterner than usual with Eudora, who chafed under the firm rein held upon her, and longed to be free.

The Colonel had it in his mind to take her to Europe, hoping to secure a desirable marriage for her. He should tell her husband, of course, who she was, knowing that money and position would atone for the Harris blood, and feeling that in this way he would be entirely freed from the page of life which did not now trouble him much. He was still Crompton of Crompton, with his head as high as ever. The Civil War had swept over the land like a whirlwind. Tom Hardy had been among the first to enlist in the Southern army, and been killed in a battle. The Colonel had heard of his death with a pang, and also with a certain feeling of relief, knowing that he was about the only one who possessed a knowledge of his folly, or his whereabouts. There was still Jake, who wrote occasionally, asking for his *lill Miss* and telling of Mandy Ann, whom the war had made free, and who had married Ted, and was living in her own house outside the clearing. Everything was out of the way except Eudora, who, before he had proposed his trip to Europe, took herself from him in a most summary manner. The restraint laid upon her was becoming more than she could bear, and she rebelled against it.

"I shall elope some day—see if I don't," she said to Peter, who still remained in the family, and was her confidant in most things. "I shall say 'yes' to the first man who proposes, and leave this prison for the world, and the grand sights which Adolph says are everywhere. Here I am, cooped up with no young society, and seldom allowed to attend a picnic, or party, or concert, and I do so enjoy the latter, only I often feel as if I could do better than the professionals. Adolph says I can, and he knows."

Adolph Candida was her music teacher, who, alone of the young men in Crompton, had free access to the house. He was a fine fellow as well as teacher, and had done much to develop Dora's taste and love for music, which had strengthened with her years, until her voice was wonderful for its scope and sweetness. Naturally there sprang up between the young people an affection which ripened into love, and Candida was told by Eudora to ask her father's sanction to their marriage. That she could stoop to care for her music teacher the Colonel never dreamed, and was speechless with surprise and anger when asked by the young Italian for her hand. To show him the door was the work of a moment, and then Dora was sent for. She came at once, with a look in her eyes which

made the Colonel hesitate a little before he told her
what he had done, and what he expected her to do.

"If you disobey me in the slightest, you are no
longer a daughter of my house," he said, in the cold,
hard tone which Dora knew so well, and had feared
so much.

But the fear was over now. Something had transformed the timid girl into a woman, with a courage
equal to the Colonel's. For a time she stood perfectly
still, with her eyes fixed upon the angry man, listening
to him until he spoke of her as the daughter of the
house; then, with a gesture of her hands, which bade
him stop, she exclaimed, "I did not know I was
daughter of anything. For fifteen years I have lived
here, and though you have been kind to me in your
way, you have surrounded yourself with an air of re-
serve so cold and impregnable that I have never dared
ask you who I am, since I was a child, and asked
you about my mother. You told me then never to
mention that subject again, and I never have. But
do you think I have forgotten that I had a mother?
I have not. I do forget some things in a strange
way. They come in a moment and go, and I cannot
bring them back, but the face I think was mother's
is not one of them. Of my father I remember nothing. I have been told that when you brought me here
you said he was a scoundrel! Are you he? Are you
my father?"

The Colonel was white as a sheet, and his lips
twitched nervously, as if it were hard for them to
frame the word No, which came at last decidedly.
Over Dora's face a look of disappointment passed,
and her hands grasped the back of a chair in front of
her, as if she needed support.

" If you are not my father, who and what was my mother? " was her next question, and the Colonel replied, " She was an honest woman. Be satisfied with that."

" I never for a moment thought her dishonest," the girl exclaimed, vehemently. " I remember her as some one seen in a dream—a frail little body, with a sweet face which seldom smiled. There were other faces round us—dusky ones—negroes, weren't they?"

Her eyes compelled the Colonel to bow assent, and she continued, " I thought so, and our home was South; not a grand home like this, but a cabin, I think. Wasn't it a cabin? "

Again the Colonel bowed, and Dora went on, " There came a day when it was full of people, and somebody was in a box, and I sat in Shaky's lap. I have never forgotten him. He was all the father I knew."

The Colonel drew a long breath, and she went on, " He held me up, and bade me kiss the white face in the box. That was my mother? "

Again her eyes made the Colonel bow assent, and she continued, " After that there is a blank, with misty recollections of another box on the table, and a walk across hot sands with Shaky, and then I came here, where you have tried hard to blot all the past from my memory, as if it were something of which to be ashamed. But I shall find my mother's family some day, and Shaky, if he is living, and shall know all about it. There was a girl, too—Mandy Ann. I called the doll you gave me for her. She took care of me when Shaky didn't. He is more distinct. He took you to the graves the day you came for me, and I went with you and showed you my play-house under the palm tree—the poor little thing, but dearer to me than the best you have ever given me, because it was hedged round with love, even if it were the love of negroes. Things are coming back to me now so vividly, pressing on my brain which feels as if it would burst, and I remember the blacks, and their prayer meetings, and the songs they sang, and their hallelujahs and amens sound in my ears, and I think they always have, and helped me on and up when I have been practising difficult music. When a child at school I was often taunted and mocked for what the children called my negro brogue and talk. We had several battles in which I generally beat, although I was one against a dozen. There is a good deal of fight in me which I must have inherited from my father, who, I suppose, was a Southerner, if you are not he."

The Colonel only glared at her, and she continued, " I have been told, too, that there is a negro twang in my voice, and I am glad of it, and try to imitate the sounds which come to me from a past I so dimly remember, and which I think are echoes from some negro *prar* meeting. You see I have not forgotten the dialect of my early surroundings, and some day— I tell you again, I shall find the place and the graves of my people, and know what you have kept from me so carefully."

" Better not. You'll be sorry if you do. Your mother's family were Crackers," the Colonel said. " You would not be proud of the connection, although they were respectable people."

If Dora had ever heard of Crackers she knew very little about them, and cared less. She was greatly excited, and her eyes flashed and glowed with that light which Mr. Mason and Peter had noticed years before, and from which the Colonel turned away as from something dangerous.

" My mother was a Cracker? My father was a Mr. Harris—a Cracker, too. I am not your daughter, as I have been weak enough at times to believe, and—yes, I will confess it—I was weak enough to be proud that I was a Crompton; but that is over now; my father and mother were Crackers. I am a Cracker, and Eudora Harris. I am eighteen, and my own mistress—amenable to the authority of no one. I am glad for that, as it makes me free to do as I please. Good evening."

She bowed and left the room, leaving him stunned that she dared defy him, and half resolved to call her back and tell her the truth. But he didn't, and it was years before he saw her again.

The next morning she was missing. She had gone with Candida—where, he took no pains to inquire. She sent him a New York paper, with a notice of her marriage, and the names of herself and husband in the list of passengers sailing on the Celtic. He put the paper in the fire with the tongs, and after that a great silence fell upon the house, and the Colonel grew more reserved than ever, and more peculiar. He forbade the servants to mention Dora's name, or tell him where she was, if they knew. They didn't know, and many years went by, and to all intents and purposes she was dead to those who had known her as a bright, beautiful girl. Jake, who wrote to inquire for her, was told that she had run away and married, and the Colonel neither knew nor cared where she was, and was not to be troubled with any more letters, which he should not answer. Jake was silenced, and there

8

was no link connecting the Colonel with the past, except his memory which lashed him like the stings of scorpions. His hair turned white as snow; there was a stoop between his shoulders, and his fifty-five years might have been sixty-five, he aged so fast, as time went on, and his great house became so intolerable to him that he at last hailed with delight an event which, sad as it was in some respects, brought him something of life and an interest in it.

PART II

CHAPTER I

" Crompton House, June ——, 18—.

" Dear Jack:

" I have bearded the lion in his den and found him a harmless old cove, after all, with many of his fangs extracted.   You know, I am the son of his half-brother, who was many years his junior.   I fancy the two never agreed very well, and when I wrote, proposing that I should visit Crompton House, I was surprised at the cordial reply, bidding me pack up my traps and come at once.   I packed up and came, and, if I know myself, I shall stay.   I am the only near relative he has in the world.   He has a large estate to dispose of, was never married, and, of course, has no children, unless——

" There must everlastingly be an *unless*, or a *but* somewhere, and here it is—a big one in the shape of a woman—a lovely woman, too, if she is nearer forty than twenty.   Don't you remember I once told you of a girl whom my uncle brought home from the South, and who ran off with her music teacher, an Italian. Well, she is here—a wreck physically and mentally in one sense; not exactly insane, but with memory so impaired that she can tell nothing of her past, or perhaps she does not wish to. She always says, when questioned about it, ' I don't remember, and it makes my head ache to try.'

"It seems her first husband, Candida, took her abroad and gave her every advantage in music, both in Paris and Italy. When he died she married Homer Smith, an American, who was associated with him in some way. After his return to America he got up what was known as the 'Homer Troupe.' He dropped his last name, thinking the *Smith* Troupe would not sound as well as Homer. His wife was the drawing card. She had a wonderful voice as a girl, they say, with a peculiarly pathetic tone in it, like what you hear in negro concerts, and it was this and her beauty which took with the people. She hated the business, but was compelled to sing by her husband, who, I fancy, was a tyrant and a brute. They starred it in the far West mostly, until her health and mind gave way, and she went raving mad on the stage, I believe. He put her in a private asylum in San Francisco. How long she was there I don't know, and she don't know. She was always a little queer, they say, and people predicted she would be crazy some time. Her husband died suddenly in Santa Barbara. Just before he died he tried to say something, but could only manage to give his physician the Colonel's address, and say, ' Tell him where my wife is.'

"Off started the Colonel, lame, and gouty, and rheumatic as he is, and brought her home, and has set her up as a kind of queen whose slightest wish is to be obeyed. To do her justice she has not many wishes. She is very quiet, talks but little, and seems in a kind of brown study most of the time. Occasionally she rouses up and asks if we are sure he is dead—the he being her husband—the last one, presumably. When we tell her he is she smiles and says, ' I think I'm glad, for now I shall never have to sing again in public.' Then she says in a very different tone, ' Baby is dead, too; and my head has ached so hard ever since that I cannot think or remember, only it was sudden and took my life away.'

" She has an old red cloak which at times she wraps around a shawl, and cuddles it as if it were a baby, crooning some negro melody she heard South. There must have been a little child who died, but she is not clear on the subject. Sometimes it is a baby; sometimes a grown girl; sometimes it died in one place; sometimes in another; but always just before she was going to sing, and the room was full of coffins until she sank down, and knew no more. Whether my uncle has taken pains to inquire about the child, I don't know. He does not like children, and is satisfied to have Amy back, and is trying to atone for his former harshness. He calls her Amy, instead of Eudora, because the latter was the name by which she was known in the Homer Troupe, and he saw it flaunted on a handbill advertising the last concert in which she took part.

" Don't think I have heard all this from him. He is tighter than the bark of a tree with regard to his affairs, and I do not think any one in the town knows anything definite about her singing in public, or the asylum; but there is a servant, Peter, who has grown old in the family. He knows everything, and has told me about my uncle bringing the child home, and how she cried for days for Shaky, a colored man, and slept in the red cloak, and kept it around her in the daytime because he gave it to her. I have learned that she was never lawfully adopted, and that my uncle has made no will. Still she must be something to him, but certainly not his lawful child, or why his reticence with regard to her. I am the only near relative bearing the Crompton name. I have made myself very necessary to him—am in fact, in a way, a son of the house. He is very much broken, and if he dies without a will——

" Well, all things come to him who waits, and I can afford to wait in such comfortable quarters. Do you catch on, and call me a scamp with your Puritanical notions? Not so fast, old fellow. You have chosen to earn your living delving at the law. I earn mine by being so useful to my uncle that he will not part with me. He has already made me a kind of agent to attend to his business, so that I look upon myself as permanently fixed at Crompton House for as long as I choose to stay. It is a grand old place, with an income of I do not know how many thousands, and if I should ever be fortunate enough to be master, I shall say that for once in his life Howard Crompton was in luck. I want you to come here, Jack, when you have finished visiting your sister. I asked my uncle if I could invite you, and he said, ' Certainly; I like to have young people in the house. It pleases Amy.'

" This is wonderful, as they say he used to keep young people away, almost with lock and key, when she was young. But now anything which pleases Amy pleases him.

" And now for another matter which involves a girl, Eloise Smith. Who is she, you ask? Well, she is neither high born, I fancy, nor city bred; nor much like the girls from Wellesley and Lasell, with whom we used to flirt. She is a country school-ma'am, and is to be graduated this month in the Normal School in Mayville, where you are visiting. What is she to me? Nothing, except this: She has haunted me ever since I heard of her, and I can't get rid of an idea that in some way she is to influence my life. You know I was always given to presentiments and vagaries, and she is the last one. I might not have thought much of her if my uncle were not in a great way on her account. Long ago when they changed the name of the town from Troutburg to Crompton in his honor, he built a school-house on his premises, and gave it to the town. Since then he has felt that he had a right to control it, and say who should teach, and who shouldn't. For a long time the people humored him, and made him school inspector, whose business it was to examine the teachers with regard to their qualifications. With his old time notions, he had some very old-time questions, which with others, he always propounded. As a test of scholarship they were ridiculous; but he was Col. Crompton, and the people shrugged their shoulders and laughed at what they called the Crompton formula. Here are a few of the questions: First, What is logic? Second, Why does the wind usually stop blowing when the sun goes down? I don't know; do you? and we are both Harvarders. The third introduces a man in old Colburn's Arithmetic, driving his sheep or geese to market. The fourth is a scorcher, and has to do with the diameter of a grindstone, after a certain number of inches have been ground from it. Then comes what I call the *pièce de résistance*, but which my uncle called 'killing two birds with one stone.' He has a

fad on writing and spelling, and required his victims
to put on paper the following :
      " ' Mr. Wright has a right
        To write the rites of the church.'
      " Blamed if I didn't get stuck on that last *rite*
when he gave it to me! If the teachers got safely
through with the sheep, or geese, and the grindstone,
and Mr. Wright, and the rest of them, he gave them a
certificate declaring them qualified to teach a district
school. In these days of methods, and analysis, and
different ways of looking at things, all that is ex-
ploded, and the Crompton people have dropped my
uncle, who is furious, and charges it to young blood,
and the normal schools which have sprung up, and
in which he does not believe. ' No matter how many
diplomas a girl may have,' he says, ' proving that she
has stood up in a white gown, and read an esay nobody within four feet of the rostrum could hear, or
care to hear, if they could, she ought to pass a good
solid examination to see if she were rooted and
grounded in the fundamentals,' and when he heard
that a normal graduate was engaged for District No.
5, he swore a blue streak at the girl, the trustee who
hired her, and the attack of gout which keeps him a
prisoner in the house, and will prevent his interview-
ing Miss Smith, as he certainly would if he were able.
I tried to quiet him by offering to interview her myself. Think of me in a district school-house, talking
to the teacher about the diameter of a grindstone!
The absurdity must have struck my uncle. You
should have seen the look he gave me over his spectacles, as he said, ' You, who know nothing, except
ball games, and boat races, and raising the devil generally, interview a girl with a diploma! You would

probably end by making love to her, but I won't have it; mind, I won't have it! Remember, you are a Crompton, and no Crompton ever married beneath him!' Here he stopped suddenly, and turned so white that I was alarmed, and asked what ailed him.

" ' Nothing,' he said, ' nothing but a twinge. I had an awful one.'

" I suppose he referred to his foot, which was pretty bad that day. After a little, quite to my surprise, he said, ' If you knew anything yourself, you might manage to see if this Smith girl knows anything. Amy can coach you. She is rooted and grounded. She was taught in the old school-house, which I would never have given the town but for her.'

" What he meant I don't know. What I do know is that Amy has told me why the wind stops blowing when the sun goes down, but I'll be hanged if I understand much about the rarefaction of the air. Do you? She was very glib with the sheep and the geese, but the grindstone made her head ache, and she gave it up. I think, however, I have all the knowledge necessary to judge whether a girl is rooted and grounded, and now I want to know something about the girl. Manage to see her while you are in Mayville. Attend the commencement exercises. She is sure to read an essay in a white gown. Write me what she is like, and if I am likely to fall in love with her. Come as soon as you can.

"Always your friend,
" HOWARD CROMPTON."

·CHAPTER II

Mayville, July ——, 18—.

" Dear Howard:

" That you are a scamp of the first water goes with-out saying, insinuating yourself into an eccentric old man's confidence in hopes to be his heir! I dare say, Amy is his daughter, and you will have to work for a living after all, and serve you right, too. But have a good time while you can, and I'll help you after a little, as I accept your invitation with pleasure.

" Now for the girl! I have seen her, and if there was ever a case of love at first sight, I'm that case. It was this way. Mayville is not a very lively place, and when my sister, Mrs. Lovell, who you know has a summer home here, suggested one morning that we attend the commencement exercises of the Normal School, saying, that twenty-five or thirty young girls were to be graduated, I concluded that it was better than nothing. I hate such places, as a rule, they are so close and stuffy, and the essays so long and dull, and the girls all look pretty much alike, and I begged Bell to get a seat as near the door as possible, so I could go out when it became unendurable. Just then your letter was brought to me, and after reading it, nothing could have kept me from Eloise Smith. I asked Bell if she knew her.

" ' I don't know many of the girls by name,' she said, ' but I have heard of Eloise Smith.   She sings in the choir, and is a basket-boarder of Mrs. Brown's.'

" ' What the mischief is a basket-boarder? ' I asked, and Bell explained that girls sometimes hire a room, and bring their food from home, and have the family with whom they lodge cook it for them, or cook it themselves on the family stove. A kind of picnic to get an education, you see, and·just think of all we spent uselessly in college. Why, it would keep a lot of basket-boarders. Well, we started for the chapel, which was literally crammed, and the thermometer at ninety. You know, Mr. Lovell is wealthy, and from New York, and that makes Bell a kind of swell woman in the place, while I fancy your humble servant had something to do with the attention we received. Instead of a seat by the door, we were pushed to the front, within ten feet of the rostrum, and I was wedged in with Bell on one side of me, afraid I'd jam her sleeves, and on the other side was a woman, who weighed at least two hundred, and was equally afraid of her sleeves. In front of me was a hat so big that I couldn't begin to see all the stage, and but for Eloise I'd have got out some way, I was so uncomfortable with Bell fanning on one side till that rheumatic spot on my shoulder, which troubled me some at Harvard, began to ache, and the fat woman the other side mopping her face with a handkerchief saturated with cheap perfumery, and the big hat in front flopping and nodding this way and that, and no place to stretch my long legs.

" There was a prayer, a song circle, and *et ceteras*, and a great flutter in a row of white dresses, and many colored ribbons to my left. ' The Graduates,'

Bell whispered, and the business of the day began. There were eight in all to read essays—nice looking girls, and much like the Lasells and Wellesleys we used to know. As for the essays—well, there was either a good deal of bosh in them, or a profundity of learning and thought to which Jack Harcourt never attained. But the people cheered like mad whenever one was ended, and sent up flowers, while I grew hotter and hotter, and when the seventh went up, and unfolded the 'Age of Progress and Reason,' which looked as if it might last an age, I made up my mind to bolt, and said so to Bell.

" ' Keep still; there's only one more after this one, and that is Eloise Smith,' she said.

" I thought of you, and settled myself for another fifteen minutes, while a red-haired girl in glasses went through the 'Age of Progress and Reason' with great applause, and a basket of flowers, and bowed herself off the stage. There was a little delay. Somebody had fainted. I wonder they didn't all faint, the air was so hot and thick; and to crown all, the window near us had to be shut, because that fat woman didn't want a draught on her back! When they got the fainting person out, and the window shut, I saw the flutter of a white dress, and knew the eighth and last essay was coming.

" ' That's Eloise,' Bell said, as a slender little girl walked on to the rostrum, looking as fresh, and cool, and sweet as a—well, as the white lilies of which I am so fond.

" ' By George!' I said, so loud that those nearest me must have heard me, and wondered what ailed me.

" Perhaps she heard me, for she looked at me with her beautiful eyes, which steadied me, and kept me quiet all through her essay.   Don't ask me what it was about.   I don't know.   I was so absorbed in the girl herself, she was so graceful, and pretty, and self-possessed, and her voice was so musical that I could think of nothing but her; and when she finished I cheered louder than anybody else, and kept on cheering as they do in plays when they want them to come back, till Bell nudged my side, and whispered, 'Are you crazy?   Everybody is looking at you.'

" I was a little ashamed to be spatting away alone, but it pleased the fat woman, who proved to be Mrs. Brown, the keeper of the basket-boarders.

" ' That's Miss Smith.   She done nice, didn't she, and she or'to of had some flowers,' she said to me; and then I remembered with a pang that not a flower had been sent up to her—the flower of them all—and wished I had a whole green-house to give her.

" Did she think of it? I wondered, as I watched her after she sat down.   The big hat had moved a little, and I could see the top of Eloise's head, with its crown of reddish-brown hair, on which a gleam of sunshine from a window fell, bringing out tints of gold, as well as red.   That sounds rather poetical, don't it? for a prosy chap who professes never to have been moved by any piece of femininity, however dainty.   I'll confess I was moved by this little girl.   She is very slight and very young, I judge.   I like Mrs. Brown, and do not think her perfumery bad, or herself very fat, and am glad they had the window shut for her.   I wouldn't have her in a draught for anything, because she told me Eloise was the nicest girl she ever had in her house, and the best scholar in her class.   Of course she is; I'd swear to that.   She may not be rooted and grounded in the fundamentals your queer old uncle thinks necessary, and I doubt if she knows about the grindstone, and the rest of it. I'd laugh to see a great hulking fellow like you questioning her on such subjects. I've a great mind to write out the lingo, and send it to her anonymously, so she will be prepared to satisfy your uncle, who, I fancy, is the Great Mogul of Crompton.

" I got quite chummy with Mrs. Brown before the exercises were over, and she told me Eloise lived in North Mayville with her grandmother, and that she was real glad she had a place to teach in Crompton, for she needed it.

" ' Poor? ' I asked, feeling ashamed of myself for the question.

" But Mrs. Brown saw nothing wrong in it, and answered, ' Very.'

" Just then Bell nudged me again, and said, ' Let's go. We can get out now. You don't care to see them receive their diplomas? '

" But I did, and sat it out till Eloise had hers, and I saw her face again, and saw, too, what I had not noticed before, that her dress looked poor and plain beside the others. Of course she's poor; but what do I care for that? I am a good deal struck, you see, and if there were nothing else to bring me to Crompton, Eloise would do it. So expect me in September about the time her school commences. When will that be?

" Very truly,
" JACK HARCOURT."

CHAPTER III

It was a brown, old-fashioned house such as is common in New England, with low ceilings, high windows, and small panes of glass, and in the centre a great chimney of a fashion a hundred years ago. In the grass plot at the side, where clothes were bleached and dried, there should have been a well-sweep and curb to complete the picture, but instead there was a modern pump where an elderly woman was getting water, and throwing away three or four pails full, so that the last might be fresh and sparkling for the coffee she was to make for the early breakfast. Above the eastern hills the sun was rising, coloring everything with a rosy tinge, and the air was full of the song which summer sings, of flowers and happy insect life, when she is at her best. But the woman neither heard the song nor saw the sunshine, her heart was so heavy with thoughts of the parting which was so near.

"I can't let her know how bad I feel," she said, fighting back her tears, as she prepared the dainty breakfast which she could scarcely touch, but which her grand-daughter, Eloise, ate with the healthy appetite of youth, and then turned her attention to strapping her trunk, while her grandmother began to fill a paper box with slices of bread and butter, and whatever else she could find, and thought Eloise would like on the road.

"There, I've got it done at last, and hope it will hold till I get there, the old lock is so shaky," Eloise said, rising to her feet, and shedding back from her face a mass of soft, fluffy hair.

"Please don't put up any more lunch. I can never eat it all," she continued, turning to her grandmother; then, as she saw the tears dropping from the dim, old eyes, she sprang forward, and exclaimed, "Don't cry. You know we promised we would both be brave, and it is not so very long to Christmas. I shall certainly be home then, and Crompton is not so very far away."

With a catching kind of sob, the elder woman smiled upon the bright face uplifted to hers, and said: "I didn't mean to cry, and I am going to be brave. I am glad you have the chance."

"So am I," the girl replied, her spirits rising as her grandmother's tears were dried. "Ever since I was engaged to go to Crompton I have felt an elation of spirits, as if something were going to come of it. If it were not for leaving you, and I had heard from California, I should be very happy. When a letter comes, forward it at once, and if necessary I shall go there during the holidays, and bring her home. I am glad we have her room all ready for her. I must see it once more."

Running upstairs she opened the door of a large chamber, and stood for a moment inspecting it. Everything was plain and cheap, from the pine washstand to the rag carpet on the floor; but it was cosey and home-like, and the girl who had worked in it so much, papering and painting it herself, with her

grandmother's help, and then arranging and re-
arranging the furniture until it suited her, thought
it fine, and said to herself, " She'll like it better than
any room she ever had at the grandest hotel. I wish
she were here. Mother's room, good-by."

She kissed her hand to it and ran downstairs, for it
was time to go. . The train was drawing up at the
station, a short distance from her grandmother's
door, and in a few minutes she was speeding away
towards Crompton. At nearly the same hour Jack
Harcourt was starting from New York for his promised visit to Crompton. His letter has given some
insight into his character, but a look at his face will
give a better. It was not a very handsome face, but
it was one which every man, and woman, and child
would trust, and never be deceived. For a young
man of twenty-six he had seen a good deal of life,
both at home and abroad, but the bad side had made
but little impression upon him.

" It slips from Jack like water from a duck's back,
while we poor wretches get smirched all over,"
Howard Crompton was wont to say of him, when
smarting from some temptation to which he had
yielded, and which Jack had resisted.

They had been friends since they were boys of
eighteen in Europe, and Howard had nursed him
through a fever contracted in Rome. They had also
been chums in Harvard, where both had pulled
through rather creditably, and where Jack had acted
as a restraint upon Howard, who was fonder of larks
than of study.

" Are you sure he is the right kind of friend for
you? " Jack's sister—who was many years his senior,
and who stood to him in the place of a mother—some-

times said to him; and he always answered, " He isn't
a bad sort, as fellows go. Too lazy, perhaps, for a
chap who has nothing but expectations from a
crabbed, half-cracked old uncle, and not always quite
on the square. But he is jolly good company, and I
like him."

Something of this sort he said to his sister, who was
in her New York home on the day when he was
starting for Crompton, and had expressed her doubts
of Howard's perfect rectitude in everything.

" He isn't a saint," he said to her, " but I don't forget how he stuck to me in that beastly place on the
Riviera, while every soul of the party but him hurried off, afraid of the fever. He is having a grand
time at Crompton, and I'm going to help him a while,
and then buckle down to hard work in the office. So
good-by, and don't worry."

He kissed her and hurried off to the station, bought
the " Century," put several expensive cigars in the
pocket of his overcoat, took a chair in a parlor car,
and felt, as the train sped away out of the city, that it
was good to live, and that Crompton held some new
pleasure and excitement for him, who found sunshine everywhere.

Moving in the same direction and for the same
point was another train, in which Eloise sat, dusty
and tired, and homesick for the old grandmother and
the house under the big poplar tree. Added to this
was a harrowing anxiety for news from California.

" If I do not hear by Christmas, I shall certainly
take an extra week in my vacation, and go there,"
she thought; and then she began to wonder about
Crompton, and District No. 5, and if she would have
any trouble with the big boys and girls, and how she

would like Mrs. Biggs, who had boarded the school
teachers for twenty years, and was to board her; and
if by any chance she would ever see the inside of the
Crompton House, of which she had heard from a
friend who had visited in the town and had given
glowing descriptions of it.

At last, as the air in the car grew cooler, she fell
asleep, and did not waken till the sun was down, and
a great bank of black clouds was looming up in the
west, with mutterings of thunder, and an occasional
flash of lightning showing against the dark sky. She
might not have wakened then if the car had not given
a lurch, with a jar which brought every one to his
feet. The train was off the track, and it would be two
or three hours before it was on again, the conductor
said to the crowd eagerly questioning him. There
was nothing to do but wait, and Eloise did it philo-
sophically. She had dined from her lunch box in the
middle of the day, and was now glad that her grandmother had put so much in it, as it not only served
her for supper, but also a tired mother and two hungry children. As the car began to grow close again,
she left it for a breath of the fresh air, which blew over
the hills as the storm came nearer. She heard some
one say it was time for the New York Express, which
was to pass them at Crompton, and it soon came
thundering on, but stopped suddenly when it found
its progress impeded. She saw the passengers alight
to ascertain the cause of the hindrance, and heard
their impatient exclamations at the delay, which
would seriously inconvenience some of them.

"It may be midnight before we reach Crompton.
I wonder if Howard will meet me at that late hour,"
she heard a young man say, the smoke from his cigar

blowing in her face as he passed where she was sitting on a stump.

" He is sure to be there. I saw him day before yesterday, and he is wild to have you come. I fancy he finds it rather dull with only a cranky old man and a half-crazy woman for associates. Howard wants life and fun," was the reply of his companion, and then the two young men were out of hearing.

Who Howard was, or the cranky old man and half-crazy woman, Eloise had no idea, nor did she give them a thought. One thing alone impressed her,—the late hour when she would probably arrive at Crompton. Would any one be there to meet her, or any conveyance, and if not, how was she to find her way to Mrs. Biggs?

" Grandma says never cross a river till you reach it, when you will probably find a plank, if nothing more," she thought, and settled herself to wait through the long hours which elapsed before the welcome " All aboard ! " was sounded, and the two trains were under way,—the accommodation in front, and the express in the rear.

The storm had broken before the trains started, and it increased in such violence that when Crompton was reached it was raining in torrents. The wind was like a hurricane, with alternate flashes of lightning which lit up the darkness, and peals of thunder which seemed to shake the trains as they stopped to let off their passengers. There were but two, the young man from the parlor car, and the girl from the accommodation. The girl was almost drenched to the skin in the downpour before she could open her cotton umbrella, which was at once turned inside out. Holding her satchel with one hand and strug-

gling to keep her hat on her head with the other, she
was trying to reach the shelter of the station, where a
faint light was shining, when the violence of the wind
and rain drove her backwards, almost into the arms
of a young man hurrying past her, in a slouched hat
and water-proof coat. Thinking him an official, she
seized his arm and said, " Oh, please, sir, tell me is
there any one here from Mrs. Biggs's, or any way to
get there? "

Her question was inopportune, for at that moment
the stranger's umbrella met a like fate with her own,
and was turned inside out, while hers, loosened by
the opening of her hand, went sailing off into the
darkness and rain. She thought she heard an oath
before the stranger replied that he knew nothing of
Mrs. Biggs, and did not think any conveyance was
there at that hour.

" Hallo, Jack! Is that you? and did you ever
know such an infernal storm? Nearly takes one off
his feet. My umbrella has gone up; so will yours if
you open it. Didn't see you till I was right on you,"
was his next exclamation, as a vivid flash of lightning
lit up the platform, and showed Eloise two young
men clasping hands within three feet of her.

Howard Crompton had been to the station at the
appointed time, and learned of the delay of the train
in which he expected his friend. Later a telephone
had told him when the belated train would arrive, and
the carriage was again ordered, the coachman grumb-
ling, and the Colonel swearing to himself at having
the horses go out in such a storm. To Howard he
said nothing. That young man had so ingratiated
himself into his uncle's good opinion, as to be nearly
master of the situation. He wrote and answered most

of the Colonel's letters, collected his rents, and looked after his business generally, and did it so well that the Colonel was beginning to feel that he could not get on without him, and to have serious thoughts of making it worth his while to stay indefinitely.

Nothing could have been further from Howard's wishes than going out so late at night, and in such a storm, but the one unselfish passion of his life was his attachment to Jack Harcourt. He was not very well pleased with the wetting he got, as his umbrella was turned inside out; nor at all interested in the girl asking so timidly for Mrs. Biggs, and in his pleasure at meeting Jack he forgot her entirely, until the same flash of lightning which showed her the two men showed them her white face, with an appealing expression on it which Jack never passed by, whether it were matron or maid who needed his help. Who the drooping little figure was, with the water running down her jacket and off her hat in streams, he had no idea from the glimpse he had of her features as the lightning played over them for a moment. That she was in trouble was evident, and in return to Howard's greeting, he said, " This is a corker of a storm, and no mistake, and I do believe I am wet through, but,—" and he spoke a little lower,—" there's a girl here near us,—alone, too, I do believe."

" Yes, I know," Howard replied. " The station master will see to her. Come on to the carriage. The horses are plunging like mad. Sam can't hold them much longer."

He moved away, but Jack stood still, for a second flash of lightning had shown him Eloise's face again. It was very pale, and tears, as well as rain, were on her cheeks.

"Can I do anything for you?" he said, opening his umbrella, and holding it over her.

His voice was that of a friend, and Eloise recognized it as such, and answered, "I don't know. I am a stranger. I want to go to Mrs. Biggs's. Do you know where she lives?"

"I am a stranger, too, and have never heard of Mrs. Biggs," Jack replied; "but the station agent will know. He ought to be here. Hallo! you, sir! Why are you not attending to your business? Here is a young lady," he called out, as the agent at last appeared coming slowly toward them, holding a lantern with one hand, and his cap on with the other.

"I didn't s'pose there was anybody here but Mr. Crompton's friend. Who is she? Where does she want to go? There ain't no conveyance here for nowhere at this hour," he said, throwing the light of his lantern fully on Eloise, whose face grew, if possible, a shade paler, and whose voice shook as she replied, "I want to go to Mrs. Biggs's. I am to board with her. I am the new school teacher, Miss Smith. Can I walk there when the storm is over? How far is it?"

"Great guns!" Jack said under his breath, holding the whole of his umbrella now over the girl instead of half, while the agent replied, "Walk to Widder Biggs's! I'd say not. It's two good miles from here. You'll have to sit in the depot till it stops rainin' a little, and I'll find you a place till mornin'. Tim Biggs was here when the train or'to of come, and said he was expectin' a schoolmarm. Be you her?"

"Yes, oh, yes; thank you. Let me get into the station as soon as I can. My umbrella is gone, and I am so cold and wet," Eloise said, with catches in her breath between the words.

" Hold on a minit," the agent continued. " The Crompton carriage goes within quarter of a mile of the Widder Biggs's. I guess the young man will take you. I will ask him."

" No, let me. I'm sure he will," Jack interrupted him, and thrusting his umbrella into Eloise's hand, he stumbled through the darkness to the corner where he heard Howard calling to him, " Jack, Jack, where in thunder are you? "

" Here," Jack replied, making for the voice, and saying to Howard when he reached him, " Howard, that's Eloise Smith, the girl I wrote you about,—the school teacher. She hasn't a dry rag on her. Her umbrella is lost. She wants to go to Widow Biggs's. The agent says it is not far from the Crompton Place. Can't we take her? Of course we can. I'll go for her."

He hurried off as well as he could, leaving Howard in no very amiable frame of mind. He had laughed at Jack's rhapsodies over Eloise Smith, and said to himself, " His interest in her will never be very lasting, no matter how pretty she is. Jack Harcourt and a basket-boarder! Ha, ha! Rich. Still, I'd like to see her."

After that he had nearly forgotten her in his absorbing efforts to keep the right side of his uncle, and entertain Amy. And now she was here, and Jack was proposing to have him take her to Widow Biggs's, which was a quarter of a mile beyond the park gates, Sam said, when consulted as to the widow's whereabouts. There was no help for it, but he didn't like it, and there was a scowl on his face as he waited for Jack, who came at last with Eloise and the agent, whose lantern shed a dim light on the handsomely-cushioned carriage when the door was open.

"I'm not fit to get in there, I am so wet," Eloise said, drawing back a little.

"As fit as we are," Jack replied, almost lifting her in, and tilting his umbrella till one of the sticks struck Howard in the eye, increasing his discomposure, and making him wish both Eloise and Mrs. Biggs in a much dryer place than he was.

"Now, Howard, in with you. There's a little lull in the rain. We'll take advantage of it," Jack continued, as he followed Howard into the carriage, where both sat down opposite Eloise, who crouched in her corner, afraid she did not know of what. Certainly not of the man who had been so kind to her, and who she wished was sitting in front of her, instead of the one who did not speak at all, except to ask Sam how the deuce they were to know when they reached the Widow Biggs's.

"Easy enough. It is a squat-roofed house with lalock and piney bushes in the yard."

"Yes, but how are we to see a squat roof with la-locks and pineys on this beastly night?" Howard rejoined, in a tone which told that he was not anticipating his trip to the widder Biggs's. "Drive on, for heaven's sake," he continued, "and don't upset us. It is darker than a pocket."

"No, sir, not if I can help it. I never knew the horses so 'fraid. Easy, Cass—easy Brute," Sam answered, as in response to a flash of lightning Brutus and Cassius both stood on their hind feet and pawed the air with terror. "Easy, easy, boys. Lightnin'

can't strike you but once," Sam continued soothingly
to the restless, nervous horses, who were at last
gotten safely from the station, and started down the
road which lead through the village to Crompton
Place.

CHAPTER IV

THE ACCIDENT

For a short time the carriage went on smoothly and swiftly through the town, where the street lamps of kerosene gave a little light to the darkness. Once out of town in the country Sam became less sure of his way, and as he could not see his hand before him, he finally left the matter to the horses, trusting their instinct to keep in the road.

"I shall know when I reach the gate, and so will Brute and Cass; but we've got to go farther to the Widder Biggs's, and darned if I b'lieve they'll know the place," he thought, with a growing conviction of his inability to recognize Mrs. Biggs's squat roof and lilacs and peonies.

The storm which had abated for a short time was increasing again. The peals of thunder were more frequent, and with each flash of lightning the horses grew more unmanageable, until at last they flew along the highway at a speed which rocked the carriage from side to side, and began at last to alarm its occupants. Eloise in her corner was holding fast to the strap, when a lurid flame filled the carriage for an instant with a blaze of light. She had removed her hat, and her face, silhouetted against the dark cushions, startled both the young men with its beauty. It was very white, except the cheeks which were flushed with excitement. Her lips were apart, but her chief beauty was in her eyes, which were full of terror, and which shone like stars as they looked from one young man to the other.

" Oh, I am afraid. Let me out. I'd rather walk," she cried, starting to her feet and grasping the handle of the door.

" Please be quiet. There is no danger. You must not get out," Howard said, laying both his hands on hers, which he held for a moment, and pressed by way of reassuring her as he pushed her gently back into her seat.

She felt the pressure and resented it, and releasing her hands put them behind her, lest in the darkness they should be touched again. The same lightning which had showed her face to Howard had also given her a glimpse of his black eyes kindling with surprise and admiration at a beauty he had not expected. A lurch of the carriage sent Jack from his seat, and Eloise felt him close beside her. Was he going to squeeze her hands, too? She didn't know, and was holding them closely pressed behind her, when there was another flash, a deafening peal of thunder, a crash, and the next she knew the rain was falling upon her face, her head was lying against some one's arm, and two pairs of hands were tugging at her collar and jacket.

" Do you think she is dead?" was asked, in the voice which had told her not to be afraid.

" Dead!" a second voice replied. " She cannot be dead. She must not be. Miss Smith, Miss Smith! Where are you hurt?"

It was on the arm of this speaker she was lying, and she felt his breath on her face as he bent over her. With a great effort she moved her head and answered, ." I'm not dead, nor hurt either, except my foot, which is twisted under me."

" Thank God! " Jack said, and instantly the two pairs of hands groped in the dark for the twisted foot.

" Oh! " Eloise cried, sitting upright, as a sharp pain shot from her ankle to her head. " Don't touch me. I can't bear it. I am afraid it is broken. What has happened, and where is the carriage ? "

" Home by this time, if Brutus and Cassius have not demolished it in their mad fright," Howard said, explaining that at the last heavy peal of thunder the horses had swerved from the road and upset the carriage at the entrance to the park; that Sam had been thrown to some distance from the box, but had gathered himself up, and gone after the horses tearing up the avenue. " I shouted to him to come back with a lantern as quickly as possible. He'll be here soon, I think. Are you in great pain ? "

" When I move, yes," Eloise replied, and then, as the full extent of the catastrophe burst upon her, she began to cry,—not softly to 'herself, but hysterically, with sobs which smote both Howard and Jack like blows.

It was a novel predicament in which they found themselves,—near midnight, in a thunderstorm, with a young girl on the ground unable to walk, and neither of them knowing what to do. Howard said it was a deuced shame, and Jack told her not to cry. Sam was sure to come with a lantern soon, and they'd see what was the matter. As he talked he put her head back upon his shoulder, and she let it lie there without protest.

After what seemed a long time, Sam came up with

a lantern. The carriage was badly injured, he said, having been dragged through the avenue on its side. Brutus had a gouge on his shoulder from running into a tall shrub; he had hurt his arm when he fell from the box, and the Colonel was not in a very pious state of mind on account of his damaged property.

Eloise heard it all, but did not realize its import, her foot was paining her so badly. Jack had helped her up when Sam came, but she could not walk, and her face looked so white when the lantern light fell upon it, that both men feared she was going to faint.

"What shall we do?" Howard asked, standing first on one foot and then on the other, and feeling the water ooze over the tops of his shoes.

"Take her to the Crompton house, of course. It must be nearer than Mrs. Biggs's," Jack suggested.

Before Howard could reply, Eloise exclaimed, "Oh, no, I can hop on one foot to Mrs. Biggs's if some one helps me. Is it far?"

The two men looked inquiringly at each other and then at Sam, who was the first to speak. In the Colonel's state of mind, with regard to his carriage and his horses, he did not think it advisable to introduce a helpless stranger into the house, and he said, "I'll tell you what; did you ever make a chair with your hands crossed—so?"

He indicated what he meant, and the chair was soon made, and Eloise lifted into it.

"That's just the thing; but you'll have to put an arm around each of our necks to steady yourself," Jack said. "So! That's right! hold tight!" he continued, as Eloise put an arm around each neck.

Sam was directing matters, and taking up the lantern and Jack's umbrella, which he had found lying in the mud, he said, " I'll light the way and hold the umbrella over you. It don't rain much now."

" My hat and satchel, please," Eloise said, but neither could be found, and the strange cortége started.

For an instant the ludicrousness of the affair struck both young men, convulsing them with laughter to such an extent that the chair came near being pulled apart and Eloise dropped to the ground. She felt it giving way, and, taking her arm from Howard, clung desperately to Jack.

" Don't let me fall, please," she said.

" No danger; hold fast as you are," Jack answered cheerily, rather enjoying the feeling of the two arms clasping his neck so tightly.

What Howard felt was streams of water trickling down his back from the umbrella, which Sam held at exactly the right angle for him to get the full benefit of a bath between his collar and his neck. He did not like it, and was in a bad frame of mind mentally, when, after what seemed an eternity to Eloise, they came to three or four squat-roofed houses in a row, at one of which Sam stopped, confidently affirming it was the Widder Biggs's, although he could not see the " lalock and pineys."

" Knock louder! Kick, if necessary," Howard said, applying his own foot to the door as there came no answer to Sam's first appeal.

There was a louder knock and call, and at last a glimmer of light inside. Somebody was lighting a candle, which was at once extinguished when the door was open, and a gust of wind and rain swept in.

" Are you Mrs. Biggs? " Sam asked, as a tall figure in a very short night-robe was for a moment visible.

"Mrs. Biggs! Thunder, no! Don't you know a man from a woman? She lives second house from here," was the masculine response.

The door was shut with a bang, and the cortége moved on to the third house, which, by investigating the lilac bushes and peonies, Sam made out belonged to the Widder Biggs. It was harder to rouse her than it had been to rouse her neighbor. She was a little deaf, and the noise of the wind and rain added to the difficulty. When she did awaken her first thought was of burglars; and there was a loud cry to her son Tim to come quick and bring his gun, for somebody was breaking into the house.

"Robbers don't make such a noise as that! Open your window and see who's there," was Tim's sleepy answer, as Sam's blows fell heavily upon the door, accompanied with thuds from Howard's foot.

Mrs. Biggs opened her window cautiously, and thrust out her head, minus her false hair, and enveloped in a cotton nightcap.

"Who is it? What has happened? Anybody sick or dead?" she asked; and Sam replied, "Miss Smith is here with a broken laig, for't I know!"

"Miss Smith! A broken leg! For the land's sake, Tim, get up quick!" the widow gasped.

Closing the window and putting on a skirt, she descended to the kitchen, lighted an oil lamp, and, throwing open the door, looked at the group outside. She was prepared for Sam and Miss Smith, and did not mind her deshabille for them. But at the sight of two gentlemen, and one of them young Mr. Crompton, she came near dropping her lamp.

"Gracious goodness!" she exclaimed. "Mr. Crompton! And I half-dressed! Wait till I get on some clothes, and my hair, and my teeth. I am a sight to behold."

"Never mind your teeth, nor your hair, nor your best gown," Sam said, pushing open the door Mrs. Biggs had partially closed, and entering the house, followed by Howard and Jack, with Eloise still clinging to Jack's neck, and half fainting with the pain in her ankle which had increased from hanging down so long.

Tim had come by this time, fastening his suspenders as he came, and caring less for his appearance than his mother. She had disappeared, but soon returned with teeth, and hair, and clothes in place, and herself ready for the emergency. Following Tim's directions they had put Eloise on a couch, where she lay with her eyes closed, and so still that they thought she had fainted.

"Bring the camphire, Timothy, and the hartshorn, and start up the oil stove for hot water, and move lively," Mrs. Biggs said to her son. "I don't believe she's broke her laig, poor thing. How white she is," she continued, laying her hand on Eloise's forehead.

This brought the tears in a copious shower, as Eloise sat up and said, "It is my ankle. I think it is sprained. If you could get off my boot."

She tried to lift it, but let it drop with a cry of pain.

"I'll bet it's sprained, and a sprain is wus than a break. I had one twenty years ago come Christmas, and went with my knee on a chair two weeks, and on crutches three," was Mrs. Biggs's consoling remark, as she held the lamp close to the fast-swelling foot, to which the wet boot clung with great tenacity.

"Oh, I can't bear it," Eloise said, as the process of removing her boot commenced; then, closing her

10

eyes, she lay back upon the cushions, while one after another, Mrs. Biggs, Howard, Jack, and Tim worked at the refractory boot.

It was such a small foot, Jack thought, pitying the young girl, as he saw spasms of pain upon her face, where drops of sweat were standing. He wiped these away with Mrs. Biggs's apron, lying in a chair, and smoothed her hair, and took one of her clenched hands in his, and held it while the three tried to remove the boot.

"'Tain't no use,—it's got to be cut off,—mine did. Tim, bring me the butcher knife,—the sharpest one," Mrs. Biggs said.

Eloise shuddered, and thought of the only other pair of boots she had,—her best ones, which were to have lasted a year. But there was no alternative. The boot must be cut off, and Jack continued to hold her hands while, piece by piece, the wet leather dropped upon the floor.

"Now for the stockin'; that'll come easier," Mrs. Biggs said.

"Must you take that off now?" Eloise asked, her maidenly modesty prevailing over every other feeling.

Howard and Jack understood, and went to the window, while the stocking followed the fate of the boot; and when they came back to the couch Eloise's foot was in a basin of hot water, and Mrs. Biggs was gently manipulating it, and declaring it the worst sprain she ever knew, except her own, which, after twenty years troubled her at times, and told her when a storm was coming.

"Ought she to have a doctor?" Jack asked, and Mrs. Biggs replied, "A doctor? What for, except to

run up a bill. I know what to do. She'll have to keep
quiet a spell; wormwood and vinegar and hot water
will do the rest. Tim, go up garret and get a handful
of wormwood. It's the bundle of 'arbs to your right.
There's catnip, and horehound, and spearmint, and
sage, and wormwood. Be lively, and put it to steep
in some vinegar, and bring me that old sheet in the
under bureau drawer for bandages."

She seemed to know what she was about. Eloise
was in good hands, and the two water-soaked young
men were about to leave when she said, " I guess one
of you will have to carry her to her chamber. I can't
trust Tim, he's such a blunderhead."

" No, no! Oh, no! I can walk somehow," Eloise
said, starting to her feet, and sinking back as quickly.

" Let me. I'll carry her!" Howard and Jack both
exclaimed; but something in Eloise's eyes gave the
preference to Jack, who lifted her as easily as if she
had been a child, and carried her up the narrow stairs
to the room which at intervals had been occupied by
one teacher after another for nearly twenty years, for
it was understood that Mrs. Biggs was to board the
teachers who had no home of their own in the district.

But never had so forlorn or wretched an one been
there as poor Eloise. The world certainly looked
very dreary to her, and her lip quivered as she said
good-by to Jack, and tried to smile in reply to his
assurance that she would be better soon, and that he
would call and see her on the morrow. Then he was
gone, and Eloise heard the footsteps and voices of the
three men as they left the house and hurried away.
She was soon in bed, and as comfortable as Mrs.
Biggs could make her. That good lady was a born
nurse as well as a gossip, and as she arranged Eloise

for what there was left of the night, her tongue ran incessantly, first on her own sprain,—every harrowing detail of which was gone over,—then on the two young men, Howard Crompton and t'other one, who was he? She knew Mr. Howard,—everybody did. He was Col. Crompton's nephew, and he ruled the roost at the Crompton House, folks said, and would most likely be the Colonel's heir, with Miss Amy, as folks called her now. Had Miss Smith ever heard of her?

Eloise never had, and the pain in her ankle was so sharp that she gave little heed to what Mrs. Biggs was saying. She did not know either of the young men, she said. Both had been kind to her, and one, she thought, was a stranger, who came in the train with her.

"Oh, yes," Mrs. Biggs answered briskly. "I remember now. Cindy,—that's Miss Stiles, the housekeeper at Crompton Place,—told me Mr. Howard was to have company,—another high buck, I s'pose, though Howard don't do nothin' worse than drive horses pretty fast, and smoke most all the time. Drinks wine at dinner, they say, which I disbelieve in on account of Tim, who never took nothin' stronger'n sweet cider through a straw."

At last, to Eloise's relief, Mrs. Biggs said goodnight, and left her with the remark, "I don't s'pose you'll sleep a wink. I didn't the first night after my sprain, nor for a good many nights neither."

CHAPTER V

"If this isn't a lark I never had one," Howard said to Jack, when they were safely housed and had changed their clothes, not a thread of which was dry.

Jack, whose luggage had not come, and who was obliged to borrow from Howard's wardrobe, looked like an overgrown boy in garments too small for him. But he did not mind it, and with Howard discussed the events of the evening, as they sat over the fire the latter had lighted in his room. Naturally Eloise was the subject of their conversation.

"I wrote you I had a presentiment that she was to come into my life in some way, but I had no idea it was to be this way," Howard said, as he puffed at his cigar and talked of their adventure and Eloise.

That she was very handsome and had pretty little feet went without saying, and that both were sorry for her was equally, of course. Jack was the more so, as his was the more unselfish and sympathetic nature.

"By Jove, didn't she bear the cutting of that boot like a hero, and how is she ever to get to school with that ankle?" he said; "and I think she ought to have a doctor to see if any bones are broken. Suppose you get one in the morning, and tell him not to send his bill to her but to me."

Howard looked up quickly, and Jack went on, "I

wrote you that Mrs. Brown said she was poor, and I should know it by her boots."

"Her boots!" Howard repeated, and Jack continued, "Yes, wet as they were I noticed they were half-worn, and had been blacked many times. She can't afford to pay many doctor's bills, and I ask you again, how is she to get to school?"

Howard did not know, unless they made another chair and carried her.

"I wouldn't mind it much for the sake of her arm around my neck. I can feel it yet. Can't you?" he said.

Jack could feel it and the little wet hand which once or twice had touched his face, but something in his nature forbade his talking about it. It might have been fun for them, but he knew it was like death to the girl, and that she had shrank from it all, and only submitted because she could not help it. He was very sorry for her, and thought of her the last moment before he fell asleep, and the first moment he awoke with Howard in the room telling him it was after breakfast time, and his uncle, who did not like to be kept waiting, was already in a temper and blowing like a northeaster.

The Colonel, who was suffering from an attack of rheumatic gout, was more irritable than usual. He had not liked having his horses and carriage go out in the rain, and had sat up waiting for the return of his nephew, and when Sam came in, telling what had happened to the carriage and horses, and that he must go back with a lantern to the park gates and see if the new school mistress was alive, he went into a terrible passion, swearing at the weather, and the late train,

and the school mistress who he seemed to think was
the cause of the accident.

"What business had she in the carriage? Why
did she come in such a storm? Why didn't she
take the 'bus, and if the 'bus wasn't there, why didn't
she—?" He didn't know what, and it took all the
tact of Peter, who was still in the family and old like
his master, to quiet him.

Then next morning his gout was so bad that he was
wheeled into the dining-room, where he was fast
growing angry at the delay of breakfast, and beginning to swear again when Peter, who knew how to
manage him, went for Amy. Nothing quieted the
Colonel like a sight of Amy, with her sweet face and
gentle ways.

"Please come. It's beginning to sizzle," Peter fre-
quently said to her when a storm was brewing, and
Amy always went, and was like oil on the troubled
waters.

"What is it?" she now asked, and the Colonel replied, "What is it! I should say, what is it! There's
the very old Harry to pay. Brutus has a big hole in
his breast, the carriage is smashed, silk cushions all
stained with a girl's blue gown, and that girl the
school-teacher I didn't want; and she's broken her
leg or something when they tipped over, and Howard
and his friend carried her to Widow Biggs's, and
the Lord knows what didn't happen!"

Amy had a way of seeming to listen very attentively when the Colonel talked to her, and always
smiled her appreciation and approbation of what he
said. Just how much she really heard or understood was doubtful. Her mind seemed to run in two
channels,—one the present, the other the past,—and

both were blurred and indistinct,—especially the past.
She understood about the young girl, however, and at
once expressed her sympathy, and said, "We must
do something for her."

To do something for any one in sickness or trouble
was her first thought, and many a home had been
made glad because of her since she came to Crompton.

"Certainly; do what you like, only don't bring her
here," the Colonel replied, his voice and manner
softening, as they always did with Amy.

She was a very handsome woman and looked
younger than her years. The storm which had swept
over her had not impaired her physical beauty, but
had touched her mentally in a way very puzzling to
those about her, and rather annoying to the Colonel,
who was trying to make amends for the harshness
which had driven her from his home. Sometimes her
quiet, passive manner irritated him, and he felt that
he would gladly welcome the old imperiousness with
which she had defied him. But it was gone. Something had broken her on the wheel, killing her spirit
completely, or smothering it and leaving her a timid,
silent woman, who sat for hours with a sad, far-off
expression, as if looking into the past and trying to
gather up the tangled threads which had in a measure
obscured her intellect.

"The Harrises are queer," kept sounding in the
Colonel's ears, with a thought that the taint in the
Harris blood was working in Amy's veins, intensified
by some great shock, or series of shocks.

Once, after he brought her home, he questioned
her of her life as a singer, and of the baby, which she
occasionally mentioned, but he never repeated the

experiment. There was a fit of nervous trembling,—
a look of terror in her eyes, and a drawn expression
on her face, and for a moment she was like the girl
Eudora when roused. Then, putting her hand before
her eyes as if to shut out something hateful to her,
she said, " Oh, don't ask me to bring up a past I can't
remember without such a pain in my head and everywhere, as if I were choking. It was very dreadful,—
with *him*,—not with Adolf,—he was so kind."

" Did he ever beat you?—or what did the wretch
do? *Smith*, I mean," the Colonel asked, and Amy replied, " Oh, no; it wasn't that. It was a constant
grind, grind,—swear, swear,—a breaking of my will,
till I had none left. He never struck me but once,
and then it was throwing something instead of a blow.
It hit me here, and it has ached ever since."

She put her hand to one side of her temple, and
went on, " It was the night I heard baby was dead,
and I said I could not sing,—but he made me, and I
broke down, and I don't know much what happened
after till you came. I can't remember."

" Yes, but the baby,—where did it die, and when?"
the Colonel asked.

Amy had been getting quiet as she talked, but at
the mention of the baby, she began to tremble again,
and beat the air with her hands.

" I don't know, I don't know," she said. " He
took her away, and she died. It is so black when I
try to think how it was, and it goes from me. Wait
a bit!" She sat very still a moment, and then in
a more natural voice said, " It may come back sometime, and then I will tell you. It makes me worse to
talk about it now. It's this way: The inside of my
head shakes all over. The doctor said it was like a

bottle full of something which must settle. I *am* settling here where everybody speaks so low and kind, but when I am a little clear, with the sediment going down, if you shake up the bottle, it is thick and muddy again, and I can't remember."

"By Jove!" the Colonel said to himself, "that bottle business isn't a bad comparison. She is all shaken up, and I'll let her settle."

He did not question her again of her life with Homer Smith, or of the baby. Both were dead, and he felt that it was just as well that they were. Homer Smith ought to be dead, and as to the baby it would have been very upsetting in the house, and might have been queer, like the Harrises, or worse yet, like its *cuss* of a father. On the whole, it was better as it was, although he was sorry for Amy, and would do all he could to make her happy, and some time, perhaps, she would remember, and tell him where the baby was buried, and he'd have it brought to Crompton, and put in the Crompton vault. As for Homer Smith, his carcase might rot in the desert of Arizona, or anywhere, for aught he cared. He was very gentle and patient with Amy, and watched the settling of the bottle with a great deal of interest. Sometimes he wondered how much she remembered of her Florida life, if anything, and what effect the mention of Jaky and Mandy Ann would have upon her, and what effect it would have upon her if he took her to the palmetto clearing, and found the negroes, if living. But pride still stood in the way. More than thirty-five years of silence were between him and the past, which to all intents was as dead as poor Dory; and why should he pull aside the dark curtain, and let in the public gaze and gossip. He couldn't and he wouldn't. All he could do for Amy in other ways he would, and for her sake he controlled himself mightily, becoming, as Peter said, like a turtle dove compared to what he once was, when the slightest crossing of his will roused him into fury.

Harsh, loud tones made Amy shiver, and brought a look into her eyes which the Colonel did not like to see, and with her he was usually very docile, or if roused, the touch of her hand and the expression of her eyes subdued him, as they did now when he told her of his broken carriage and ruined cushions and the young girl for whom Amy at once wished to do something.

"Certainly," he had said; "only don't bring her here," and he was beginning to wonder where Howard was, and to feel irritated at the delay, when the latter came in with Jack, and found a tolerably urbane and courteous host.

Naturally the conversation turned upon the storm and accident, the particulars of which were briefly gone over, while Amy stirred her coffee listlessly and did not seem to listen. She was very lovely, Jack thought, with no sign of her mental disorder, except the peculiar expression of her eyes at times. Her dress was faultless, her manner perfect, her language good, and her smile the sweetest and saddest he had ever seen, and Jack watched her curiously, while the conversation drifted away from Eloise, in whom the Colonel felt no interest. She was a graduate, and probably knew nothing of what he thought essential for a teacher to know. She was not rooted and grounded in the fundamentals. Probably she had never heard of the grindstone, or the sheep, and could not work out the problems if she had. She was superficial. She belonged to a new generation which had put him and his theories on the shelf. Her blue dress had stained the cushions of his carriage, and there was a puddle of water in the hall where Sam had put down her satchel and hat, which had been found in the driveway near the stable. They had been thrown from the carriage, and lain in the rain all night. The hat was soaked through and through, and the ribbons were limp and faded; but he did not care a rap what became of them, he said to himself, when Howard spoke of them and their condition, saying that bad as they were he presumed she wanted them.

Amy on the contrary was instantly on the alert, and as they passed through the hall from the dining-room, and she saw the poor crushed hat, she said to Jack, " Is it hers? "

" Yes, and I'm afraid it is ruined," Jack answered, taking it in his hand and examining it critically.

" I will fix it," Amy replied, and, carrying it to her room, she tried to bend it into shape and renovate the bows of ribbon.

But it was beyond her skill.

" She can never wear it. I must send her one of mine," she said, selecting a hat which she wore when walking in the park. " You must take it to the young lady at Mrs. Biggs's. What is her name? I don't think I understood; they were all talking together and confused me so," she said to her maid, who had heard of the adventure from Sam, but had not caught the right name.

" It is Louise something. I don't remember what," she replied.

" Louise! That sounds like baby's name, and it makes my head ache to think of it," Amy said sadly, going to the window, and looking out at the rain and fog, for the weather had not cleared.

It was a wet morning, and Howard, who liked his ease, shrugged his shoulders when Jack suggested that they should call upon Miss Smith.

" She ought to have her satchel and her hat," Jack said, and Howard replied, " Oh, Amy sent Sarah off with a hat half an hour ago. She would send all her wardrobe if she thought the girl wanted it, and, by George! why didn't she send a pair of boots? She has dozens of them, I dare say," he continued, as he recalled the bits of leather they had cut from Eloise's foot, and left on Mrs. Biggs's floor.

Jack had spoken of her boots, and he readily acceded to Howard's proposition to ask Amy if she had any cast-offs she thought would fit Miss Smith. " They must wear about the same size, the girl is so slight," Howard said as he went to Amy's room, where he found her still standing by the window drumming upon the pane as if fingering a piano and humming softly to herself. She never touched the grand instrument in the drawing-room, and when asked to do so and sing, she answered, " I can't; I can't. It would bring it all back and shake up the bottle. I hate the memory of it when I sang to the crowd and they applauded. I hear them now; it is baby's death knell. I can never sing again as I did then."

And yet she did sing often to herself, but so low that one could scarcely understand her words, except to know they were some negro melody sung evidently as a lullaby to a child. As Howard came up to her he caught the words, " Mother's lil baby," and knew it was what she sometimes sang with the red cloak hugged to her bosom.

"Miss Amy," he said, "I wonder if you haven't a pair of half-worn boots for the young lady at Mrs. Biggs's? We had to cut one of hers off, her foot was so swollen."

Amy was interested at once, and ordered Sarah, who had returned from Mrs. Biggs's, to bring out all her boots and slippers, insisting that several pairs be sent for the girl to choose from. Sarah suggested that slippers would be better than boots, as the young lady could not wear the latter in her present condition.

"Yes," Amy said, selecting a pair of white satin slippers, with high French heels and fanciful rosettes. "I wore them the night he told me baby was dead. I've never had them on since. I don't want them. Give them to her. They are hateful to me."

Amy was in a peculiar mood this morning, such as sometimes came upon her and made Peter say she was a chip of the old block, meaning the Colonel, who he never for a moment doubted was her father. Sarah's suggestion that white satin slippers would be out of place made no difference. They must go. She was more stubborn than usual, and Sarah accounted for it by saying in a low tone to Howard, "Certain spells of weather always affect her and send her back to a night when something dreadful must have happened. Probably the baby she talks about died. She's thinking about it now. Better take the slippers. I've heard her talk of them before and threaten to burn them."

"All right," Howard said. "Miss Smith can send them back if she does not want them."

The slippers were made into a parcel so small tha Howard put them in his pocket and said he wa ready. It had stopped raining, and as the young me: preferred to walk they set off througn the park laughing over their errand and the phase of excite ment in which they found themselves. Jack liked it and Howard, too, began to like it, or said he shoul if the girl proved as good-looking by daylight as sh had been in the night.

CHAPTER VI

Notwithstanding Mrs. Biggs's prediction that she would not sleep a wink, Eloise did sleep fairly well. She was young and tired. Her ankle did not pain her much when she kept it still, and after she fell asleep she did not waken till Mrs. Biggs stood by her bed armed with hot coffee and bandages and fresh wormwood and vinegar.

"Do you feel like a daisy?" was Mrs. Biggs's cheery greeting, as she put down the coffee and bowl of vinegar in a chair and brought some water for Eloise's face and hands.

"Not much like a daisy," Eloise answered, with a smile, "but better than I expected. I am going to get up."

"Better stay where you be. I did, and had 'em wait on me," Mrs. Biggs said; but Eloise insisted, thinking she must exercise.

She soon found, however, that exercising was a difficult matter. Her ankle was badly swollen, and began to ache when she moved it, nor did Mrs. Biggs's assurance that "it would ache more until it didn't ache so bad" comfort her much. She managed, however, to get into a chair, and took the coffee, and submitted to have her ankle bathed and bandaged and her foot slipped into an old felt shoe

of Mrs. Biggs's, which was out at the toe and out at
the side, but did not pinch at all.

"Your dress ain't dry. You'll catch your death of
cold to have it on. You must wear one of mine,"
Mrs. Biggs said, producing a spotted calico wrapper,
brown and white,—colors which Eloise detested.

It was much too large every way, but Mrs. Biggs
lapped it in front and lapped it behind, and said the
length would not matter, as Eloise could only walk
with her knee in a chair and could hold up one
side. Eloise knew she was a fright, but felt that she
did not care, until Mrs. Biggs told her of the hat
which the lady from Crompton Place had sent her,
and that Sarah had said the young gentlemen would
probably call.

"I've been thinking after all," she continued, "that
it is better to be up. The committee man, Mr. Bills,
who hired you, will call, and you can't see him and
the young men here. I'm a respectable woman, and
have boarded the teachers off and on for twenty
years,—all, in fact, except Ruby Ann, who has a
home of her own,—and I can't have my character
compromised now by inviting men folks into a bedroom. You must come down to the parlor. There's
a bed-lounge there which I can make up at night, and
it'll save me a pile of steps coming upstairs."

"How am I to get there?" Eloise asked in dismay,
and Mrs. Biggs replied, "It'll be a chore, I guess,
but you can do it. I did when my ankle was bad. I
took some strong coffee, same as I brought you, had
my foot done up, and slid downstairs, one at a time,
with my lame laig straight out. I can't say it didn't
hurt, for it did, but I had to grin and bear it.
Christian Science nor mind cure wasn't invented then,

11

or I should of used 'em, and said my ankle wasn't sprained.   There's plenty of nice people believes 'em now.   You can try 'em on, and we'll manage some-how."

Eloise was appalled at the thought of going down-stairs to meet people, and especially the young men from Crompton, clad in that spotted brown and white gown, with nothing to relieve its ugliness, not even a collar, for the one she had worn the previous day was past being worn again until it had been laundered. She looked at her handkerchief.   That, too, was im-possible.

"Mrs. Biggs," she said at last, "have you a hand-kerchief you can loan me?"

"To be sure! To be sure! Half a dozen, if you like," Mrs. Biggs answered, hurrying from the room, and soon returning with a handkerchief large enough for a dinner napkin.

It was coarse and half-cotton, but it was clean, and Eloise tied it around her neck, greatly to Mrs. Biggs's surprise.

"Oh," she said, "you wanted it for that?   Why not have a lace ruffle?   I'll get one in a jiffy."

Eloise declined the ruffle.   The handkerchief was bad enough, but a lace ruffle with that gown would have been worse.

"Now, I'll call Tim to go in front and keep you from falling.   He is kind of awkward, but I'll go be-hind and stiddy you, and you grit your teeth and put on the mind cure, and down we go," Mrs. Biggs said, calling Tim, who came shambling up the stairs, and laughed aloud when he saw Eloise wrapped in his mother's gown.

"Excuse me, I couldn't help it; mother has made

you into such a bundle," he said good-humoredly, as he saw the pained look in Eloise's face. "I'll get your trunk the next train, and you can have your own fixin's. What am I to do?"

This last was to his mother, who explained the way she had gone downstairs when she sprained her ankle twenty years ago come Christmas.

"She must sit down somehow on the top stair and slide down with one before her,—that's you,—and one behind,—that's me,—and she's to put on the mind cure. Miss Jenks says it does a sight of good."

Tim looked at his mother and then at Eloise, whose pitiful face appealed to him strongly.

"Oh, go to grass," he said, "with your mind cure! It's all rot! I'll carry her, if she will let me. I could of done it last night as well as them fine fellows."

He was a rough young boy of sixteen, with uncouth ways; but there was something in his face which drew Eloise to him, and when he said, "Shall I carry you?" she answered gladly, "Oh, yes, please. I don't think I have any mind to put on."

Lifting her very gently in his strong arms, while his mother kept saying she knew he'd let her fall, Tim carried her down and into the best room, where he set her in a rocking-chair, and brought a stool for her lame foot to rest upon, and then said he would go for her trunk, if she would give him her check. There was something magnetic about Tim, and Eloise felt it, and was sorry when he was gone. The world looked very dreary with the fog and rain outside, and the best room inside, with its stiff hair-cloth furniture, glaring paper and cheap prints on the wall —one of them of Beatrice Cenci, worse than anything she had ever seen. She was very fastidious in her tastes, and everything rude and incongruous offended it, and she was chafing against her surroundings, when Mrs. Biggs came bustling in, very much excited, and exclaiming, " For the land's sake, they are comin'! They are right here. They hain't let much grass grow. Let me poke your hair back a little from your forehead,—so! That's right, and more becomin'."

" Who are coming? " Eloise asked.

" Why, Mr. Crompton and his friend. I don't know his name," Mrs. Biggs replied, and Eloise felt a sudden chill as she thought of the figure she must present to them.

If she could only look in the glass and adjust herself a little, or if Mrs. Biggs would throw something over the unsightly slipper and the ankle smothered in so many bandages. The mirror was out of the question. She had combed her hair with a side comb which had come safely through the storm, but she felt that it was standing on end, and that she was a very crumpled, sorry spectacle in Mrs. Biggs's spotted gown, with the handkerchief round her neck. Hastily covering her foot with a fold of the wide gown, she clasped her hands tightly together, and leaning her head against the back of her chair, drew a long breath and waited.

She heard the steps outside, and Mrs. Biggs's " Good-mornin'; glad to see you. She is expectin' you, or I am. Yes, her laig is pretty bad. Swelled as big as two laigs, just as mine was twenty years ago come Christmas, when I sprained it. Tim brought her downstairs where she can see folks. She's in the parlor. Walk in."

Eloise's cheeks were blazing, but the rest of her face was very pale, and her eyes had in them a hunted look as the young men entered the room, preceded by Mrs. Biggs in her working apron, with her sleeves rolled up.

"Miss Smith, this is Mr. Crompton," she said, indicating Howard; "and the t'other one is—his name has slipped my mind."

"Harcourt," Jack said, feeling an intense sympathy for the helpless girl, whose feelings he guessed and whose hand he held a moment with a clasp in which she felt the pity, and had hard work to keep the tears back.

Howard also took her hand and felt sorry for her, but he did not affect her like Jack, and she did not like his eyes, which she guessed saw everything. He had a keen sense of the ridiculous, and the contrast between Eloise and the gown which he knew must belong to Mrs. Biggs struck him so forcibly that he could scarcely repress a smile, as he asked how she had passed the night. Mrs. Biggs answered for her. Indeed, she did most of the talking.

"She slep' pretty well, I guess; better'n I did when I sprained my ankle twenty years ago come Christmas. I never closed my eyes, even in a cat nap, and she did. I crep' to her door twice to see how she was gettin' on, and she was—not exactly snorin'—I don't s'pose she ever does snore,—but breathin' reg'lar like, jess like a baby, which I didn't do in a week when I sprained my ankle."

She would have added "twenty years ago come Christmas," if Jack had not forestalled her by asking Eloise if her ankle pained her much.

"Yes," she said, while Mrs. Biggs chimed in, "Can't help painin' her, swelled as 'tis,—big as two ankles; look."

She whisked off the bottom of her dress which Eloise had put over her foot, and disclosed the shapeless bundle encased in the old felt slipper.

"Look for yourselves; see if you think it aches," she said.

This was too much for Eloise, who, regardless of pain, drew her foot up under the skirt of her dress, while her face grew scarlet. Both Howard and Jack were sorry for her, and at last got the conversation into another channel by saying they had brought her satchel and hat, which they feared were ruined, and asking if she had seen the hat Miss Amy had sent her.

"Land sakes, no! I told her about it, but I hain't had time to show it to her," Mrs. Biggs exclaimed, starting from the room, while Howard explained that his cousin had tried in vain to renovate the drenched hat, and, finding it impossible, had sent one of her own which she wished Miss Smith to accept with her compliments.

"How do you like it?" Mrs. Biggs asked, as she came in with it.

It was a fine leghorn, with a wreath of lilacs round the crown, and Eloise knew that it was far more expensive than anything she had ever worn.

"It is very pretty," she said, "and very kind in the lady to send it. Tell her I thank her. What is her name?"

Jack looked at Howard, who replied, "She has had a good many, none of which pleased my uncle, the last one least of all; so he calls her Miss Amy, and wishes others to do so."

Eloise was puzzled, but the sight of Mrs. Biggs tugging at her wet satchel to open it diverted her mind.

"Your things is sp'ilt, most likely, but you'd better

have 'em out. For the mercy's sake, look!" she said, passing the satchel to Eloise, who was beyond caring for what was spoiled and what was not. "There's somebody knockin'. It's Mr. Bills, most likely, the committee man, come to see you; I told Tim to notify him," Mrs. Biggs exclaimed, hurrying out, and saying to Howard as she passed him, " You can visit a spell before I fetch him in. She needs perkin' up, poor thing."

It proved to be a grocer's boy instead of Mr. Bills, and Mrs. Biggs came back just as Howard was presenting the slippers.

" I did not think they were just what you wanted," Howard explained, as he saw the look of surprise on Eloise's face. " Miss Amy is not always quite clear in her mind, but rather resolute when it is made up; and when we told her we had to cut off your boot, she insisted upon sending these."

At this point Mrs. Biggs appeared, throwing up both hands at what she saw, and exclaiming, " Wall, if I won't give up! Satin slips for a spraint laig. Yes, I'll give up!"

She looked at Howard, who did not reply, but turned his head to hide his laugh from Eloise, while Mrs. Biggs went on, " I don't see how she can ever get her feet into 'em. I can't mine, and I don't b'lieve she can. Better send 'em back;" and she looked at Eloise, who, if she was proud of any part of her person, was proud of her feet.

Flushing hotly she said, " They are not suitable for me, of course, but I think I *could* get one on my well foot."

" I know you could; try it," Jack said.

Stooping forward Eloise removed her boot, although the effort brought a horrible twinge to her lame ankle and made her feel faint for a moment.

" Put it on for me, please," she said to Mrs. Biggs, who, mistaking the right-hand slipper for the left, began tugging at it.

" I told you so," she said. " Your foot is twice as big."

" Try this one," Jack suggested, " or let me; " and he fitted the slipper at once to the little foot, while Mrs. Biggs exclaimed, " Wall, I vum, it does fit to a T! If anything, it's too big."

In spite of her pain and embarrassment there was a look of exultation in Eloise's eyes, as they met those of Jack, who was nearly as pleased as herself.

" You will keep them and wear them some time," he said; and when Eloise declined, saying they would be of no use to her, Howard, who had been watching this Cinderella play with a good deal of interest, and wishing he had been the prince to fit the slipper instead of Jack, said to Eloise, " I think it better for you to keep them. Miss Amy will not like to have them returned, and if they were, she'd give them to some one else, or very likely send them to the Rummage Sale we are to have in town."

" That's so," Mrs. Biggs chimed in. " There is to be a rummage sale, and Ruby Ann has spoke for Tim's old clothes and mine, especially our shoes. Keep 'em by all means."

Eloise was beginning to feel faint again, and tired with all this talk and excitement, and painfully conscious that Howard's eyes were dancing with laughter at the sight of her feet,—one swollen to three times its natural size and pushed into Mrs. Biggs's old felt shoe, and the other in Miss Amy's white satin slipper.

"Oh, I wish you would take it off!" she gasped, feeling unequal to leaning forward again, and closing her eyes wearily.

She meant Mrs. Biggs, but Jack forestalled that good woman, and in an instant had the slipper off and the boot on, doing both so gently that she was not hurt at all.

"Thanks!" Eloise said, drawing her well foot under the spotted calico, and wishing the young men would go.

How long they would have staid is uncertain if there had not come a second knock at the kitchen door. This time it was really Mr. Bills, and Mrs. Biggs went out to meet him, while Eloise felt every nerve quiver with dread. She must see him and tell him how impossible it would be for her to commence her duties on Monday. Perhaps he would dismiss her altogether, and take another in her place, and then—"What shall I do?" she thought, and, scarcely knowing what she said, she cried, "Oh, I can't bear it!" while the tears rolled down her cheeks, and Howard and Jack gathered close to her,—the laugh all gone from Howard's eyes, and a great pity shining in Jack's.

"Excuse me," she continued, "I don't mean to be childish, but everything is so dreadful! I don't mind the pain so much; but to be here away from home, and to lose the school, as I may, and—and,—I want a handkerchief to wipe my face,—and this is ruined."

She said this last as she took from her satchel the handkerchief which had been so white and clean when she left home, and which now was wet and stained from a bottle of shoe blacking which had come uncorked and saturated everything. She had borne a great deal, and, as is often the case, a small matter upset her entirely. The spoiled handkerchief was the straw too many, and her tears came faster as she held it in one hand, and with the other tried to wipe them away.

"Take mine, please; I've not used it," Jack said, offering her one of fine linen, and as daintily perfumed as a woman's.

She took it unhesitatingly. She was in a frame of mind to take anything, and smiled her thanks through her tears.

"I know I must seem very weak to you to be crying like a baby; but you don't know how I dread meeting Mr. Bills, or how much is depending upon my having this school, or what it would be to me to lose it, if he can't wait. Do you think he will?"

She looked at Jack, who knew nothing whatever of the matter, or of Mr. Bills, but who answered promptly, "Of course he will wait; he must wait. We shall see to that. Don't cry. I'm awfully sorry for you; we both are."

He was standing close to her, and involuntarily laid his hand on her hair, smoothing it a little as he would have smoothed his sister's. She seemed so young and looked so small, wrapped up in Mrs. Biggs's gown, that he thought of her for a moment as a child to be soothed and comforted. She did not repel the touch of his hand, but cried the harder and wiped her face with his handkerchief until it was wet with her tears.

"Mr. Bills wants to know if he can come in now," came as an interruption to the scene, which was getting rather affecting.

"In just a minute," Jack said. Then to Eloise, "Brace up! We'll attend to Mr. Bills if he proves formidable."

She braced up as he bade her, and gave his handkerchief back to him.

"I shan't need it again. I am not going to be foolish any longer, and I thank you so much," she said, with a look which made Jack's pulse beat rapidly.

"We'd better go now and give Mr. Bills a chance," he said to Howard, who had been comparatively silent and let him do the talking and suggesting.

Howard could not define his feeling with regard to Eloise. Her beauty impressed him greatly, and he was very sorry for her, but he could not rid himself of the conviction which had a second time taken possession of him that in some way she was to influence his life or cross his path.

He bade her good-by, and told her to keep up good courage, and felt a little piqued that she withdrew her hand more quickly from him than she did from Jack, who left her rather reluctantly. They found Mr. Bills outside talking to Mrs. Biggs, who was volubly narrating the particulars of the accident, so far as she knew them, and referring constantly to her own sprained ankle of twenty years ago, and the impossibility of Miss Smith's being able to walk for some time.

With his usual impetuousness Jack took the initiative, and said to Mr. Bills: "Your school can certainly wait; it must wait. A week or two can make no difference. At the end of that time, if she cannot walk, she can be taken to and from the school-house every day. To lose the school will go hard with her, and she's so young."

Jack was quite eloquent, and Mr. Bills looked at him curiously, wondering who this smart young fellow was, pleading for the new school-teacher. He knew Howard, who, after Jack was through, said he hoped Mr. Bills would wait; it would be a pity to disappoint the girl when she had come so far.

"Perhaps a week or two will make no difference," Mr. Bills said, "though the young ones are getting pretty wild, and their mothers anxious to have them out of the way, but I guess we'll manage it somehow."

He knew he should manage it when he saw Eloise. She could not tell him of the need there was of money in her grandmother's home, or the still greater need if she took the trip to California which she feared she must take. She only looked her anxiety, and Mr. Bills, whose heart Mrs. Biggs said was "big as a barn," warmed toward her, while mentally he began to doubt her ability to "fill the bill," as he put it, she looked so young and so small.

"I'll let her off easy, if I have to," he thought, and he said, "Folks'll want school to begin as advertised. You can't go, but there's Ruby Ann Patrick. She'll be glad to supply. She's kep' the school five years runnin'. She wanted it when we hired you. She's out of a job, and will be glad to take it till you can walk. I'll see her to-day. You look young to manage unruly boys, and there's a pile of 'em in Deestrick No. 5 want lickin' half the time. Ruby Ann can lick 'em. She's five feet nine. You ain't more'n five."

Eloise did not tell him how tall she was. In fact, she didn't know. She must look very diminutive in Mr. Bills's eyes, she thought, and hastened to say, "I taught boys and young men older than I am in the normal at Mayville, and never had any trouble. I had only to speak to or look at them."

" I b'lieve you, I b'lieve you," Mr. Bills said. " I should mind you myself every time if you looked at me, but boys ain't alike. There's Tom Walker, ringleader in every kind of mischief, the wust feller you ever see. Ruby Ann had one tussle with him, and came off Number One. He'd most likely raise Cain with a schoolmarm who couldn't walk and went on crutches."

" Oh-h!" Eloise said despairingly. " I shall not have to do that!"

" Mebby not; mebby not. Sprained ankles mostly does, though. I had to when I sprained mine. I used to hobble to the well and pump cold water on it; that's tiptop for a sprain. Well, I must go now and see Ruby Ann. Good-day. Keep a stiff upper lip, and you'll pull through. Widder Biggs is a fust-rate nurse, and woman, too. Little too much tongue, mebby. Hung in the middle and plays both ways. Knows everybody's history and age from the Flood down. She'll get at yours from A to izzard. Good-day!"

He was gone, and Eloise was alone with her pain and homesickness and discouragement. Turn which way she would, there was not much brightness in her sky, except when she thought of Jack Harcourt, whose hand on her hair she could feel just as he had felt her wet hand on his neck hours after the spot was dried. It seemed perfectly natural and proper that he should care for her, just as it did that the lady at the Crompton House should send her a hat. It was lying on a chair near her with the slippers, and she took it up and examined it again very carefully, admiring the fineness of the leghorn, the beauty of the lilac wreath, and the texture of the ribbons.

" I shall never wear it," she thought. " It is too handsome for me; but I shall always keep it, and be glad for the thoughtfulness which prompted the lady to send it."

Then she wondered if she would ever see the lady and thank her in person, or go to the Crompton House; and if her trunk would ever come from the station, so that she could divest herself of the detestable cotton gown and put on something more becoming, which would show him she was not quite so much a guy as she looked in Mrs. Biggs's wardrobe. The him was Jack, not Howard. He was not in the running. She cared as little for him as she imagined he cared for her. And here she did him injustice. She interested him greatly, though not in the way she interested Jack, whom he chaffed on their way home, telling him he ought to offer his services as nurse.

" I wonder you did not wipe her eyes as well as give her your handkerchief," he said. . " I dare say you will never have it laundered, lest her tears should be washed out of it."

" Never! " Jack replied, and, taking the handkerchief from his pocket and folding it carefully, he put it back again, saying, " No, sir; I shall keep it intact. No laundryman's hands will ever touch it."

" Pretty far gone, that's a fact," Howard rejoined, and then continued: " I say, Jack, we'd better not talk of Miss Smith before the Colonel. It will only rouse him up, and make him swear at normal graduates in general, and this one in particular. You know I wrote you that he gave the lot and built the school-house, and for years was inspector of Crompton schools,—boss and all hands,—till a new generation came up and shelved him. He fought hard,.but had to give in to young blood and modern ideas. He had no voice in hiring Miss Smith,—was not consulted. His choice was a Ruby Ann Patrick, a perfect Amazon of an old maid; weighs two hundred, I believe, and rides a wheel. You ought to see her. But then she is rooted and grounded, and uncle does not think 'Miss Smith is, though she was pretty well grounded last night when she sat on that sand heap with her foot twisted under her. I'm not a soft head like you, to fall in love with her at first sight; but I'm awfully sorry for her, and I don't wish to hear the Colonel swear about her."

Jack had never seen Howard more in earnest, and his mental comment was, " Cares more for her than I supposed. He'll bear watching. Poor little girl! How white she was at times, and how tired her eyes looked; and bright, too, as stars. I wonder if she really ought not to have a doctor."

He put this question to Howard, who replied: " No, that Biggs woman is a full team on sprained ankles. She'll get her up without a doctor, and I don't suppose the girl has much to spend on the craft."

" Yes, but what is a little money to you or me, if she really needs a doctor?" Jack said thoughtfully, while Howard laughed and answered, " Don't be an idiot, and lose your heart to a schoolma'am because she happened to have had her arm around your neck when we carried her in that chair. I can feel it yet, and sometimes put up my hand when half awake to see if it isn't there, but I am not going to make a fool of myself."

As they were near home Jack did not reply, but he could have told of times when half awake and wide awake he felt the arms and the hands and the hot breath of the girl clinging to him in the darkness and rain, and saw the eyes full of pain and dumb entreaty not to hurt her more than they could help, as they cut the soaked boot from the swollen foot. But he said nothing, and, when the house was reached, went at once to his own room, wondering what he could do to make her more comfortable.

Acting upon Howard's advice, Eloise was not mentioned, either at lunch or at dinner. Amy had evidently forgotten her, for she made no inquiry for her. Neither did the Colonel. She was, however, much in the minds of the young men, and each was wondering how he could best serve her. Howard thought of a sea chair, in which his uncle had crossed the ocean. He had found it covered with dust in the attic, and brought it to his room to lounge in. It would be far more comfortable for Eloise than that stiff, straight-backed, hair-cloth rocker in which she had to sit so upright. He would send it to her with Amy's compliments, if he could manage it without the knowledge of Jack, who he would rather should not know how much he was really interested in Eloise. Jack was also planning what he could do, and thought of a wheel chair, in which she could be taken to and from school. He might possibly find one in the village by the shore. He would inquire without consulting Howard, whose joking grated a little, as it presupposed the impossibility of his really caring for one so far removed from his station in life as Eloise seemed to be.

Could she have known how much she was in the minds of the young men at Crompton Place, she would not have felt quite as forlorn and disconsolate as she did during the long hours of the day, when she sat helpless and alone, except as Mrs. Biggs tried to entertain her with a flow of talk and gossip which did not interest her. A few of the neighbors called in the evening, and it seemed to Eloise that every one had had a sprained ankle or two, of which they talked continually, dwelling mostly upon the length of time it took before they were able to walk across the floor, to say nothing of the distance from Mrs. Biggs's to the school-house. That would be impossible for two or three weeks at least, and even then Miss Smith would have to go on crutches most likely, was their comforting assurance.

"I've got some up garret that I used twenty years ago. Too long for her, but Tim can cut them off. They are just the thing. Lucky I kept them," Mrs. Biggs said, while Eloise listened with a feeling like death in her heart, and dreamed that night of hobbling to school on Mrs. Biggs's crutches, while Jack Harcourt helped and encouraged her, and Howard Crompton stood at a distance laughing at her.

12

CHAPTER VII

RUBY ANN PATRICK

She had taught the school in District No. 5 summer and winter for five years. She had been a teacher for fifteen years, her first experience dating back to the days when the Colonel was school inspector, and his formula in full swing. She had met all his requirements promptly, knew all about the geese and the grindstone, and the wind, and Mr. Wright, and had a certificate in the Colonel's handwriting, declaring her to be rooted and grounded in the fundamentals, and qualified to teach a district school anywhere. As Mr. Bills had said to Eloise, she was five feet nine inches high and large in proportion, with so much strength and vital force and determination, that the most unruly boy in District No. 5 would hesitate before openly defying her authority. She had conquered Tom Walker, the bully of the school, and after the day when he was made to feel the force there was in her large hand, he had done nothing worse than make faces behind her back and draw caricatures of her on his slate.

As a rule, Ruby Ann was popular with the majority of the people, and there had been some opposition to a change. It was hardly fair, they said to the Colonel, who took so much interest in the school, and who was sure to feel angry and hurt if deprived of

the privilege of catechising the teachers in the office
he had erected for that purpose on his grounds. He
had not only built the school-house, but had kept it
in repair, and had added a classroom for the older
scholars because somebody said it was needed, and
had not objected when it was only used for wraps and
dinner pails, and balls and clubs in the summer, and
in the winter for coal and wood and sleds and skates
and other things pertaining to a school of wide-awake
girls and boys.

This was the conservative party, but there was another which wanted a change. They had been in a
rut long enough, and they laughed at the Colonel's
formula, which nearly every child knew by heart.
The Colonel was too old to run things,—they must
have something up to date, and when the president
of Mayville Normal School applied for a situation
for Eloise she was accepted, and Ruby Ann went to
the wall. She was greatly chagrined and disappointed when she found herself supplanted by a normal graduate, of whom she had not a much higher
opinion than the Colonel himself. When she heard
of the accident and that her rival was disabled, she
was conscious just for a moment of a feeling of exultation, as if Eloise had received her just deserts.
She was, however, a kind-hearted, well-principled
woman, and soon cast the feeling aside as unworthy
of her, and tried to believe she was sorry for the girl,
who, she heard, was very young, and had been carried in the darkness and rain to Mrs. Biggs's house
in Howard Crompton's arms.

" I would almost be willing to sprain my ankle for
the sake of being carried in that way," Ruby thought,
and then laughed as she tried to fancy the young

man bending beneath the weight of her hundred and ninety pounds.

It was at this juncture that Mr. Bills came in asking if she would take Miss Smith's place until she was able to walk. It might be two weeks, and it might be three, and it might be less, he said. Any way, they didn't want a cripple in the school-house for Tom Walker to raise Hail Columby with. Would Ruby Ann swaller her pride and be a substitute?

" It is a good deal to ask me to do after I have been turned out of office," she said, " but I am not one to harbor resentment. Yes, I'll take the school till Miss Smith is able. How does she look? I hear she is very young."

" Well, she's some younger than you, I guess, and looks like a child as she sits down," Mr. Bills replied. " Why, you are big as two of her,—yes, three,—and could throw her over the house."

Ruby's face clouded, and Mr. Bills went on: " She is handsome as blazes, with a mouth which keeps kind of quivering, as if she wanted to cry, or something, and eyes—well, you've got to see 'em to know what they are like. They are just eyes which make an old man like me feel,—I don't know how."

Ruby laughed, but felt a little hurt as she thought of her own small, light-blue eyes and lighter eyebrows, which had never yet made any man, young or old, feel " he didn't know how." She knew she was neither young nor handsome nor attractive, but she had good common sense, and after Mr. Bills was gone she sat down to review the situation, and resolved to accept it gracefully and to call upon Eloise. It would be certainly *en regle* and Christian-like to do so, she thought, and the next afternoon she presented herself at Mrs. Biggs's door and asked if Miss Smith were able to see any one.

Mrs. Biggs belonged to the radical party which favored a change of teachers. Five years was long enough for one person to teach in the same place, she said, and they wanted somebody modern and younger. She laid a great deal of stress upon that, and on one occasion, when giving her opinion over her gate to a neighbor, had added " smaller and better-looking." Ruby was not a favorite with Mrs. Biggs, whom she had called an inveterate gossip, hunting up everbody's history and age, and making them out two or three years older than they were. She had lived at home and kept Mrs. Biggs out of a boarder five years. She had called Tim a lout, and kept him after school several times when his mother needed him. Consequently Mrs. Biggs's sympathies were all with Eloise, who was young and small and good-looking, and she flouted the idea of having Ruby hired even for a few days.

" It's just a wedge to git her in again," she had said to Tim, with whom she had discussed the matter. " I know Ruby Ann, and she'll jump at the chance, and keep it, too. She can wind Mr. Bills round her fingers. I'd rather have Miss Smith with one laig than Ruby Ann with three. Tom Walker ain't goin' to raise Ned with such a slip of a girl."

"I ruther guess not, when I'm there," Tim said, squaring himself up as if ready to fight a dozen Tom Walkers, when, in fact, he was afraid of one, and usually kept out of his way.

Mrs. Biggs had not expected Ruby Ann to call, and her face wore a vinegary expression when she opened the door to her.

"Yes, I s'pose you can see her, but too much company ain't good for sprained ankles," she replied in response to Ruby's inquiry if she could see Miss Smith. "You'll find her in the parlor, but don't stay long. Talkin' 'll create a fever in her laig."

Ruby was accustomed to Mrs. Biggs's vagaries, and did not mind them.

"I'll be very discreet," she said, as she passed on to the parlor, curious to see the girl who had been preferred to herself.

She had heard from Mr. Bills that Eloise "was handsome as blazes," but she was not prepared for the face which looked up at her as she entered the room. Something in the eyes appealed to her as it had to Mr. Bills, and any prejudice she might have had melted away at once, and she began talking to Eloise as familiarly as if she had known her all her life. At first Eloise drew back from the powerfully built woman, who stood up so tall before her, and whose voice was so strong and masculine, and whose eyes travelled over her so rapidly, taking in every detail of her dress and every feature of her face. Mrs. Biggs's disfiguring cotton gown had been discarded for a loose white jacket, which, with its knots of pink ribbon, was very becoming, and Ruby found herself studying it closely, and wondering if she could make one like it, and how she would look in it. Then she noticed the hands, so small and so white, and felt an irresistible desire to take one of them in her broad palm.

"I do believe I could hold three like them in one of mine," she thought, and sitting down by Eloise's side, she laid her hand on the one resting on the arm of the chair.

There was something so friendly and warm and so sympathetic in the touch that Eloise wanted to cry. With a great effort she kept her tears back, but could not prevent one or two from standing on her long lashes, and making her eyes very bright as she answered Ruby's rapid questions with regard to the accident.

"And I hear Mr. Howard Crompton brought you here himself. That was something of an honor, as he seldom goes out of his way for any one," she said, with a keen look of curiosity in her eyes.

"I never thought of the honor," Eloise replied. "I could think of nothing but the pain, which was terrible, and now everything is so dreary and so different from what I hoped. Do you think it will be long before I can walk?"

"No; oh no," Ruby answered cheerily. "Let me see your foot. It is swollen badly," she said, as she replaced the old shawl Mrs. Biggs had thrown across it. "What have you on it? Wormwood and vinegar, I know by the odor. You should have a rubber band, and nothing else. It is cleaner and saves trouble. That's what I used, and was well in no time."

"Have you had a sprained ankle, too?" Eloise asked, and Ruby Ann replied, "Certainly. Nearly every one has at some time in his life. It is as common as the measles."

"I believe it," Eloise rejoined with a laugh. "So many have called to see me, and almost every one had had a sprain,—some as many as three; and each one proposed a different remedy."

"Naturally; but you try the rubber band. I'll

bring you one, and massage your ankle, and have you well very soon."

These were the first hopeful words Eloise had heard, and her heart warmed towards this great blond woman, who was proving herself a friend, and who began to tell her of the school and her own experience as teacher in District No. 5, which, she said, was the largest and most important district in town, with the oldest scholars both summer and winter. " There are some unruly boys, especially Tom Walker, but I am so big and strong that I conquered him by brute force, and had no trouble after one battle. You will conquer some other way. Tom is very susceptible to good looks,—calls me a hayseed, and a chestnut, and a muff. It will be different with you," and Ruby pressed the hand she was holding. Then she spoke of Col. Crompton, who used to examine the teachers, and before whom she had been five times; usually answering the same questions, especially those contained in the " Formula," and to which Eloise would not be subjected.

" What is the Formula?" Eloise asked, and Ruby told her, while Eloise listened bewildered, and glad she was to escape an ordeal she could never pass with credit.

It was easy to be confiding with Ruby, and Eloise found herself talking freely of her life and school in Mayville, and the necessity there was for her and the bitter disappointment it would be to lose the school on which so much depended.

" My father is dead," she said, " and my mother," she hesitated, while a deep flush came to her cheek, " is an invalid, and there is no one to care

for her now but me. She is in California, and I may
have to go for her, and must have the money."

Just for a moment, when Mr. Bills asked her to
take Eloise's place, there had been in Ruby's mind
a half-formed hope that she might be wholly rein-
stated in her old place as a teacher. But it was gone
now, and Jack Harcourt himself was not more kindly
disposed to the helpless girl than she was.

"You shall not lose the school, nor the time
either," she said impulsively. "I am to take it till
you are able, and then I shall step out. In the mean
time, I shall do all I can for you,—shall enlist Tom
Walker on your side, and you will have no trouble."

She arose to go, then sat down again and said, "I
hope you will be able to attend our Rummage Sale."

"Rummage Sale!" Eloise repeated, remembering
to have heard the word in connection with the slippers Miss Amy had sent her. "I don't think I quite
understand."

"Don't you know what a Rummage Sale is?"
Ruby Ann asked, explaining what it was, and saying
they were to have one in a vacant house not far from
Mrs. Biggs's, the proceeds to go for a free library
for District No. 5. "I am one of the solicitors," she
continued, "but as you are a stranger you may not
have anything to contribute."

As Rummage Sales were just beginning to dawn
on the public horizon Eloise had never heard of
them, but she became interested at once, because
Ruby Ann was so enthusiastic, and said, "I have two
or three white aprons I made myself. You can have
one of them if you think anybody will buy it."

"Buy it!" Ruby repeated, rubbing her hands in
ecstasy. "It will bring a big price when they know

it was yours and you made it. I'll see that it has a conspicuous place. And now I must go and see Mrs. Biggs again about the sale. Good-by, and keep up your courage."

She stooped and kissed Eloise, who heard her next in the kitchen talking to Mrs. Biggs, first of rubber bands and massage, and then of the Rummage Sale. When she was gone Mrs. Biggs came in and sat down and began to give her opinion of the Rummage Sale, and massage and rubber bands, and first the Rummage. A good way to get rid of truck, and Ruby Ann said they took everything. She had a lot of old chairs and a warming pan and footstove, and she s'posed she might give the spotted brown and white calico wrapper which Eloise had worn. It was faded and out of style. Yes, on the whole, she'd give the wrapper. She never liked it very well, she said; and then she spoke of the rubber band Ruby Ann had recommended instead of wormwood and vinegar, and of which she did not approve. What did Ruby Ann know? though, to be sure, she was old enough. How old did Eloise think she was? Eloise had not given her age a thought, but, pressed for an answer, ventured the reply that she might be verging on to thirty.

"Verging on to thirty! More likely verging on to forty," Mrs. Biggs said, with a savage click of the needles with which she was knitting Tim a sock. "I know her age, if she does try to look young and wear a sailor hat, and ride a wheel in a short gown! I'd laugh to see me ridin' a wheel, and there ain't so much difference between us neither. I know, for we went to school together. She was a little girl, to be sure, and sat on the low seat and learnt her a-b-c's.

I was four or five years older, and sat on a higher seat with Amy Crompton, till the Colonel took her from the district school and kep' her at home with a governess."

Mrs. Biggs was very proud of the acquaintance she had had with Amy Crompton, when the two played together under the trees which shaded the school-house the Colonel had built as *expiatory* years before, and she continued: "Amy, you know, is the half-cracked lady at the Crompton House who sent the hat and slippers. She's been married twice,—run away the first time. My land! what a stir there was about it, and what a high hoss the Colonel rode. Who her second was nobody knows,—some scamp by the name of Smith,—that's your name, and a good one, too, but about the commonest in the world, I reckon. There's four John Smiths in town, and Joel Smith, who brings my milk, and George Smith I buy aigs of, and forty odd more. They say the Colonel hates the name like pisen. Won't have anybody work for him by that name. Dismissed his milkman because he was a Smith, and between you and I, I b'lieve half his opposition to you was your name. Why, it's like a red rag to a bull."

"I didn't know he was opposed to me personally," Eloise said, and Mrs. Biggs replied, "Of course not; how could he be? He never seen you. It's the normal, and bein' put out of office—he and Ruby Ann. They've run things long enough. They say he did swear offel at the last school meetin' about normals and ingrates and all that,—meanin' they'd forgot all he'd done for 'em; but, my land, you can't b'lieve half you hear. I don't b'lieve nothin', and try to keep a close mouth 'bout what I do b'lieve. I ain't none

o' your gossips, and won't have folks sayin' the Widder Biggs said so and so."

Here Mrs. Biggs stopped to take breath and answer a rap at the kitchen door, where George Smith
was standing with a basket of eggs. Eloise could
hear her badgering him because he charged too
much and because his hens did not lay larger eggs,
and threatening to withdraw her patronage if there
was not a change. Then items of the latest news
were exchanged, Mrs. Biggs doing her part well for
one who never repeated anything and never believed
anything. When George Smith was gone she returned to her seat by Eloise and resumed her conversation, which had been interrupted, and which was
mostly reminiscent of people and incidents in Crompton, and especially of the Crompton House and its
occupants, with a second fling at Ruby Ann.

CHAPTER VIII

" Maybe I was too hard on Ruby Ann," she said, measuring the heel of Tim's sock to see if it were time to begin to narrow. " She's a pretty clever woman, take her by and large, but I do hate to see a dog frisk like a puppy, and she's thirty-five if she's a day. You see, I know, 'cause, as I was tellin' you, there was her and me and Amy Crompton girls together. I am forty, Amy is thirty-eight or thirty-nine, and Ruby Ann is thirty-five."

Having settled Ruby's age and asked Eloise hers, and told her she looked young for nineteen, the good woman branched off upon the grandeur of the Crompton House, with its pictures and statuary and bric-à-brac, its flowers and fountains, and rustic arbors and seats scattered over the lawn. Eloise had heard something of the place from a school friend, but never had it been so graphically described as by Mrs. Biggs, and she listened with a feeling that in the chamber of her childhood's memory a picture of this place had been hung by somebody.

" Was it my father? " she asked herself, and answered decidedly, " No," as she recalled the little intercourse she had ever had with him. " Was it my mother? " she next asked herself, and involuntarily her tears started as she thought of her mother, and

how unlikely it was that she had ever been in Crompton.

Turning her head aside to hide her tears from Mrs.
Biggs, she said, " Tell me more of the place.   It almost seems as if I had been there."

Thus encouraged, Mrs. Biggs began a description
of the lawn party which she was too young to remember, although she was there with her mother,
and had a faint recollection of music and candy and
lights in the trees, and an attack of colic the night
after as a result of overeating.

" But, my land! " she said, " that was nothin' to the
blow-out on Amy's sixteenth birthday.   The Colonel
had kep' her pretty close after he took her from
school.   She had a governess and she had a maid,
but I must say she didn't seem an atom set up, and
was just as nice when she met us girls.   ' Hello,
Betsey,' she'd say to me.   That's my name, Betsey,
but I call myself 'Lisbeth.   ' Hello, Betsey,' I can hear
her now, as she cantered past on her pony, in her
long blue ridin' habit.   Sometimes she'd come to the
school-house and set on the grass under the apple
trees and chew gum with us girls.   That was before
her party, which beat anything that was ever seen in
Crompton, or will be again.   The avenue and yard
and stables were full of carriages, and there were
eighteen waiters besides the *canterer* from Boston."

" The what? " Eloise asked, and Mrs. Biggs replied, " The *canterer*, don't you know, the man who
sees to things and brings the vittles and his waiters.
They say he alone cost the Colonel five hundred dollars; but, my land! that's no more for him than five
dollars is for me.   He fairly swims in money.   Such
dresses you never seen as there was there that night,

and such bare necks and arms, with a man at the door, a man at the head of the stairs to tell 'em where to go, and one in the gentlemen's room, and two girls in the ladies' rooms to button their gloves and put on their dancing pumps. The carousin' lasted till daylight, and a tireder, more worn-out lot of folks than we was you never seen. I was nearly dead."

" Were you there? " Eloise asked, with a feeling that there was some incongruity between the Crompton party and Mrs. Biggs, who did not care to say that she was one of the waitresses who buttoned gloves and put on the dancing pumps in the dressing-room.

" Why, yes, I was there," she said at last, " though I wasn't exactly in the doin's. I've never danced since I was dipped and jined the church. Do you dance, or be you a perfessor? "

Eloise had to admit that she did dance and was not a professor, although she hoped to be soon.

" What persuasion? " was Mrs. Biggs's next question, and Eloise replied, " I was baptized in the Episcopal Church in Rome."

" The one in York State, I s'pose, and not t'other one across the seas? " Mrs. Biggs suggested, and Eloise answered, " Yes, the one across the seas in Italy."

" For goodness' sake! How you talk! You don't mean you was born there? " Mrs. Biggs exclaimed, with a feeling of added respect for one who was actually born across the seas. " Do you remember it, and did you know the Pope and the King? "

Eloise said she did not remember being born, nor did she know the Pope or the King.

" I was a little girl when I left Italy, and do not re-

member much, except that I was happier there than
I have ever been since."

"I want to know! I s'pose you've had trouble in
your family?" was Mrs. Biggs's quick rejoinder, as
she scented some private history which she meant to
find out.

But beyond the fact that her father was dead and
her mother in California, she could learn nothing
from Eloise, and returned to the point from which
they had drifted to the Episcopal Church in Rome.

"I kinder mistrusted you was a 'Piscopal. I do'
know why, but I can most always tell 'em," she said.
"The Cromptons is all that way of thinkin'. Old
Colonel is a vestedman, I b'lieve they call 'em, but
he swears offul. I don't call that religion; do you?
But folks ain't alike. I don't s'pose the Church is
to blame. There's now and then as good a 'Piscopal
as you'll find anywhere. Ruby Ann has jined 'em,
and goes it strong. B'lieves in candles and vestures;
got Tim into the choir one Sunday, and now you
can't keep him out of it. Wears a—a—I don't know
what you call it,—something that looks like a short
night-gown, and I have to wash it every other week.
I don't mind that, and I do b'lieve Tim is more of a
man than he was, and he sings beautiful. And hain't
learnt nothin' bad there yet, but the minister does
some things I don't approve; no, don't approve.
What do you think he does right before folks, in
plain sight, sittin' on the piazza?"

Eloise could not hazard a guess as to the terrible
sin of which Mr. Mason, the rector of St. John's, was
guilty, and said so.

"Well," and Mrs. Biggs's voice sank to a whisper
as she leaned forward, "*he smokes a cigar in broad*

daylight! What do you think of that for a minister of the gospel?"

She was so much in earnest, and her manner so dramatic, that Eloise laughed the first real, hearty laugh she had indulged in since she came to Crompton. Smoking might be objectionable, but it did not seem to her the most heinous crime in the world, and she had a very vivid remembrance of a coat in which there lurked the odor of many Havanas, and to which she had clung desperately in the darkness and rain on the night which seemed to her years ago. She did not, however, express any opinion with regard to the Rev. Arthur Mason's habits, or feel especially interested in him. But Mrs. Biggs was, and once launched on the subject, she told Eloise that he was from the South, and had not been long in the place; that he was unmarried, and all the girls were after him, Ruby Ann with the rest, and she at least half a dozen years older.

"But, land's sake! What does that count with an old maid when a young minister is in the market," she said, adding that, with the exception of smoking, she believed the new minister was a good man, though for some reason Col. Crompton did not like him, and had only been to church once since he came, and wouldn't let Miss Amy go either.

This brought her back to the Cromptons generally, and during the next half hour Eloise had a pretty graphic description of the Colonel and his eccentricities, of Amy, when she was a young girl, of the way she came to the Crompton House, and the mystery which still surrounded her birth.

"My Uncle Peter lived there when she came, and lives there now,—a kind of vally to the old Colonel,"

she said, " and he's told me of the mornin' the Colonel
brung her home, a queer-looking little thing,— in her
clothes, I mean,—and offul peppery, I judge, fightin'
everybody who came near her, and rollin' on the
floor, bumpin' and cryin' for a nigger who had took
care of her somewhere, nobody knows where, for the
Colonel never told, and if Uncle Peter knows, he
holds his tongue. She was a terrible fighter at school,
if things didn't suit her, but she's quiet enough now;
seems 's if she'd been through the fire, poor thing,
and they say she don't remember nothin', and begins
to shake if she tries to remember. The Colonel is
very kind to her; lets her have all the money she
wants, and she gives away a sight. Sent you a hat
and slips, almost new, and had never seen you.
That's like Amy, and, my soul, there she is now,
comin' down the road with the Colonel in the b'rouch.
Hurry, and you can see her; I'll move you."

Utterly regardless of the lame foot, which dragged
on the floor and hurt cruelly, Mrs. Biggs drew Eloise
to the window in time to see a handsome open carriage drawn by two splendid bays passing the house.
The Colonel was muffled up as closely as if it were
midwinter, and only a part of his face and his long,
white hair were visible, but he was sitting upright,
with his head held high, and looked the embodiment
of aristocratic pride and arrogance. The lady beside
him was very slight, and sat in a drooping kind of
posture, as if she were tired, or restless, or both. To
see her face was impossible, for she was closely veiled,
and neither she nor the Colonel glanced toward the
house as they passed.

" I am so disappointed. I wanted to see her face,"
Eloise said, watching the carriage until it was hidden

from view by a turn in the road. "You say she is lovely?" and she turned to Mrs. Biggs.

"Lovely don't express it. Seraphic comes nearer. Looks as if she had some great sorrow she was constantly thinking of, and trying to smile as she thought of it," Mrs. Biggs replied. Then, as Eloise looked quickly up, she exclaimed, "Well, if I ain't beat! It's come to me what I've been tryin' to think of ever sense I seen you. They ain't the same color; hers is darker, but there is a look in your eyes for all the world as hers used to be when she was a girl, and wan't wearin' her high-heeled shoes and ridin' over our heads. Them times she was as like the Colonel as one pea is like another, and her eyes fairly snapped. Other times they was soft and tender-like, and bright as stars, with a look in 'em which I know now was kinder,—well, kinder crazy-like, you know."

Eloise had heard many things said of her own eyes, but never before that they were crazy-like, and did not feel greatly complimented. She laughed, however, and said she would like to see the lady whose eyes hers were like.

Before Mrs. Biggs could reply there was a step outside, and, tiptoeing to the window, she exclaimed, in a whisper, "If I won't give it up, there's the 'Piscopal minister, Mr. Mason, come to call on you! Ruby Ann must of told him you belonged to 'em."

She dropped her knitting, and, hurrying to the door, admitted the Rev. Arthur Mason, and ushered him at once into the room where Eloise was sitting, saying as she introduced him, "I s'pose you have come to see her."

It was an awkward situation for the young man, whose call was not prompted by any thought of

Eloise. His business was with Mrs. Biggs, who had the reputation of being the parish register and town encyclopædia, from which information regarding everybody could be gleaned, and he had come to her for information which he had been told she could probably give him. He had been in Crompton but three months, and had come there from a small parish in Virginia. On the first Sunday when he officiated in St. John's he had noticed in the audience a tall, aristocratic-looking man, with long white hair and beard, who made the responses loud and in a tone which told the valuation he put upon himself. In the same pew was a lady whose face attracted his attention, it was so sweet and yet so sad, while the beautiful eyes, he was sure, were sometimes full of tears as she listened with rapt attention to what he was saying of our heavenly home, where those we have loved and lost will be restored to us. It scarcely seemed possible, and yet he thought there was a nod of assent, and was sure that a smile broke over her face when he spoke of the first meeting of friends in the next world, the mother looking for her child; and the child coming to the gates of Paradise to meet its mother. Who was she, he wondered, and who was the old man beside her, who held himself so proudly? He soon learned who they were, and hearing that the Colonel was very lame, and the lady an invalid, he took the initiative and called at the Crompton House. The Colonel received him very cordially, and made excuses for Amy's non-appearance, saying she was not quite herself and shy with strangers. He was very affable, and evidently charmed with his visitor, until, as the conversation flowed on, it came out that the rector was a South-

erner by birth, although educated for the ministry at
the North, and that his father, the Rev. Charles Mason, was at present filling a vacancy in a little country
church in Enterprise, Florida, where he had been before the war.   The Rev. Arthur Mason could not
tell what it was that warned him of an instantaneous
change in the Colonel's manner, it was so subtle and
still so perceptible.   There was a settling himself
back in his chair, a tighter clasping of his gold-headed
cane with which he walked, and which he always kept
in his hand.   He was less talkative, and finally was
silent altogether, and when at last the rector arose to
go, he was not asked to stay or call again.   Peter was
summoned to show him the door, the Colonel bowing very stiffly as he went out.   How he had offended, if he had done so, the rector could not guess,
and, hearing within a week or two that the Colonel
was indisposed, he called again, but was not admitted.   Col. Crompton was too nervous to see any
one, he was told, and there the acquaintance had
ended.   The Crompton pew was not occupied until
Howard came and was occasionally seen in it.   Evidently the new rector was a *persona non grata*, and he
puzzled his brain for a reason in vain, until a letter
from his father threw some light upon the subject
and induced him to call upon Mrs. Biggs.

As usual she was very loquacious, scarcely allowing him a word, and ringing changes on her own and
Eloise's sprained ankle, until he began to fear he
should have no chance to broach the object of his
visit without seeming to drag it in.   The chance came
on the return of the Crompton carriage, with the
Colonel sitting stiff and straight and Amy drooping
under her veil beside him.   ˊHere was his opportu-

nity, and the rector seized it, and soon learned nearly all Mrs. Biggs knew of Amy's arrival at Crompton House and the surmises concerning her antecedents.

"She's a Crompton if there ever was one, and why the Colonel should keep so close a mouth all these years beats me," was Mrs. Biggs's closing remark, as she bowed the rector out and went back to Eloise, who felt that she was getting very familiar with the Crompton history, so far as Mrs. Biggs knew it.

CHAPTER IX

"Enterprise, Fla., Sept. —, 18—.

" My dear Arthur:

" I was glad to hear that you were so pleasantly situated and liked your parish work. I trust it is cooler there than here in Florida, where the thermometer has registered higher day after day than it has before in years. I rather like it, however, as I am something of a salamander, and this, you know, is not my first experience in Florida. I was here between thirty and forty years ago, before I was married. In fact, I met your mother here at the Brock House, which before the war was frequented by many Southerners, some of whom came in the summer as well as in the winter.

" It was while I was here that an incident occurred which made a strong impression upon my mind, and was recalled to it by your mention of *Crompton* as the town where you are living. On one of the hottest days of the season I attended a funeral, the saddest, and, in some respects, the most peculiar I ever attended. It was in a log-house some miles from the river, and was that of a young girl, who lay in her coffin with a pathetic look on her face, as if in death she were pleading for some wrong to be righted. I could scarcely keep back my tears when

I looked at her, and after all these years my eyes grow moist when I recall that funeral in the palmetto clearing, with only Crackers and negroes in attendance, a demented old woman, a dark-eyed little girl, the only relatives, and a free negro, Jake, and Mandy Ann, a slave, belonging to Mrs. Harris, the only real mourners. Mandy Ann attended to the child and old woman, while Jake was master of ceremonies, and more intelligent than many white people I have met. Such a funeral as that was, with the cries and groans and singing of both whites and blacks! One old woman, called Judy, came near having the *power*, as they call a kind of fit of spiritual exaltation. But Jake shook her up, and told her to behave, as it was a 'Piscopal funeral and not a pra'r meetin'. Mandy Ann also shook up the old lady, Mrs. Harris, and screamed in her ear through a trumpet, while the little dark-eyed child joined in the refrain of the negroes' song,

> " ' Oh, it will be joyful
> When we meet to part no more.'

" It was ludicrous, but very sad, and Jake's efforts to keep order were pitiful. He called his young mistress Miss Dory, and was most anxious to screen her from the least suspicion of wrong. When I questioned him with regard to the parentage of the little girl, he wrung his hands and answered, 'I do' know for shu', but fo' God it's all right. She tole me so, fo' she died, an' Miss Dory never tole a lie. She said to find Elder Covil, who knew, but he's done gone off Norf, or somewhar.'

" I felt sure it was all right when I saw the girl's

face.   It must have been beautiful in life, and no taint
of guilt had ever marred its innocence.   There could
have been no fault at her door, except concealment,
and the reason for that was buried in her grave.   I
heard of a stranger who visited the clearing three
or four years before the funeral.   Jake was away, but
Mandy Ann was there and full of the ' gemman,' who,
I have no doubt, was the girl's husband and a great
scamp.   I left Florida within a week after that funeral, and have never been here since, until I came
to take charge for a time of the church which has
been erected here.   I should never have known the
place, it has changed so since the close of the war
and the influx of visitors from the North.   The hotel,
which has been greatly improved and enlarged, is
always full in the season, and it is one of the most
popular winter resorts on the river.

" One of my first inquiries was for the negroes Jake
and Mandy Ann.   The latter is married and lives
near the hotel, with as many children, I thought, as
the old woman who lived in a shoe, the way they
swarmed out when I called to see their mother.   She
had gone to Jacksonville to see ' ole Miss Perkinses,
who was dyin', and had sent for her 'case she done
live with her when she was a girl,' one of the picka-
ninnies said.   When I asked for Jake I was told he
was still in the palmetto clearing.   No one could tell
me anything about the little girl who must now, if
living, be a woman of nearly forty.   Indeed, no one
seemed to remember her, so changed are the people
since the war.   Jake, I was sure, had not forgotten,
and a few days ago I went to see him.   He is an old
man now, and if there is such a thing as an aristocratic negro, he is one; with his face black as ebony,

his hair white as snow, and his eyes full of intelligence and fire, especially when he talks of Miss Dory and ' de good ole times fo' she went to Georgy and met de Northern cuss.' That is what he calls the man who came for the little girl after the old grandmother died.

"I will tell you the story of his coming as Jake told it to me in the little enclosure where Miss Dory is buried, and where there is a very pretty monument to her memory, with 'Eudora, aged 20,' upon it. He was working in the yard, which was a garden of bloom, and over the grave and around the monument a Marshal Niel had twined itself, its clusters of roses filling the air with perfume. Pushing them a little aside, so that I could see the lettering more distinctly, he said, 'That's what he tole me to put thar, jess "Eudora, aged 20." I've left room for another name when I'm perfectly shu'. I don't want to put no lie on a grave stun, if her name wan't Crompton.'

"'Crompton!' I repeated, thinking of your parish.

"'Yes, Mas'r Mason, fo' God I b'lieve it's Crompton shu'. He comed an' fotched lil chile Dory, the lil girl you seen at the funeral, what seems only yestiddy, one way and in another a big lifetime sense we buried her mother here.'

"'Who is Mr. Crompton, and how did he know about the child?' I asked, and Jake replied, 'He is somebody from the Norf, and he'd sent money to Mas'r Hardy in Palatka for Miss Dory, who put it away for de chile. After she died Mas'r Hardy was gwine to Europe, an' tole me 'twas Col. Crompton, Troutburg, Massachusetts, who sent the money, but he wouldn't say nothin' else, 'cept that Col. Crompton had gin him his confidence and he should keep it. I'm shoo that Miss Dory sent letters through Mas'r Hardy to de Colonel, an' he writ to her. Not very offen, though. She'd sen' one to Mas'r Hardy, an' he'd sen' it Norf, an' then she'd wait and wait for de answer, an' when it came you or'to seen her face light up like sun-up on de river in a May mornin'. An' her eyes,—she had wonnerful eyes,—would shine like de stars frosty nights in Virginny. Maybe 'twas mean, but sometimes I watched her readin' de letter, her han's flutterin' as she opened it like a little bird's wings when it's cotched. I think she was allus 'spectin' sumptin' what never comed. The letters was short, but it took her a mighty time to read 'em, 'case you see she wasn't good at readin' writin', an' I 'specs de Colonel's handwrite wasn't very plain. She used to spell out de long words, whisperin' 'em out sometimes, her face changin' till all de brightness was gone, an' it was more like a storm on de river than sun-up. Den she'd fold de letter, an' take up de lil chile an' kiss it, an' say, " I've got *you*. We'll never part." Den she'd burn de letter. I specs he tole her to, an' she was shoo to mind. Den she'd go at her readin' book agin, or writin', tryin' to larn, but 'twixt you an' I 'twan't in her, an', no direspec' nuther, de Harrises couldn't larn from books. Dey's quick to 'dapt theirselves to what they seen, an' she didn't see nothin'.

" ' Once she said to me when de big words troubled her an' floor'd me, " I can never be a lady dis way. Ef he'd take me whar he is, an' 'mongst his people, I should larn thar ways, but what can I do here wid—" She didn't say " wid Jake an' Mandy Ann an' ole granny, an' de rest of 'em," but she meant it.

If it hadn't been for the lil chile she could of gone to school. I tole her oncet I'd sen' her an' take care of de lil chile an' ole Miss,—me an' Mandy Ann. The tears come in her eyes as she ast whar I'd git de money, seein' we was layin' up what come from de Norf for de chile. I'd done thought that out lyin' awake nights an' plannin' how to make her a lady. I'se bawn free, you know, an' freedom was sweet to me an' slavery sour, but for Miss Dory I'd do it, an' I said, " I'll sell myself to Mas'r Hardy, or some gemman like him." Thar's plenty wants me, an' would give a big price, an' she should have it all for her schoolin'.

" ' You orter have seen her face then. Every part of it movin' to oncet, an' her eyes so bright I could not look at 'em for the quarness thar was in 'em, an' I'll never forget her voice as she said, " That can't be; but, Jakey, you are de noblest man, black or white, I ever seen, an' my best frien', an' I loves you as if you was my brodder."

" ' Dem's her very words, an' I would of sole myself for her if I could. But de lam gin up after a while. All de hope an' life went out of her, an' she died' an' you done 'tended her funeral,—you 'members it,—as fust class as I could make it. I tole you sumptin' den, but not all this. It wasn't a fittin' time, but seein' you brings it all back. Mandy Ann an' me said we'd keep lil chile a while, bein' ole Miss was alive, though she was no better than a broomstick dressed in her clothes. She didn't know nothin', not even that Miss Dory was dead, an' kep' askin' whose chile it was,—ef it was Mandy Ann's, an' why it was hyar. It kinder troubled her, I think, it was so active an' noisy, an' sung so much. Used to play at pra'r meetin' an' have de pow' powerful, as she had seen de blacks have it when Mandy Ann took her to thar meetin's. Seems ef she liked thar ways better than what I tried to teach her from de Pra'r Book, an' they is rather more livelier for a chile. All de neighbors was interested in her, an' ole Miss Thomas most of all. She's de one what stood out de longest agin Miss Dory, 'case she didn't tell squar what she'd promised not to. But she gin in at de funeral, an' was mighty nice to the lil chile. When ole Miss Lucy died she comed in her democrat wagon, as she did for Miss Dory, an' coaxed lil chile inter her lap, an' said she showed she had good blood, an' or'to be brung up a lady, an' it wasn't fittin' for her to stay whar she was, an' if I knew de fader I mus' write to him.

" ' I knew dat as well as she did, an' after consultin' wid Mandy Ann an' prayin' for light, it come dat I must sen' on, an' I did, hopin' he wouldn' come, for to part wid de lil chile was like tearin' my vitals out, an' Mandy Ann's, too. He did come,—a big, gran' man, wid a look which made me glad Miss Dory was in heaven 'stead of livin' wid him. He'd been hyar oncet before. Mebby I tole you, at de funeral. My mind gets leaky, an' I can't 'member exactly, an' so repeats.'

" ' I think not,' I said, ' and if you did, I have forgotten, and am willing to hear it again.'

" We were sitting now on a bench close by what Jake said had been the little girl's play-house, which she called her *Shady*, because it was under a palm tree.

" ' Yes, he comed,' Jake said, ' two or three weeks after Miss Dory comed home from Georgy, whar she was visitin' her kin. Mandy Ann tole me 'bout him,—how he walked an' talked to Miss Dory, till when he went away her face was white as the gown she put on when she hearn he was comin'. You see, Mandy Ann was on de boat wid him, an' tole her. She was all of a twitter, like you've seen de little hungry birds in de nest when dar mudder is comin' wid a worm,—an' she was jess as cold an' slimpsy an' starved when he went away as dem little birds is when de mudder is shot on de wing an' never comes wid de worm. You know what I mean. She s'pected somethin' an' didn't get it.'

"Jake was very eloquent in his illustrations, and I looked admiringly at him as he went on: 'I was in Virginny vallyin' for Mas'r Kane, a fine gemman who gin me big wage, an' I was savin' it up to buy some things for de house, 'case I reckoned how Miss Dory seen somethin' different in Georgy. Her kin was very 'spectable folks, an' she might want some fixin's. Thar was nobody hyar but ole Miss Lucy, who'd had some kind of a spell an' lost most of her sense, an' didn't know more'n a chile. Mandy Ann got somebody to write me that Miss Dory had a beau,—a gran' man, an' I was that pleased that I ast the price of a second-han' pianny, thinkin' mebby she'd want to larn, 'case she sung so nice. Den I never hearn anoder word, 'cept from Miss Dory, till Mas'r Hardy writ Mas'r Kane to sen' me home, 'case I was needed. I s'posed ole Miss Lucy had had another fit, an' started thinkin' all de way up de river how I'd see Miss Dory standin' in de do' wid de smile on her face, an' de light in her eyes, an' her pleasant voice sayin' to me, " How d'ye, Jake, I'se mighty glad to see you." 'Stid o' that she wasn't thar, an' Mandy Ann come clatterin' down de stars,

an' I hearn a baby cry.   In my s'prise I said, " What's
dat ar?   Has ole Miss got a baby?"

" 'Mandy Ann laughed till she cried, den cried
without laughin', an' tole me wid her face to de wall,
an' I was so shamed I could of hid in de san'; an'
Mandy Ann, they tole me, did run inter de woods
at fust to hide herself.   Den she smarted up an' fit
for Miss Dory, who said nothin' 'cept, " Wait, it will
all be right.   I tole him I would wait.   I'm a good
girl," an' fo' Heaven, I b'lieved her, though some o'
de white trash didn't at fust, but they all did at the
last.   Maybe I'm tirin' you?'

" ' No,' I said, ' go on,' and he continued: ' I'se
tole you most all dat happened after dat till she died
an' you comed to de funeral.

" ' When ole miss died, I writ to de Colonel, as I
tole you, an' he comed, gran', an' proud, an' stiff, an'
I tole him all 'bout Miss Dory same as I have you,—
p'raps not quite so much,—p'raps mo'.   I don't remember, 'case as I said my memory is ole an' leaky,
and mebby I ain't tellin' it right in course as I tole
him.   Some was in de house, an' some out hyar,
whar I said, " Dis is her grave.   She's lyin' under
de san', but I'll fix her up in time an' she shall sleep
under de roses."

" ' I tole him everything was done in order, an' how
you preached about de Resurrection an' de Life, an'
how sweet she look in her coffin, an' Mandy Ann's
puttin' her ring on de weddin' finger, an' his mouf
trembled like, up and down, an' I b'lieve ef thar had
been a tear in his dried-up heart he'd of shed it.

" ' Oncet, when he seemed kinder softened, I ast
him squar, " Ain't you her husband?"

" ' Thar was such a quar look in his eyes,—a starin'

at me a minit,—an' then he said, " I am nobody's husband, an' never shall be."

" ' I b'lieve he lied, an' wanted to knock him down,
but wouldn't right thar by her grave. He tole me
I was to have all the money Miss Dory had been
layin' up, an' he would send me mo' for the stun.
I ast what I should put on it, an' he said, " What was
on her coffin plate ? "

" ' " Eudora, aged 20," I tole him.   " Put the same
on the stun," he said.   He tole me I was to stay on
de place, an' have all I made.   Then thar was Mandy
Ann, who 'longed to de lil chile.   She was to stay
hyar, he said, an' he'd pay her wage which she could
keep herself.   He'd settle wid de lil chile when de
time come, an' set Mandy Ann free.   I think he
meant it, but he was spar'd de trouble, for de wah
comed like a big broom an' swep' slavery away, an'
mos' everyting souf wid it, an' Mandy Ann was free
any way widout de Colonel.

" ' After de chile went away I got to broodin' over
Miss Dory's wrongs, till I'se so worked up agin de
Colonel, dat when de wah broke out I was minded
to 'list, hopin' I'd meet him somewhar in battle an'
shoot him.   Den I cooled down an' staid home an'
raised things an' worked for de poor folks hyar,—
de women, whose husban's an' brudders had gone to
de wah.   Ted,—dat's de boy on de " Hatty " long
ago,—went to de wah wid a great flourish, promisin'
Mandy Ann he'd shoot the Colonel shu' ef he got a
chance.   An' what do you think ? At de fust crack of
de cannon in de fust battle he seen, he cut an' run, an'
kep' on runnin' till he got hyar, beggin' me an' Mandy
Ann to hide him, 'case he was a deserter.   I held my
tongue, an' let Mandy Ann do as she pleased, an'

she hid him till de Federals come, when he jined them, an' did get hit, but 'twas on de back or shoulder, showin' which way he was runnin'.

" ' Den Mandy Ann married him, an' has ten chillenses, an' washes an' scrubs for de Brock House an' everybody, while Ted struts roun' wid a cigar in his mouf, an' says he has neber seen a well day sense de wah,—dat his shoulder pains him powerful at times,—an' he is tryin' to get a pension, an' Mandy Ann is helpin' him. Beats all what women won't do for a man if they love him, no matter how big a skunk he is. Miss Dory died for one, an' Mandy Ann is slavin' herself to deff for one. I'se mighty glad I'se not a woman.'

" Here Jake stopped a moment, presumably to reflect on the waywardness of Miss Dory and Mandy Ann caring for two skunks,—one the Colonel and one Ted, whose last name I did not know till I asked Jake, who replied, ' Hamilton—a right smart name, I'm told, an' 'long'd to de quality. Ole man Hamilton come from de norf somewhar, an' bought Ted's mother, a likely mulatto. Who his fader was I doan know. He's more white dan black, an' is mighty proud of his name,—Hamilton,—'case somebody tole him thar was once a big man, Hamilton, an' when Mandy Ann had twin boys, she was tole to call 'em Alexander an' Aaron,—sumptin',—I doan justly remember what. It makes me think óf a chestnut.'

" ' Burr,' I suggested, and he replied, ' Yes, sar, dat's it,—Aaron Burr,—anoder big man,—an' dey calls de twins Alex and Aaron. Fine boys, too, wid Mandy Ann's get-up in 'em. Dar's two mo' twins,— little gals; beats all what a woman Mandy Ann is for twins,—an' she calls 'em Judy and Dory,—one for

14

young Miss, an' t'other for de rag doll lil chile took norf wid her and called Judy, for an ole woman who has gone to de Canaan she used to sing about—" Oh, I'se boun' for de lan' of Canaan." She was powerful in pra'r, an' at de fust meetin' after de wah, an' she knew she was free, I b'lieve you could of hearn her across de lake to Sanford, she shout " Glory, bress de Lawd! " so loud. But for all she was free, she wouldn't leave ole Miss Thomas. " I likes my mistis, an' I ain't gwine to leave her wid somebody else to comb her har, an' make her corn bread," she said, when dey tried to persuade her to go to Palatky. She staid wid ole Miss, who buried her decent, an' has gone herself to jine her an' Miss Dory in de better land, which seems to me is not far away; an' offen, when I sees de sun go down in a glory of red an' purple an' yaller,—I'se mighty fond of yaller,— I says to myself, " It's dat way dey goes to de udder world, whar, please God, I'll go some day fore berry long,—for I tries to be good.'

" There was a rapt look in Jake's face as he turned it to the west, and I would have given much to know that my future was as assured as his."

Here the first part of Mr. Mason's letter closed abruptly, as a friend came to call, but he added hastily, " To-morrow I'll finish, and tell you about the child who now occupies all Jake's thoughts, praying every day that he may see her again."

CHAPTER X

" I was interrupted yesterday, and hardly know where to begin again, or what I have written, as Jake was a little mixed and went forward and back at times, showing that his memory was, as he said, leaky, but when he struck the child he was bright as a guinea. ' Lil Chile ' and ' Honey Bee ' he calls her. He told me of her running into the house to meet the Colonel, with her soiled frock, and her face and hands besmeared with molasses; of her tussle with Mandy Ann, who wanted to wash her face and change her clothes, and of her fine appearance at the last in a white gown, her best, which he had bought and Mandy Ann made not long before, and which the Colonel would not take with him. So they kept it, and Mandy Ann washed and ironed it, and put it away with some sweet herbs, and aired it every year till she was married, when Jake cared for it till Mandy Ann's twins were born,—Alex and Aaron. Then Mandy Ann borrowed it for them to be christened in, one of them one Sunday and one the next, so that both had the honor of wearing it, while Jake was sponsor, ' For,' said he, ' Mandy Ann has gin up them hollerin' meetin's whar white folks done come to see de ole darkies have a kind of powow, as dey use to have befo' de wah. Clar for't if de

folks from de Norf don't gin de blacks money to sing
de ole-time songs an' rock an' weave back an' forth
till dey have de pow'.   I don't think much of dat ar,
jess 'musin' theyselves wid our religion;' and Jake
looked his disgust, and continued:

"'Mandy Ann like mighty well to jine 'em, but
I hole her back, an' now she's 'Piscopal, ef she's
anything,—an' when de girl twins come,—Dory an'
Judy,—she borrowed lil chile's gown agin.   Dat
make fo' times, an' then I shet de gates, an' said, " No
mo' gown, an' no mo' twins," an' thar hain't been
no mo'.

"'But I'se got a good ways from lil chile, who
wan't an atom shy of de Colonel, though he was of
her, an' when he took her han' I could almost see
him squirm like.   I think he tried to be kind, an' he
gin her a lil ivory book he had on his watch-chain,
but you see he didn't feel it.   He didn't care for
children, and it seemed as if he wanted to get away
from this one.   But he couldn't.   She was his'n; I'd
bet my soul on dat.   He had to come after her an'
took her, though 'twas 'bout the wust job he ever
did, I reckon.   She fit like a tiger cat about gwine
wid him, an' 's true's you bawn, I don't b'lieve she'd
gone ef he hadn't took me wid him to Savannah.   I
can't tell you, Mas'r Mason, 'bout de partin' thar.
'Twas drefful, an' I kin see her now rollin' on de flo',
wid her heels an' han's in de air, an' she a-sayin' she
mus' stay wid Shaky.   I bought her such a pretty
red cloak, all lined wid white silk, an' wrapped her
in it, an' took her on to de boat, an' left her thar,
she thinkin' I was comin' back, an' the last I seen of
her, as the boat moved off, she was jumpin' up an'
down, an' stretchin' her arms to me, an' the Cunnel

holdin' her tight, or I b'lieve she'd sprung over-
board.   He'd a good time gettin' her home, I reckon.
She was the very old Harry when her dander was
up,' and the old negro laughed as he thought of what
the Colonel must have borne on that journey with his
troublesome charge.

"There came a few lines to him, he said, telling of
Col. Crompton's safe arrival home, and that the child
was well.   After a while the war broke out, and communication with the North was cut off.   The friend
in Palatka, who had returned from Europe and joined
the Confederate Army, was killed, and the letter
which Jake sent to Col. Crompton when peace was
restored was not answered for a long time.   At last
the Colonel wrote that Eudora had married against
his wishes and gone to Europe, and Jake was not to
trouble him with any more letters concerning her.

"An' that's all I knows of her,' he said, ' whether
she's dead or alive, or whar she is; but if I did know
I b'lieve I'd walk afoot to de Norf to see her.   She
ain't my lil chile Dory no mo', but I allus thinks of
her like dat, an' I keeps de cradle she was rocked in
by my bed, an' sometimes, when I'se lonesome nights,
an' can't sleep for thinkin' of her, I puts my han' out
an' jogs it with a feelin' the lil one is thar, an' every
day I prays she may come back to me, an' I b'lieve
she will.   Yes, sar, it comes to me that she will.'

"The tears were running down the old man's face
when, on our going to the house, he showed me the
cradle close to his bed, a rude, old-fashioned, high-
topped thing, such as the poorest families used years
ago.   There was a pillow, or cushion, in it, and a
little patchwork quilt, which, he said, Mandy Ann
pieced and made.   He showed me, too, a second or

third school reader, soiled and worn and pencil
marked, and showing that it had been much used.

" ' This was Miss Dory's,' he said; ' the one she
studied de most, tryin' to learn, an' gettin' terribly
flustered wid de big words.   I can see her now,
bendin' over it airly an' late; sometimes wid de chile
in her lap till she done tuckered out, an' laid it away
with a sithe as if glad to be shet of it.   She couldn't
larn, an' de Lord took her whar dey don't ask what
you knows,—only dis: does you lub de Lord? an' she
did, de lamb.'

" Jake was still crying, and I was not far from it
as I saw in fancy that poor young girl trying to learn,
trying to master the big words and their meaning,
in the vain hope of fitting herself for companionship
with a man who had deserted her, and who probably
never had for her more than a passing fancy, of which
he was ashamed and would gladly ignore.

" ' I showed him de book,' Jake said, ' an' tole him
how she tried to larn, an' I tried to help her all I
could, an' then he did have some feelin' an' his eyes
got red, but he didn't drap a tear; no, sar, not a
drap!   He ast me could he have de book, an' I said,
" No, sar, not for nothin'.   It's mine," an' he said,
proud-like, " As you please."   He was mighty good
to me an' Mandy Ann 'bout money, an' when I writ
him she was married, he sent her two hundred dollars, which she 'vested in a house, or Ted would of
spent it for fine close an' cigarettes.   He must be
gettin' ole, as I be, an' they call de town Crompton,
after him, 'stid of Troutburg.'

" Remembering your parish, I told him I had a
son settled in Crompton, Massachusetts.   I hardly

thought there were two towns of the same name in one State, and I'd inquire if Col. Crompton lived there. His face brightened at once, and when I left him, he grasped my hand and said, ' Bress de Lawd for de grain of comfort you done give me. If she is thar I'd walk all de road from Floridy to see her, if I couldn't git thar no other way. Thankee, Mas'r Mason, for comin' to see me. I'se pretty reg'lar at church, an' sets by de do', an' allus gives a nickel for myself an' one for Miss Dory dead an' for Miss Dory livin', an' I makes Mandy Ann 'tend all I can, though she'd rather go whar she says it's livelier. She is mighty good to me,—comes ebery week an' clars up an' scoles me for gittin' so dirty. She's great on a scrub, Mandy Ann is. Muss you go? Well, I'm glad you comed, an' I s'pec's I've tole you some things twiste, 'case of my memory. Good-by.'

"He accompanied me to the door, and shook hands with all the grace of a born gentleman. Then I left him, but have been haunted ever since by a picture of that old negro in his lonely cabin, jogging that empty cradle nights when he cannot sleep, and contrasting him with Col. Crompton, whoever and wherever he may be. Perhaps you can throw some light on the subject. The world is not so very wide that our sins are not pretty sure to find us out, and that some Col. Crompton has been guilty of a great wrong seems certain. Possibly he is one of your parishioners, and you may know something of the second Dory. I shall await your answer with some anxiety.

"Your father,
"CHARLES MASON."

This was the letter which had sent the Rev. Arthur
to call on Mrs. Biggs, with no thought of Eloise in
his mind. She was not yet an active factor in the
drama which was to be played out so rapidly. Returning to his boarding place, the rector read his
father's letter a second time, and then answered it.
A part of what he wrote we give:

" I have just come from an interview with a woman
who is credited with knowing the history of the place
forty years back, and I have no doubt that Shaky's
Col. Crompton is living here in Crompton Place, the
richest man in town and largest contributor to the
church.   There is a lady living with him who people believe is his daughter, although he has never
acknowledged her as such.   Mrs. Biggs, the woman
I interviewed, gave me a most graphic account of the
manner of her arrival at Crompton Place, when she
was a little girl like the one you describe.   She has a
lovely face, but is a little twisted in her brain.   She
did run away with her music teacher, and her name
is Amy Eudora.   There was no mention made of
Harris.   They call her Miss Amy.   There can't be
much doubt of her identity with Jaky's lil chile.
Send him on, and Mandy Ann, too,—and the four
twins, Alex and Aaron, Judy and Dory.   I'll pay
half their fare!   There's enough of the old Adam in
me to make me want to see them confront the proud
Colonel, who ignores me for reasons I could not
fathom, until I received your letter.   Then I suspected that because I am your son he feared that
some pages of his life, which he hoped were blotted
out by time and the ravages of war, might be re-
vealed.   He is an old man, of course, but distin-
guished-looking still, though much broken with

rheumatic gout, which keeps him mostly at home. My respects to Shaky, whom I hope before long to hear ringing the bell at Crompton Place.   Is that wicked?   I suppose so, but I cannot help it.

"ARTHUR."

CHAPTER XI

The day following the rector's call on Mrs. Biggs was Sunday, and the morning was wet and misty, with a thick, white fog which crept up from the sea and hid from view objects at any distance away.

"This is nearly as bad as London," Howard said to Jack when, after breakfast, they stood looking out upon the sodden grass and drooping flowers in the park. "Have you a mind to go to church?"

Jack shrugged his shoulders, and replied, "Not I; it's too damp. Are you going?"

Howard had not thought of doing so until that moment, when an idea came suddenly into his mind, and he answered, "I think so,—yes. · Some one ought to represent the Crompton pew. It is out of the question for my uncle to go, and he would not if he could. He has taken a violent prejudice against the new rector, for no reason I can think of. He is a good fellow,—the rector, I mean,—and not too straight-laced to smoke a cigar, and he knows a fine horse when he sees one, and preaches splendid sermons. I think I shall go and encourage him."

He did not urge Jack to accompany him, nor would Jack have done so if he had. There was an idea in his mind, as well as in Howard's, which he intended to carry out, and half an hour after Howard started for church, he, too, left the house and walked slowly through the park in the direction of Mrs. Biggs's.

" I don't know as it is just the thing to call on Sunday," he thought, hesitating a little as he came in sight of the house, " but it seems an age since I saw her. I'll just step to the door and inquire how she is."

His knock was not answered at first, but when he repeated it he heard from the parlor what sounded like—" The key is under the mat," in a voice he knew did not belong to Mrs. Biggs. That good woman was in church. Tim had gone to the choir in St. John's, and Eloise was alone. Ruby Ann had been to see her the night before with her massage and rubber band, both of which had proved so successful that Eloise was feeling greatly encouraged, and the outlook was not quite so forlorn as when she first landed at Mrs. Biggs's, helpless and homesick and half crazed with pain. Her ankle was improving fast, although she could not walk ; but she had hopes of taking her place in school within a week or ten days. Mrs. Biggs had wondered why the young men from Crompton Place did not call on Saturday, and Eloise had felt a little disappointed when the day had passed and she did not see them.

" 'Tain't noways likely they'll come to-day. Folks know my principles, and that I don't b'lieve in Sunday visiting," she said as she tidied up the room before starting for church. " Nobody'll come, unless it is Ruby Ann with her massage, that's no more good than a cat's foot; so I'll just give the parlor a lick and a promise till to-morrow, and 'fise you I'd be comfortable in that wrapper."

But Eloise insisted upon the white dressing jacket with pink ribbons, in which Mrs. Biggs said she looked " like a picter," regretting that the young men could not see her.

" If it wasn't for desiccating the Sabbath I wish them high bucks would call," she added, as she gave a final whisk to the duster and went to prepare for church. " I'm goin' to lock the door and put the key under the mat, so nobody can get in if they want to. I might lose it if I carried it to meetin'. I did once, and had to clamber inter the butry winder," was her last remark as she left the house; and Eloise heard the click of the key and knew she was locked in and alone.

She was not afraid, but began to imagine what she could do in case of a fire, or if any one were to come knocking at the door. " Sit still and not answer," she was thinking when Jack came rapidly up the walk. She saw his shadow as he passed the window, and her heart gave a great bound, for she knew who was " desiccating " the Sabbath by calling upon her. The first knock she did not answer, but when the second came, louder and more imperative than the first, she called out, " The key is under the mat," regretting her temerity in an instant, and trembling as she thought, " What if I am doing something improper to admit him, and Mrs. Biggs should disapprove ! "

The thought sent the blood to her cheeks, which were scarlet as Jack came in, eager and delighted to find her alone.

" Locked up like a prisoner," he said, as he took her hand, which he held longer than was at all necessary, while he looked into her eyes, where the gladness at seeing him again was showing so plainly.

When he last saw her she was arrayed in Mrs. Biggs's spotted calico, and he was quick to note the change. He had thought her lovely before; she was beautiful now, with the brightness in her eyes and the color coming and going so rapidly on her cheeks. Drawing a chair close to her, he sat down just where he could look at her as he talked, and could watch the varying expression on her face. Once he laid his hand on the arm of her chair, but withdrew it when he saw her troubled look, as if she feared he was getting too familiar. He asked her about her sprain, and was greatly interested, or seemed to be, in the massage and rubber band which were helping her so much. Then he spoke of Ruby Ann, the biggest woman he ever saw, he believed, and just the one for a school-teacher. He was past the school-house the day before, he said. It seemed they had half a day on Saturday and half a day on Wednesday. It was the boys' recess, and he never heard such a hullaballoo as they were making. A tall, lanky boy seemed to be the leader, whom the others followed.

"That must be Tom Walker, the one who makes all the trouble, and whom Mr. Bills and Mrs. Biggs think I can't manage," Eloise said, with a little gasp, such as she always felt when she thought of Tom, who, Tim had reported, was boasting of what he meant to do with the lame schoolmarm when she came.

Jack detected the trouble in her voice, and asked who Tom Walker was. It did not take long for Eloise to tell all she knew, while Jack listened thoughtfully, resolving to seek out Tom, and by thrashing, or threatening, or hiring, turn him from any plan he might have against this little girl, who seemed to him far too young and dainty to be thrown upon the mercy of the rabble he had seen by the school-house with Tom Walker at their head.

"Don't worry about Tom. Big bullies like him are always cowards. You'll get along all right," he said encouragingly, with a growing desire to take the helpless girl in his arms and carry her away from Tom Walker and Mr. Bills and Mrs. Biggs, and the whole of her surroundings, which she did not seem at all to fit.

He wanted to entertain her, and told her of an excursion on the water he had taken the previous day with Howard Crompton,—the last of the season, he said, and very enjoyable. He wished she had been there. Then he spoke of the Colonel, laughing at his peculiarities, and asking if she had ever heard of the Crompton "Formula." She said she had from Ruby Ann, and was glad she was not to be subjected to questioning on it, as she knew she should fail in everything except the four *rights*. She might manage them, but it was not necessary for her to be examined by anybody, since her normal school diploma was a license to teach anywhere in the State.

"Hanged if I think I could manage the *rights !*" Jack said. "Spelling is not my forte, and Howard, who is great at it, missed the last one."

"How is Mr. Howard?" Eloise asked, and Jack replied, "All right. Has gone to church like a good Christian. I ought to have gone, but I thought I'd come here, as you might be lonely here alone."

It flashed through Eloise's mind to wonder how he knew she was alone, but she made no comment, except to say that the rector, Mr. Arthur Mason, called upon her the day before.

"Did he?" Jack said. "I believe he is a fine fellow. Howard likes him, but for some reason the Colonel does not, and when Howard said he was going to church, and suggested bringing Mr. Mason home to lunch, he growled out something about not liking company on Sunday. He is a queer old cove, and does not seem to care for anybody but Miss Amy. He is devoted to her, and she is a lovely woman, and must once have been brilliant, but she puzzles me greatly. She seems to be rational on every subject except her life in California. If any allusion is made to that she looks dazed at once, and says, 'I can't talk about it. I don't remember.'"

"My father died in California, and my mother is there now," Eloise said sadly.

Jack had not supposed she had a mother. Mrs. Brown, who sat beside him at the commencement exercises in Mayville, had spoken of her as an orphan, and he replied, "I had somehow thought your mother dead."

"No; oh, no!" Eloise answered quickly. "She is not dead; she is——"

She stopped suddenly, and Jack knew by her voice that her mother was a painful subject, and he began at once to speak of something else. He was a good talker, and Eloise a good listener, and neither took any heed to the lapse of time, until there was the sound of wheels before the house. A carriage had stopped to let some one out; then it went on, and Howard Crompton came up the walk and knocked at the door just as Jack had done an hour before.

"Pull the bobbin and come in," Jack called out,

and, a good deal astonished, Howard walked in, looking unutterable things when he saw Jack there before him, seemingly perfectly at home and perfectly happy, and in very close proximity to Eloise, who wondered what Mrs. Biggs would say if she came and found both the " high bucks " there.

" Hallo! " Jack said, while Howard responded, " Hallo! What brought you here? "

" A wish to see Miss Smith. What brought you? " was Jack's reply, and Howard responded, " A wish to see Miss Smith, of course. You didn't suppose I came to see Mrs. Biggs, did you? Where is the old lady? "

Eloise explained that she had gone to church, and Jack told of the key under the mat, and the talk flowed on; and Eloise could not forbear telling them of Mrs. Biggs's wish not to have the Sabbath " desiccated " by visitors.

" A regular Mrs. Malaprop," Jack said, while Howard suggested that they leave before she came home. " We can put the key under the mat, and she'll never know of the ' desiccation,' " he said.

Jack looked doubtfully at Eloise, who shook her head.

" No," she said, " I shall tell her you have been here. It would be a deception not to."

" As you like. And it's too late now, for here she comes! " Howard said, as Mrs. Biggs passed the window and stooped to find the key.

It was not there. Turning the mat upside down, she failed to discover it. The key was gone!

" For goodness' sake, what can have happened? " they heard her say, as she pushed the door open and entered the room, where the two young men stood, one on either side of Eloise, as if to protect her. "Well, if I ain't beat!" the widow exclaimed, dropping into a chair and beginning to untie her bonnet strings as if they choked her. "Yes, I am beat. Hain't you been to meetin'?" she asked rather severely, her eyes falling on Howard, who answered quickly, "Yes, I have, and on my way home called to inquire for Miss Smith, and found this rascal here before me. He had unlocked the door and taken possession. You ought to have him arrested as a burglar, breaking into your house on Sunday."

"I s'pose I or'ter," Mrs. Biggs said, "and I hope none of the neighbors seen you come in. Miss Brown acrost the way is a great gossip, and there hain't a speck of scandal ever been on my house in my life, and I a-boardin' schoolma'ams for fifteen years!"

Mrs. Biggs was inclined to be a little severe on the two young men invading her premises, but Jack was equal to the emergency. She was tugging at her bonnet strings, which were entangled in a knot, into which the cord of her eyeglasses had become twisted.

"I can swear that neither Mrs. Brown, nor any one else was looking from the window when I came in. She was probably at church," Jack said, offering to help her, and finally undoing the knot which had proved too much for her. "There you are," he said, removing the bonnet, and setting her false piece, which had become a little askew, more squarely on her head. "You are all right now, and can blow me up as much as you please. I deserve it," he added, beaming upon her a smile which would have disarmed her of a dozen prejudices.

Jack's ways were wonderful with women, both

15

young and old, and Mrs. Biggs felt their influence
and laughed, as she said, "I ain't goin' to blow,
though I was took aback to see two men here, and
I'd like to know how you knew where to find the
key."

"I told him," Eloise answered rather shamefacedly.

Mrs. Biggs shot a quick glance at her, and then
said, with a meaning nod, "I s'pose I'd of done the
same thing when John and me was courtin', and
young folks is all alike."

Eloise's face was scarlet, while Jack pretended suddenly to remember the lateness of the hour, and
started to leave the room. As he did so his eyes
fell upon a table on which a few books were lying.

"You must find these lively," he said, turning them
over and reading their titles aloud. "'Pilgrim's
Progress,' 'Foxe's Martyrs,' 'Doddridge's Rise and
Fall,' 'Memoir of Payson,' all solid and good, but a
little heavy, 'United States History,' improving, but
tedious,—and,—upon my word, 'The Frozen Pirate'! That is jolly! Have you read it?"

Before Eloise could reply Mrs. Biggs exclaimed,
"Of course she hasn't, and I don't know how under
the sun it got in here, unless Tim put it here unbe-
knownst to me. I never read novels, and that is the
wust I ever got hold of, and the biggest lie. I told
Tim so."

She took it from the table and carried it from the
room, followed by the young men, who laughed as
they thought how the widow, who never read novels,
betrayed the fact that she had read "The Frozen
Pirate."

CHAPTER XII

THE MARCH OF EVENTS

"I say, Howard," Jack began, when they were out upon the road, "that girl ought to have something besides 'The Frozen Pirate' and 'Foxe's Martyrs' to brighten her up,—books and flowers, and other things. Do you think she'd take them?"

Howard's head was cooler than Jack's, and he replied, "She would resent gifts from us, but would take them from Amy. Anyhow, we can try that dodge."

"By Jove, you are right! We can send her a lot of things with Mrs. Amy's compliments," Jack exclaimed. "Flowers and books and candy, and——"

He did not finish what was in his mind, but the next morning, immediately after breakfast, he pretended that he had an errand in the village, and started off alone, preferring to walk, he said, when Howard suggested the carriage, and also declining Howard's company, which was rather faintly offered. Howard never cared to walk when he could drive, and then he had a plan which he could better carry out with Jack away than with him present. He was more interested in Eloise than he would like to confess to Jack or any one, and he found himself thinking of her constantly and wishing he could do something to make her more comfortable than he was sure she could be even in Mrs. Biggs's parlor. He was very fastidious in his tastes, and Mrs. Biggs's parlor was a horror to him, with its black hair-cloth furniture, and especially the rocker in which Eloise sat, and out of which she seemed in danger of slipping every time she bent forward. He had thought of his uncle's sea chair on the occasion of his first call, and now he resolved to send it in Amy's name. Something had warned him that in Eloise's make-up there was a pride equal to his own. She might receive favors from Amy, as she had the hat, and although a chair would seem a good deal perhaps, he would explain it on the ground of Amy's great desire to help some one when he saw her. He'd send it at once, he thought, and he wrote a note, saying, " Miss Smith: Please accept this sea chair with the compliments of Mrs. Amy, who thinks you will find it more comfortable than the hair-cloth rocker, of which I told her. As she seldom writes to any one, she has made me her amanuensis, and hopes you will excuse her. Yours, very truly, Howard Crompton, for Mrs. Amy."

It was a lie, Howard knew, but that did not trouble him, and calling Sam, he bade him take it with the chair and a bunch of hothouse roses to Miss Smith. Sam took the chair and the note and the roses, and started for Mrs. Biggs's, stopping in the avenue to look at the shrub where Brutus had received the gouge in his shoulder, and stopping again at a point where some bits of glass from the broken window of the carriage were lying. All this took time, so that it was after eleven when he at last reached Mrs. Biggs's gate, and met a drayman coming in an opposite direction with Jack Harcourt on the cart, seated in a very handsome wheel chair, and looking supremely happy.

Jack had been very busy all the morning visiting furniture stores and inquiring for wheel chairs, which he found were not very common. Indeed, there were only three in the town, and one of these had been sent from Boston for the approval of Col. Crompton when his rheumatic gout prevented him from walking. Something about it had not suited him, and it had remained with the furniture dealer, who, glad of a purchaser, had offered it to Jack for nearly half the original price. Jack did not care for the cost if the chair was what he wanted. It was upholstered with leather, both the seat and the back, and could be easily propelled from room to room by Eloise herself, while Jack thought it quite likely that he should himself some day take her out for an airing, possibly to the school-house, which he had passed on his way to the village. There was a shorter road through the meadows and woods than the one past the school-house, but Jack took the latter, hoping he might see Tom Walker again, in which case he meant to interview him. Nor was he disappointed, for sauntering in the same direction and chewing gum, with his cap on the back of his head and his hands in his pockets, was a tall, wiry fellow, whom Jack instantly spotted as Tom Walker, the bully, who was to terrorize Eloise.

"Now is my time," Jack thought, hastening his steps and soon overtaking the boy, who, never caring whether he was late or early at school, was taking his time, and stopping occasionally to throw a stone at some bird on the fence or a tree. "Hallo, Tom!" Jack said in his cheery way as he came up with the boy, whose ungracious answer was, "How do you know my name is Tom?"

At heart Tom was something of an anarchist, jealous of and disliking people higher in the social scale than he was, and this dislike extended particularly to the young gentlemen from the Crompton House, who had nothing to do but to enjoy themselves. He did not like to be patronized, but there was something in Jack's voice which made him accompany his speech with a laugh, which robbed it of some of its rudeness.

"Oh, I know you, just as, I dare say, you know me, Jack Harcourt, from New York, visiting at present at the Crompton House," was Jack's reply, which mollified Tom at once.

If Jack had called himself Mr. Harcourt Tom would have resented it as airs. But he didn't; he said *Jack*, putting himself on a par with the boy, who took the gum from his mouth for a moment, looked at it, replaced it, and began to answer Jack's questions, which at first were very far from Eloise. But they struck her at last as they drew near the school-house.

"I'm late, as usual," Tom said, rolling his gum from side to side in his mouth. "I presume I'll catch thunder, but I don't care. I'm not afraid of any schoolmarm I've ever seen, and I mean to carry the new one out on a couple of chips if she tries to boss me."

There was a look on Tom's face which Jack did not like, but he said pleasantly, "No, you won't, when you see how helpless she is, and how she needs a young gentleman like you to stand by her."

"I ain't a gentleman," Tom answered, but his voice was a good deal softened. "I'm just Tom

Walker, who they lay everything to, and who the
boys expect to do all their dirty work for them."

"I see," Jack answered; "you pick off the hot
chestnuts. *I* used to do that when a little shaver, till
I got my fingers blistered so badly I decided to let
some one else get burned in my place."

"Did you ever cut up at school?" Tom asked,
with a growing interest in and respect for Jack, who
replied, "Oh, yes, I was pretty bad sometimes, and
am ashamed of it when I remember how I annoyed
some of my teachers. I have asked pardon of one
or two of the ladies when I have chanced to meet
them, but I never could have annoyed Miss Smith,
nor will you when you know her. You haven't seen
her yet?"

"Nope!" Tom answered. "I hear she ain't big-
ger than my thumb, and awful pretty, Tim Biggs says,
and he is threatening to thrash anybody who is mean
to her. I'd laugh to see him tackle me!"

"He'll have no occasion to, for I predict you will
be the warmest champion Miss Smith has. See if
you are not," Jack said, offering his hand to Tom, as
they had now reached the school-house.

"He is certainly a good deal of a ruffian," Jack
said to himself as he went on his way, while Tom
was not quite so sure of the two chips on which he
was to carry Eloise out if she tried to boss him. He'd
wait and see. That city chap from Crompton Place
had certainly been very friendly, and had not treated
him as if he was scum; and after taking his seat and
telling Ruby Ann, with quite an air when she asked
why he was so late, that he had been detained by Mr.
Harcourt, who wanted to talk with him, he took from
his desk his slate and rubbed out the caricature he

had drawn the day before of a young girl on crutches trying to get up the steps of the school-house. He was intending to show it to Tim Biggs and make him angry, and to the other scholars and make them laugh, and thus ferment a prejudice against Eloise, for no reason at all except the natural depravity of his nature.

The word " champion " kept sounding in his ears, and he wrote it two or three times on his slate, where the girl on crutches had been. " I always supposed champion belonged to prize-fighters, but Mr. Harcourt didn't mean that kind. He meant I was to stand up for her and behave myself. Well, I'll see what kind of craft she is," he thought.

With this decision Tom took up his lessons, and had never been more studious and well behaved than he was that day.

Meanwhile Jack had gone on his way to the village and bought his chair, with some misgivings as to how Eloise would receive it, even from Mrs. Amy. " I guess I'd better go with it, and make it right somehow," he thought, getting into the chair and riding along in state, while the people he met looked curiously at him. It was recess again when they reached the school-house, where, as usual, Tom Walker was leading the play. At sight of the dray he stopped suddenly, and then went swiftly forward to the cart, and said to Jack, " Goin' to take her out in that? "

Jack reddened a little, but answered pleasantly, " Perhaps."

" Well, I guess she'll like it better than the chips I told you about. I've thrown 'em away."

A ring from Ruby Ann's bell told the boys their

recess was over, and with a bow Tom hurried off, while Jack and his chair went on till they reached Mrs. Biggs's door, just as Sam came up with the sea chair. That good woman was washing in her back kitchen, but in response to the drayman's knock she came hurriedly, wiping the soap-suds from her arms as she came, and holding up both hands as she saw the two chairs deposited at the door, while Sam held the note and roses, and Jack stood looking a little shamefaced, as if he hardly knew what to say.

" For the pity sakes and the old Harry, are you moving a furniture store, or what ? " she asked.

Jack began to explain that Mrs. Amy thought, or he thought— He could not quite bring himself to lie as glibly as Howard would have done, had he been there, and he stammered on, that he thought Miss Smith would soon be able to get round in a wheel chair, which he hoped she would accept with the compliments of— He didn't say Mrs. Amy, but Mrs. Biggs understood, and nodded that she did, helping him out by saying it was just like Mrs. Amy, and adding that it looked a good deal like the chair the Colonel had for a spell and then returned to Lowell & Brothers, where she saw it a few days ago in the window.

Jack made no reply, and Mrs. Biggs continued, " I s'pose t'other chair is Mrs. Amy's compliments, too. I'm sure I'm greatly obliged to her, and Miss Smith will be. She is quite peart this morning. Come in and see her."

Jack did not think he would. He'd rather have Mrs. Biggs present his chair, feeling sure that her conscience was of the elastic kind, which would not stop at means if a good end was attained.

"Thanks," he replied. "Later in the day I may come in. Good-morning."

He walked away, leaving Mrs. Biggs alone with Sam, who was told to take the chairs into Eloise's room.

"Something from the Crompton House. From Mrs. Amy, they say. It is like her to be sending things where she takes a notion as she has to you," Mrs. Biggs said, while Eloise looked on in astonishment.

She read Howard's note, and her surprise increased as she said, " I ought not to keep them. Col. Crompton would not like it if he knew."

" Yes, you ought. Mrs. Amy does what she likes without consulting the Colonel," Mrs. Biggs rejoined. " It would not do to send them back and upset her, and isn't there a verse somewhere in the Bible about taking what the gods give ye? "

Eloise knew what she meant, and replied, " ' Take the good the gods provide,' and they are certainly providing for me bountifully, but I must at least write a note of thanks to Mrs. Amy for her thoughtfulness and kindness."

To this Mrs. Biggs, who felt that she was in league with the young men, also objected.

" Better not," she said. " Better wait till you can go and thank her in person. I'll have Tim wheel you up some day. He'd like nothing better."

To this Eloise finally assented, and at once exchanged the hair-cloth rocker for the sea chair, which she found a great improvement. When Tim came from school he was told of the addition to the furniture in the parlor by his mother, who added, " I smelt a rat at once, and thought it a pity to spoil the young men's fun. Mrs. Amy don't know nothin' about them chairs, no more than the man in the moon, and if Miss Smith had much worldly sense she'd know they never came from Mrs. Amy. But she hain't. She's nothin' but a child, and don't dream that both them young men is jest bewitched over her. I don't b'lieve Mr. Howard means earnest, but t'other one does. He's got the best face. I'd trust myself with him anywhere."

Tim laughed at the idea that his mother could not trust herself with anybody, but said nothing. He was Eloise's devoted slave, and offered to wheel her miles if she cared to go; but she was satisfied with a few turns up and down the road, which gave her fresh air and showed her something of the country. The wheel chair was a great success, as well as the sea chair, in which she was sitting when the young men came in the afternoon to call, bringing some books which Mrs. Amy thought would interest her, and a box of candy, which Jack presented in his own person. He could not face her with Mrs. Amy as Howard could, and he felt himself a great impostor as he received her thanks for Mrs. Amy, who, he was sure, had entirely forgotten the girl.

No mention was ever made of her in Amy's presence or the Colonel's. He was not yet over his wrath at the accident to his carriage and horse, which, with strange perversity, he charged to the Normal. Brutus was getting well, but there would always be a scar on his shoulder, where the sharp-pointed shrub had entered the flesh. The carriage had been repaired, the stained cushions had been re-covered, and the Colonel had sworn at the amount of the bill, and said it never would have happened if the trustees had hired Ruby Ann in the first place, as they should have done. He knew she now had the school, and felt a kind of grim satisfaction that it was so. She was rooted and grounded, while the other one, as far as he could learn, was a little pink and white doll, with no fundamentals whatever. He had forgotten that Howard was to sound her, and did not dream how often that young man and his friend were at Mrs. Biggs's, not sounding Eloise as to her knowledge, but growing more and more intoxicated with her beauty and sweetness and entire absence of the self-consciousness and airs they were accustomed to find in most young ladies.

But for the non-arrival of the letter she was so anxious to get Eloise would have been comparatively happy, or at least content. Her ankle was gaining rapidly, and she hoped soon to take her place in school, Tim having offered to wheel her there every day and back, and assuring her that, mean as he was, Tom Walker was not mean enough to annoy her in her helpless condition. For some reason Eloise had not now much dread of Tom Walker, and expressed a desire to see him.

" Tell him to call," she said to Tim, who delivered her message rather awkwardly, as if expecting a rebuff.

" Oh, get out," was Tom's reply, " I ain't one of your callin' kind, with cards and things, and she'll see enough of me bimeby."

The words sounded more ungracious than Tom intended. He said he was not the calling kind, but the fact that he had been asked to do so pleased him, and two or three times he walked past Mrs. Biggs's in hopes to see the little lady in whom he was beginning to feel a good deal of interest. He met Jack occasionally, and always received a bow of recognition and a cheery "How are you, Tom?" until he began to believe himself something more than a loafer and a bully whom every hand was against. He was rather anxious for the little Normal to begin her duties, and she was anxious, too, for funds were low and growing less all the time.

"Wait till the Rummage is over. That is coming next week. You will want to go to that and see the people you have not seen, and your scholars, too. They are sure to be there," Ruby Ann said to her.

Ruby Ann was greatly interested in the Rummage Sale, as she was in anything with which she had to do, and all her spare time from her school duties was given to soliciting articles for it, and arranging for their disposition in the building where the sale was to be held. Eloise was interested because those around her were, and she offered her white apron a second time as the only thing she had to give.

"I guess I'll do it up and flute the ruffles," Mrs. Biggs said. "'Tain't mussy, but a little rinse and starch won't harm it."

She had given it a rinse and starch, and was ironing it when Jack came in, rather unceremoniously, as was his habit now that he came so often. This time he went to the kitchen door, as the other was locked, and found Mrs. Biggs giving the final touches to the apron, which she held up for his inspection.

"Rummage," she said. "Miss Smith's contribution. Ain't it a beauty?"

Jack was not much of a judge of aprons, but something in this dainty little affair interested him, and he wished at once that he knew of some one for whom he could buy it.   His sister Bell never wore aprons to his knowledge, neither did Mrs. Amy.   It was too small for Ruby Ann, and it would never do to give it back to Eloise.   But he did not want any money but his own spent for it, and he believed he'd speak to Ruby Ann and have it put aside for him.   He could tell her he had a sister, and she could draw her own inference.

"I swan, if I was a little younger, I'd buy it myself," Mrs. Biggs said, holding it up and slipping the straps over her shoulders and her hands into its pockets.

Jack felt relieved when she took it off, gave it another smooth with her iron, and folded it ready for the sale.

"I am going to put it in a box," she said, "with a card on it saying it is Miss Smith's contribution, and that she made every stitch herself."

Jack was now resolved that it should be his at any cost.   As to its real value he had no idea, and when Mrs. Biggs said it "or'to bring a good price, and probably will seein' whose 'tis," he replied, "I should say so,—four or five dollars at least."

"For the Lord's sake," Mrs. Biggs exclaimed, dropping her flatiron in her surprise.   "Four or five dollars!   Are you crazy?"

"Do you think it ought to bring more?" Jack asked, and Mrs. Biggs replied, "Was you born yesterday, or when?   If it brings a dollar it'll do well. Rummages ain't high priced.   Four or five dollars! Well, if I won't give up!"

Jack did not reply, but he was beginning to feel a good deal of interest in the Rummage Sale, and his interest increased when he went in to see Eloise, and heard from her that she was going down in the evening, as Ruby Ann said it would be more lively then, with more people present and possibly an auction.

" Tim is to wheel me," she said, " and has promised not to run into any one, or tip me over. I feel half afraid of him, as he does stumble some."

Jack looked at her a moment as she leaned back in her chair, her blue dressing sacque open at the throat showing her white neck.

" Miss Smith," he said, " *I* shan't stumble. I'll take you. I'd like to. I'll make it right with Tim."

Eloise could not mistake the eagerness in his voice, and her cheeks flushed as she replied, " It is very kind in you and kind in Tim, who perhaps will be glad to be rid of the trouble."

" Of course he will," Jack said quickly. " Day after to-morrow, isn't it? I'll see you again and arrange just when to call for you, and now I must go. I'd forgotten that I was to drive with Howard this morning. Good-by."

He went whistling down the walk, thinking that a Rummage Sale was more interesting than anything which could possibly happen in the country, and that he'd telegraph to his sister to send something for it. As he started on his drive with Howard, he said, " Let's go first to the telegraph office, I want to wire to Bell."

They drove to the office, and in a few minutes there flashed across the wires to New York, " We are going to have a Rummage Sale for the poor. Send a lot of things, old and new, it does not matter which; —only send at once."

" I believe I made a mistake about the object of the sale. I said ' For the poor,' and it's for a public

library, isn't it?" he said to Howard, who replied,
" Seems to me you are getting daft on the Rummage.
I don't care for it much. It will be like a Jews' or
pawnbroker's bazaar, with mostly old clothes to sell."

" No, sir," Jack answered quickly. " It will not be
at all like a pawnbroker's shop. Bell will send a pile
of things. I know her, and Miss Smith is to be there
in the evening, and it's going to be a great success."

" I see," and Howard laughed immoderately. " It
is going to be a great success because Miss Smith
is to be there. Is she for sale, and how is she going?
Are we to take her in a hand chair, as we carried her
that night in the rain?"

" No, sir!" Jack answered, " I am to wheel her and
have heaps of fun, while you mope at home."

Howard thought it very doubtful whether he
should mope at home. It would be worth something to see Jack wheeling Eloise, and worth a good
deal more to see her, as he knew she would look
flushed and timid and beautiful, with all the strangers
around her. He had not felt much interest in the
Rummage. Old clothes were not to his fancy, but he
had promised a pair of half-worn boots to Ruby Ann,
who had cornered him on the street, and wrung from
him not only his boots, but half a dozen or more of
the fifty neckties she heard he had strung on a wire
around his room, so as to have them handy when he
wanted to choose one to wear. Neckties were his
weakness, and he never saw one which pleased him
without buying it, and his tailor had orders to notify
him of the last fashion as it came out. It was quite
a wrench to part with any of them, but as some were
passée he promised them to Ruby, but told her he
hardly thought he should attend the sale. Now,

however, he changed his mind. Eloise's presence would make a vast difference, and he should go; and he thought of a second pair of boots, and possibly a vest and a few more neckties he might add to the pile which he had heard from Peter was to be sent the next day from the Crompton House to the Rummage.

16

CHAPTER XIII

GETTING READY FOR THE RUMMAGE SALE

Never had District No. 5 been so stirred on the subject of any public entertainment as on the Rummage Sale. It was something entirely new and unique, and the whole neighborhood entered into it with great enthusiasm. Between the little village by the sea, which numbered about two thousand, and the radius known as District No. 5, which could not boast half that number, there was a kind of rivalry, the district claiming that it excelled the village in the quality of its inhabitants, if not in quantity. Its people were mostly well educated and intelligent, and they had Col. Crompton, with his fine house and grounds. He was gouty and rheumatic and past his prime it was true, but he was still a power among them, and they were proud of him and proud of themselves, and delighted that they had been the first to carry out the idea of a Rummage Sale, which had been brought to them by a visitor from western New York, who explained its workings, and gave almost fabulous accounts of the money made by such sales. The village had intended to have one, but District No. 5 was ahead, with the result that many of the villagers joined in, glad to be rid of articles which had been stowed away as useless.

At first it seemed incredible that any one would

buy clothing which for years had hung in closets, or
been packed in trunks away from moths and carpet
bugs.   But what had been done in other places could
be done in District No. 5, and never was a more
heterogeneous mass of goods of every description
gathered together than was sent to the Rummage
rooms the day before the sale, and dumped upon
tables and chairs and boxes, until they nearly reached
the rather low ceiling.   There were old bonnets and
hats, and boots and shoes and dresses, and coats and
trousers and vests, and draperies and dishes, and
stoves and chairs and tables and bedsteads, with
books and old magazines and toys.

There was Mrs. Biggs's foot-stove and warming-
pan, which had been her mother's, and a brass kettle,
which had belonged to her grandmother, and which
Mrs. Parker, the lady from western New York, said
was the most valuable of all the articles sent.   Antiques were sure to sell to relic hunters, and a big
price must be put upon them, she told the committee who looked in dismay at the piles of goods as
they came pouring in, wondering how they were
ever to bring anything like order out of the confu-
sion.   They could not have done it without Mrs.
Parker and Ruby Ann, the latter of whom had obtained permission to dismiss school for two days, and
worked early and late.   She had laid siege to the
Crompton House, from which most of the others
shrank.   The Colonel was a rather formidable old
fellow to meet, if he was in a mood with twinges in
his foot, while Mrs. Amy was scarcely well enough
known to the people generally to make them care to
interview her.

On the strength of having been to school with her

and known her since " she was knee high," Mrs.
Biggs offered to call upon her, but declined seeing
the Colonel, who, she heard, didn't believe in the
Rummage. Ruby Ann, however, was selected as the
fittest person to see both, and had undertaken the
task with her usual assurance and energy. She
found Amy a fine subject. The idea of giving always appealed to her, and she began at once to think
of what she would send. The dresses she had worn
as a concert singer were hateful to her, and she
brought them from a closet and spread them upon
chairs· and tables, while Ruby looked on admiringly
and wonderingly, too, as fans and gloves and sashes
and ribbons were laid with the dresses, and Amy grew
more excited and eager every moment.

" We'll go to the attic now," she said; " my doll
house is there."

They climbed the stairs and found the house
packed away as it had been for years.

" It may as well be sold and make some child
happy," Amy said as she took off its wrappings.

In it was Mandy Ann, the doll the Colonel had
bought in Savannah, and Judy, lying on her face in
a pile of dust. Amy took her up tenderly, saying,
" Do you think anybody will buy her? "

There was a little choke in her voice as she asked
the question, for the sight of Judy had stirred memories which often flitted through her weak brain and
puzzled her, they were so misty and yet so sweet,
like the negro melodies she hummed to herself or
sang to an imaginary baby.

" Buy her? I guess they would," Ruby Ann replied, all her blood astir at the thought of the doll
house, with Judy and Mandy Ann.

She knew nothing of their antecedents, or how they were connected with Amy's childhood, but she felt intuitively that almost any price put upon them would be paid because they belonged to Mrs. Amy, and particularly because of the dilapidated appearance of Judy, which was sure to rouse the mirth of the spectators. She was very doubtful as to whether she ought to take the dresses without consulting some one besides Amy, to whom she said, " Are you sure you want to give these away? They are different from anything we shall have, and will seem out of place."

For a moment Amy looked at her with a strange glitter in her eyes, as she said, " I hate them! I have been going to burn them more than once. You don't know what they represent to me. I shall burn them, or tear them, if you don't take them."

She made a motion as if she were going to tear one of the lace flounces, when Ruby Ann stopped her by saying, " Don't, Mrs. Amy,—please don't. I'll take the dresses, of course. I only feared you might be giving too much, with the doll house and Mandy Ann and Judy. I want *them*, sure."

" Yes," Amy said, her mood changing. " Take them all; but don't try to improve them,—Mandy Ann and Judy, I mean."

There was another choke in her voice as she smoothed Judy's old brown dress, and brushed a bit of bran from her face. There was no danger that Ruby would try to change either Mandy Ann or Judy. They were perfect as they were, and telling Amy when the articles would be sent for, she left her and went to interview the Colonel, anticipating a different reception from what she had received from Mrs. Amy.

"Better not handle him to-day; he had some awful twinges this morning," Peter said, after she had "picked him clean," as he expressed it, "and scarcely left him a shoe to his foot or a coat to his back."

Ruby knew she could not come again, and in spite of Peter's advice, resolved to beard the lion at once. She found him, with his lame foot on a cushion, and a not very encouraging look on his face. He had liked Ruby ever since she first came to be examined as to her qualifications for a teacher, and he had found her rooted and grounded in the fundamentals, and he had taken sides stoutly for her when the question of normal graduates came up and Eloise had won the day. Ruby Ann's head was level, he always said, and when she was ushered into his room, he greeted her with as much of a smile as he could command, with his foot aching as it did. But the smile faded when she told him her errand, and said she was sure he would be glad to contribute either in money or clothing to so good a cause as the public library. The Colonel had not been consulted with regard to the library, except to be asked if he didn't think it would be a fine thing for the school and neighborhood generally. He was not very often consulted about anything now. Plans were made without him, and he was only asked to contribute, which he generally did.

Now, however, his back was up, Peter said to Ruby Ann, warning her of what she was to expect. He didn't believe in turning attics and cellars and barns inside out and scattering microbes by the millions. How did any one know what germs were lurking in old clothes? He knew a man who died of smallpox, and twenty-five years after his death a coat, which had hung in his closet, was given away, taking the disease with it to three or four people. No, he didn't believe in a Rummage. It was just a fad, got up by those who were always seeking for something new, and he wouldn't give a thing, not even an old stock such as he used to wear, and of which Ruby Ann knew he must have several.

"Who under heavens would buy an old stock, and why?" he asked, and Ruby Ann replied, "Just because it is an old stock and belonged to you."

The "belonged to you" mollified him a little, as it flattered his vanity, but the idea struck him as ridiculous, and he would not give in, and as Ruby Ann grew more and more persistent, telling of the antiques gathered up, and among them Mrs. Biggs's warming-pan and foot-stove and brass kettle,—old Mrs. Baker's quill wheel, and some other old lady's wedding bonnet, he grew furious and swore about the Rummage Sale, and might have sworn at Ruby Ann if she had not discreetly withdrawn and left him to himself and his twinges.

She was rather chagrined over her failure with the Colonel, from whom she had expected so much, but her success with Amy and the other members of the household made amends, and she left tolerably well satisfied with her work. She had not been gone long when Peter was summoned by a sharp ring to his master's room, and found him sitting very erect in his chair, listening intently to sounds overhead, where there was the scurrying of feet mingled with Amy's voice and that of her maid, as box after box was dragged across the floor.

"Peter!" the Colonel began, "shut the door!"

Peter had shut it and stood with his back against it, as the Colonel went on, "What in thunder is all that racket in the attic? Has the Rummage come up there? It commenced some time ago. Sounded as if they were pulling out trunks, then it stopped, and now they are at it again."

"That's just it. Mrs. Amy and Sarah were looking for something for the sale, and now, I suppose, they are pushing the boxes back. Mrs. Amy is greatly interested. I've never seen her so much like herself since she was a girl," was Peter's reply, whereupon the Colonel consigned the Rummage to perdition, with its old pots and kettles, and Mrs. Biggs's warming-pan and foot-stove and brass kettle, and Granny Baker's quill wheel and Mrs. Allen's wedding bonnet. Who was going to buy such truck? "And Peter," he said, in a lower tone of voice, "what do you think? Ruby Ann actually asked for my trousers! Yes, my trousers! And when I told her I hadn't any but what were shiny at the knees, she said it didn't matter; in fact, the shine would be all the better, showing they had been worn. They'd label 'em 'Col. Crompton's,' and hang them up with the valuables,—meaning Widow Biggs's warming-pan and foot-stove, and Widow Allen's bonnet, and that other old woman's quill wheel, I dare say. Think of it, Peter. My coat and trousers! She asked for a coat, too,—strung on a line with warming-pans and quill wheels and bonnets a hundred years old, and the Lord only knows what else, and labelled 'Col. Crompton.' If it had been anybody but Ruby Ann, I'd turned her from the room. I thought she had more sense,—upon my soul, I did! What did she get out of you?"

"Nothing much but some old clothes and shoes and a boot-jack; she thought a good deal of that," Peter said, and with a sniff of contempt the Colonel replied, "Old clothes and a boot-jack; and what is Mrs. Amy sending? Half the attic, I should think from the noise they make up there."

Hesitating a moment Peter said, "She is giving the fancy gowns she used to wear, with the tops of the waists and bottoms of the sleeves cut off. She says they are hateful to her."

The Colonel guessed what she meant, and replied, "Quite right; Rummage and rag-bags good places for them; but I say, Peter, I won't have them strung up with warming-pans and quill wheels and my trousers. You must stop it. Do you hear?"

"I didn't know your trousers were going," Peter suggested, and the Colonel answered curtly, "Who said they were, you blockhead? They are not going unless Ruby gets them in the night. Upon my soul, she is equal to it. I think I shall put them under my pillow. It is Mrs. Amy's dresses I mean. What else is she going to send?"

"You remember the doll house you bought her when she was a little girl?" Peter said.

"Good thunder, yes! Will she give that away?" the Colonel asked, with something in his tone which was more than surprise.

It hurt him that Amy should be willing to part with the doll house. She must be queerer than usual, and he thought of the Harris blood. Suddenly he remembered Mandy Ann and Judy, and

asked if she was going to give them to the Rummage.

"She means to. Yes, sir. They go with the doll
house, one as mistress, the other as maid. I heard
her say so. They are downstairs now," was Peter's
reply.

The Colonel's countenance fell, and there was an
awful twinge in his foot, but he didn't mind it. His
thoughts flew back to the palmetto clearing, where
he first saw the little girl and Judy. Then they
travelled on to Savannah and the store where he
bought Mandy Ann, and so on through the different
phases of Amy's childhood, and he was surprised to
find how unwilling he was to part with what had been
so intimately associated with years which, on the
whole, had been happy, although at times a little
stormy. And Amy was going to send them to a
Rummage Sale!

"I may be a weak old fool, but I won't have them
sold down there with quill wheels and warming-
pans!" he thought.

But what could he do? They were Amy's, and if
she had made up her mind to send them, it would
take more than his opposition to prevent it. She
was very gentle and yielding as a whole, but behind
the gentleness and sweetness he knew there was a
spirit he did not like to rouse. He must manage
some other way. He had told Ruby he would
neither give his clothes nor money to the farce, and
he prided himself on never going back on his word.
But he didn't tell her he wouldn't buy anything, and
his face brightened as he said, very briskly, "Peter!"

"Yes, sir," was the prompt reply.

"Hold your tongue!"

"Yes, sir," was Peter's still more prompt reply, and his master continued, " I don't care a rap about those dresses, but I won't have Mandy Ann and the nigger baby and the doll house sold. I may be a hard old cur. I s'pose I am, but I have now and then a streak of,—I don't know what,—clinging to the years of Mrs. Amy's childhood. She turned the house upside down. She raised the very old Harry sometimes, but she got into our hearts somehow, didn't she?"

"Yes, a long ways," was Peter's reply, as he waited for what was next to come, and looked curiously at the Colonel, who sat with his eyes closed, clutching the arms of his chair tightly, as if suffering from a fearful twinge.

But if he were, he did not think of it. His mind was again in the palmetto clearing, and he was standing by Dory's grave in the sand, and a little child was holding his hand, and looking at him with eyes which had in them something of the same expression which had once quickened his pulse, and made his heart beat with a thrill he fancied was love, but which had died almost as soon as it was born. As a result of that episode he had Amy, whom he did love, and because he loved her so much, he clung to the mementoes of her babyhood, when she had been a torment and a terror, and still a diversion in his monotonous life.

"Peter!" he said again. "Hold your tongue, but get them somehow. Who is head of this tomfoolery?"

"Ruby Ann is about as big a head as there is, I guess. She and a woman from York State," Peter replied, and the Colonel continued, "Well, I s'pose

those things will have to go to the sale, if Mrs. Amy
says so, but I won't have them mixed with the quill
wheels and boot-jacks and Widow Biggs's foot-stove
and brass kettle, and I won't have a pack of idiots
looking them over and buying them and saying they
belonged to the Cromptons. Mandy Ann Crompton and Judy Crompton would sound fine,—both
niggers! No, sir! You are to go quietly to Ruby
Ann and buy 'em! Do you hear? Buy 'em! You
knew Mrs. Amy when she played with 'em. You
want 'em, and you'll pay the price, no matter what
it is. Lord Harry! I'll bet they'll put a big one on
'em, but no matter. I paid thirty dollars for the doll
house and five for Mandy Ann. I don't s'pose Judy
cost anything, but the child liked it best, and I believe I'd rather have it than both the others, because——"

He did not say why, but he gripped the arms of
his chair tightly, while drops of sweat stood upon his
forehead. He was in the clearing again with Dora
living, instead of dead, and the moon was shining
on her face as she stood in the turn of the road and
gave him the promise she had kept so faithfully.
Judy belonged to that far-off time, and he'd keep
her at any cost. He called himself a sentimental old
fool after Peter left him, and wondered why his eyes
grew misty and there was a lump in his throat as his
thoughts kept going back to the South he wished
he had never seen.

"Poor little Dora!" he said to himself; "but for
me she might have been alive and married to some
respectable— No, by George!" he added suddenly, with a start which made his foot jump as he
recalled the class into which Dora would probably

have married if he had not crossed her path. " No, by George, I believe I'd rather she died in her youthful beauty, and was buried by Jake in the sand, than to see her the wife of some lout, and rubbing her gums with snuff."

He was roused from his reverie by wheels crunching on the gravel walk up to a side door, and he heard Sarah's voice and Cindy's, the cook's, and finally Amy's giving directions, and felt sure some one had come for whatever was to go from the Crompton Place to the sale. Ruby had not intended sending so soon when she left the house, but chancing to meet a drayman who had just deposited a load in the salesrooms, she bade him go for whatever was ready, thinking, " I'll strike while the iron is hot, and before Mrs. Amy has time to change her mind."

There was no danger of that, at least as far as the dresses were concerned. Like everything connected with her stage life, they had been to her a kind of nightmare whenever she thought of them, and she was glad to be rid of them. Mandy Ann and Judy did give her a few pangs, and especially the latter, and as she wrapped it in tissue paper she held it for a moment pressed close to her, and began a song she had heard from the negroes as they sat around their light-wood fire after their day's work was done. It was a weird melody which Homer Smith had caught up and revised and modernized, with a change of words in some places, and made her sing, knowing it would bring thunders of applause. She heard the roar now, and saw the audience and the flowers falling around her, and with an expression of disgust she put Judy into Sarah's hands, and said, " Take her away, and quick, too. She, or something, brings it back."

Sarah took poor, discarded Judy, tied her in her chair in the old doll house, which was placed on top of the two trunks containing Amy's concert dresses, and then the drayman started up his horse, and the Colonel heard the wheels a second time coming past his window. With a great effort he succeeded in getting upon his well foot, and, dragging the other after him, hobbled on his crutches to the window in time to see the cart as it turned into the avenue. As far as he could see it he watched it as the doll house swung from side to side, and the drayman held it to keep it from falling off.

" I don't see how Amy could have done it," the Colonel said to himself when the dray disappeared from view, and then becoming conscious of the pain in his foot, he dragged himself back to his chair, and ringing for Peter, said to him: " I think I'll lie down a spell,—and, bring me a hot-water bag, I'm pretty cold, and my foot just jumps; and, Peter, go to-day and buy those things as if they were for yourself. You mustn't lie, of course,—but get 'em somehow, and bring them here to this big closet. The chances are when Mrs. Amy comes to her senses she'll want 'em, and raise Ned, as she used to. I'd give a good deal to see her in a tantrum. I'd rather have her that way than passive, as she is now. Will nothing ever rouse her out of her apathy? Curse that Homer Smith! "

He was talking to himself rather than to Peter, who got him on to the lounge, adjusted the cushions, brought a hot-water bag, covered him up, and then left him, saying, " Don't fret, I'll go this afternoon and get Judy and Mandy Ann by fair means or foul."

"All right," the Colonel said drowsily. "Fair means or foul, but don't lie, and don't let them think they are for me. *You* want them, and must get them, fair means or foul. You know where my purse is. Hold your tongue, and go!"

CHAPTER XIV

Order was being brought out of chaos in the Rummage rooms, where twenty ladies were working industriously, sorting, pricing, and marking the multitudinous articles heaped upon the counters. Not only District No. 5, but the village had emptied itself, glad to be rid of the accumulations of years. Nearly every room was occupied, and the committees were showing great skill in assigning things to the different departments. The antiques had a niche by themselves; the quill wheel, the warming-pan, the foot-stove, the brass kettle with Peter's boot-jack, and many more articles of a similar character were placed together. Jack's sister had responded quickly, and a large box had arrived with articles curious and new, which elicited cries of delight from the ladies in charge, who marked them at a ridiculously low price, less even, in some instances, than had been paid for them, and labelled their corner "The New York Store."

Scarcely was this completed when the drayman arrived from Crompton Place with the doll house and the two trunks, the last of which were pounced upon first, as Ruby Ann had reported what was in them. Her description, however, had fallen far short of the reality, and the ladies held their breath, as one after another of the beautiful gowns was taken out for exhibition. Few had ever seen anything just like them. Homer Smith had prided himself upon being a connoisseur in ladies' costumes and had directed all of Amy's, taking care that there was no sham about them. Everything was real, from the fabric itself to the lace which trimmed it, and which alone had cost him hundreds of dollars. And now they were at a Rummage Sale, and the managers did not know what to do with them. It was scarcely possible that any one would buy them, and it would be greatly out of place to exhibit them in the dry-goods department with Mrs. Biggs's brown and white spotted gown which she had contributed rather unwillingly, insisting that it should not be sold for less than a dollar. Ruby Ann suggested that they be carefully folded in boxes and laid away by themselves for inspection by any one who had a thought of buying them. If they did not sell, and probably they would not, they were to be returned either to Amy or to the Colonel,—the latter most likely, as Amy had expressed so strong a desire to be rid of them. Her suggestion was acted upon, and the dresses laid aside, and the attention of the managers turned to the doll house and its occupants, Mandy Ann and Judy, the latter of whom was greeted with shrieks of laughter.

Here was something that would sell, but what price to put upon it was a puzzle. No one had any idea of the original cost. Mrs. Biggs, who had joined the working force and whose voice was loudest everywhere, suggested ten dollars, with the privilege of falling, but was at once talked down, as low prices were to be the rule for everything, and five was quite

17

enough. There were few who would pay that for a mere plaything for their children, so the card upon it was marked five dollars, with the addition that it had once belonged to Mrs. Amy Crompton Smith. It was then placed conspicuously in a window before which a group of eager, excited children gathered, and to which early in the afternoon Peter came leisurely.

The Colonel had asked him several times why he didn't go, and had finally grown so petulant that Peter had started, wondering how much he'd have to pay and what excuse he was to make for wanting it himself. His instructions were not to lie, but get it somehow without using the Colonel's name. Finding Ruby Ann alone, he began, " I say, do you make any sales before the thing opens? "

" Why, yes, we can," Ruby answered. " Several antiques are promised, if not actually sold, your boot-jack with the rest. Could sell another if we had it. Any particular thing you want? "

" Yes, I want that house in the window and the two women in it,—Mandy Ann and Judy. It's marked five dollars. Here's your money," and he laid a crisp five-dollar bill in her hand.

" Why, Peter,—why, Peter," Ruby exclaimed in surprise, with a sense of regret that more had not been asked, and a feeling of wonder as to why Peter wanted it. " Are you buying it for yourself? " she asked, and Peter replied, " Who should I buy it for? I knew Mrs. Amy when she was a little girl and played with it and slept with that nigger baby Judy. I've bought it. It's mine, and I'll take it right away. There's a drayman now, bringing a worn-out cook-stove and an old lounge."

"Oh, but, Peter,—please leave it till the sale is over. It draws people to look at it, and then they'll come in," Ruby said, while others of the ladies joined their entreaties with hers.

But Peter was firm. He had bought the doll house and paid for it. It was his, and in spite of the protests of the entire committee which gathered round him like a swarm of bees he took it away, and an hour later it was safely deposited in the Colonel's room without Amy's knowledge. The Colonel was delighted.

"Bring it close up," he said, "but first take off that infernal card that it belonged to 'Mrs. Amy Crompton Smith.' That's the way they'd marked my trousers! Give me Mandy Ann and Judy. I haven't seen them in more than twenty years,—yes, nearer thirty. Upon my soul they wear well, especially the old lady. She was never very handsome, but Amy liked her best," he said, laughing a little as Peter put Judy in his lap.

He did not know that he had ever touched her before, and he held her between his thumb and finger, with something which felt like a swelling in his throat, —not for Judy, nor for Amy, but for poor Dory, thoughts of whom were haunting him these days with a persistency he could not shake off.

"What did you give?" he asked, and Peter replied, "Five dollars,—just what it was marked."

"Five dollars! Heavens and earth!" and Judy fell to the floor, while the Colonel grasped his knees with his hands and sat staring at Peter. "Five dollars! Are you an idiot, and have none of them common sense?" he asked, and Peter replied, "That was the price, and I didn't like to beat them down.

Ruby Ann isn't easy to tackle, and Mrs. Biggs was there with her gab, if she is my niece, and said I got it dirt cheap."

" Go to thunder with your Ruby Ann and Mrs. Biggs and dirt cheap! " the Colonel roared. " Who said I wanted you to beat 'em down? Why, man, I told you I gave thirty for the house and five for Mandy Ann, and here they have sold the whole caboodle, Judy and all, for five dollars! Five dollars! Do you hear? Five dollars, for what cost thirty-five! I consider they've insulted Mandy Ann and Judy both. Five dollars! I'll be——"

He didn't finish his sentence, for he heard Amy's voice in the hall. She might be coming, and he said hastily to Peter, " Put them in the closet. Don't let her see them, or there'll be the old Harry to pay."

Peter obeyed, but Amy did not come in, and after a moment the Colonel continued, " We will keep them here a while. I dare say she'll never think of them again. She doesn't think much. Do you believe she will ever be any better? "

The Colonel's voice shook as he asked the question, and Peter's shook a little as he replied, " Please God she may. A great shock of some kind might do it."

" Yes, but where is the shock to come from, hedged round as she is from every rough wind or care? " the Colonel said, little thinking with what strides the shock was hastening on, or through what channel it was to come.

CHAPTER XV

AT THE RUMMAGE

The rooms were ready at last, and twenty tired ladies went through them to see that every thing was in its proper place, and then went home with high anticipations of the morrow and what it would bring. It opened most propitiously and was one of those soft, balmy September days, more like early June than autumn. There were brisk sales and crowds of people all day, with the probability of greater crowds and brisker sales in the evening. Jack Harcourt was in and out, watching the sale of what his sister had sent, drinking cups of chocolate every time a pretty girl asked him to do so, and buying toys and picture books and candy, and distributing them among the children gathered around the door and windows. He thought he had looked at everything on sale, but had failed to find the white apron. Where was it? he wondered. He would not ask Ruby Ann or Mrs. Biggs, as that would be giving himself away. It would certainly be there in the evening when he was to bring Eloise in her chair. He had settled that with Tim, who gave up rather unwillingly, but was consoled by being hired as errand boy,—an office he could not have filled had he been hampered with a wheel chair.

The night was glorious, with a moon near its full,

and a little before seven Jack presented himself at Mrs. Biggs's, finding Eloise ready and alone. Tim was at the rooms, running hither and thither at everybody's beck and call, and his mother was there, running the whole thing,—judging from her manner as she moved among the crowd filling the rooms nearly to suffocation. Eloise had more than once changed her mind about going, as she sat waiting for Jack. She was shy with strangers, and there would be so many there, and she would be so conspicuous in her chair, with Mr. Harcourt in attendance, that she began to doubt the propriety of going.

"If it were Tim who was to take me, I believe I should feel differently," she was thinking, when Jack came in, breezy and excited,—full of the Rummage and anxious to be off.

"You are ready, I see," he said. "That's right. We have no time to lose. And there's no end of fun. I've been there half the day, and drank chocolate, and eaten cake and candy till I never want to see any more. But you will."

He was adjusting her dress and getting the chair in motion as he talked, and Eloise had no time to suggest that she ought not to go, before she found herself out upon the piazza, and Jack, who had locked the door, was putting the key under the mat.

"You see I remember where I found it that time Howard and I desiccated the Sabbath by calling upon you," he said, with a laugh in which Eloise joined.

"Is Mr. Howard going?" she asked, and Jack replied, "He is a kind of lazy fellow, but he'll be there all right;" and the first one they saw distinctly as they drew near the house was Howard, struggling with the crowd.

Howard had gone down on purpose to see Eloise, and was wondering how with her chair she could ever be gotten through that mass of people, when she appeared at the door, and, with Howard, wondered how she was to get in. She might not have accomplished it if he had not come to the rescue with two boys,—one Tim Biggs, the other a tall, freckled-faced, light-haired fellow whom Jack greeted as Tom, saying, "Can you manage to find a good position for Miss Smith?"

"You bet," came simultaneously from both boys, and immediately four sharp elbows were being thrust into the sides of the people, who moved all they could and made a passage for Eloise and her chair near the middle of the room, and in a comparatively sheltered place where she could see everything without being jostled.

If she could see everything and everybody, so everybody could see her, and for a moment there was a hush in the large room where every eye was turned upon Eloise, who began to feel very uncomfortable, and wish she had not come. She had wondered what she ought to wear, and had decided upon black as always suitable. When she left California her mother had urged her to take a small velvet cape lined with ermine. It was the only expensive article of dress she had, and she was very choice of it, but to-night she wore it about her shoulders, as later the air was inclined to blow up cool and damp from the sea. Just as they reached the house Jack stooped to arrange it, throwing it back on either side so that more of the ermine would show.

"There! You look just like a queen! Ermine is

very becoming to you," he said, and the people staring at her thought so, too.

Her head was uncovered, and her hair, which waved softly around her forehead, was wound in a flat knot low in her neck, making her look very young, as she sat shrinking from the fire of eyes directed towards her and saw, if she did not hear, the low whispers of the people, many of whom had never seen her before, and were surprised at her extreme youth and beauty. Ruby Ann was at a distance, trying to sell Mrs. Biggs's spotted brown and white wrapper to a scrub woman who was haggling over the price which Mrs. Biggs had insisted should be put upon it. That good woman was busy in the supper-room, or she would have made her way at once to Eloise, who, as she looked over the sea of faces confronting her, saw no one she knew except Howard Crompton, who had been very uncomfortable in the heat and air of the place until she came, and with her fresh, fair young face seemed at once to change the whole atmosphere. Jack, who was not used to much exertion and had found even Eloise's light weight a trifle heavy, especially up the hill near the Rummage house, was sweating at every pore, and fanning himself with a palm leaf he had bought at the entrance.

"By George!" he said to Howard, who was standing by them. "It's hotter than a furnace in here. I believe I'll have to go outside and cool off a minute, if you'll stay and keep guard over Miss Smith."

"Certainly;—with pleasure," Howard said, putting his hand on Eloise's chair and asking if there was anything he could do for her.

She was watching the brown and white spotted

gown, and to Howard's question she shook her head, while he continued, " Jack says the chocolate is pretty fair. He ought to know —he has drank six cups. I am going to bring you some."

Before she could protest that she did not care for chocolate, he left her and his place was at once taken by the tall, lank, light-haired boy, whose elbows had done so good execution in forcing a passage for the chair. Tom had been watching her ever since she came in, and making up his mind. He had heard she was pretty, but that did not begin to express his opinion of her, as she sat with the ermine over her shoulders, the soft sheen on her hair, the bright color on her cheeks, and a look in her eyes which fascinated him, boy though he was, as it did many an older man, from Mr. Bills to Jack, and Howard Crompton. If his two chips had not been thrown away he would have thrown them now, and still the feeling in him which people called *cussedness* was so strong that he could not repress a desire " to see what stuff she was made off."

Taking Howard's vacant place he pushed himself forward until he was nearly in front of her, where he could look into her face. She recognized him as the boy Jack had called Tom, and guessed who he was,—her eyes drooping under his rather bold gaze, and her color coming and going. Tom was not sure what he was going to say to her, and could never understand why he said what he did. He had been told so often by Mr. Bills and others that he needed *licking*, and so many teachers had *licked* him, to say nothing of his drunken father, that the idea was in his mind, but as something wholly at variance with this dainty little girl, who at last looked at him fearlessly.

She knew he was going to speak to her, but was not prepared for his question.

"You are the new schoolmarm, ain't you? Do you think you could *lick* me?"

Just for an instant Eloise was too much surprised to answer, while the hot blood surged into her face, then left it spotted here and there, making Tom think of pink rose petals with white flecks in them. But she didn't take her eyes from the boy, who was ashamed of himself before she said with a pleasant laugh, " I know I couldn't; and I don't believe I shall ever wish to try. I am the new school-teacher, and you are Mr. Thomas Walker!"

She did not know why she put on the Mr. It came inadvertently, but was the most fortunate thing she could have done. To be called Thomas was gratifying, but the Mr. was quite overpowering and made Tom her ally at once.

"I'm Thomas Walker,—yes," he said. "Miss Patrick has told you about me, I dare say,—and Mr. Bills, and Widder Biggs, and Tim. Oh, I know he's told you a lot what I was goin' to do,—but it's a lie. I have plagued Miss Patrick some, I guess, and she whaled me awful once, but I've reformed. I didn't s'pose you was so little. I could throw you over the house, but I shan't. Say, when are you going to begin? I'm tired of Miss Patrick's everlasting same ways of doing things, and want something new,—something modern, you know."

He was getting very familiar, and Eloise was chatting with him on the most friendly terms, when Howard came back with a cup of chocolate, a part of which was spilled before he reached her. Howard knew who the young blackguard was, and glowered

at him disapprovingly, but Eloise said, " Mr. Crompton, this is Thomas Walker, one of my biggest
scholars that is to be. Some difference in our height,
isn't there? but we shall get on famously. I like big
boys and taught a lot of them in Mayville."

She smiled up at Tom and gave him her empty cup
to take away. He would have stood on his head i
she had asked him to, and he hurried off with the cup,
meeting Jack, who had cooled himself, bought a
pound of candy at one table and some flowers at
another, and was making his way back to Eloise.
He had also looked round a little for the apron he
was going to buy, but could not find it. He'd make
another tour of inspection later, he thought, for he
meant to have it, if it were still there. Taking his
stand on one side of Eloise's chair while Howard
stood on the other, the three made a striking tableau
at which many looked admiringly, commenting upon
the beauty of the young girl,—the kind, good-
humored face of Jack, and the haughty bearing of
Howard, who, an aristocrat to his finger tips, watched
the proceedings with an undisguised look of contempt showing itself in his sarcastic smile and the expression of his eyes.

Eloise was greatly interested and so expressed
herself. She had seen the scrub woman haggling
with Ruby Ann over the brown and white spotted
wrapper, and had seen it laid aside until another cus-
tomer came, when the same haggling took place with
the same result, for Mrs. Biggs, who darted in and
out, still clung to the price put upon it and so re-
tarded the sale. The last time Ruby Ann brought it
out Howard and Jack both recognized it.

"By Jove! I've half a mind to buy it myself as a

kind of souvenir," Jack said, but a look of disgust in Eloise's face and a frown on Howard's deterred him, and he kept very quiet for a while, wondering where that apron was and if by any possibility it could have been sold.

The box of articles which Jack's sister had sent from New York had been sold early in the day, and Amy's dresses had not been opened. Nearly everything of any value was gone. Two of Howard's neckties still remained conspicuously near the young men, who watched Tom Walker as he examined them very critically, and they heard the saleswoman say, " They belonged to Mr. Howard Crompton. They say he has dozens of them and all first-class. This suits you admirably,"—and she held up a white satin one with a faint tinge of blue.

Tom took it, disappeared for a few minutes, and when he came back to the chair he was resplendent in his new necktie which he had adjusted in the dressing-room, adding to it a Rhine-stone pin bought at the jewelry counter. Howard's vanity told him he was complimented, and that restrained the laugh which sprang to his lips at the incongruity between Tom's dress and the satin necktie bought for a grand occasion in Boston, which Howard had attended a few months before. On his way back to the group to which he felt he belonged Tom had stopped at the candy table and inquired the price of the fanciful boxes, his spirits sinking when told the pounds were fifty cents and the half-pounds twenty-five. Money was not very plenty with Tom, and what he had he earned himself. The necktie had made a heavy draft on him, and twenty cents was all he could find in either pocket.

"I say, Tim, lend me a nickel. I'll pay it back. I hope to die if I don't," he said to Tim, who was hurrying past him on some errand for his mother.

"I hain't no nickels to lend," was Tim's answer, as he disappeared in the crowd, leaving Tom hovering near the candy table and looking longingly at the only half-pound box left.

"I say," he began, edging up to the girl in charge, "can't you take out a piece or two and let me have it for twenty cents? All the money I have in the world! 'Strue's I live, and I want it awfully for the new schoolmarm over there in the chair with them swells standin' by her."

It was the last half-pound box and the girl was tired.

"Yes, take it," she said, and Tom departed, happier if possible with his candy than with his necktie.

"I bought it for you. It's chocolate. I hope you like it," he said, depositing his gift in Eloise's lap, where Jack's box was lying open and half empty, for Eloise's weakness was candy.

"Oh, thank you, Thomas," she said, beaming upon him a smile which more than repaid him for having spent all his money for her.

She was really very happy and thought a good deal of Rummage Sales. She had the best place in the hall;—a good many people had spoken to her. She had won Tom Walker, body and soul, and she knew that her escorts, Howard and Jack, added *éclat* to her position. She had scarcely thought of her foot, which at last began to ache a little. She was getting tired and wondered how much longer the sale would last. Jack wondered so, too; not that he was tired. He could have stood all night looking at Eloise and seeing the people admire her; but he was rather stout and apt to get very warm in a room where the atmosphere was close as it was here, and he wanted to be out in the fresh air again. He could take his time wheeling Eloise home, and if Mrs. Biggs staid at the rooms, as he heard her say she was going to do "till the last dog was hung," he could stay out in the porch and enjoy the moonlight with Eloise's eyes shining upon him. But where was that apron? Perhaps it hadn't come after all. He'd inquire. But of whom? Mrs. Biggs was in the supper-room. He did not care to go there again, for every time he appeared somebody was sure to get off on him a cup of chocolate or coffee, and he could not drink any more.

Ruby Ann was busy,—her face very red and her eyes very tired, as she tried to sell the most unsalable articles to old women who wanted something for nothing, and quarrelled with the quality and quarrelled with the price. His only recourse was Eloise, and he planned a long time how to approach the subject without mentioning her apron. At last a happy inspiration came to him, and when Howard's attention was diverted another way he bent over her and began.

CHAPTER XVI

THE AUCTION

"Astonishing, isn't it, where all the stuff comes from? Somebody must have given very freely. I never gave a thing except money. Bell sent a lot to be sure, and it's all sold. They had a pile from the Crompton House. They were good at begging. They didn't expect anything of you, a stranger, of course?"

"Oh, yes," Eloise replied. "I had an apron which Miss Patrick seemed to think might sell for something. It was rather pretty, and I made it myself. I haven't seen it, and think it may have been sold, or perhaps Mrs. Biggs, who had it in charge, forgot it. She has had a great deal on her mind."

Jack did not hear more than half Eloise was saying. One fact alone was clear. She had expected the apron to be there and he would look it up.

"Excuse me," he said, and going into the room where Mrs. Biggs was trying to make half a loaf of bread do duty as a whole loaf to a party just arrived, he said to her, "Pardon me, Mrs. Biggs, but did you send or bring Miss Smith's contribution to the sale? I believe it was an apron. She has not seen it."

The bread fell from Mrs. Biggs's hand to the table, and the knife followed it to the floor as she exclaimed,

"Lord of heavens! I forgot it till this minute. Where's Tim?"

She darted from the room and found Tim bringing two pails of water, "the last gol darned thing he was going to do that night," he said, as he put them down. Seizing him by the collar his mother almost shrieked, "Run home for your life, Tim!"

"Why-er,—what-er! Is our house afire?" Tim asked, and his mother replied, "No, but Miss Smith's apron is there. I clean forgot it. You'll find it in a paper box on my bed, or in my bureau, or on the closet shelf, pushed away back, or somewhere. Now clip it."

Tim started without his hat, and the last thing he heard was his mother's voice shrill as a clarion, "If you don't find the key under the mat, climb inter the but'ry winder, but don't upset the mornin's milk!"

Business was beginning to slacken and sales were few. Some of the people had gone home and others were going, and still there were quantities of goods unsold. An auction was the only alternative and Mr. Bills, who, to his office of school commissioner, added that of auctioneer, was sent for. There was no one like him in Crompton for disposing of whatever was to be disposed of, from a tin can to a stove-pipe hat. He could judge accurately the nature and disposition of his audience,—knew just what to say and when to say it, and had the faculty of making people bid whether they wanted to or not. To hear him was as good as a circus, his friends said, and when it became known that he was to auction off the goods remaining from the sale, many who had left came back, filling the rooms again nearly as full as they were early in the evening.

Eloise's chair was moved a little more to the front,—a long counter was cleared, and on it Mr. Bills took his stand, smiling blandly upon the crowd around him and then bowing to Eloise and her escorts, Jack and Howard. He was bound to do his best before them and took up his work eagerly. He was happiest when selling clothes which he could try on, or pretend to, and after disposing of several bonnets amid roars of laughter he took up Mrs. Biggs's gown, which Ruby Ann had not been able to sell. Here was something to his mind and he held it out and up, and tried its length on himself and expatiated upon its beauty and its style and durability until he got a bid of twenty-five cents, and this from Howard, who said to Eloise, " It seems a pity not to start the old thing at something, and I suppose the Charitable Society will take it. I believe there is one in town."

Eloise did not answer. The spotted gown was an offence to her, and she shut her eyes while Mr. Bills, delighted that he had a bid at last and from such a source, began, " Thank you, sir. You know a good thing when you see it, but only twenty-five cents! A mere nothing. Somebody will give more, of course, for this fine tea gown to put on hot afternoons. Just the thing. Twenty-five cents! Twenty-five cents! Do I hear more? Twenty-five! Did you say thirty? " and he looked at Jack, who half nodded, and the bids, raised five cents at a time, rolled on between Jack and Howard and another young man, who cared nothing for the gown, but liked the fun. Fifty cents was reached at last, and there the bidding ceased and Mr. Bills was ringing the changes on half a dollar, half a dollar, for a *robe de chambre ;*—he called it that

18

sometimes, and sometimes a tea gown, and once a *robe de nu-it*, which brought peals of laughter from those who understood the term, as he certainly did not. In the dining-room Mrs. Biggs was busy washing dishes, but kept her ears open to the sounds in the next room, knowing Mr. Bills was there and anxious to get in and see the fun. When the last shouts reached her she dropped her dish towel, saying to her companion, " I can't stand it any longer. I've got to go and see what Bills is up to! "

Elbowing her way in she caught sight of her gown held aloft by Mr. Bills, and heard his voluble " Going, going, at fifty cents."

She had thought it low at a dollar, and here it was as good as gone for fifty cents,—to whom she did not know or care,—probably the scrub woman who had looked at it earlier in the evening and offered sixty. Her blood was up, and making her way to Mr. Bills she snatched at her gown, exclaiming, " It's mine, and shall never go for fifty cents, I tell you! "

Here was a diversion, and Mr. Bills met it beautifully.

" Jess so, Miss Biggs," he said, bowing low to her. " I admire your taste and judgment. I've told 'em time and time over it was worth more than fifty. The fact is they don't know what is what, but you and I do. Shall we double right up and shame 'em by sayin' a dollar? A dollar! A dollar! and going! "

Mrs. Biggs did not know that she assented, she was so excited, and afterwards declared she didn't: but the final Going was said, with " Gone! to Mrs. Biggs, for one dollar. Cheap at that! "

At this juncture, when the hilarity was at its height and Mrs. Biggs was marching off with her property, which she said she should never pay for, Tim appeared, hatless and coatless, but with the box in his hand. When Jack locked the door he pushed the key further under the mat than was usual, and failing to find it at once, and being in a hurry, Tim made his entrance into the house through the pantry window, upsetting the pan of milk and a bowl of something, he did not stop to see what, in his haste to find the box. It was not on the bed, nor on the bureau, nor pushed back on a shelf in the closet. It was on a chair near the door where his mother had put it and then forgotten it. As the key was outside Tim made his exit the way he came in, stopping a moment to look at the milk the cat was lapping with a great deal of satisfaction.

"Bobbs, you'll have a good supper, and I shall catch old hundred for giving it to you," he said, picking up the pan and springing through the window.

He was very warm, and taking off his coat he threw it across his arm and started rapidly for the sale, knowing before he reached it that Mr. Bills was there by the sounds he heard. He had no thought that the apron was not to be sold at auction. Probably that was why it was wanted, and pushing through the crowd to Mr. Bills he handed him the box, saying, " Here 'tis. I 'bout run my legs off to get it. Make 'em pay smart."

"Mr. Bills! Mr. Bills!" came excitedly from Ruby Ann, but Mr. Bills did not hear, the buzz of voices was so great.

He had opened the box and taken out the apron, which he handled far more carefully than he had the spotted gown.

"Now this is something like first-class business,"

he said, holding it up. "The prettiest thing you ever saw,—a girl's apron, all ruffled and prinked, and, —yes,—made by——"

He had glanced at the card, which said it was made by Miss Smith, and was about to announce that fact, feeling sure it would bring bidders, when he chanced to look at Eloise, whose face was nearly as white as the apron, and in whose eyes he saw an expression which checked the words. But he had no idea of relinquishing the article, and misunderstood the motion of Jack's hand to stop him.

"Now, give me an offer," he began,—"a first-rate one, too; none of your quarters, nor halves. Bid high and show you know something. 'Tain't every day you have a chance to buy as fine a thing as this. You who have wives, or daughters, or sisters, or sweethearts, or want it for yourselves, speak up! Walk up! Roll up! Tumble up! Any way to get up, only come up and bid!"

He was looking at Jack, whose face was as red as Eloise's was pale.

"If the thing must be sold at auction it shall bring a good price, and I'll get it, too," he thought.

Standing close to him was Tom Walker, who all the evening had hovered near Eloise.

"Tom," Jack said. "I have a sister, you know."

Tom didn't know, but he nodded, and Jack went on: "That apron is the only thing I've seen that I really want for her. I am not worth a cent to bid. Will you do it for me?"

Tom nodded again, and Jack continued, "Well, start pretty high. Keep your eyes on me, and when I look at you raise the bid if there is any against you. Understand?"

"Yes, sir," Tom answered, understanding more than Jack thought he did.

He guessed whose apron it was and did not believe much in the sister, but he had his instructions and waited for the signal. Howard had watched the sale of the spotted gown with a great deal of amusement, but was beginning to feel tired with standing so long, and was wondering when Jack proposed taking Eloise home. That he would go with them was a matter of course, and he was about to speak to Jack when Tim came in and the apron sale began. He had no idea whose it was until he saw the halt in Mr. Bills's manner, and looked at Eloise. Then he knew, and knew, too, that nothing could get Jack away till the apron was disposed of. That Jack would buy it he did not for a moment dream, for what could he do with it? "But yes, he is going to buy it," he thought, as he heard Jack's instructions to Tom, "and I mean to have some fun with him, and run that apron up."

Close to him was Tim, and the sight of him put an idea into Howard's mind. It would be jolly for Tom and Tim to bid against each other, while he and Jack backed them.

"Tim," he said, laying his hand on the boy's arm, "I am going to buy that apron for Mrs. Amy, and I want you to bid for me against Tom Walker and everybody. I have no idea what it is worth, but when I squeeze your arm *so*, bid higher!"

He gave Tim's arm a clutch so tight that the boy started away from him, saying, "Great Peter, don't pinch like that! You hurt! 'cause I'm in my shirt sleeves."

"All right. I'll be more careful," Howard said. "Now begin, before Tom has time to open the ball."

" Yes, but-er, what-er shall I bid?" Tim stammered.

" How do I know? It's Miss Smith's, and on that account valuable. Go in with a dollar."

All this time Mr. Bills had been talking himself hoarse over the merits of the apron, while his audience were watching Howard and Jack, with a feeling of certainty that they were intending to bid, but they were not prepared for Tim's one dollar, which startled every one and none more so than his mother, who, having rolled up her spotted gown " in a *wopse*," as she said, and put it with her dish pan and towels, had come back in time to hear Tim's astonishing bid. She could not see him for the crowd in front of her, but she could make him hear, and her voice was shrill and decided as she called out, " Timothy Biggs! Be you crazy? and where are you to get your dollar, I'd like to know!"

" Tell mother to mind her business! I know what I'm about!" Tim said to some one near him, while Mr. Bills rang the changes on that dollar with astonishing volubility, and Tom kept his eyes on Jack for a signal to raise.

Jack was taken by surprise, but readily understood that it was Howard against whom he had to contend and not Tim.

" All right, old chap," he whispered, then looked full at Tom, who, eager as a young race horse, shouted a dollar and a half!

" All right," Jack said again, and turned to Eloise on whose face there was now some color, as she began to share in the general excitement pervading the room and finding vent in laughter and cheers when Tom's bid was raised to two dollars by Tim, and two and a quarter was as quickly shrieked by Tom. Everybody now understood the contest and watched it breathlessly, a great roar going up when Tim lost his head and mistaking a slight movement of Howard's hand on his arm, raised his own bid from three dollars to three and a half!

"That's right," Mr. Bills said; "you know a thing or two. We are getting well under way. Never enjoyed myself so well in my life. Three and a half! three and a half! Who says four?"

"I do," Tom yelled, his yell nearly drowned by the cheers of the spectators, some of whom climbed on chairs and tables to look at Tom and Tim standing, one next to Howard and the other next to Jack, with Eloise the central figure, her ermine cape thrown back, and drops of sweat upon her forehead and around her mouth.

She almost felt as if it were herself Howard and Jack were contending for instead of her apron, which Mr. Bills was waving in the air like a flag, with a feeling that he had nearly exhausted his vocabulary and didn't know what next to say. Four dollars was a great deal for an apron, he knew, but he kept on ringing the changes on the four dollars,—a measly price for so fine an article, and for so good a cause as a Public Library. And while he talked and repeated his *going, going,* faster and faster, Tim stood like a hound in a leash fretting for a sign to raise.

"You ain't goin' to be beat by Tom Walker, be you?" he said, in a whisper to Howard, who gave him a little squeeze, with the words "Go easy," spoken so low that Tim did not hear them, and at once raised the four dollars to four and a half, while quick as lightning Tom responded with five dollars.

Jack hadn't really looked at him, but it did not matter. He was going to have the apron, and turning to Howard he said, " I don't know how long you mean to keep this thing up. I am prepared to go on all night."

Howard felt sure he was and decided to stop, and his hand dropped from Tim's shoulder quite to the disgust of that young man, who said, " You goin' to let 'em lick us? "

" I think I'll have to," Howard replied, while "Five dollars, and going! " filled the room until the final " Gone! " was spoken, and the people gave gasps of relief that it was over.

" Sold for five dollars to Thomas Walker, who will please walk up to the captain's office and pay," Mr. Bills said, handing the apron to Tom, who held it awkwardly, as if afraid of harming it.

" I guess it's yourn," he said, giving it to Jack, who knew as little what to do with it as Tom.

Ruby came to his aid and took it from him. She had watched the performance with a great deal of interest, comprehending it perfectly and feeling in a way sorry for Eloise, whose lips quivered a little when she went up to her, and bending over her said, " You should feel complimented, but I'm afraid you are very tired."

" Yes, very tired and warm. I want to get into the fresh air," Eloise said, shivering as if she were cold instead of warm.

Jack had gone to the cashier's desk to pay for the apron, and Tom undertook the task of getting the wheel chair through the crowd, running against the people promiscuously, if they impeded his progress, and caring little whom he hit if he got Eloise safely outside the door. The night was at its best, almost as light as day, as they emerged from the hot, close room, and Eloise drew long breaths of the cool air which blew up from the sea, the sound of whose waves beating upon the shore could be heard even above the din of voices inside the building. The auction was still going on, and Mr. Bills was doing his best, but the interest flagged with the sale of the apron and the breaking up of the group which had attracted so much attention. Even Mrs. Biggs's grandmother's brass kettle, on which so many hopes were built, failed to create more than a ripple, as Mr. Bills rang changes upon it both with tongue and knuckles, and when his most eloquent appeals could not raise a higher bid than ten cents, it was withdrawn by the disgusted widow, who put it aside with her dish pan and towels and gown, and then went to find Tim to take them home.

Howard had been called by Ruby into the room where Amy's dresses were lying in the boxes just as they came, and asked what they were to do with them.

"We could not offer them for sale, and she does not want them back," she said.

"Send them to the Colonel. She'll never know it, and the chance is will never think of them again," Howard said, and then hurried outside to where Eloise was still waiting and talking to Tom.

"That apron went first rate," he said. "You must have felt glad they thought so much of you, 'cause 'twas you and not the apron, though that was pretty enough."

"Oh!" Eloise replied, drawing her ermine cape around her shoulders, "I don't know whether I was glad or not. I felt as if I were being sold to the highest bidder."

"That's so," Tom said. "It was something like it. Ain't you glad 'twas Mr. Harcourt bought you instead of t'other?"

Eloise laughed as she replied, "Why, Thomas, it was *you* who bought me! Have you forgotten?"

She seemed so much in earnest that for a moment Tom thought she was, and said, "You ain't so green as not to know that 'twas Mr. Harcourt eggin' me on,—winkin' to me when to raise, and tellin' me to go high! You are his'n, and I'm glad on't! I like him better than t'other; ain't so big feelin'. Here they come, both on 'em."

Howard had finished his business with Ruby Ann, and Jack had paid his five dollars and received the apron, slightly mussed, but looking fairly well in the box in which they put it. A good many people were leaving the rooms again, and among them Tim, laden with his mother's dish pan and towels, and dress and brass kettle, and one or two articles which she had bought.

"Hallo, Tim! You look some like a pack horse," Tom said, but Tim did not answer.

He was very tired, for with so many calling upon him through the day and evening; he had run miles and received only seventy cents for it. He was chagrined that he had raised his own bid, and wondered Tom did not chaff him. It would come in time, he knew, and he felt angry at Tom, and angry with the brass kettle and dish pan and dress which kept him from wheeling Eloise instead of Tom, who, when they finally started, took his place behind the chair as a matter of course, while Howard and Jack walked on either side. It was a splendid night, and when Mrs. Biggs's house was reached Howard and Jack would gladly have lingered outside talking to Eloise, if they could have disposed of the boys. But the boys were not inclined to be disposed of. Tom had become somebody in his own estimation, and intended to stay as long as the young men did, while Tim, having found the key, this time instead of entering by the pantry window, unlocked the door, deposited his goods, and then came back, saying to Eloise with a good deal of dignity for him, " Shall I take you in? "

" Yes, please. I think it's time," she said, and Howard and Jack knew they were dismissed. "Thank you all so much for everything," she continued, giving her hand to each of them in turn, and pressing Tom's a little in token of the good feeling she felt sure was established between them.

It was not long before Mrs. Biggs came home, rather crestfallen that her spotted gown and brass kettle had not been more popular, but jubilant over the sale, the proceeds of which, so far as known when she left, were over two hundred and fifty dollars.

" Never was anything like it before in Crompton," she said, as she helped Eloise to her bed lounge. " That apron sale beat all. Them young men didn't care for the apron, of course, except that it was yours, and what Mr. Harcourt will do with it I don't know. Said he was goin' to send it to his sister. Maybe he is. He paid enough for it. Five dollars! I was in hopes they'd run it up to ten! and I was sorry when 'twas over. Mr. Bills kinder wilted after you all went out, and the whole thing flatted. Well, goodnight! You was the star! the synacure,—is that the word?—of all eyes, and looked awful pretty in that white cape. I see you've got Tom Walker, body and soul, but my land! you'd get anybody! Good-night, again."

She was gone at last, and Eloise was glad to lay her tired head upon her pillow, falling asleep nearly as soon as she touched it, but dreaming of the Rummage Sale and that she was being auctioned off instead of her apron. It was a kind of nightmare, and her heart beat fast as the bids came rapidly,—sometimes on Howard's side and sometimes on Jack's. She called him *Jack* in her dreams, and finally awoke with a start, saying aloud, " I am glad it was Jack who bought me! "

PART III

CHAPTER I

THE BEGINNING OF THE END

The Rummage Sale was a great success and netted fully two hundred and fifty dollars, besides quantities of goods of different kinds which were left and given either to the poor or to the Charitable Society in Crompton. The trunks containing Amy's dresses had been sent home without Amy's knowledge, and deposited in the closet with Mandy Ann and Judy, the Colonel swearing at first that he would have nothing pertaining to Homer Smith so near him. The apron sale had been an absorbing topic of conversation, the people wondering what Mr. Harcourt was going to do with his purchase, and if he wouldn't give it back to Eloise. Nothing was further from his thought. He had bought it to keep, and he laid it away in the bottom of his trunk with the handkerchief Eloise had used when he first called upon her.

He was growing more and more in love with her and more unwilling to leave Crompton. He had already staid longer than he had at first intended, but it did not need Howard's urgent invitation for him to prolong his visit. Every day he went to Mrs. Biggs's, and sometimes twice a day, and took Eloise out in her arm-chair for an airing,—once as far as to the school-house where Ruby Ann still presided, and where Eloise hoped soon to take up her duties. She was very happy, or would have been if she could have heard from California. Every day she hoped for news, and every day was disappointed, until at last nearly a week after the Rummage a letter came forwarded by her grandmother from Mayville. It was from a physician to whom Eloise had twice written with regard to her mother, and this was his reply:

" Portland, Oregon, September —, 18—.
" My Dear Miss Smith:
" I left San Francisco several months ago and have been stopping in several places, and that is why your letters were so long in reaching me. They both came in the same mail, and I wrote to San Francisco to see what I could learn with regard to your mother. It seems that the private asylum of Dr. Haynes was broken up, as there were only three patients when Mrs. Smith left, and it did not pay. Soon after your father died in Santa Barbara, your mother was removed from the asylum by a gentleman whose name I have thus far been unable to learn. I thought it must have been some relative, but if you know nothing of it my theory is wrong. Dr. Haynes went at once with his family to Europe, and is travelling on the continent. His address is, Care of Munroe & Co., Bankers, 7 Rue Scribe, Paris. Write him again, as he must know who took your mother from his care. He may not be in Paris now, but your letter will reach him in time. If there is anything I can do to help you, I will gladly do it. If you were in San Francisco you might find some of the attendants in

the asylum, who could give you the information you desire.

" Yours, very truly,

" J. P. ALLING, M.D."

It was Ruby who brought the letter one evening two or three days before Eloise expected to make her first appearance in school. Mrs. Biggs and Tim were out and Eloise was alone. Tearing open the envelope, she read it quickly, and then with the bitterest cry Ruby had ever heard, covered her face with her hands and sobbed: " My mother! Oh, my mother!"

" Is she dead? " Ruby asked, and Eloise replied, " Worse than that, perhaps. I don't know where she is. Read what it says."

She gave the letter to Ruby, who read it twice; then, sitting down by Eloise and passing her arm around her, she said, " I don't understand what it means. Was your mother in a lunatic asylum? "

" Oh, don't call it that! " Eloise answered. " It was a private asylum in San Francisco,—very private and select, father said, but I never quite believed her crazy. She was always quiet and sad and peculiar, and hated the business, and so did I."

" What was the business? " Ruby asked, and Eloise answered hesitatingly, as if it were something of which to be ashamed, " She sang in public with a troupe,—his troupe. He made her. She was the star and drew big houses, she was so beautiful and sang so sweetly, without any apparent effort. It was just like a bird, and when she sang the Southern melodies she seemed to be in a trance, seeing things we could not see. It made me cry to hear her. I know many good women are public singers, but mother shrank from it, and when they cheered like mad there used to be a frightened look in her eyes, as if she wondered why they were doing it and wanted to hide, and when she got to our rooms she'd tremble and be so cold and cry, while father sometimes scolded and sometimes laughed at her. He tried to make me sing once. I have a fair voice, but I rebelled and said I'd run away before I'd do it. He was very angry, and sent me North to my grandmother, saying I was too great an expense to keep with him unless I would help, and was a hindrance to my mother, who was always so anxious about me. It nearly killed her to part with me. I was all the comfort she had, she said, and she always called me Baby. Father was not kind to her, and it seemed as if he hated me, and was jealous of mother's love for me. When I heard he was dead, I could not feel badly, as I ought, and did not cry. He was a very handsome man, and very nice with people, who thought my mother a most fortunate woman to have so polished and courteous a husband. They should have seen him as I saw him at times, and heard him swear, as I have heard him, and call her names till she was white as a corpse and fainted. I never saw her turn upon him but once. I had asked her why she didn't leave him and go home, if she had any to go to. That was when I was a little girl.

"'I have no home or friends in all the wide world to go to' she said, and then, with a sneer which was maddening, it meant so much, my father said, 'Ask her who her father was and see if she can tell you.'

"I didn't know then what he meant to insinuate, but mother did, and there came a look into her eyes which frightened me, and her voice was not mother's

at all, as she walked straight up to him and said,
' How dare you insult my mother ! '

" She looked like an enraged animal, and my father
must have been afraid she would attack him, for he
tried to soothe her and succeeded at last in doing so.
I think there was some mystery about her father and
mother, as she would never talk of them.   Once I
asked her about them, and she said she hadn't any;
and she looked so strange that I never asked her
again.   I knew she was born South, that her people
were poor, and her name Harris, and that is all I
know, except that no better or lovelier woman ever
lived, and if she is really crazy father made her so, and
I cannot feel any love for him, or respect.   If I ever
had any, and I suppose I must have had, he killed it
long ago.   The first thing I remember of him in
Rome, where I was born, he was practising some
music with mother,—playing for her while she sang,
and I was standing by him, putting my hands on his
arm and trying to hum the tune.   With a jerk he said
to my nurse, ' Take her away and keep her away.'

" I am wicked, I know, to talk as I am doing, but
it seems as if there was a spell over me urging me
to say things I never thought of saying.   It's a comfort to talk to some one who I know is my friend, and
you are so strong every way and have been so good
to me."

She laid her head on Ruby's arm like a tired child,
and continued, " I wrote to mother very often after
I came to Mayville, and she replied, telling me how
,she missed me, and how she always fixed her eyes on
some part of the house, fancying she saw me, and was
singing to me, and I used to listen nights and think
I heard her grand voice as it rose and fell, and the

19

people cheering, and she so beautiful standing there for the crowd to gaze at, and wishing she could get away from it all.

"At last her letters ceased and father wrote that her mind had given way suddenly;—that she was a raving maniac,—dangerous, I think he said,—and I thought of the way she looked at him once when I was a child, and he told me to ask her about her father. He said she was in Dr. Haynes's private asylum, where she had the kindest of care. I think I died many deaths in one when I heard that. I wrote her again and again, and wanted to go to her, but my father forbade it. No one saw her, he said, except her attendant and the physician,—not even himself, as the sight of him threw her into paroxysms. I didn't wonder at that. He sent my letters back, telling me she would not sense them, and they would excite her if she did. Her only chance of recovery was in her being kept perfectly quiet, with nothing to remind her of the past.

"A few months ago he died suddenly in Santa Barbara. One of the troupe wrote to grandma, and, as I told you, I did not cry; I couldn't. I was too anxious about mother, and wrote at once to Dr. Haynes, but received no answer. I waited a while and wrote again, with the same result. Then I remembered Dr. Alling, who had attended me for some slight ailment, and wrote to him, with the result you know. Some one has taken my mother away. Who was it, and where is she? I feel as if I were going mad when I think of the possibilities."

She pressed her hands to her head and rocked to and fro, while Ruby tried to quiet and comfort her.

"I must go to San Francisco and find my mother.

I would start to-morrow, lame as I am, only I haven't the money, and grandma hasn't it, either," she said. " Father made a great deal of money at times, but he spent it as freely. Always stopped at the best hotels; had a suite of rooms, with our meals served in them; drank the costliest wines, and smoked the most expensive cigars, and bought mother such beautiful dresses. I did not fare so well. Anything was good enough for me after I refused to sing in public, and that was an added source of trouble to my mother. I was always a bone of contention and it was, perhaps, as well in some respects that I was sent away, only mother missed me so. I was so glad to get this school, because it would give me something for my mother, whom I hoped to bring home before long. And now, I don't know where she is, but I must find her. Oh, what shall I do? "

It was not often that Eloise talked of herself and her affairs. At school in Mayville she had been very reticent with regard to her past, and had seldom mentioned either her father or her mother. With Mrs. Biggs she had been equally silent, and, try as she would, the good woman had never been able to learn anything beyond what Eloise had first told her,— that her father was dead and her mother in California;—in a sanitarium, Mrs. Biggs had finally decided, and let the matter drop, thinking she should some time know " if there was anything to know." Ruby Ann had from the first seemed to Eloise like one to be trusted, and she felt a relief in talking to her, and said more than she had at first intended to say.

For a moment Ruby was silent, while Eloise's head lay on her arm and Eloise's hand was holding hers.

She was thinking of the piano she wanted to buy, the money for which was in the Crompton bank. There was a struggle in her mind, and then she said, " I can loan you the money. I know you will pay it back if you live, and if you don't, no matter. I will not call it a loss if it does you any good."

At first Eloise demurred, longing to accept the generous offer, and fearing that she ought not. But Ruby overcame her scruples.

" Naturally I shall keep your place in school, so I owe you something for the business, don't you see? " she said.

Eloise did not quite see, but she yielded at last, for her need was great.

" I don't think I'd tell Mrs. Biggs all the sad story, unless you want the whole town to know it. Tell her you have had bad news from your mother, and are going to her," Ruby suggested, when at last she said good-night and went out, just as Mrs. Biggs came in.

" Goin' away! Goin' to Californy! Your mother sick! What's the matter, and how under the sun are you goin' alone, limpin' as you do? I knew Ruby Ann would manage to keep the school if she once got it! " were some of Mrs. Biggs's exclamations when told Eloise was to leave her.

Eloise parried her questions very skilfully, saying nothing except that her mother needed her and she was going to her, and Mrs. Biggs left her more mystified than she had ever been in her life, but re-solved " to get at the bottom if she lived."

That night Eloise, who was now sleeping in the chamber to which she had first been taken, sat a long time by her window, looking out upon the towers and chimneys of Crompton Place, which were visible above the trees in the park, and wondering at the feeling of unrest which possessed her, and her unwillingness to leave.

" If I could only see him once more before I go," she thought, the " him " being Jack, who, with Howard Crompton, was in Worcester, attending a musical festival.

Not to see him was the saddest part of leaving Crompton, and for a moment hot tears rolled down her cheeks,—tears which, if Jack could have seen and known their cause, would have brought him back from Worcester and the prima donna who that night was entrancing a crowded house with her song. Dashing her tears away, Eloise's thoughts reverted to Amy, who had been so kind to her.

" I hoped to thank her in person," she said, " but as that is impossible. I must write her a note for Tim to take in the morning, together with the chairs."

The note was written, and in it a regret expressed that Eloise could not have seen her.

" Maybe when she reads it she will call upon me to-morrow," she thought, as she directed the note, and that night she dreamed that Amy came to her, with a face and voice so like her mother's that she woke with a start and a feeling that she had really seen her mother, as she used to stand before the footlights, while the house rang with thunders of applause.

CHAPTER II

Col. Crompton was in a bad way, both mentally and bodily. The pain in his gouty foot had extended to his knee, and was excruciating in the extreme; but he almost forgot it in the greater trouble in his mind. In the same mail which had brought Eloise's letter from California there had been one for him, which in the morning Peter had taken from the postman and examined carefully, until he made out its direction.

"Mister Kurnel Krompton, of Krompton Plais, Krompton, Massachusetts."

So much room had been taken up on one side of the envelope with the address, that half of "Massachusetts" was on the other side, and Peter's memory instantly went back to years before, when a letter looking like this and odorous with bad tobacco had come to the Colonel. He had a copy of the letter still, and could repeat it by heart, and knew that it was from Jake Harris,—presumably the "Shaky" for whom the little girl Eudora had cried so pitifully. This was undoubtedly from the same source. "What can he want now? and what will the Colonel say?" he thought, as he took the letter to his master's room.

"A letter for you, sir," he said, putting it down upon the table by the Colonel's chair, and then lingering on the pretence of adjusting a curtain and brushing up the hearth, but really waiting to see what effect the letter would have.

It was different from what he expected. With one glance at the superscription, the Colonel grew deathly pale, and his hands shook so that the letter dropped upon the floor. Peter picked it up and handed it to him, saying, " Can I help you, sir? "

" Yes, by leaving me, and holding your tongue! There's the devil to pay! " was the answer.

Peter was accustomed to hearing of his master's debts in that direction, and to being told to hold his tongue, and he answered, " All right, sir," and left the room. For some moments the Colonel sat perfectly still, his heart beating so fast that he could scarcely breathe. Then he opened Jake's letter, and read as follows:

" Palmetto Clarin', Oct. —, 18—.

" Mister Kurnel Krompton,

" Deer Sir:

" Glory to God. I'se done sung all day for his mussy in lettin' me heer from lil Miss Dory onc't mo' an' 'noin' she ain't ded as I feared she was. Mas'r Minister Mason, who done 'tended the funeral of t'other Miss Dory done tole me how she's livin' with you, an' a lil off in her mind. The lam'! What happened her, I wonder? Her granny, ole Miss Lucy, was quar. All the Harrises was quar. Mebby she got it from them. A site of me will cure her sho'. Tell her I'se comin' to see her as soon as I hear from you that it is her, sho'. Thar might be some mistake, an' I doan' want to take the long journey for nothin', 'case I'm ole, tho' I feels mighty peart now wid de

news. Rite me wen you git this. I shall wait till I
har, an' then start to onc't.
                    " Yours to command,
                              " JAKE HARRIS."

" P. S.—Mandy Ann, you 'members her, what took
care of lil chile. She's a grown woman now in course,
an' has ten chillen, 'sides Ted. You 'members Ted,
on de ' Hatty.' No 'count at all; but Mandy Ann,
wall, she's a whopper, an' when she hears de nuse,
she 'most had de pow'. She sen's her regrets, an'
would come, too, if she hadn't so many moufs to feed,
an' Ted doin' nothin' but playin' gemman.
                    " Onc't mo', yours,
                              " JAKE."

To describe the Colonel's state of mind as he read
this letter is impossible. He forgot the pain in his
leg and knee in the greater sensation of the cold,
prickly feeling which ran through his veins, making
his fingers feel like sticks, and powerless to hold the
letter, which dropped to the floor. With every year
he had hugged closer and closer the secret of his life,
becoming more and more morbid and more fearful,
lest in some way his connection with the palmetto
clearing should be known and he fall from the high
pedestal on which he had stood so long, and from
which his fall would be greater because he had been
there so long. It would all be right after he was
dead. He had seen to that, and didn't care what the
world would say when he was not alive to hear it.
But he was very much alive now, and his sin bade
fair to find him out.
    " Just as I feared when that rector told me who

his father was," he thought, cursing the chance which had sent the Rev. Arthur Mason to Crompton,—cursing the Rev. Charles for giving information to Jake,—and cursing Jake for the letter, which he spurned with his well foot, as it lay on the floor. He had hoped the negro might be dead, as he had heard nothing from him in a long time; and here he was, alive and waiting for a word to come. " If he waits for that he will wait to all eternity," he said to himself. " I shall write and make it worth his while to stay where he is. He knows too much of Amy's birth and her mother's death to be trusted here. Uncertainty is better than the truth. I have made matters right for Amy, and confessed everything. They'll find it when I'm gone, and can wag their tongues all they please. It won't hurt me then, but while I live I'll keep up the farce. It might have been better to have told the truth at first, but I didn't, and it's too late now. Who in thunder is that knocking at the door? Not Amy, I hope,—and I can't reach that letter," he continued, as there came a low rap at the door.

" Come in ! " he called, when it was repeated, and Cora, the housemaid, entered.

She had been in the family but a few days and did not yet understand her duties with regard to the Colonel, and know that she was not to trouble him. Tim Biggs had been commissioned by Eloise to take her note to Mrs. Amy, together with the chairs.

" You can't carry both at one time, so take the sea this morning, and the wheel this afternoon," Mrs. Biggs said, just as Tom Walker appeared.

He had been to the house two or three times since the Rummage, ostensibly to ask when Eloise was going to commence her duties as teacher, but really to see her and hear her pleasant " Good-morning, Thomas, I am glad to see you."

Whatever Mrs. Biggs knew was soon known to half of District No. 5, and the news that Eloise was going to California had reached Tom, and brought him to inquire if it were true.

" And won't you come back? " he asked, with real concern on his homely face.

" Perhaps so. I hope so," Eloise replied, and he continued, " I'm all-fired sorry you are goin', because, —well, because I am ; and I wish I could do something for you."

" You can," Eloise said. " You can take the wheel chair back to the Crompton House and save Tim one journey."

Tom cared very little about saving Tim, but he would do anything to serve Eloise, and the two boys were soon on their way, quarrelling some as they went, for each was jealous of the other's attention to the " little schoolmarm," as they called her. Tom reached the house first, but Tim was not far behind, and both encountered Cora, who bade them leave the chairs in the hall, while she inquired as to their disposition. Had Peter been in sight she might have consulted him, but he was in the grounds, and, entering the Colonel's room she said, " If you please, sir, what shall I do with the chairs? "

" What chairs? " the Colonel asked, and Cora replied, " A sea chair, I think, and a wheel chair, which Tom Walker and Tim Biggs have just brought home."

" My sea chair, and my wheel chair! How in thunder can that be, when I'm sitting in the wheel, and how came Tom Walker, the biggest rascal in town, by my chairs, or Tim Biggs either?" the Colonel exclaimed; and Cora replied, "I think they said the schoolma'am had them. Here's a note from her to Mrs. Amy."

Since his last attack of the gout the Colonel had in a measure forgotten Eloise, and ceased to care whether she were rooted and grounded in the fundamentals or not. That Howard and Jack had been in the habit of calling upon her he did not suspect, and much less that for the last two weeks or more she had been enjoying his sea chair, and the fruit and flowers sent her with Mrs. Amy's compliments. At the mention of her he roused at once.

"That girl had my chair! How the devil came she by it? A note for Mrs. Amy! Give it to me, and pick up that paper on the floor and go!"

Cora was not long in obeying, and the irascible old man was again alone. First tearing Jake's letter in strips, he turned Eloise's note over in his hand, and read, "Mrs. Amy Smith, Crompton Place." The name "Smith" always made him angry, and he repeated it with a quick shutting together of his teeth.

"Smith!" he said, "I can't abide it! And what has she to say to Mrs. Smith?"

The note was not sealed, and without the least hesitancy he opened it and read, commenting as he did so.

"My dear Mrs. Smith." (Her dear Mrs. Smith! I like that.) "I am going away (Glad to hear it) and I wish to thank you for the many things you have sent me. (The deuce she has! I didn't know it.) The pretty hat I want to keep, with the slippers, which remind me of my mother. (Slippers,—remind her of her mother, who, I dare say, never wore anything but big shoes, and coarse at that," the Colonel growled, and read on.) The chairs I return, with my thanks for them, and the fruit and flowers and books. I would like so much to see you, and thank you personally, but as this cannot be I must do it on paper. Be assured I shall never forget your kindness to me, a stranger.

" Your very truly,
" E. A. SMITH."

"Smith again! E. A. Smith!" the Colonel said. "Why couldn't she write her whole name? E. A., ELIZA ANN, of course! That's who she is, ELIZA ANN SMITH!"

If there was one name he disliked as much as he did Smith, it was Eliza Ann, and he repeated it again: "ELIZA ANN SMITH! Fruit and flowers and books, and shoes and my sea chair and a wheel chair sent to her by Amy! Where did she get the wheel, I'd like to know? I don't believe it!" he added, as a sudden light broke upon him. "It's that dog Howard's work, and that other chap."

Ringing the bell which stood on the table beside him, he bade Cora, who appeared, to send Mrs. Amy to him. Amy had not slept well, and was more easily confused than usual, but she came and asked what he wanted. It did not occur to him to give her the note, which he kept in his hand while he said, in a much softer tone than that in which he had been talking to himself, "Have you sent things to Eliza Ann Smith,—fruit and flowers and books, and my sea chair and a wheel chair, and a bonnet and shoes, and the Lord knows what else?"

Amy was bewildered at once.

" Eliza Ann Smith ! " she repeated. " I don't know her. Who is she? "

" Why, the girl that jammed a hole in Brutus's neck and stained the cushions of my carriage, and broke her leg at Mrs. Biggs's," the Colonel replied.

At the mention of Mrs. Biggs, Amy's face brightened. Since the day after the accident, when she sent the hat and slippers, Eloise had not been mentioned in her presence, and she had entirely forgotten her. Now she was all interest again, and said, " Oh, yes; I remember now, Poor girl! I did send her a hat and some slippers, which I hated because I wore them when I sang. Did they fit her? "

" Lord Harry! How do I know? It isn't likely your shoes would fit her. They would be a mile too small! " the Colonel said, and Amy asked, " Does she want anything? "

" No," the Colonel replied. " Somebody has sent her flowers and chairs and books and things. She thought it was you and wished to thank you."

" It was not I, and I am sorry I forgot her," Amy rejoined, as she turned to leave him, with a confused feeling in her brain, and a pang of regret that she had perhaps neglected the little girl at Mrs. Biggs's.

Once the Colonel thought to call her back and give her the note. Then, thinking it did not matter, he let her go without it. Just what influence was at work in Amy's mind that morning it were difficult to tell. Whatever it was, it prompted her on her return to her room to take the little red cloak from the closet where it was kept and examine it carefully. It had been the best of its kind when it was bought, and, though somewhat faded and worn, had withstood the ravages of time wonderfully. It had en-

circled her like a friend, both when she was sad and
when she was gay. It had been wrapped around the
Baby, of whom she never thought without a pang
and a blur before her eyes. It was the dearest article
she had in her wardrobe, and because of that and
because she had been so forgetful, she would send it
to Eliza Ann Smith!

"But not for good," she said to Sarah, who was
commissioned to take it to Eloise the next morning.
"She can keep it till she is well. Somebody told
me she had a sprained ankle. I had one once, and I
put it across my lap and foot, it was so soft and warm.
Tell her I am sorry I forgot about her. I am not
always quite myself."

.   .   .   .   .   .

"Sent that old red cloak she's had ever since she
was knee high! I shouldn't s'pose there'd be a rag
of it left! She must be crazy as a loon to-day," was
Mrs. Biggs's comment, when Sarah told her errand.
"What possessed her?"

Sarah only knew that her mistress was more dazed
than usual that morning, and had insisted upon her
bringing the cloak.

"I think it rattled her when the chairs came back.
She didn't know anything about 'em, nor the Colonel
either," Sarah said.

Mrs. Biggs laughed, and replied, "I didn't s'pose
they did. Them young men, I b'lieve, was at the
bottom of it, and I or'to have told Miss Smith to
send her thanks to them, but I wasn't quite sure
about the sea chair. So I let it slide, thinkin' it was
a good joke on 'em to thank Amy. They pretended
the things was from her."

Taking the cloak from the girl, she carried it into

the room where Eloise had fallen asleep, with her foot resting upon a hassock, and a shawl thrown over it. Removing the shawl and putting the red cloak in its place, Mrs. Biggs stole noiselessly out, saying to herself, " I guess she'll wonder where that came from when she wakes up."

CHAPTER III

For an hour or more Eloise slept on, and then awoke suddenly and saw the scarlet cloak across her foot. At first it was the color which attracted her. Then taking it in her hands she began to examine it, while drops of sweat came out upon her forehead and under her hair. She knew that cloak! She had worn it many and many a time when she was a child. She had seen her mother fold and pack it far more carefully, when they were starting on a starring tour, than she did the fine dresses she wore on the stage.

"It is my mother's, but how came it here?" she thought, as she took it into the kitchen where she heard Mrs. Biggs at her work. "Where did you get my mother's cloak?" she asked.

Mrs. Biggs, who always washed on Saturdays, had just put Tim's shirt through the wringer. Holding it at arm's length with one hand and steadying herself on the side of the tub with the other, she stared blankly at Eloise for a moment, and then said, "Your mother's cloak! Child alive, that's Mrs. Amy's. I've seen her wear it a hundred times when she was a little girl. She has got on a spell of givin' this mornin', and sent it to you by Sarah. She's kep' it well all these years. What ails you?" she continued, as

Eloise's face grew as white as the clothes in Mrs. Biggs's basket.

Ray after ray of light was penetrating her mind, making her wonder she had not seen it before, and bringing a possibility which made her brain reel for a moment.

"Sit down," Mrs. Biggs continued, "and tell me why you think this is your mother's cloak."

"I know it is," Eloise answered. "I have worn it so many times, and once I tore a long rent in the lining and mother darned it. It is here,—see!"

She showed the place in the silk lining where a tear had been and was mended.

"For the Lord's sake, who be you?" Mrs. Biggs exclaimed, still flourishing Tim's shirt, which she finally dropped back into the tub, and in her excitement came near sitting down in a pail of bluing water instead of a chair.

"I am Eloise Albertina Smith, and my father was Homer Smith, and my mother was Eudora Harris from Florida, and sang in concerts, and lost her mind, and was in a private asylum in San Francisco, and my father died, and a strange man took her out a few months ago. I did not know where she was, and was going to California to find her. I believe your Mrs. Amy is she, and I am going to the Crompton House to inquire!"

"For Heaven's sake!" was Mrs. Biggs's next ejaculation. "Harris was Amy's name before she was called Crompton, and her name is Amy Eudora, too; but I never heard she had a girl."

"Yes, she had, and I am that girl," Eloise said, "and I am going up there now, right off!"

"You can't walk," Mrs. Biggs suggested. "That

20

ankle would turn before you got half way there. If you must go,—and I believe I would,—Tim will git a rig from the livery. Here, Tim," she called, as she heard him whistling in the woodshed, "run to Miller's and git a carriage and a span, quick as you can,— a good one, too," she added, as the possibility grew upon her that Eloise might belong to the Cromptons, and if so, ought to go up in style.

It did not take long for Tim to execute his mother's order, and the best turn-out from Miller's stable soon stood before the door.

"I b'lieve I'll go, too. The washin' will keep, and this won't," the widow said, beginning to change her work-dress for a better one.

Eloise was too much excited to care who went with her, and with Mrs. Biggs she was soon driving up the broad avenue under the stately maples to the door of the Crompton House. Peter saw the carriage, and thinking it came from town with callers on Amy, went out to say she could not see them, as she was not feeling well and was lying down.

"But I must see her," Eloise said, alighting first and brushing past him, while he stood open-mouthed with surprise.

"She thinks she is Amy's girl, and, I swan, I begin to think so, too," Mrs. Biggs said, trying to explain and getting things a good deal mixed, and so bewildering the old man that he paid no attention to Eloise, who, with the cloak on her arm, was in the hall and saying to a maid who met her, "Take me to Mrs. Amy."

All her timidity was gone, as she gave the order like one who felt perfectly at home.

"Mrs. Amy is asleep, and I don't like to disturb

her. She is unusually nervous this morning. Will you see the Colonel instead?" the girl said, awed by Eloise's air of authority.

"My business is with Mrs. Amy, but perhaps I'd better see Col. Crompton first," she replied.

Mrs. Biggs and Peter were in the house by this time, and heard what Eloise was saying.

"Better not," Peter began. "I don't know as you can see him. You stay here. I'll inquire."

He started up the stairs, followed by Eloise, who had no idea of staying behind.

"Wait," he said, motioning her back as he reached the Colonel's door, and saw her close beside him. "Let me go in first."

He left the door ajar and walked into the room where the Colonel was sitting just as he had sat the morning before, when Jake's letter and Eloise's note were brought to him. He had not slept at all during the night, and was in a trembling condition, with a feeling of numbness in his limbs which he did not like.

"Well?" he said sharply, as Peter came in, and he saw by his face that something had happened. "What's up now?"

"Nothing, but Miss Smith, the teacher," Peter replied. "She wants to see you."

"Miss Smith, the normal? Do you mean Eliza Ann? Tell her to go away. I can't see anybody," the Colonel said.

"I'll tell her, but I'm afraid she won't go," Peter replied, starting for the door, through which a little figure came so swiftly as nearly to knock him down, and Eloise, who had forgotten her lameness, stood before the astonished Colonel, her face glowing with excitement, and her eyes shining like stars as she confronted him.

Old as he was, the Colonel was not insensible to female beauty, and the rare loveliness of this young girl moved him with something like admiration, and made his voice a little softer as he said, " Are you Eliza Ann Smith? What do you want? "

" I am not Eliza Ann," Eloise answered quickly. " I am Eloise Albertina Smith. My father was Homer Smith; my mother was Eudora Harris, from Florida, a concert singer, till she lost her mind and was put in a private asylum in San Francisco. You took her out, and she is here. You call her Mrs. Amy. She never told me of you. I don't know why. She never talked much of her girlhood. I don't think she was very happy. She sent me this cloak, and that's how I knew she was here. I have worn it many times when a child. I knew it in a moment, and I have come to see her. Where is she? "

This was worse than Jake's letter, and every nerve in the Colonel's body was quivering with excitement, and he felt as if a hundred prickly sensations were chasing each other up and down his arms and legs, and making his tongue thick as he tried to call for Peter. Succeeding at last, he said faintly, " Take this girl away before she kills me."

" I shall not go," Eloise rejoined, " until I see my mother. I tell you she is my mother. Has she never spoken of me? "

" Never," the Colonel answered. " She has talked of a baby who died, and you are not dead."

" No, but I am Baby,—her pet name for me always. Why she should think me dead, I don't know. Send for her, and see if she does not know me."

She had come close to the trembling old man, and put one of her hands on his cold, clammy one. He didn't shake it off, but looked at her with an expression in his eyes which roused her sympathy.

" I don't mean any harm," she said. " I only want my mother. Send for her, please."

There was a motion of assent toward Peter, who left the room, encountering Mrs. Biggs outside the door. There was too much going on for her not to have a hand in it, and she stood listening and waiting till Amy came down the hall, her white cashmere wrapper trailing softly behind her, and her hair coiled under a pretty invalid cap. She had been roused from a sound sleep, which had cleared her brain somewhat, and when told the Colonel wished to see her, she rose at once and started to go to him, fearing he was worse. He heard her coming, and braced himself up. Eloise heard her, and, with her head thrown back and her hands clasped together, stood waiting for her. For a moment Amy did not see her, so absorbed was she in the expression of the Colonel, who was watching her intently. When at last she did see her, she started suddenly, while a strange light leaped into her eyes. Then a wild, glad cry of " Baby! Baby!" rang through the room, and was answered by one of " Mother! Mother!" as the two women sprang to each other's arms.

Amy was the first to recover herself. Turning Eloise around and examining her minutely, she said, " I thought you dead. He told me so, and everything has been a blank to me since."

" You see she is my mother!" Eloise said to the Colonel; " and if she is your daughter, you must be my grandfather!"

If the Colonel had been carved in stone he could not have sat more motionless than he did, giving no sign that he heard.

"No matter! I shall find it all out for myself," Eloise continued, as she turned again to her mother, who was examining the red cloak as if she wondered how it came there.

The mention of "finding it out" affected the Colonel more than anything else had done. Amy had said the same thing to him once. She had not found it out, but this slip of a girl would, he was sure, and with something like a groan he sank back in his chair with a call for Peter.

"Take them away," he said huskily. "I can't bear any more, and,—and,—the girl must stay, if Amy wants her, and bring me a hot-water bag,—two of them,—I was never so cold in my life."

Peter nodded that he understood, and, ringing the bell for Amy's maid, bade her take her mistress to her room, and the young lady, too. "She is Mrs. Amy's daughter," he added.

There was no need to tell this, for Mrs. Biggs had done her duty, and every servant in the house had heard the news and was anxious to see the stranger. Amy was always at her best in her own room, where Sarah left her alone with Eloise, and hastened away to gossip with Mrs. Biggs and Peter. The shock, instead of making Amy worse, had for the time being cleared her brain to some extent, so that she was able to talk quite rationally to Eloise, whose first question was why she had thought her dead. "I was so homesick for you, and cried so much after you went away that he was angry and hard with me,— very hard,—and I said at last if he didn't send for you I'd never sing again, and meant it, too," Amy replied. " It was at Los Angeles on a concert night. I must have been pretty bad, and he seemed half afraid of me, and finally told me you were dead, and had been for three weeks, and that he had meant to keep it from me till the season was over. I believed him, and something snapped in my head and let in a pain and noise which have never left it; but they will now I have found you. I went before the footlights once that night, and the stage was full of coffins in which you lay, and I saw the little grave in the New England cemetery where he said you were buried. At last I fainted, and have never sung again. They were very kind to me at Dr. Haynes's, where he came often to see me till I heard he was dead. I was not sorry; he had been so,—so— I can't explain."

" I know," Eloise said, remembering her father's manner toward this weak, timid woman, who went on: " Then Col. Crompton came and brought me home. I used to live here years ago and called him father, till he said he was not my father. I never told you of him, or that this was once my home, although I described the place to you as something I had seen. If he were not my father I did not want to know who was, and did not want to talk about it, and after I married Mr. Smith it was very dreadful. He hated the Colonel when he found he could not get money from him, and sometimes taunted me with my birth, saying I was a Harris and a Cracker; but the cruelest of all was telling me you were dead. Why did he do it? "

" I think your fretting for me irritated him, and he feared you might never sing again unless he sent for me, and he did not want me," Eloise said. " He never wanted me. He was a bad man, and I could not feel sorry when he died."

"You needn't," Amy exclaimed excitedly, and, getting up she began to walk the floor as she continued, "It is time things were cleared up. I am not afraid of him now, although I was when he was living. He broke all the spirit I had, till the sound of his voice when he was angry made me shake. Thank God he was not your father! there has been a lie all the time, and that wore upon me. Your father,—Adolph Candida,—is lying in the Protestant burying-ground in Rome."

Grasping her mother's arm Eloise cried, "Oh, mother, what is this you are saying, and why have I never heard it before?"

Amy had been tolerably clear in her conversation up to this point, but she was getting tired, and it was a long, rambling story she told, with many digressions and much irrelevant matter, but Eloise managed to follow her and get a fairly correct version of the truth. Candida, whom Amy loved devotedly, and with whom she had been very happy, had died after a brief illness when Eloise was an infant. Homer Smith, the handsome American, who had attached himself to the Candidas, was very kind to the young widow, whom he induced to marry him, and to let her little girl take his name.

"I don't know why I did that," Amy said; "only he always made me do what he pleased, and he pretended to love you so much, and he didn't want his friends to know he was my second husband when he came to America. I couldn't understand that, but I yielded, as I did in everything. He seemed to hate the name of Candida, and was jealous of him in his

grave, and would never let me speak of him.   I think
he was crazy, and he said I was, and shut me up.   He
once wrote to Col. Crompton for money and got a
dreadful letter, telling him to go to that place where
I am afraid he has gone, and saying I was welcome
to come home any time, if I would leave the singing
master.   There was a bad word before the ' singing,'
which I can't speak.   I meant to go home some time
and take you with me.   I hated the stage, and the
pain got in my head, and I forgot so many things
after he said you were dead, but never forgot you,
although I didn't talk about you much.   I couldn't,
for a bunch came in my throat and choked me, and
my head seemed to open and shut on the top when
I thought of you.   Col. Crompton has been very
kind to me since I came.   I think now he is my
father.   I asked him once, and he said, No.   I believed him then, and accepted in my mind some Mr.
Harris, for I knew my mother was a true woman.
We will find it all out, you and I."

"Yes," Eloise replied, "and the pain will go away,
and you will tell me more of my own father.   I know
now why I never could feel a daughter's love for the
other one.   Does grandmother know?   She was always kind to me, and I love her."

Amy shook her head, and said, "I think not, but
am not sure.   It will be clearer by and by.   I must
sleep now."

When she was tired she always slept, and, adjusting the cushions on the sofa, Eloise made her lie
down, and spread over her the little red cloak which
had been the means of bringing them together.

"Yes, that's right.   Cover me with the dear old

cloak Jakey gave me," Amy said sleepily. "You'll help me find him."

Eloise didn't know who Jakey was, or what connection he had with the cloak; but she answered promptly, "Yes, I'll help you find him and everything."

Thus reassured, Amy fell asleep, while Eloise sat by her until startled by the entrance of Mrs. Biggs. That worthy woman had been busy telling the servants everything she knew about Eloise since she came to Crompton, and that she had always mistrusted she was somebody out of the common. Then, as Eloise did not appear, and the carriage from Miller's was still waiting at a dollar and a half an hour, it occurred to her thàt if Eloise should not prove to be somebody out of the common she would have to pay the bill, as she had ordered the turn-out. Going to Amy's room, she walked in unannounced, and asked, "Be you goin' home with me, or goin' to stay?"

"I don't know what I am to do," Eloise said, starting to her feet.

Amy decided for her. Mrs. Biggs had roused her, and, hearing what was wanted, she protested so vehemently against Eloise's leaving her even for an hour, that Mrs. Biggs departed without her, thinking to herself as she rode in state behind the fleet horses, "It beats the Dutch what luck some folks have. I've lost my boarder, and Ruby Ann has got the school, just as I knew she would, and mebby I'll have to pay for the rig. I wonder how long I've had it."

CHAPTER IV

THE SHADOW OF DEATH

This was on Saturday, and by Monday the whole town of Crompton, from District No. 5 to the village on the seashore, was buzzing with the news told eagerly from one to another. The young girl who had sprained her ankle while coming to take charge of the school in District No. 5 had, it was told, turned out to be the daughter of Mrs. Amy, and was at the Crompton House with her mother, who had thought her dead. This some believed and some did not, until assured by Mrs. Biggs, who, having done her washing on Saturday, was free on Monday to call upon her neighbors and repeat the story over and over, ending always with, "I mistrusted from the first that she was somebody."

The second piece of news was scarcely less exciting, but sad. After his interview with Eloise, the Colonel had complained of nausea and faintness, and had gone early to bed. Before going, however, he had asked if Eliza Ann were still in the house. An idea once lodged in his brain was apt to stay, and Eliza Ann had taken too strong a hold upon his senses to be easily removed.

"Bring her here," he said.

She came at once and asked what she could do for him.

" Sit down," he said. " You seem to be lame."

He had evidently forgotten about the accident, and Eloise did not remind him of it, but sat down while he catechised her with regard to what she had told him of herself. Some of his comments on Homer Smith were not very complimentary, and this emboldened Eloise to tell him who her real father was.

" Thank God!" he said emphatically. " I'm glad you are not that rascal's, and because you are not you can stay with Amy and fare as she fares. But why did she think you dead?"

Eloise told him all she thought necessary to tell him, while his face grew purple with anger, and his clenched fists beat the air as if attacking an imaginary Homer Smith.

" It's a comfort to know, if there is a God—and I know there is—he is getting his deserts," he said. Then, as his mood changed, he continued, " And you are the little normal I didn't want, and you board with Mrs. Biggs?"

" Yes," Eloise replied. " I am the normal you did not want, and I board with Mrs. Biggs, where I heard a great deal of Mrs. Amy, as they call her. I must have a slow, stupid mind, or I should have suspected who she was. I never heard the name Harris connected with her. If I had I should have known. It is so clear to me now."

The Colonel looked at her a moment, and then said, " If you are Amy's daughter you are a Harris, and they are queer, with slow minds,—and now go. I am infernally tired, and cannot keep up much longer."

He moved his hand toward her, and Eloise took it and pressed it to her lips.

"D-don't," the Colonel said, but held fast to the soft, warm hand clasping his. "If one's life could roll back," he added, more to himself than to Eloise, as his head dropped wearily upon his breast, and he whispered, "I am sorry for a great deal. God knows I am sorry. Call Peter."

The old servant came and got him to bed, and sat by him most of the night. Toward morning, finding that he was sleeping quietly, he, too, lay down and slept until the early sun was shining into the room. Waking with a start, he hurried to his master's side, to find him with wide-open eyes full of terror as he tried to ask what had happened to him. All power to move except his head was gone, and when he tried to talk his lips gave only inarticulate sounds which no one could understand.

"Paralysis," the doctor said when summoned. "I have expected it a long time," he continued, and would give no hope to Amy and Eloise, who hastened to the sick-room.

The moment they came in the Colonel's eyes brightened, and when Amy stooped and kissed him he tried to kiss her back. Then he fixed his eyes on Eloise with a questioning glance, which made her say to him, "Do you know me?"

He struggled hard for a moment, and then replied, "Yesh, 'Lisha Ann! Stay!" and those were the only really intelligible words he ever spoke.

They telegraphed to Worcester for Howard, and learning that he was in Boston, telegraphed there, and found him at the Vendome. "Come at once. Your uncle is dying," the telegram said, and Howard read it with a sensation for which he hated himself, and which he could not entirely shake off. He tried to believe he did not want his uncle to die, but if he did die, what might it not do for him, the only direct heir, if Amy were not a lawful daughter? And he did not believe she was. She had not been adopted, and he had never heard of a will, and before he was aware of it a feeling that he was master of Crompton Place crept over him. Amy would live there, of course, just as she did now, even if he should marry, as he might, and there came up before him the memory of a rainy night and a helpless little girl sitting on a mound of stones and dirt and crying with fear and pain. He had seen Jack's interest in Eloise with outward indifference, but with a growing jealousy he was too proud to show. He admired her greatly, and thought that under some circumstances he might love her. As a Crompton he ought to look higher, and if he proved to be the heir it would never do to think of her even if Jack were not in his way. All this passed like lightning through his mind as he read the telegram and handed it to Jack, who, he insisted, should return with him to Crompton.

"I feel awfully shaky, and I want you there if anything happens," he said, while Jack, whose first thought had been that he would be in the way, was not loath to go.

Eloise was in Crompton, and ever since he left it, a thought of her had been in his mind.

"If I find her as sweet and lovely as I left her, I'll ask her to be my wife, and take her away from Mrs. Biggs," he was thinking as the train sped on over the New England hills toward Crompton, which it reached about two P.M.

Peter was at the station with Sam, and to Howard's eager questions answered, " Pretty bad. No change since morning. Don't seem to know anybody except Mrs. Amy and Miss Eloise. She's with him all the time, and he tries to smile when she speaks to him."

" Who?" both the young men asked in the same breath, and Peter told them all he knew of the matter during the rapid drive to the house.

Howard was incredulous, and made Peter repeat the story twice, while his brain worked rapidly with a presentiment that this new complication might prove adverse to him.

" What do you think of it?" he asked Jack, who replied, " I see no reason to doubt it," and he was conscious of a pang of regret that he had not asked Eloise to be his wife before her changed circumstances.

" She would then know that I loved her for herself, and not for any family relations," he thought.

He had no doubt that Amy was Col. Crompton's daughter, and if so, Eloise's position would be very different from what it had been.

" I'll wait the course of events, as this is no time for love-making," he decided, as they drove up to the door, from which the doctor was just emerging.

" Matter of a few hours," he said to Howard. " I am glad you have come. Evidently he wants to see you, or wants something, nobody can make out what. You have heard the news?"

Howard bowed, and entering the house, ran up to his uncle's room. The Colonel was propped on pillows, laboring for breath, and trying to articulate words impossible to speak, while, if ever eyes talked,

his were talking, first to Amy and then to Eloise, both
of whom were beside him, Amy smoothing his hair
and Eloise rubbing his cold hands.

They had been with him for hours, trying to understand him as he struggled to speak.

"There is something he wants to tell us," Eloise
said, and in his eyes there was a look of affirmation,
while the lips tried in vain to frame the words, which
were only gurgling sounds.

What did the dying man want to say? Was he
trying to reveal a secret kept so many years, and
which was planting his pillow with thorns? Was he
back in the palmetto clearing, standing in the moonlight with Dora, and exacting a promise from her
which broke her heart? No one could guess, and
least of all the two women ministering to him so
tenderly,—Amy, because she loved him, and Eloise,
because she felt that he was more to her than a mere
stranger.   She was very quiet and self-contained.
The events of the last two days had transformed her
from a timid girl into a fearless woman, ready to
fight for her own rights and those of her mother.
Once when Amy was from the room a moment she
bent close to the Colonel and said, "You are my
mother's father?"

There was a choking sound and an attempt to
move the head which Eloise took for assent.

"Then you are my grandfather?" she added.

This time she was sure he nodded, and she said, "It
will all be right. You can rest now," but he didn't
rest.

There was more on his mind which he could not
tell.

"I believe it is Mr. Howard," Eloise thought, and

said to him, " He is coming on the next train. I
hear it now. He will soon be here. Is that what
you want ? "

The dying man turned his head wearily. There
was more besides Howard he wanted, but when at
last the young man came into the room, his eyes
shone with a look of pleased recognition, and he
tried to speak a welcome. In the hall outside Jack
was waiting, and as Eloise passed out he gave her his
hand, and leading her to a settee, sat down beside
her, and told her how glad he was for the news he
had heard of her, but feeling the while that he did
not know whether he were glad or not. She had
never looked fairer or sweeter to him than she did
now, and yet there was a difference which he detected, and which troubled him. It would have been
easy to say " I love you," to the helpless little school-
teacher at Mrs. Biggs's, and he wished now he had
done so, and not waited till she became a daughter
of the Crompton House, as he believed she was.
Now he could only look his love into the eyes which
fell beneath his gaze, as he held her hand and questioned her of the Colonel's sudden attack, and the
means by which she had discovered her relationship
to Amy.

Again he repeated, " I am so glad for you," and
might have said more if Howard had not stepped
into the hall, his face clouded and anxious.

" He wants you, I think," he said to Eloise. " At
least he wants something,—I don't know what."

Eloise went to him at once, and again there was
a painful effort to speak. But whatever he would
say was never said, and after a little the palsied
tongue ceased trying to articulate, and only his

21

eyes showed how clear his reason was to the last. If there was sorrow for the past, he could not express it. If thoughts of the palmetto clearing were in his mind, no one knew it. All that could be guessed at was that he wanted Amy and Eloise with him.

"Call him father. I think he will like it," Eloise said to her mother, while Howard looked up quickly, and to Peter, who was present, it seemed as if a frown settled on his face as a smile flickered around the Colonel's mouth at the sound of the name Amy had not given him since she came from California.

All the afternoon and evening they watched him, as his breathing grew shorter and the heavy lids fell over the eyes, which, until they closed, rested upon Amy, who held his hand and spoke to him occasionally, calling him father, and asking if he knew her. To the very last he responded to the question with a quivering of the lids when he could no longer lift them, and when the clock on the stairs struck twelve, the physician who was present said to Eloise, "Take your mother away; he is dead."

CHAPTER V

LOOKING FOR A WILL

For three days the Colonel lay in the great draw-ing-room of the Crompton House, the blinds of which were closed, while knots of crape streamed from every door, and the servants talked together in low tones, sometimes of the dead man and some-times of the future, wondering who would be master now of Crompton Place. Speculation on this point was rife everywhere, and on no one had it a stronger hold than on Howard himself. He would not like to have had it known that within twenty-four hours after his uncle's death he had gone through every pigeon-hole and nook in the Colonel's safe and pri-vate drawers, and turned over every paper search-ing for a will, and when he found none, had con-gratulated himself that in all human probability he was the sole heir. He was very properly sad, with an unmistakable air of ownership as he went about the place, giving orders to the servants. To Amy he paid great deference, telling the undertaker to ask what she liked and abide by her decisions. And here he was perfectly safe. With the shock of the Colonel's death Amy had relapsed into a dazed, silent mood, saying always, " I don't know; ask Eloise," and when Eloise was asked, she replied, " I have been here too short a time to give any orders. Mr. Howard will tell you."

Thus everything was left to him, as he meant it should be, stipulating that Eloise meet the people who came, some to offer their sympathy, and more from a morbid curiosity to see whatever there was to be seen. This Eloise did with a dignity which surprised herself, and if Howard were the master, she was the mistress, and apparently as much at home as if she had lived there all her life. Ruby was the first to call. She had not seen Eloise since the astounding news that she was Amy's daughter.

" I am so glad for you," she said, and the first tears Eloise had shed sprang to her eyes as she laid her head on Ruby's arm, just as she had done in the days of her trouble and pain.

Mrs. Biggs came, too,—very loud in her protestations of delight and assertions that she had always known Eloise was above the common.

Never since the memorable lawn party many years ago had there been so great a crowd in the house and grounds as on the day of the funeral. In honor of his memory, and because he had given the schoolhouse to the town, the school was closed, and the pupils, with Ruby Ann at their head, marched up the avenue with wreaths of autumn leaves and bouquets of flowers intended for the grave. The Rev. Arthur Mason read the burial service, and as he glanced at the costly casket, nearly smothered in flowers, and at the crowd inside and out, he could not keep his thoughts from his father's description of another funeral, where the dead woman lay in her cheap coffin, with Crackers and negroes as spectators; and only a demented woman, a little child, and black

Jake and Mandy Ann as mourners. The mourners here were Amy and Howard, Eloise and Jack, and next to him a plain-looking, elderly woman, who, Mrs. Biggs told every one near her, was old Mrs. Smith, Eloise's supposed grandmother from Mayville.

Eloise had sent for her, and while telling the story of deception and wrong which had been practised so long, and to which the mother listened with streaming eyes, she had said, " But it makes no difference with us. You are mine just the same, and wherever I live in the future, you are to live, too, if you will."

Mrs. Smith had smiled upon the young girl, and felt bewildered and strange in this grand house and at this grand funeral, unlike anything she had ever seen. It seemed like an endless line of carriages and foot passengers which followed the Colonel to the grave, and when the services were over, a few friends of the Colonel, who had come from a distance, returned to the house, and among them Mr. Ferris, the lawyer, who had been the Colonel's counsel and adviser for years, and managed his affairs. This was Howard's idea. He could not rest until he knew whether there was in the lawyer's possession any will or papers bearing upon Amy. When lunch was over he took the old man into his uncle's library, and said, hesitatingly, " I do not want to be too hasty, but it is better to have such matters settled, and if I have no interest in the Crompton estate I must leave, of course. Did my uncle leave a will? "

Lawyer Ferris looked at him keenly through his glasses, took a huge pinch of snuff, and blew a good deal of it from him and some in Howard's face, making him sneeze before he replied, " Not that I know of; more's the pity. I tried my best to have him make one. The last time I urged it he said, ' There's no need. I've fixed it. Amy will be all right.' I was thinking of her. If there is no will, and she wasn't adopted and wasn't his daughter, it's hard lines for her."

" But she was his daughter," came in a clear, decided voice, and both the lawyer and Howard turned to see Eloise standing in the door.

Rain was beginning to fall, and she had come to close a window, with no thought that any one was in the library, until she heard the lawyer's last words, which stopped her suddenly. Where her mother was concerned she could be very brave, and, stepping into the room, she startled the two men with her assertion, " She was his daughter."

" He told me so," she continued.

" He did? When? " Howard asked, and Eloise replied, " I asked him, and his eyes looked yes, and when I said, ' You are my grandfather? ' I was very sure he nodded. I know he meant it."

The lawyer smiled and answered her, " That is something, but not enough. We must have a will or some document. He might have been your mother's father. I think he was; and still, she may not be—be——"

He hesitated, for Eloise's eyes were fixed upon him, and the hot blood of shame was crimsoning her face. After a moment he continued, " A will can set things right; or, if we can prove a marriage, all will be fair sailing for your mother and you."

" I was not thinking of myself," Eloise returned. " I am thinking of mother. I know all the dreadful gossip and everything. Mrs. Biggs has told me, and I am going to find out. Somebody knows, and I shall find them."

She looked very fearless as she left the room, and Howard felt that she would be no weak antagonist if he wanted to contest his right to the estate. But he didn't, he told himself, and Mr. Ferris, too. He was willing to abide by the law. If there was a will he'd like to find it; and, in any case, should be generous to Amy and—Eloise!

"No doubt of it," the lawyer said, looking at him now over his spectacles, and taking a second pinch of snuff preparatory to the search among the dead man's papers, which Howard suggested that he make.

Every place Howard had gone through was gone through again,—every paper unfolded and every envelope looked into. There was no will or scrap of writing bearing upon Amy. There were some receipts from Tom Hardy, of Palatka, for money received from the Colonel and paid over to Eudora Harris, and at these the lawyer looked curiously.

"Harris was the name Amy sometimes went by before her marriage, I believe," he said. "Eudora was probably her mother. Now, if we can find Tom Hardy we may learn something. Shall I write to Palatka and inquire?"

"Certainly," Howard replied, with a choke in his throat which he managed to hide from the lawyer.

He didn't mean to be a scoundrel. He only wanted his own, and he meant to do right if chance made him master of Crompton, he said to himself, as he went to the drawing-room, where Jack and Eloise were sitting with a few friends who seemed to be waiting for something. Ruby and Mrs. Biggs, who, on the strength of their intimacy with Eloise, had remained in the house while the family was at the grave, were there, evidently expectant. It was not Howard's idea to broach the subject at once. He wanted to talk it over with Jack and Eloise, and make himself right with them. The lawyer had no such scruples. He had read wills after many funerals, and now that there was none to read, he spoke up:

"Ladies and gentlemen, I'm sorry I can't oblige you, but there ain't any will as we can find, and nothing to show who Mrs. Amy is, and matters must rest for a spell as they are. Meanwhile, Mr. Howard Crompton, as the Colonel's nephew and only known heir, must take charge of things."

Eloise's face flushed, and Jack, who stole a look at her, saw that her hands trembled a little. No one spoke until Mrs. Biggs rose and said, "'Squire Ferris, if no will ain't found, and nothin' is proved for Mrs. Amy,—adoption nor nothin',—you know what I mean,—can't she inherit?"

"Not a cent!" was the reply.

"You mean she'll have nothin'?"

"Legally nothing!"

"And Mr. Howard will have everything?"

"Yes, everything, as he is sole heir and next of kin."

"Get out with your 'sole heir and next of kin' and law!" Mrs. Biggs exclaimed vehemently. "There ain't no justice in law. Look a-here, Squire; when women vote we'll have things different. Here is Amy, been used to them elegancies all her life." She swept her arm around the room, and, still keeping it poised, continued: "And now she's to be turned out because there ain't no will and you can't prove nothin'! And that's law! It makes me so mad! Who is goin' to take care of her, I'd like to know?"

"I am!" and Eloise sprang to her feet, the central figure now in the room. "I shall take care of my mother! I don't care for the will, nor anything, except to prove that she is Col. Crompton's legitimate daughter, and that I will do. I am going where she was born, if I can find the place, and take her with me. I am not very lame now, and I would start to-morrow if——"

She stopped, remembering that in her purse were only two and one half dollars, and this she owed to Mrs. Biggs for board; then her eyes fell upon Ruby, the friend who had stood by her in her need, and who had been the first to congratulate her on finding her mother. Ruby had offered her money for the journey to California, and something in Ruby's face told her it was still ready for her, and she went on: "I was foolish enough to think Crompton Place was her rightful home, and be glad for her, but if it is not, I shall take her away at once. No one need worry about mother! I shall care for her."

"Bravo!" Mrs. Biggs rejoined, as Eloise sank back in her chair. "That's what I call pluck! Law, indeed! It makes me so mad! You can fetch her to my house any minit. Your old room is ready for you, and I won't charge a cent till you find something to do and can pay. Maybe Ruby'll give up the school. Won't you, Ruby Ann?"

"Certainly, if she wishes it," Ruby answered, and going over to Eloise, she said, "You are a brave little girl, and the money is still waiting for you if you want it."

As for Jack, he was ready to lay himself at her feet, but all he could do then was to say to Ruby, " Perhaps Miss Smith had better go to her room; she seems tired," and taking her arm, he went with her to the door, which Howard opened for her. That young man did not feel very comfortable, and as soon as Eloise was gone he said to the inmates of the room, " If any of you think me such a cad as to turn Mrs. Amy and her daughter from the house, or to allow them to go, you are mistaken. If it should prove that I am master here, they will share with me. I can do no more."

" Good for you! " Jack said, wringing Howard's hand, while the party began to break up, as it was time for those who lived at a distance to take the train.

Among those who arose to go was the Rev. Arthur Mason, whom Howard had asked to lunch after the burial. As he left the house he said to Jack, who stood for a moment with him on the piazza, " Please say to Miss Smith that I can direct her to her mother's birthplace in Florida. My father is preaching there."

" Thanks! I will tell her," Jack replied, in some surprise, and then went in to where Howard was standing, with an expression on his face not quite such as one ought to have when he has just come into possession of a fortune.

" I congratulate you, old boy," Jack said cheerily, as he went up to him.

" Don't! " Howard   answered   impetuously. " Nothing is sure. A will may be found, or my uncle's marriage proved; in either case, I sink back into the cipher I was before. I cannot say I'm not glad to have money, but I don't want people blaming me. I can't help it if my uncle made no will and did not marry Amy's mother, and I don't believe he did, or why was he silent so many years?"

Jack could not answer him and left the room, taking his way, he hardly knew why, to the village, where he fell in again with the rector. To talk of the recent events at the Crompton House was natural, and before they parted Jack knew the contents of the Rev. Charles's letter to his son, and in his mind there was no doubt of a secret marriage and Amy's legitimacy.

"It will be hard on Howard," he thought, "but Amy ought to have her rights,—and,—Eloise! And she shall!" he added, as he retraced his steps to the Crompton House.

Chancing to be alone with her, he told her in part what he had heard from the rector, keeping back everything pertaining to the poverty of the surroundings, and speaking mostly of Jakey and Mandy Ann, whom Amy might remember.

"She does," Eloise replied, "and at every mention of them her brain seems to get clearer. Peter has brought me a copy of a letter which Col. Crompton received from Jake just before he went for my mother, and which he has kept all these years. It may help me to find whatever there is to be found, good or bad." She handed him the copy, and continued, "The letter was mailed in Palatka, but from what you tell me, Jakey is farther up the river. Shall I have any trouble in finding him, do you think?"

"None whatever," Jack replied, a plan rapidly maturing in his mind as to what he would do if Eloise persisted in going to Florida. "Better leave your mother here," he said, when she told him of her determination to unravel the mystery.

"No," she answered. "Mother must go. I expect much from a sight of her old home and Jakey."

Jack shivered as he recalled the Rev. Charles Mason's picture of that home, but he would not enlighten her. She must guess something from Jakey's note to the Colonel, he thought. Evidently she did, for she asked him what a Cracker was.

"I ought to know, of course, and have some idea," she said. "I asked mother, and she said she was one. What did she mean?"

"If you go to Florida you will probably learn what a Cracker is," Jack replied, as he bade her good-night, pitying her for what he knew was in store for her.

The next day a telegram from New York called him to the city. But before he went he had an interview with Ruby with regard to the journey which Eloise was designing to take as soon as her mother should have recovered from the shock of the Colonel's death.

For a few days after his departure matters moved on quietly at the Crompton House, where Howard assumed the head unostentatiously, and without giving offence to any of the servants. The Crompton estate, as reported to him by Lawyer Ferris, was larger than he had supposed, and if it were his he would be a richer man than he had ever hoped to be. He liked money, and what it would bring him, and if he had been sure of his foothold he would have been very happy. And he was nearly sure. There was no will in the house, he was certain, for he had gone a second and third time through every place where one could possibly have been put, and found nothing. He was safe there, and as he did not know all which Mr. Mason had written to his son, he did not greatly fear the result of Eloise's trip to the South, which he thought a foolish undertaking. But she was bent upon going and the day was fixed. Grandmother Smith had returned home to await developments. Amy was ready. Eloise's lameness was nearly gone, "And to-morrow we start," she said to him one evening, when, after dinner, she joined him in the library, where he spent most of his time.

Every day since his uncle's death, and he had seen so much of Eloise, Howard's interest in her had increased, until it amounted to a passion, if not positive love. Jack was a formidable rival, he knew, but now that he was probably master of Crompton Place, where her mother would be happier than elsewhere, she might think favorably of him. At all events he'd take the chance, and now was his time. Looking up quickly as she came in, and drawing a chair close to him for her, he said, " Sit down a moment while I talk to you." She sat down, and he continued, "I wish you would give up this journey, which can only end in disappointment. I have no idea there was a marriage, or that you could prove it if there was. My uncle was not a brute. He loved Amy, and would not have kept silent till he died if she had been his legitimate daughter. Give up the project. I will gladly share the fortune with you, and be a son to your mother.

Will you, Eloise? I must call you that, and I ask you to be my wife. It is not so sudden as you may think," he continued, as he saw her look of surprise. " I do not show all I feel. I admired you from the first, but Jack seemed to be ahead, and I gave way to him, not understanding until within the last few days how much you were to me. I love you, and ask you again to be my wife."

He had one of her hands in his, but it was cold and pulseless, and it seemed to him it told her answer before she said, very kindly, as if sorry to give him pain:

" I believe you are my cousin, or, rather, my mother's, and I can esteem you as such, but I cannot be your wife."

" Because you love Jack Harcourt, I suppose," Howard said, a little bitterly, and Eloise replied, " I do not think we should bring Mr. Harcourt into the discussion. When he asks me to be his wife it will be time to know whether I love him or not. I cannot marry you."

She arose to go, while Howard tried to detain her, feeling every moment how his love was growing for this girl who had so recently come into his life, and was crossing his path, as he had felt she would when he first heard of her from his uncle, and had promised to sound her as to her fitness for a teacher. There had been no need for that; his uncle was dead, and she was going from him, perhaps to return as a usurper.

" Eloise," he said again, with more feeling in his voice than when he first spoke, " you must listen to me. I cannot give you up. I would rather lose Crompton, if it is mine, than to lose you."

Rising to his feet, he took her face between his hands and kissed it passionately.

"How dare you!" she said, wresting herself from him.

"Because I dare! Jack may have the second kiss, but I have had the first," he replied. Then his manner changed, and he said, entreatingly, "Forgive me, Eloise, I was beside myself for a moment. Don't give me an answer now. Think of what I have said while you are gone, if you will go; and if you fail, remember this is your home and your mother's, just as much as it will be if you succeed. Promise me you will come back here whatever happens. You will come?"

"For a time, yes; till I know what to do if I fail," she replied.

Then she went out and left him alone, to go again through the pigeon-holes and drawers and shelves he had been through so often and found nothing.

CHAPTER VI

IN FLORIDA

The Boston train was steaming into the Central
Station in New York, and Eloise was gathering up
her satchels and wraps, and looking anxiously out
into the deepening twilight, wondering if the cars
would be gone from the Jersey side, and what she
should do if they were. She had intended taking a
train which reached New York earlier, but there was
some mistake in her reading of the time-table, and
now it was growing dark, and for a moment her
courage began to fail her, and she half wished herself back in Crompton, where every one had been so
kind to her, and where every one had looked upon
the journey as useless, except the rector and Ruby.
These had encouraged her to go, and Ruby had furnished the money and had been very hopeful, and
told her there was nothing to fear even in New York,
which Eloise dreaded the most. Howard had seen
her to the train and got her seats in the parlor car,
and said to her, as he had once before:

" I'd like to offer you money, but you say you have
enough."

" Oh, yes," Eloise answered; " more than enough.
Ruby has been so kind."

Then he said good-by, and went back to the house,
which seemed empty and desolate.

"I ought at least to have gone to New York with them, but that little girl is so proud and independent, I dare say she would not have let me," he said to himself, and all day his thoughts followed them, until by some clairvoyant process he seemed to see them at the station alone and afraid, just as for a short time Eloise was afraid and wished she had not come.

Then, rallying, she said to herself, "This won't do. I must keep up," and she helped her mother from the car, and began to walk through the long station toward the street. Only half the distance had been gone over when a hand was laid upon her shoulder, and a voice which made her heart bound with delight, said to her, "Here you are! I was afraid I had missed you in the crowd."

"Oh, Mr. Harcourt, I am so glad! How did you know we were coming?" Eloise exclaimed, her gladness showing in her eyes and sounding in her voice.

"Oh, I knew," Jack answered, taking her satchel and wraps and umbrella from her, and giving his disengaged arm to her mother. "I have a friend at court who lets me know what is going to happen. It is Ruby. She telegraphed."

Calling a carriage, which was evidently waiting for him, Jack put the ladies into it, attended to the baggage, and then sprang in himself. With him opposite her, Eloise felt no further responsibility. Everything would be right, she was sure, and it was. They were in time for the south-bound train, and after a word with the porter, were ushered into a drawing-room compartment, which Jack said was to be theirs during the long journey.

22

"Yes, I know," Eloise said. " It is large and comfortable, and away from the people, but I'm afraid it costs too much."

" It's all right," Jack answered, beginning to remove Amy's jacket, with an air of being at home.

Just then Eloise glanced from the window and saw they were moving.

"Oh, Mr. Harcourt!" she screamed. " We have started! You will be carried off! Do hurry!"

She put both hands on his arm to force him from the room, while he laughed and said, " Did you think I would let you go to Florida alone? I am going with you. I have a section all to myself outside, where you can sit when you are tired in here. Are you sorry?"

" Sorry!" she repeated. " I was never so glad in my life. But are you sure you ought to go? Is it right?"

" You mean proper? Perfectly!" he answered. " Your mother is with us. Your friend Ruby knows I am going, and Mr. Mason, and Mrs. Biggs, and everybody else by this time. It's all right. Mrs. Grundy will approve."

Eloise was too happy to care for Mrs. Grundy, and her happiness increased with every hour which brought her nearer to Florida, and she saw more and more how thoroughly kind and thoughtful Jack was. Sometimes he sat with her and her mother in the compartment he had engaged for them, but oftener when Amy was resting she sat with him in his section, planning what she was to do first when Florida was reached, and how she was to find Jakey. Jack knew exactly what to do, but he liked to listen to her and watch the expression of her face, which seemed to him to grow more beautiful every hour. On the last evening they were to be upon the road, she was sitting with him just before the car lamps were lighted, and he said to her, " Suppose you don't succeed? What will you do? "

For a moment Eloise was silent; then she replied, " I shall take mother home to my grandmother's. I call her that still, although you know she is not really mine, but I love her just the same, and shall take care of her and mother. I can do it. Ruby will let me have the school, I am sure, if I ask her, but I couldn't take it from her now. I can get another somewhere, or if not a school, I can find something to do. I am not afraid of work."

She was trying to be very brave, but there was a pathetic look in her face which moved Jack strangely. Her hands were lying in her lap, and taking the one nearest to him, he said, " Eloise, I'll tell you what you are going to do, whether you succeed or not. You are going to be my wife! Yes, my wife! "

" Mr. Harcourt! " Eloise exclaimed, trying to withdraw her hand from him.

But he only held it closer, while he said, " Don't Mr. Harcourt me! Call me Jack, and I shall know you assent. I think I have loved you ever since I saw you on the rostrum in Mayville,—at any rate, ever since that stormy night when you came near being killed. I did not mean to speak here in the car, but I am glad I have settled it."

He was taking her consent for granted, and was squeezing her hand until she said involuntarily, " Oh, Jack, you hurt me! "

Then he dropped it and, stooping, kissed her, saying, " I am answered. You have called me Jack.

You are mine,—my little wife,—the dearest a man ever had."

He kissed her again, while she whispered, " Oh, Jack, how can you, with all the people looking on? and it isn't very dark yet."

" There are not many to look on, and they are in front of us, and I don't care if the whole world sees me," Jack replied, passing his arm around her and drawing her close to him.

" You must not, right here in the car; besides that, I haven't told you I would," she said, making an effort to free herself from him, as the porter began to light the lamps.

He was satisfied with her answer, and kept his arm around her in the face of the porter, who was too much accustomed to such scenes to pay any attention to this particular one. He had spotted them as lovers from the first and was not surprised, but when eleven o'clock came and every berth was made up except that of Jack, who still sat with Eloise beside him, loath to let her go, the negro grew uneasy and anxious to finish his night's work.

" Sir," he said at last to Jack, " 'scuse me, but you might move into the gentlemen's wash-room whiles I make up the berth; it's gwine on toward mornin'."

In a flash Eloise sprang up, and without a word went to her mother, who was sleeping quietly, just as she had left her three hours before. A lurch of the train awoke her, and, kneeling beside her, Eloise said to her, " Mr. Harcourt has asked me to be his wife. Are you glad?"

" Yes, daughter, very glad. Are we in Florida?" Amy replied.

" Yes, mother, and before long we shall reach

your old home and Jakey," was Eloise's answer, as she kissed her mother good-night and sought her own pillow to think of the great happiness which had come to her in Jack Harcourt's love, and which would compensate for any disappointment there might be in store for her.

CHAPTER VII

IN THE PALMETTO CLEARING

There were not many guests at the Brock House as the season had not fully opened, and Jack had no trouble to find rooms for the ladies and himself. Amy's was in front, looking upon the St. John's, which here spreads out into Lake Monroe. She had had glimpses of the river from the railway car, but had not seen it as distinctly as now, when she stood by the window with an expression on her face as if she were thinking of the past, before her reason was clouded.

" Oh, the river!—the beautiful river!" she said. " It brings things back,—the boat I went in; not like that," and she pointed to a large, handsome steamboat lying at the wharf. " Not like that. What was its name? "

Jack, who was in the room, and who had read Mr. Mason's letter to his son, suggested, " The 'Hatty'? "

" Yes, the ' Hatty '! " Amy said. " Strange, I remember it when I have forgotten so much. And he was with me,—my father. Wasn't he my father? "

She looked at Eloise, who answered promptly, " Yes, he was your father."

" I thought so. He said I was to call him so," Amy went on, more to herself than to Eloise. " I didn't always, he was so cold and proud and hard with me, but he was kind at the last, and he is dead, and this is Florida, where the oranges and palm trees grow. They are there,—see!" and she pointed to the right, where a tall palm tree raised its head above an orange grove below.

She was beginning to remember, and Eloise and Jack kept silent while she went on: "And we are here to find my mother and Jakey."

She looked again at Eloise, who answered her: "To find Jakey,—yes; and to-morrow we shall see him. To-night you must rest."

"Yes, rest to-night, and to-morrow go to Jakey," Amy replied, submissive as a little child to whatever Eloise bade her do.

She was very tired, and slept soundly without once waking, and her first question in the morning was, "Is it to-morrow, and are we in Florida?"

"Yes, dearest, we are in Florida, and going to find Jakey," was Eloise's reply, as she kissed her mother's face, and thought how young and fair it was still, with scarcely a line upon it.

Only the eyes and the droop of the mouth showed signs of past suffering, and these were passing away with a renewal of old scenes and memories. Jack had found the Rev. Mr. Mason, who received him cordially.

"I was expecting you," he said. "A telegram from my son told me you were on the way. I have not seen Jake, as it was only yesterday I had the despatch. I have one piece of news, however, for which I am sorry. Elder Covil died in Virginia soon after the war, and nothing can be learned from him."

Jack was greatly disappointed. His hope had

been to find Elder Covil, if living, or some trace of him, and that was swept away; but he would not tell Eloise. She was all eagerness and excitement, and was ready soon after breakfast for the drive to the palmetto clearing, and Amy seemed almost as excited and eager. Born amid palms and orange trees, and magnolias and negroes, the sight of them brought back the past in a misty kind of way, which was constantly clearing as Eloise helped her to remember. Of Mr. Mason she of course had no recollection, and shrank from him when presented to him. He did not tell her he had buried her mother. He only said he knew Jakey, and was going to take her to him, and they were soon on their way. The road was very different from the one over which he had been driven behind the white mule, and there were marks of improvement everywhere,—gardens and fields and cabins with little negroes swarming around the doors, and these, with the palm trees and the orange trees, helped to revive Amy's memories of the time when she played with the little darkys among the dwarf palmettos and ate oranges in the groves.

In the doorway of one of the small houses a colored woman was standing, looking at the carriage as it passed. Recognizing Mr. Mason, she gave him a hearty " How d'ye, Mas'r Mason? " to which he responded without telling his companions that it was Mandy Ann. He wished Amy to see Jake first.

" Here we are," he said at last. " This is the clearing; this is the house, and there is Jake himself."

He pointed to a negro in the distance, and to a small house,—half log and half frame, for Jake had added to and improved it within a few years.

"I'se gwine to make it 'spectable, so she won't be 'shamed if she ever comes back to see whar she was bawn," he had thought, and to him it seemed almost palatial, with its addition, which he called a "linter," and which consisted of a large room furnished with a most heterogeneous mass of articles gathered here and there as he could afford them.

Conspicuous in one corner was "lil Dory's cradle," which had been painted red, with a lettering in white on one side of it, "In memory of lil chile Dory." This he had placed in what he called the parlor that morning, after dusting it carefully and putting a fresh pillow case on the scanty pillow where Amy's head had lain. He was thinking of her and wondering he did not hear from the Colonel, when the sound of carriage wheels made him look up and start for his house. Mr. Mason was the first to alight; then Jack; then Eloise; and then Amy, whose senses for a moment left her entirely.

"What is it? Where are we?" she said, pressing her hands to her forehead.

Evidently the place did not impress her, except as something strange.

"Let's go!" she whispered to Eloise. "We've nothing to do here; let's go back to the oranges and palmettos."

"But, mother, Jakey is here!" Eloise replied, her eyes fixed upon the old man to whom Mr. Mason had been explaining, and whose "Bress de Lawd. I feels like havin' de pow', ef I b'lieved in it," she heard distinctly.

Then he came rapidly toward them, and she could see the tears on his black face, which was working nervously.

"Miss Dory! Miss Dory! 'Tain't you! Oh, de Lawd,—so growed,—so changed! Is it you for shu'?" he said, stretching his hands toward Amy, who drew closer to Eloise.

"Go gently, Jake; gently! Remember her mind is weak," Mr. Mason said.

"Yes, sar. I 'members de Harris's mind mostly was weak. Ole Miss didn't know nuffin', an' Miss Dory was a little quar, an' dis po' chile is like 'em," was Jake's reply, which brought a deep flush to Eloise's face.

She had felt her cheeks burning all the time she had been looking round on her mother's home, wondering what Jack would think of it. At Jake's mention of the Harrises she glanced at him so appealingly, that for answer he put his arm around her and whispered, "Keep up, darling, I see your mother is waking up."

Jake had taken one of her hands, and was looking in her face as if he would find some trace of the "lil chile Dory" who left him years ago. And she was scanning him, not quite as if she knew him, but with a puzzled, uncertain manner, in which there was now no fear.

"Doan' you know me, Miss Dory? I'm Shaky,— ole Shaky,—what use' to play b'ar wid you, an' tote you on his back," he said to her.

"I think I do. Yes. Where's Mandy Ann?" Amy asked.

"She 'members,—she does!" Jake cried, excitedly. "Mandy Ann was de nuss girl what looked after her an' ole Miss." Then to Amy he said, "Mandy Ann's done grow'd like you, an' got chillen as big as you. Twins, four on 'em, as was christened in your gown.   Come into de house.   You'll 'member then.   Come inter de gret room, but fust wait a minit.   I seen a boy out dar,—Aaron,—one of Mandy Ann's twins, an' I'se gwine to sen' for Mandy Ann.

"Hello, you flat-footed chap!" he called.   "Make tracks home the fastest you ever did, an' tell yer mother to come quick, 'case lil Miss Dory's hyar. Run, I say."

The boy Aaron started, and Jake led the way to the door of the "gret room," which he threw open with an air of pride.

"Walk in, gemmen an' ladies, walk in," he said, holding Amy's hand.

They walked in, and he led Amy to a lounge and sat down beside her, close to the red cradle, to which he called her attention.

"Doan' you 'member it, Miss Dory?" he said, giving it a jog.   "I use' ter rock yer to sleep wid you kickin' yer heels an' doublin' yer fists, an' callin' me ole fool, an' I singin':

> "'Lil chile Dory, Shaky's lil lam',
>   Mudder's gone to heaven,
>   Shaky leff behime
>   To care for lil chile Dory, Shaky's lil lam'.'

Doan' you 'member it, honey,—an' doan' you 'member me?   I'm Shaky,—I is."

There was a touching pathos in Jakey's voice as he sang, and it was intensified when he asked, "Doan' you 'member me, honey?"

Both Mr. Mason and Jack turned their heads aside to hide the moisture in their eyes, while Eloise's tears fell fast as she watched the strange pair,—the wrinkled old negro and the white-faced woman, in whom a wonderful transformation seemed to be taking place. With the first sound of the weird melody and the words " Lil chile Dory, Shaky's lil lam'," she leaned forward and seemed to be either listening intently or trying to recall something which came and went, and which she threw out her hands to retain. As the singing went on the expression of her face changed from one of painful thought to one of perfect peace and quiet, and when it ceased and Jakey appealed to her memory, she answered him, " Yes, Shaky, I remember." Then to Eloise she said, " The lullaby of my childhood, which has rung in my ears for years. He used to want me to sing a negro melody to the people, and said it made them cry. That's because I wanted to cry, as I do now, and can't. I believe I must have sung it that last night in Los Angeles before everything grew dark."

Moving closer to Jakey she laid her head upon his arm and whispered to him, " Sing it again, Shaky. The tightness across the top of my head is giving way. It has ached so long."

Jake began the song again, his voice more tremulous than before, while Amy's hands tightened on his arm, and her head sank lower on his breast. As he sang he jogged the cradle with one foot, and kept time with the other and a swaying motion of his body, which brought Amy almost across his lap. When she lifted up her head there were tears in her eyes, and they ran at last like rivers down her cheeks, while a storm of hysterical sobs shook her frame and brought Eloise to her.

" Don't cry so," she said. " You frighten me."

Amy put her aside, and answered, " I must cry; it cools my brain. There are oceans yet to come,—all the pent-up tears of the years—since he told me you were dead. I am so glad to cry."

For some moments she wept on, until Jakey began to soothe her with his " Doan' cry no mo', honey. Summat has done happened you bad, but it's done gone now, an' we're all here,—me an' I do' know her name, but she's you uns, an' Mas'r Mason an' de oder gemman. We're all here, an' de light is break-in'. Doan' you feel it, honey? "

" Yes, I feel it," she said, lifting up her head and wiping away her tears. " The light is breaking; my head is better. This is the old home. How did we get here? "

Her mind was misty still, but Eloise felt a crisis was past, and that in time the films which had clouded her mother's brain would clear away, not wholly, perhaps, for she was a Harris, and " all the Harrises," Jake said, " were quar." She was very quiet now, and listened as they talked, but could recall noth-ing of her mother or the funeral, which Mr. Mason had attended. She seemed very tired, and at Eloise's suggestion lay down upon the lounge and soon fell asleep, while Jack put question after question to Jake, hoping some light would be thrown upon the mys-tery they had come to unravel.

CHAPTER VIII

THE LITTLE HAIR TRUNK

Jake could tell them but little more than he had told Mr. Mason on a former visit. This he repeated with some additions, while Eloise listened, sometimes with indignation at Col. Crompton, and sometimes with shame and a thought as to what Jack would think of it. Her mother's family history was being unrolled before her, and she did not like it. There was proud blood in her veins, and she felt it coming to the surface and rebelling against the family tree of which she was a branch,—the Harrises, the Crackers, and, more than all, the uncertainty as to her mother's legitimacy, which she began to fear must remain an uncertainty. It was not a very desirable ancestry, and she glanced timidly at Jack to see how he was taking it. His face was very placid and unmoved as he questioned Jake of the relatives in Georgia, whom Amy's mother had visited.

"We must find them," he said. "Do you know anything of them? Were they Harrises, or what?"

Jake said they were "Browns an' Crackers; not the real no 'counts. Thar's a difference, an' I'm shu' ole Miss Lucy was fust class, 'case Miss Dory was a lady bawn."

"Are there no papers anywhere to tell us who they were?" Jack asked, and Jake replied, "Thar's papers in de little har trunk whar I keeps de writin' book Miss Dory used, an' de book she read in to learn, but dem's no 'count. Some receipts an' bills an' some letters ole Mas'r Harris writ to Miss Lucy 'fo' they was married,—love letters, in course, which I seen Miss Dory tie up wid a white ribbon. I've never opened dem, 'case it didn't seem fittin' like to read what a boy writ to a gal."

"Why, Jake," Jack exclaimed, "don't you see those letters may tell us where Miss Lucy lived in Georgia? and that is probably where Miss ·Dory visited. Bring us the trunk."

"'Clar for't. I never thought of that," Jake said, rising with alacrity and going into the room where he slept.

Mr. Mason, too, stepped out for a few moments, leaving Eloise alone with Jack. Now was her time, and, going up to him, she said, "Jack, I want to tell you now, you mustn't marry me!"

"Mustn't marry you!" Jack repeated. "Are you crazy?"

"Not yet," Eloise answered with a sob, "but I may be in time, or queer, like all the Harrises,— mother and her mother and 'old Miss.' We are all Harrises, and,—and,—oh, Jack, I know what a Cracker is now; mother is one; I am one, and it is all so dreadful; and mother nobody, perhaps. I can't bear it, and you must not marry me."

"I shall marry you," Jack said, folding her in his arms. "Do you think I care who your family are, or how queer they are? You'll never be queer. I'll shield you so carefully from every care that you can't even spell the word."

He took her hands and made her look at him,

while he kissed her lips and said, " It is you I want, with all the Harrises and Crackers in Christendom thrown in, if necessary. Are you satisfied? "

He knew she was, and was kissing her again when Jake appeared with the trunk, which he said had held Miss Dory's clothes when she went to Georgia. There was a musty odor about it when he opened it, and the few papers inside were yellow with age.

" Dis yer is de reader Miss Dory use' to go over so much," Jake said, handing the book to Eloise, who turned its worn pages reverently, as if touching the hands of the dead girl, who, Jake said, " had rassled with the big words an' de no 'count pieces. She liked de po'try, an' got by heart 'bout de boy on de burnin' deck, but de breakin' waves floo'd her, 'case 'twan't no story like Cassy-by-anker."

He pointed the latter poem out to Eloise, who said, " Will you give me this book? "

Jake hesitated before he replied, " He wanted it, the Colonel, an' I tole him no, but you're different. I'll think about it."

Mr. Mason had returned by this time, and with Jack was looking at the bundle of letters tied with a satin ribbon which Jake said Miss Dory had taken from her white dress, the one he believed she was married in, as it was her bestest. There were four letters and a paper which did not seem to be a letter, and which slipped to the floor at Eloise's feet as Jack untied the ribbon. There was also a small envelope containing a card with " James Crompton " upon it, the one Mandy Ann had carried her mistress on a china plate, and which poor Dora had kept as a souvenir of that visit. With the card were the remains of what must have been a beautiful rose. The

petals were brown and crumbling to dust, but still
gave out a faint perfume, which Eloise detected.
While she was looking at these mementos of a past,
Jack was running his eyes over the almost illegible
directions on the letters, making out "Miss Lucy
Brown, Atlanta, Ga."

"That doesn't help us much," he said to Mr. Mason. "Brown is a common name, and the Atlanta
before the war was not like the Atlanta of to-day."

"Perhaps something inside will give a cue," Mr.
Mason suggested, and Jack opened one of the letters
carefully, for it was nearly torn apart.

The spelling was bad and the writing was bad, but
it rang true with a young man's love for the girl of his
choice, and it seemed to Jack like sacrilege to read
it. Very hurriedly he went through the four letters,
finding nothing to guide him but "Atlanta," and a
few names of people who must have been living in
the vicinity.

"Here's another," Eloise said, passing him the
paper which she had picked from the floor.

Jack took it, and opening it, glanced at the contents. Then, with a cry of "Eureka!" he began a
sort of pirouette, while Eloise and Mr. Mason wondered if he, too, had gone quar, like the Harrises.

"It's the marriage certificate," he said, sobering
down at last, and reading aloud that at the Hardy
Plantation, Fulton County, Georgia, on December
—, 18—, the Rev. John Covil united in marriage
James Crompton, of Troutburg, Massachusetts, and
Miss Eudora Harris, of Volucia County, Florida.

Upon no one did the finding of this certificate pro-
duce so miraculous an effect as upon Jake.

"Fo' de Lawd!" he exclaimed, "I feels as if I mus'"

23

have de pow',—what I hain't had since I jined de 'Piscopals. To think dat ar was lyin' in thar all dis time, an' I not know it. I 'members now dat Elder Covil comed hyar oncet after the lil chile was bawn, to see Miss Dory, an' I seen him write a paper an' give it to 'her, an' she put it in her bosom. I axed no questions, but I know now 'twas this. The Cunnel tole her not to tell, an' if she said she wouldn't, she wouldn't. Dat's like de Harrises,—dey's mighty quar, stickin' to dar word till they die like that Cassy-by-anker on de burnin' ship. Glory to God, glory! I mus' shout, I mus' hurrah. Glory!"

He went careering round the room like one mad, knocking over a chair, waking up Amy, and bringing her to the scene of action.

"Bress de Lawd!" he said, taking her by the arm and giving her a whirl, "we've done foun' your mudder's stifficut in de letters whar she put it an' tied 'em wid her weddin' ribbon. Glory 'hollerluyer!"

Amy looked frightened, and when Eloise explained to her she did not seem as much impressed as the others. Her mind had grasped Jake and the old home, and could not then take in much more. Still, in a way she understood, and when Eloise said to her, "Col. Crompton was really your father,—married to your mother,—and you were Amy Crompton, and not Harris," she said, "I am glad, and wish he knew. He used to taunt me with my low birth and call me a Cracker. When are we going home?"

Her mind had reverted at once to Crompton Place, now hers in reality, although she probably did not think of that.

"I am very glad, and congratulate you that

Crompton Place is your home without a doubt,"
Jack said to her. Then, turning to Eloise, he continued, in a low tone, " I can't tell you how glad I
am for you, provided you don't feel so high and
mighty that you want to cast me off."

" Oh, Jack," Eloise replied, " don't talk such non-
sense. I am still of the Harris blood and part
Cracker, and maybe quar. If you can stand that I
think I can stand you."

At this point there was the sound of hurrying feet
outside, and a woman's voice was heard saying,
" Now, mind your manners, or you'll cotch it." Then
four woolly heads were thrust in at the door and with
them was Mandy Ann.

" Hyar she comes wid de fo' twins," Jake said,
going forward to meet her. " Mandy Ann," he began, " hyar's de lil chile Dory. Miss Amy they done
call her. Would you know'd her?"

" Know'd her? I reckon so,—anywhar in de
dark. Praise de Lawd, an' now let His servant 'part
in peace, 'case my eyes has seen de lil chile oncet
mo'," Mandy Ann exclaimed, going up to Amy and
putting her hands on her shoulders.

" She's 'peatin' some o' de chant in de Pra'r Book.
Mandy Ann is mighty pious, she is," Jake said in a
low tone, while Amy drew back a little, and looked
timidly at the tall negress calling her lil chile Dory.

" Mandy Ann wasn't so big," she said, turning to
the twins, Alex and Aaron, Judy and Dory, who
brought the past back more vividly when Mandy
Ann was about their size.

A look of inquiry passed from Mandy Ann to Jake,
who touched his forehead, while Mandy whispered,
" Quar, like ole Miss an' all of 'em. Oh, de pity of

it! What happened her?" Then to Amy she said, with all the motherhood of her ten children in her voice, " Doan' you 'member me, Mandy Ann, what use' to dress you in de mornin', an' comb yer har, an' wass yer face?"

" Up, instead of down," Amy said quickly, while everybody laughed instead of herself.

" To be shu'," Mandy Ann rejoined. " I reckon I did sometimes wass up 'sted of down. I couldn't help it, 'case you's gen'rally pullin' an' haulin' an' kickin' me to git away, but you 'members me, an' Judy, wid dis kind of face?"

She touched her eyes and nose and mouth to show where Judy's features were marked with ink, and then Amy laughed, and as if the mention of Judy took her back to the vernacular of her childhood, she said, " Oh, yes, I done 'members Judy. Whar is she?"

This lapse of her mother into negro dialect was more dreadful to Eloise than anything which had gone before, but Mr. Mason, who read her concern in her face, said to her, " It's all right, and shows she is taking up the tangled threads."

No one present knew of Judy's sale at the Rummage, and no one could reply to the question, " Whar is she?" Amy forgot it in a moment in her interest in the twins, whom Mandy presented one after another, saying, " I've six mo' grow'd up, some on 'em, an' one is married, 'case I'se old,—I'se fifty-three, an' you's about forty."

To this Amy paid no attention. She was still absorbed with the twins, who, Mandy Ann told her, had worn her white frock at their christening. Mandy Ann had not yet heard of the finding of the marriage certificate, and when Jake told her she did not seem greatly surprised.

"I allus knew she was married, without a stifficut," she said. "I b'lieved it the fust time he come befo' lil Miss Dory was bawn."

"Tell me about his coming," Eloise said, and Mandy Ann, who liked nothing better than to talk, began at the beginning, and told every particular of the first visit, when Miss Dora wore the white gown she was married in and buried in, and the rose on her bosom. "And you think this is it?" Eloise asked, holding carefully in a bit of paper the ashes of what had once been a rose.

"I 'clar for't, yes," Mandy said, "I seen her put it somewhar with the card he done gin me. You'se found it?"

Eloise nodded and held fast to the relics of a past which in this way was linking itself to the present. "Tell us of the second time, when he took mother," Eloise suggested, and here Mandy Ann was very eloquent, describing everything in detail, repeating much which Jake had told, telling of the ring,—a real stone, sent her from Savannah, and which she had given her daughter as it was too small for her now. From a drawer in the chamber above she brought a little white dress, stiff with starch and yellow and tender with time, which she said "lil Miss Dory wore when she first saw her father."

This Eloise seized at once, saying, "You will let me have it as something which belonged to mother far back."

Mandy Ann looked doubtful. There would probably be grandchildren, and Jake's scruples might be overcome and the white gown do duty again as a christening robe. But Jake spoke up promptly.

"In course it's your'n, an' de book, too, if you wants it, though it's like takin' a piece of de ole times. Strange Miss Dora don't pay no 'tention, but is so wropp'd up in dem twins. 'Specs it seems like when de little darkys use' to play wid her," he continued, looking at Amy, who, if she heard what Mandy Ann was saying, gave no sign, but seemed, as Jake said, "wropp'd up" in the twins.

There was not much more for Mandy Ann to tell of the Colonel, except to speak of the money he had sent to her and Jake, proving that he was not "the wustest man in the world, if she did cuss him kneeling on Miss Dory's grave the night after the burial." She spoke of that and of "ole Miss Thomas, who was the last to *gin in*," and wouldn't have done it then but for the ring on her finger. At this point Jake, who thought she had told enough, said to her, "Hole on a spell. Your tongue is like a mill wheel when it starts. Thar's some things you or'to keep to your self. Ole man Crompton is dead, an' God is takin' keer of him. He knows all the good thar was at the last, an' I 'specs thar was a heap."

By this time Amy had tired of the twins, who had fingered her rings and buttons, and stroked her dress and hair, and called her a pretty lady, and asked her on the sly for a nickel. She was getting restless, when Jakey said, "If you'd like to see your mudder's grave, come wid me."

From the house to the enclosure where the Harrises were buried he had made a narrow road, beside which eucalyptus trees and oleanders were growing, and along this walk the party followed him to Eudora's grave.

"I can have 'Crompton' put hyar now that I am shu'," Jake said, pointing to the vacant space after Eudora. "I wish dar was room for 'belobed wife of Cunnel Crompton.' I reckons, though, she wasn't 'belobed,' or why was he so dogon mean to her?" he added, kneeling by the grave and picking a dead leaf and bud which his quick eye had detected amid the bloom. "Couldn't you done drap a tear 'case your mother is lyin' here?" he said to Amy, who shook her head.

The dead mother was not as real to her as the living Jake, to whom she said, "As you talk to me I remember something of her, and people making a noise. But it is long ago, and much has happened since. I can't cry. Is it wrong?"

She looked at Eloise, who replied, "No, darling; you have cried enough for one day. Some time we will come here again, and you'll remember more. Let us go."

"What is your plan now?" Mr. Mason asked Jack when, after a half hour spent with Jake, they were driving back to the Brock House.

"I have been thinking," Jack replied, "that I will leave the ladies for a few days at the hotel, while I go to Palatka and Atlanta, and see if anything can be learned of the Browns, or Harrises, or the Hardy plantation, where the marriage took place. I wish to get all the facts I can, although the certificate should be sufficient to establish Mrs. Amy's right to the estate. I don't think she realizes her position as heir to the finest property in Crompton."

She didn't realize it at all, but was very willing to

stay at the Brock House with Eloise, while Jack went to Palatka and Atlanta to see what he could find. It was not much. Tom Hardy had been killed in the war, and had left no family. This he was told in Palatka. In Atlanta he learned that before the war there had been a plantation near the city owned by a Hardy family, all of whom were dead or had disappeared. There were Browns in plenty in the Directory, and Jack saw them all, but none had any connection with the Harrises. At last he struck an old negress, who had belonged to the Hardys, and who remembered a double wedding at the plantation years before, and who said that an Andrew Jackson Brown, who must have been present, as he was a son of the house, was living in Boston, and was a conductor of a street car. With this information as the result of his search Jack went back to Enterprise, where he found Amy greatly improved in mind and body. Every day Jake and Mandy Ann had been to see her, or with Eloise she had driven to the clearing, where her dormant faculties continued to awaken with the familiar objects of her childhood. Many people and much talking still bewildered her, and her memory was treacherous on many points, but to a stranger who knew nothing of her history she seemed a quiet, sane woman, " not a bit quar," Eloise said to Jack as she welcomed him back. "And I believe she will continue to improve when we get her home, away from the people who talk to her so much and confuse her. When can we go?"

"To-morrow, if you like," Jack said, and the next day they left Enterprise, after bidding an affectionate good-by to Mandy Ann, with whom they left a substantial remembrance of their visit.

Amy would have liked to take the twins with her, but Eloise said, "Not yet, mother; wait and see, and perhaps they will all come later."

It was sure that Jakey was to follow them soon and spend as much time with them as he pleased. "Stay always, if you will. We owe you everything," Eloise said to him, when at parting he stood on the platform with his "God bress you, Mas'r Harcourt an' Miss Amy, an' Miss t'other one," until the train was out of sight.

They made the journey by easy stages, for Amy was worn with excitement, and it was a week after leaving Florida when a telegram was received at the Crompton House saying they would arrive that evening.

CHAPTER IX

WHAT HOWARD FOUND

Jack had sent Howard a postal on the road to Florida, and a few lines from Enterprise on the day of their arrival. Since that time he had been so busy that he had failed to write, thinking he could tell the news so much better, and Howard argued from his silence that the errand had been unsuccessful. Crompton Place was undoubtedly his, and still he had not been altogether happy in his rôle as heir. The servants had been very respectful; people had treated him with deference; trades-people had sought his patronage; subscription papers had poured in upon him from all quarters, and in many ways he was made to feel that he was really Crompton of Crompton, with a prospective income of many thousands. He had gone over his uncle's papers, and knew exactly what he was worth, and when his dividends and rents were due. He was a rich man, unless they found something unexpected in Florida, and he did not believe they would. It seemed impossible that if there were a marriage it should have been kept secret so long. " My uncle would certainly have told it at the last and not left a stain on Amy," he said to himself again and again, and nearly succeeded in making himself believe that he had a right to be where he was,—his uncle's heir and head of the house. Why no provision was made for Amy he could not imagine. "But it will make no difference," he said; "I shall provide for her and Eloise."

At the thought of her his heart gave a great throb, for she was dearer to him than he had supposed. " I believe I'd give up Crompton if I could win her," he thought, " but that cannot be; Jack is the lucky fellow," and then he began to calculate how much he would give Amy out and out. " She can live here, of course, if she will, but she must have something of her own. Will twenty thousand be enough, or too much? " he said, and from the sum total of the estate he subtracted twenty thousand dollars, with so large a remainder that he decided to give her that amount in bonds and mortgages, which would cause her as little trouble as possible. There were some government bonds in a private drawer, through which he had searched for a will. He would have a look at them and see which were the more desirable for Amy. He had been through that drawer three or four times, and there was no thought of the will now as he opened it, wondering that it came so hard, as if something were binding on the top or side. It shut harder, or, rather, it didn't shut at all, and with a jerk he pulled it out to see what was the matter. As he did so a folded sheet of foolscap, which had been lodged between the drawer and the side of the desk, fell to the floor. With a presentiment of the truth Howard took it up and read, " THE LAST WILL AND CONFESSION OF JAMES CROMPTON ! "

It had come at last, and, unfolding the sheet, Howard began to read, glancing first at the date, which was a few weeks after Amy came from California.

" KNOW ALL MEN BY THESE PRESENTS," it began,

"that I, JAMES CROMPTON, am a coward and a sneak and a villain, and have lived a lie for forty years, hiding a secret I was too proud to divulge at first, and which grew harder and harder to tell as time went on and people held me so high as the soul of honor and rectitude. Honor! There isn't a hair of it on my head! I broke the heart of an innocent girl, and left her to die alone. AMY EUDORA SMITH is my own daughter, the lawful child of my marriage with EUDORA HARRIS, which took place December —, 18—, on the Hardy Plantation, Fulton County, in Georgia, several miles from Atlanta."

Up to this point Howard had been standing, but now the floor seemed to rise up and strike him in the face. Sitting down in the nearest chair, he breathed hard for a moment, and then went on with what the Colonel called his CONFESSION, which he had not had courage to make verbally while living.

When in college he had for his room-mate Tom Hardy from Atlanta. The two were fast friends, and when the Colonel was invited to visit Georgia he did so gladly. Some miles from the town was the plantation owned by the Hardys. This the Colonel visited in company with his friend. A small log-house on a part of the farm was rented to a Mr. Brown, a perfectly respectable man, but ignorant and coarse. His family consisted of himself and wife and son, and daughter Mary, a pretty girl of twenty, and a cousin from Florida, Eudora Harris, a beautiful girl of sixteen, wholly uneducated and shy as a bird. There was about her a wonderful fascination for the Colonel, who went with his friend several times to the Brown's, and mixed with them familiarly for the sake of the girl whose eyes welcomed him so gladly, and in which he at last read unmistakable signs of love for himself, while the broad jokes of her friends warned him of his danger. Then his calls ceased, for nothing was further from his thought than marriage with Eudora. At last there came to him and Tom a badly written and spelled invitation to Mary's wedding, which was to take place on the afternoon of the nineteenth day of December, 18—.

"Let's go; there'll be no end of fun," Tom said, but when the day came he was ill in bed with influenza, and the Colonel went without him, reaching the house just as the family were taking a hasty lunch, preparatory to the feast which was to follow the wedding.

"I sat down with them," the Colonel wrote, "and made myself one of them, and drank vile whiskey and home-made wine until my head began to feel as big as two heads, and I do not think I knew what I was about. As bad luck would have it, the man who was to stand with Eudora as groomsman failed to come, and I was asked to take his place.

"'Certainly, I am ready for anything,' I said, and my voice sounded husky and unnatural, and I wondered what ailed me.

"'Then, s'posin' you and Dory get spliced, and we'll have a double weddin'. You have sparked it long enough, and we don't stand foolin' here,' Mr. Brown said to me, in a half-laughing, half-threatening tone.

"I looked at Eudora, and her beautiful eyes were shining upon me with a look which made my pulses quicken as they never had before. I don't know what demon possessed me, unless it were the demon of the whiskey punch, of which I had drank far too much, and which prompted me to say, ' All right, if Eudora is willing.'

" To do her justice, she hesitated a moment, but when I kissed her she yielded, and with the touch of her lips there came over me a feeling I mistook for love, and everything was forgotten except the girl. Elder Covil performed the double ceremony, and looked questioningly at me, as if doubtful whether I were in my right mind or not. I thought I was, and felt extremely happy, until I woke to what I had done, and from which there was no escape. I was bound to a girl whose sweet disposition and great beauty were her only attractions, and whose environments made me shudder. I could not bring her to Crómpton Place and introduce her to my friends, and I did not know what to do.

" Tom was furious when he heard of it, and suggested suicide and divorce, and everything else that was bad. But Dora's eyes held me for two weeks, and then I became so disillusionized and so sick of my surroundings, that I was nearly ready to follow Tom's advice and blow out my brains.

" ' If you won't kill yourself,' he said, ' send the girl home to Florida, and leave her there till you make up your mind what to do. There must be some way to untie that knot. If not, you are in for it.'

" I sent her home, and after two or three weeks, during which Tom and I revolved a hundred plans, I decided on one, and went to see her in her home— and such a home! A log-house in a palmetto clearing, with a foolish old grandmother who did not know enough to ask or care what I was to Eudora.

I could not endure it, and I told Eudora how impossible it was for me to take her North until she had some education and knowledge of the world. I would leave her, I said, until I could decide upon a school to which I would send her, and, as it would be absurd for a married woman to be attending school, she was to retain her maiden name of Harris, and tell no one of our marriage until I gave her permission to do so. I think she would have jumped into the river at my bidding, and she promised all that I required.

"'I shall never tell I am your wife until you say I may,' she said to me when I left her, but there was a look in her eyes like that I once saw in a pet dog I had shot, and which in dying licked my hands.

"Through Tom Hardy, who left Atlanta for Palatka, I sent her money regularly and wrote occasionally, while she replied through the same medium. Loving, pitiful letters they were, and would have moved the heart of any man who was not a brute and steeped to the dregs in pride and cowardice. I burned them as soon as I read them, for fear they might be found. I told her to do the same with mine, and have no doubt she did. I did mean fair about the school, and was making inquiries, slowly, it is true, as my heart was not in it, and I had nearly decided upon Lexington, Kentucky, when the birth of a little girl changed everything, but did not reconcile me to the situation. I never cared for children,—disliked them rather than otherwise,—and the fact that I was a father did not move me a whit.

"There was a letter imploring me to come and see our baby, and I promised to go, with a vague idea that I might some time keep my word. But I didn't.

I had no love for Eudora, none for the child; and still a thought of it haunted me continually, and was the cause of my giving the grounds and the school-house to the town. I wanted to expiate my sin, and at the same time increase my popularity, for at that time I was trying to make up my mind to acknowledge my marriage and bring Eudora home. The poor girl never knew it, for on the day of the lawn party she was buried. Tom Hardy wrote me she was dead, and that he was about starting for Europe, and had given Jake, a faithful servant of the family, my address. God knows my remorse when I heard it, and still I put off going for the child until Jake wrote me that the grandmother, too, had died, and added that it was not fitting for the little girl to be brought up with Crackers and negroes. He did not know that I had heard of Eudora's death from Tom, and was waiting for—I did not know what, unless it was to hear from him personally. There was more manliness in that negro's nature than in mine, and I knew it, and was ashamed of myself, and went for my daughter and stood by my wife's grave, and heard from Jake the story of her life, and knew she had kept her promise and never opened her lips, except to say that ' it was all right.'

"The people believed her for the most part, and anathematized the unknown man who had deserted her, but they could not heap upon me all the odium I deserved. Why the story has never reached here I hardly know, except that intercourse between the North and the extreme South was not as easy as it is now, and then the war swept off Tom Hardy and most likely all who knew of the marriage.

"When I brought Amy home I was too proud to

acknowledge her as my daughter. The Harrises and the palmetto clearing stood in the way, and I let people think what they chose, hating myself with an added hatred for allowing a stain to rest on her birth. I was fond of her in a way, and angry when she married Candida, who died in Rome. Then she married a Smith, who took her round the country to sing in concerts, until her mind gave way, when he put her in a private asylum in San Francisco. I was very proud of her, and loved her more than she ever knew, but could not confess my relationship to her. When she married Candida I cast her off. She must have some of my spirit, for she never came begging for favors. Her rascally second husband wrote once for money, but I shut him up so that he never wrote again, and the next I heard was a message from Santa Barbara, where he died, and where, before he died, he had bidden his physician to write to me that his wife was in an asylum in San Francisco. I found her and brought her home, shattered in health and in mind, but I think she will recover. If she does before I die, I have sworn to tell her the truth, and will do it, so help me God!

" She has at times spoken of a baby who died,— Smith's probably, and I hated him and did not care for his child. I have thought to make my will, but would rather write this confession, which will explain things and put Amy right as my heir. I have, however, one request to make to her, or those who attend to her affairs. I want my nephew, Howard, to have twenty thousand dollars,—enough for any young man to start on if there is any get-up in him, and Howard has considerable.

24

"Written by me and signed this —— day of July, 18—, the anniversary of Eudora's funeral and the big picnic on my grounds.

"JAMES M. CROMPTON."

CHAPTER X

HOWARD'S TEMPTATION

Howard did not know how long it took him to read this paper. It seemed to him an age, and when it was read he felt as if turning into stone. There was a fire in the grate before which he sat, and something said to him, " Burn it," so distinctly, that he looked over his shoulder to see who was there. " It's the devil," he thought, and his hand went toward the flame, then drew back quickly. He knew now what his uncle had tried so hard to tell them, and remembered how often his eyes had turned in the direction of the private drawer. He had put his confession there, and it had become wedged in and was out of sight, until frequent opening and shutting the drawer had brought it into view. He read the document again, and felt the perspiration oozing out of every pore. The twenty thousand recommended for him made him laugh, as he thought that was the sum he had intended for Amy, and which looked very small for his own needs. " Six times two are twelve," he said, calculating the interest at six per cent. " Twelve hundred a year is not much when one expected as many thousands. I believe I'll burn it!" and again the paper was held so near the fire that a corner of it was scorched.

" I can't do it," he said, drawing it back a second

time. "It would do no good, either, if they find out in Florida. I don't see, though, how they can, and if they have, Jack would have written, but I can't burn it yet. I must think a while."

He put the paper aside, and, without his overcoat, went out into the cold, sleety rain, which was falling heavily. It chilled him at once, but he did not think of it as he went through the grounds and gardens and fields of the Crompton Place, where everything was in perfect order and bespoke the wealth of the owner. It was a fair heritage, and he could not give it up without a pang. He never knew how many miles he walked back and forth across the fields and through the woods. Nor did he know that he was cold, until he returned to the house with drenched garments and a chill which he felt to his bones. He had taken a heavy cold, and staid in-doors the next morning, shivering before the grate, which he told Peter to heap with coal until it was hot as——. He didn't finish the sentence, but added, "I'm infernally cold,—influenza, I reckon, but I won't have any nostrums brought to me. All I want is a good fire."

Peter heaped up the fire until the room seemed to him like a furnace, and then left the young man alone with his thoughts and his temptation, which was assailing him a second time, stronger than before. He firmly believed the devil was there, urging him to burn the paper, and held several spirited conversations with him, pro and con, the cons finally gaining the victory.

Late in the afternoon Jack's telegram was brought to him. "We'll be home this evening."

"That means seven o'clock, and dinner at half-past seven," he said to Peter. " Send Sam with the carriage, and see that there are fires in their rooms."

He had given his orders and then sat down to decide what he would do.

" I know the Old Harry is here with me, but his company is better than none," he said, wishing he had a shawl, he was so cold, with the room at 90 degrees.

The short day drew to a close. Peter came in and lighted the gas, and put more coal on the grate, and said Sam had gone to the station. Half an hour later Howard heard the whistle of the train, and then the sound of wheels coming up the avenue.

" Now or never! " was whispered in his ear, and his hand, with the paper in it, went toward the fire.

There was a fierce struggle, and Howard felt that he was really fighting with an unseen foe; then his hand came back with the paper in it, safe except for a second scorch on one side.

" By the great eternal, it is never! I swear it! " he said, as his arm dropped beside him and the paper fell to the floor.

There was a sound below of people entering the house. They had come, and he heard Eloise's voice as she passed his door on her way to her room with Amy. Was Jack there too? he was wondering— when Jack came in, gay and breezy, but startled when he met the woe-begone face turned toward him.

" By George! old man," he said, " Peter told me you were shut up with a cold, but I didn't expect this. Why, you look like a ghost, and are sweating like a butcher, and no wonder. The thermometer must be a hundred. What's the matter? "

" Jack," Howard said, " for forty-eight hours I

have had a hand-to-hand tussle with the devil. He was here bodily, as much as you are, but I beat him, and swore I wouldn't burn the paper. Read it!"

He pointed to it upon the floor at his feet.

"I had it pretty near the fire twice, and singed it some," he continued, as Jack took it up, and, glancing at the first words, exclaimed, "A will! You found one, then?"

"Not a regularly attested will, but answers every purpose," Howard replied, while Jack read on with lightning rapidity, understanding much that was dark before, and guessing in part what it was to Howard to have all his hopes swept away.

"By Jove!" he said, as he finished reading, "there was good in the old man after all. I didn't think so when I heard Jakey's story, and saw where his wife lived and died. We found the marriage certificate."

"You did!" Howard exclaimed, a great gladness that he had not destroyed the paper taking possession of him. "Why didn't you write and tell me? It would have saved me that fight with the devil."

"I don't know why I didn't," Jack replied. "I was awfully busy, and went at once to Palatka to see if Tom Hardy left any family there, and found he was never married. Then I went to Atlanta to find some trace of the Browns and the Hardy plantation. The latter had been sold, the Hardys were all gone, and the Browns, too,—killed in the war, most likely, except one who is a street-car conductor in Boston, and I am going to hunt him up, as I believe he was at the wedding, although he must have been quite young. Yes, I ought to have written, and I'm sorry for you, upon my soul. You look as if you'd had a taste of the infernal regions. I'm glad you didn't burn it."

He took Howard's hand and held it, while he told him, very briefly, the circumstances of their finding the certificate, of whose existence Col. Crompton could not have known. " And, Howard," he added, " I've something else to tell you. Eloise is to be my wife. We settled it in the train before I knew she was a great heiress. Can't you congratulate me? " he asked, as Howard did not speak.

" I expected it. You've got everything,—money, and girl, too," Howard said at last. " You are a lucky dog, and, whether you believe me or not, I'd rather have the girl than the money. I asked her to marry me. Did she tell you? "

" Of course not," Jack replied, and Howard went on, " Well, I did, and kissed her, too! "

" Did she kiss you? " Jack asked a little sharply, and Howard replied, " No, sir; she was madder than a hatter; you've no cause to be jealous."

" All right," Jack answered, his brow clearing. " All right. I'm more sorry for you now than I was before. I didn't know you really cared for her that way; but, I say, aren't you coming to dinner? The bell has rung twice, and I still in my travelling clothes and you in your dressing-gown."

Howard shook his head. " Don't you see, I am sick with an infernal cold," he said. " Got it tramping in the rain without my overcoat, and that fight I told you of has unstrung me. It was a regular battle. But you go yourself, and perhaps Eloise will come to see me. I shall show her the Colonel's confession, and she can do as she pleases about telling her mother."

Jack left him and went to the dinner, which had been kept waiting some time, and at which Amy did not appear. She had gone at once to bed, Eloise explained, when she took her seat at the table with Jack. When told of Howard's message, she said, " Of course I'll go to him," and half an hour later she was in his room, and greatly shocked at his white, haggard face, which indicated more than the cold of which he complained. He did not tell her of his temptation. It was not necessary. He congratulated her upon her success, and upon her engagement, of which Jack had told him. Then he gave her the paper he had found, and watched her as she read it, sometimes with flashes of indignation upon her face, and again with tears of pity in her eyes.

" He was a bad man," she said, with great energy, and then added, " A good one, too, in some respects, although I cannot understand the pride which made him such a coward."

" I can," Howard rejoined. " It's the Crompton pride, stronger than life itself. I know, for I am a Crompton. You, probably, are more Harris than Crompton, and do not feel so deeply."

He did not mean to reflect upon her mother's family, but Eloise's face was very red as she said, " The Harrises and Browns are not people to be proud of, I know, but they were as honest, perhaps, as the Cromptons, and they are mine, and if they all came here to-night I would not disown them."

She looked every inch a Crompton as she spoke, and Howard laughed and said, " Good for you, little cousin; I believe you would, and if Jack finds the conductor in Boston, I dare say you will have him at your wedding. When is it to be? "

"Just as soon as arrangements can be made," Jack replied, coming in in time to hear the last of Howard's remark, " and, of course, we'll have the street conductor if he will come. I start to-morrow to find him."

He took an early train the next morning for Boston, and two days after he wrote to Eloise: " I believe there are a million street cars in the city and fifty conductors by the name of Brown. Fortunately, however, there is only one Andrew Jackson, or Andy, as they call him, and I found him on one of the suburban trains, rather old to be a conductor, but seemed young for his years. He is your grandmother's cousin, and was present at the double wedding, when Eudora Harris was married by Elder Covil to James Crompton, ' a mighty proud-lookin' chap,' he said, ' who deserted her in less than a month. I remember him well. Pop threatened to shoot him if he ever cotched him, but the wah broke out and pop was killed, and all of us but me, who married a little Yankee girl what brought things to us prisoners in Washington. She's right smart younger than I am, and I've got eight children and five grandchildren, peart and lively as rabbits. And you want me to swear that I seen Eudory married? Wall, I will, for I did, and I'd like to see her girl— Amy you call her. Mabby Mary Jane an' me will come to visit her when I have a spell off.'

" All this he said in a breath, and when I told him I was to marry Amy's daughter, he called me his cousin, and asked when the wedding was to be. If it had not been for those eight children and five grandchildren, thirteen Browns in all, which I felt sure he would bring with him, I should have promised him and Mary Jane an invitation. As it was, I did nothing rash. I got his affidavit, and we parted the best of friends, he urging me to call at his shanty and see Mary Jane and the kids. I had to decline, but told him perhaps I'd bring my wife to see them. What do you say? Expect me to-morrow.

"Lovingly,
"Jack."

CHAPTER XI

CONCLUSION

It did not take long for all Crompton to know that Amy was Col. Crompton's daughter, and that the Colonel had left a paper to that effect, which Mr. Howard had found, and that Eloise had also found the marriage certificate, proving her mother's legitimacy beyond a doubt, and making her sole heir to the Crompton estate. It was Friday night when the travellers returned from the South, and on Saturday morning, Mrs. Biggs's washing day, she heard the news. Leaving her clothes in the suds, and her tubs of rinsing and bluing water upon the floor, she started for the Crompton House, which she reached breathless with haste and excitement, and eager to congratulate Amy and Eloise.

"I swan, it 'most seem's if I was your relation," she said, shaking Eloise's hand, and telling her she always mistrusted she was somebody more than common, "and I hope we shall be neighborly. I s'pose you'll live here?"

Eloise received her graciously, and said she should never forget her kindness, and told her some incidents of her journey, and, as Mrs. Biggs reported to Tim, "treated me as if I was just as good as she, if she is a Crompton."

Ruby Ann came later in the day, genuinely glad

for Eloise, and sure that nothing would ever change the young girl's friendship for herself, no matter what her position might be. Many others called that day and the following Monday, and Eloise received them with a dignity of which she was herself unconscious, and which they charged to the Crompton blood. Howard, who was still suffering from a severe cold, kept his room until Jack returned. Then he came out with a feeling of humiliation, not so much that he had lost the estate, as that he had thought to burn the paper which took it from him. This feeling, however, gradually wore off under Jack's geniality and Eloise's friendliness, and Amy's sweetness of manner as she called him Cousin Howard, and said she hoped he would look upon Crompton as his home. Then he was to have twenty thousand dollars when matters were adjusted, and that was something to one who, when he came to Crompton, had scarcely a dollar. His visit had paid, and, though he was not the master, he was the favored guest and cousin, who, at Eloise's request, took charge of affairs after Jack went home to New York.

Early in December Jake came from the South, and was welcomed warmly by Amy and Eloise. To the servants he was a great curiosity, with his negro dialect and quaint ways, but no one could look at the old man's honest face without respecting him. Even Peter, who detected about him an ordor of the bad tobacco which had so offended his nostrils in the letters to his master, and who on general principles disliked negroes, was disarmed of his prejudices by Jake's confiding simplicity and thorough goodness. Taking him one day for a drive around the country and through the village, he bought him some first-class cigars with the thought "Maybe they'll take that smell out of his clothes."

"Thankee, Mas'r Peter, thankee," Jake said, smacking his lips with his enjoyment of the flavor of the Havanas. "Dis yer am mighty fine, but I s'pecks I or'to stick to my backy. I done brought a lot wid me."

He smoked the Havanas as long as they lasted, with no special diminution of odor as Peter could discover, and then returned to his backy and his clay pipe.

In the love and tender care with which she was surrounded, Amy's mind recovered its balance to a great extent, with an occasional lapse when anything reminded her of her life in California as a public singer, or when she was very tired. She was greatly interested in Eloise's wedding, which was fixed for the 10th of January, her twentieth birthday. Jack, who came from New York every week, would have liked what he called a blow-out, but the recent death of the Colonel and Amy's mourning precluded that, and only a very few were bidden to the ceremony, which took place in the drawing-room of the Crompton House, instead of the church. Amy gave the bride away, and a stranger would never have suspected that she was what Jakey called quar. After Eloise left for her bridal trip she began to assume some responsibility as mistress of the house and to understand Mr. Ferris a little when he talked to her on business. Jake was a kind of ballast to her during Eloise's absence, but a Northern winter did not agree with the old man, who wore nearly as much clothing to keep him warm as Harry Gill, and then complained of the cold.

" Florida suits me best, and I've a kind of hankerin' for de ole place whar deys all buried," he said, and in the spring he returned to his Lares and Penates, leaving Amy a little unsettled with his loss, but she soon recovered her spirits in the excitement of going abroad.

It was Jack who suggested this trip, which he thought would benefit them all, and early in May they sailed for Europe, taking Ruby with them, not in any sense as a waiting maid, as some ill-natured ones suggested, but as a companion to Amy, and as the friend who had been so kind to Eloise in her need.

That summer Howard was a conspicuous figure at a fashionable watering place with his fast horse and stylish buggy, and every other appearance of wealth and luxury. He had received his twenty thousand dollars and more, too, for Eloise was disposed to be very generous toward him, and Amy assented to whatever she suggested.

" I'll have one good time and spend a whole year's interest if I choose," he said, and he had a good time and made love to a little Western heiress, whose eyes were like those of Eloise, and first attracted him to her, and who before the season was over promised to be his wife.

Just before she left for Europe Eloise brought her grandmother, Mrs. Smith, from Mayville, and established her in Crompton Place as its mistress, but that good woman had little to say, and allowed the servants to have their way in everything. The change from her quiet home to all the grandeur and ceremony of the Crompton House did not suit her, and she returned, like Jakey, to her household gods when the family came back in the spring.

. . . . . .

Several years have passed since then, and Crompton Place is just as lovely as it was when we first saw it on the day of the lawn party. Three children are there now; two girls, Dora and Lucy, and a sturdy boy, who was christened James Harris Crompton, but is called Harry. The doll-house has been brought to light, with Mandy Ann and Judy, to the great delight of the little girls, and Amy is never brighter than when playing with the children, and telling them of the palms and oranges, alligators and negroes in Florida, which she speaks of as home.

Eloise is very happy, and if a fear of the Harris taint ever creeps into her mind, it is dissipated at once in the perfect sunshine which crowns her life. Nearly every year Jakey comes to visit " chile Dory an' her lil ones," and once Mandy Ann spent a summer in Crompton as cook in place of Cindy, who was taking a vacation. But Northern ways of regularity and promptness did not suit her.

" 'Clar for't," she said, " I jess can't git use't to de Yankee Doodle quickstep nohow. At Miss Perkinses dey wasn't partic'lar ef things was half an hour behime."

Her mind dwelt a good deal on what she had seen at Miss Perkins's, more than forty years before, and on her children and Ted, and when Cindy returned in the autumn she went back to him and the twins, laden with gifts from Amy and Eloise, the latter of whom saw that her mother gave more judiciously than she would otherwise have done. Both Amy and Eloise are fond of driving, and nearly every day the carriage goes out, but the coachman is no longer Sam. He is married and lives in the village, and his place is filled by Tom Walker, who wears a brown livery, and fills the position with a dignity one would scarcely expect in the tall, lank boy, once the bully in school and the blackguard of the town.

There have been three or four different teachers in District No. 5,—all normal graduates, and all during their term of office boarding with Mrs. Biggs, who is never tired of boasting of her intimacy with the Cromptons, and Eloise in particular. Every detail of the accident is repeated again and again, with many incidents of Amy's girlhood. Then she takes up the Colonel and his private marriage, and with his introduction we end our story and leave her to tell hers in her own way.

THE END.

CPSIA information can be obtained
at www.ICGtesting.com
Printed in the USA
BVHW042021011022
648390BV00002BA/23